Fury:
Surviving the Zombie Apocalypse

SHAWN CHESSER

ISBN: 978-1-7371106-2-0

CONTENTS

ACKNOWLEDGEMENTS

Dedicated to the Uyghurs imprisoned in China's labor camps and the billion-plus Lao Beijing languishing daily under the thumb of the CCP.

Maureen, Raven, and Caden ... I couldn't have done this without your support. Thanks to our military, LE and first responders for your service. To the people in the U.K. and elsewhere around the world who have been in touch, thanks for reading my yarns! Lieutenant Colonel Michael Offe, thanks for your service as well as your friendship. Beta readers, you rock, and you know who you are. Thanks George Romero for introducing me to zombies. To my friends and fellows at S@N and Monday Steps On Steele, thanks as well. Lastly, thanks to Bill W. and Dr. Bob … you helped make this possible. I am going to sign up for another 24.

Special thanks to John O'Brien, Mark Tufo, Joe McKinney, Craig DiLouie, Heath Stallcup, Eric A. Shelman, David P. Forsyth, and Nicholas Sansbury Smith. I truly appreciate your continued friendship and always invaluable advice. Thanks to Marsha and Hal Lohmeyer for their help fleshing out Colorado Springs and Pueblo, Colorado. Thanks to Jason Swarr and Straight 8 Custom Photography for another awesome cover. Once again, extra special thanks to Monique Happy for her work editing "FURY." Mombie, as always, you came through like a champ! Working with you for close to a decade has been nothing but a pleasure. I truly appreciate having a confidante I can trust. If I have accidentally left anyone out ... I am truly sorry.

***

Edited by Monique Happy Editorial Services
mohappy@att.net

Prologue

Queen Anne District

Seattle, Washington

Wednesday, July 4th, 2012

Army Lt. Colonel Ret. Remember "Alamo" Baker was a modern-day Colonel Andy Tanner. He considered the Chinese communist invaders his Soviets, and this was *his* Red Dawn. Named after American Revolutionary War hero Remember Baker—one of the Continental Army's Green Mountain Boys—the retired colonel was known as a hard-charger in the War on Terror. Wounded by an IED in Mosul, Iraq, he was retired and living in Washington State when the dead began to walk.

Having recovered fully from multiple torture sessions the enemy invaders had subjected him to at the OMSI museum in Portland, Oregon, Baker was now directing all of his energy into training up his small band of self-titled Wolverine resistance fighters. When the Chicom's purported spring offensive failed to materialize, Baker took the fight to the enemy, conducting hit-and-run raids with impunity in and around Seattle—a city he knew like the back of his hand.

"What do you think, sir?" asked John McGrath, a middle-aged former Alaskan wilderness guide. He was standing with his back to an interior wall, gray eyes locked on the trussed and bound Chinese soldier writhing on the floor in the center of the great room. The Chicom soldier's foraging partner, a whip-thin corporal, was lying dead on the floor in the next room.

Speaking in passable Mandarin, Baker said, "I think Sergeant Lei needs another swift kick to the head."

Eyes darting between the two camo-clad Wolverines, the prisoner exhaled sharply, then ceased struggling.

Baker pinned the sheer curtains to the window casing and craned to see down Highland Drive. "No sign of them yet, John," he answered. "I hear them, though. Loud and clear. Two vehicles … maybe three."

Since sound traveled far and wide across the once-bustling city, Baker couldn't quite put a finger on how far away the patrol was. If he had to venture a guess, something he was loath to do, he'd put the approaching vehicles at no more than half a mile out.

The radio taken from Lei wasn't offering up much in the way of intel, either. Every few minutes a call would go out demanding the sergeant check in. Knowing a string of failures to do so would precipitate a search being mounted, Baker had let the calls go unanswered.

The third-floor window overlooking Highland was on the southeast corner of a rectangular brownstone that had been partitioned into ten separate apartments. The apartment Baker and his lifelong friend were holed up in was one of two top-floor "penthouse" units. While it wasn't exactly spacious, Baker supposed that before the fall, in the super-high-priced Seattle housing market, the three-bedroom with rooftop access probably carried a million-dollar price tag.

Across the street from the brownstone, Kerry Park was an unkempt mess. Growing out of control for nearly a year, the waist-high grass encroached mightily on the brick paths and all but swallowed up the dozen or so benches scattered about the gently sloping hillside.

Some kind of modern sculpture, two huge brick squares with viewing ports bored through them, sat forlornly at the park's main entrance.

A pair of weathered corpses, locked in an embrace as if the two adults had died professing their undying love for one another, lay at the base of the sculpture. In the long grass beside the corpses, stubby black suppressor on her Colt Commando AR-15 barely visible, was another of Baker's fighters. Kylee Dorn, a former Washington National Guard soldier in her mid-twenties, had joined Baker's Wolverines a week after her unit fell to the dead. Snohomish County 3-Gun Champion two years running, Dorn was the best all-around shooter Baker had.

Baker lifted his eyes from the park entrance, then walked his gaze from right to left. Considering the unobstructed views of downtown Seattle and Elliott Bay, the fifty-seven-year-old former Special Forces Green Beret added another million dollars to his previous assessment. Before the fall and subsequent Chicom invasion, when lying low wasn't tantamount to remaining on the good side of the grass, waking up to a view like this would have been worth every penny to Baker. Now, with only two egress points and noon fast approaching, he felt as exposed as a streaker sprinting across Safeco Field during a Mariners' game. Or one of those fools who climbs, willingly, into the bear enclosure at the zoo. To say he didn't like being in the city during the day would be a massive understatement.

Parked at the curb beside the brownstone, its rear end facing east, was an American Spirit horse trailer. It sat on dual axles and sported a drop-down rear ramp. Spelled out in a red font meant to look like neon tubing were the words "Seattle Police Mounted Patrol." Measuring roughly thirty feet from front to back, eight feet from ground to roof, and nearly eight feet across, the trailer took up more than its fair share of the narrow residential street.

The trailer's gooseneck hitch was empty. The police department's Dodge Ram pickup the trailer had been hitched to when Baker and his small band of fighters had found it, four miles away in the Magnolia district, was now parked at the curb directly across the street from the trailer. Uncoupled, the truck and trailer created a perfect chokepoint on Highland. Add in the dozen or so Zs crowded around the trailer and you had a scene that even the usually non-curious PLA soldiers should take notice of.

Inside the trailer, its speaker ports covered by duct tape, the orange, golf-ball-sized Screamer was playing a looped recording of a woman dying a gruesome death. While Baker couldn't hear the noisemaker from his position, the zombies on the street sure could.

The muffled wails and shrieks were just loud enough to keep the first turns enticed, to keep them convinced that a meal of fresh meat was contained within the trailer. The only drawback to the setup was the stink of rotten flesh wafting in through the condo's open window.

The waiting, the stench, the sight of the living, breathing Chicom soldier five feet away … all of it worthwhile if the cards fell the way Baker hoped they would. Best case scenario: The Chicom patrol would find the trailer enough of a curiosity to halt their patrol, dismount their vehicles, and investigate.

Lifting the Steiner binoculars to his face, Baker glassed the bay, right to left, stopping only when the Space Needle came into view.

"Motherfuckers," he growled. "The audacity. And on Independence Day, no less."

Two tiny forms were in the process of hanging a massive Chinese flag off the wire railing encircling the Space Needle's observation deck. The crimson herald, thrashed about mightily by wind lifting off the bay, was roughly four times the height of the soldiers securing its upper corners to the handrail. In one corner of the flag, four small gold stars formed an arc around front of a much larger gold star.

Baker dipped the binoculars a few degrees. Clustered near the dual mouths of the Duwamish Waterway, at the southernmost edge of the bay, where man-made Harbor Island dominated the shoreline, was a flotilla of Chinese warships. They stood at anchor, light gray hulls aligned and bows pointing north. The jagged superstructures atop the handful of frigates and destroyers closest to shore stood out starkly against the charred ruins of Seattle's westside neighborhoods.

The oilers and supply ships necessary to keep the large fleet on the move were moored at slips jutting from Harbor Island's north tip. Multiple cranes and a massive petroleum tank farm rose up from behind the support ships.

As the sound of engines drew nearer, Baker peered down Highland. Seeing the first of two AM General Humvees, both painted in dark woodland camouflage, he spoke into his two-way radio. "I have eyes on. Two commandeered Humvees. Soft tops … no armor. I count four tangos. Two in each victor. Both victors westbound on Highland. They're single file and moving five mikes per. Stand by."

Informing Baker that his SITREP had been heard, a pair of clicks sounded over the secure channel. One was from Dorn, the other from the radio of the Wolverine on the roof above him.

Baker knew Dorn was ready. The young woman had been born ready. He sometimes wondered if the blonde-haired blue-eyed sharpshooter was decorated Vietnam sniper Carlos Hathcock reincarnated.

The man on the roof behind the FN M240 belt-fed machinegun was another story. Though Steve Lawless, twenty-six-year-old son of a local longshoreman and a lifelong hunter, always gave it his all when outside the wire, he *was* prone to distraction—Kylee Dorn, chief among them.

Below Baker's perch, the zombies also heard the approaching vehicles. Torn between the anguished wails coming from the Screamer and noises mechanical in nature also associated with the possibility of fresh meat, the Zs simply about-faced and stood rooted in place.

Two minutes crept by at a glacial pace. When the search party finally crested the hill, the lead Humvee came to a complete stop in the center of Highland.

"They onto us?" asked McGrath through gritted teeth. The sight of the Chinese flag stenciled onto the sides of vehicles that used to be deployed by the Washington Army National Guard started his blood pressure rising.

Baker shook his head. "Negative," he said, "they're eyeballing the zeds. Probably counting heads." He removed his ball cap and ran a hand through his dark hair. The high-and-tight cut was hours old and contrasted sharply with a bushy beard shot through with gray.

"I hid the wires real good."

"No doubt," replied Baker. "Patience, friend." Though his words belayed a steely calmness, the combat veteran's face was a mask of barely contained fury. His free hand went to the moon-shaped scar running from cheek to brow, a byproduct of the beating suffered in Portland. Whenever the white-hot rage born from that final torture session welled within him, the simple act of touching the inches-long rope of scar tissue pushed the emotion back down to where it belonged: in the imaginary strongbox tucked away in the farthest reaches of his mind.

The vehicular pause lasted all of ten seconds.

As those ten seconds ticked by, someone in one of the vehicles came on over the radio, trying once again to hail their missing comrades.

Baker listened to this and detected a hint of fear in the rapid-fire Mandarin coming out of the speaker. He imagined the driver of the lead Humvee contemplating getting his vehicle turned around. Since this was the only passable route over the high point in the district, Baker had a gut feeling the urge to push forward, to follow orders and find the missing foraging party, would win out over fear.

Sure enough, as soon as the radio went silent, the lead Humvee began to creep forward.

As expected, the zombies held their ground.

Only when both Humvees had crossed the nearby intersection and were nearing the chute between the horse trailer and curbed Dodge pickup did the zombies forget about the noisemaker still doing its thing inside the trailer.

At about the same time the lead Humvee braked again and ceased all forward movement, Baker said, "For Scully," and rapidly squeezed the handle on the M57 pulse generator clutched in his left hand.

In milliseconds a 3-volt pulse had transited the hundred feet of firing wire connecting the firing device to the pair of daisy-chained M18A1 Claymore anti-personnel mines deployed on the horse trailer's rear bumper.

When the pulse detonated the blasting caps inserted into the Claymores, a combined three pounds of C4 plastic explosive detonated, sending a swarm of fourteen hundred steel ball bearings scything the air toward the static Humvees.

As the twin thunderclaps shook the penthouse windows in their frames, Baker witnessed the hail of steel tear a majority of the zombies to pieces, then go on to implode the lead vehicle's near vertical front windshield.

There was a sound like hail hitting a tin roof as debris and ball bearings ricocheted off of vehicles and structures.

The two CCP soldiers in the first Humvee also bore the full brunt of the blast. They were dead or soon would be. Slumped forward, helmets ripped from their heads, faces a bloody mess of shredded flesh, they were truly a vision from hell.

No sooner had the wind begun to whirl away the dust and rising smoke tendrils than the driver in the second Humvee wised up to his situation and started his vehicle reversing from the kill box.

Too little, too late. With a perfect angle on the driver's window, Dorn rose up on her elbows, put the Leupold optic's crosshairs over the wide-eyed soldier's left cheek, and squeezed off three closely spaced rounds.

Just as the driver was receiving his lead facial, Lawless was stitching the Humvee's roof with controlled bursts fired from the M240 Bravo.

Taking the better part of a dozen rounds to the top of his helmeted head, three more in the right shoulder, and a pair to the meaty part of his inner left thigh, the PLA captain in the passenger seat died instantly.

Seeing the rear passenger door swing open, Baker shouldered the Chicom QBZ-95 bullpup carbine and aimed for the spot on the road he expected to see the responsible party come into view. A beat after throwing the safety and applying a few pounds of pressure to the trigger, a helmeted soldier slithered out, went to one knee, and shouldered a rifle identical to the one currently targeting him.

Simultaneously, Baker leaned into his weapon and finished pressing the trigger. *Oh the irony*, he thought as he held the trigger back, *to be cut down in a foreign country by ammo manufactured in your own.*

The sustained burst stitched the soldier from crotch to sternum, leaving a half-dozen crimson blooms on the urban-camo blouse, but not before the soldier fired a salvo of his own.

The errant shots plowed harmlessly into the bricks framing the brownstone's front entryway.

"Spray and pray," noted McGrath.

Ignoring the accurate observation, Baker spoke into his radio. "Dorn, Alamo Actual. How copy?"

"Good copy," replied Dorn.

"SITREP?"

"Nothing's moving but the deaders that were outside the kill zone."

Baker said, "Wait one. What do you got, Lawless?"

The man on the roof said, "Five tangos down. Four KIA. The one you just hit is down and bleeding out. Only other movement on our side is a crawler. Want me to smoke it?"

Baker poked his head out the window. "I see it." The Z Lawless spoke of had been in the kill zone and was cut in half just below the navel by the deadly spray of ball bearings. It was clawing its way toward the gut-shot soldier, whose weapon was now lying on the road well outside of his reach. Though the undead creature was trailing intestines and leaving a wide crimson track in its wake, its forward progress was admirable.

"Stand down," Baker ordered. "Let the zed finish the fucker."

"Copy that," replied Lawless.

The soldier was holding his guts in with both hands. Now and again he would tear his eyes off the encroaching zombie and look longingly at his dropped weapon.

The entire ambush, from the Claymores popping to the final radio interaction between Baker and Lawless, had lasted all of forty-five seconds. It took the crawler double that to reach the dying man.

During that time, Dorn put down the remaining zombies and began the grisly task of collecting intel from the torn-up PLA soldiers.

Having finally arrived at the dying soldier, the crawler dragged itself atop the man's heaving chest. Tilt to its head, like that of a curious dog, the Z opened its maw wide, then dove down on the soldier's blood-spattered neck.

No screams escaped the soldier's throat as dirty, clawlike hands plunged into the jagged bite wound and ripped it wide open. The only fight on the part of the PLA soldier came in the form of a couple of lazy kicks at the road and the fingers on one hand threading weakly into the zombie's wispy tangle of hair.

Addressing Dorn, Baker said, "Let him suffer. Once he's gone, finish the Z. You know the drill after that."

The *drill* consisted of collecting intel, ammo, weapons, and food.

The PLA soldier lasted another thirty seconds or so.

Two minutes after the enemy drew his last breath, Dorn was finished with her tasks and dropping her haul on the penthouse floor.

Looking to Baker, McGrath said, "Want me to call Lawless down?"

Baker knew what his friend was thinking. Under normal circumstances, after a daylight attack, especially one involving explosives whose reports traveled great distances, a helicopter would soon be launching from the deck of one of the ships anchored in the bay.

These weren't normal circumstances. Consulting his stainless Rolex Submariner, Baker said, "We're staying another five minutes. Call Lawless down so we can all watch the fireworks together." Hauling the prisoner to the window, he added, "I think Lei needs to see this, too."

As the hands on Baker's Rolex neared high noon, he focused his attention on the second hand. As it swept silently past the twelve, he lifted his gaze to the ships on the bay.

Five seconds past noon a huge fissure opened up on the deck of one of the battleships. As ammunition in its below-deck magazines touched off, it heaved sideways, orange flames and thick black smoke belching from stressed and bowed hull plates.

Similar scenes were playing out all over the bay. Backs broken, a pair of cruisers began to slip beneath the choppy water.

Still lashed to pilings beside Harbor Island, an oiler disappeared after a trio of explosions rocked her from bow to stern.

Hit by shockwaves pushed out by the multiple explosions, the penthouse windows rattled mightily in their casings. A beat later, a freight-train-like rumble reached Baker's ears. With the booms from secondary explosions rolling up off the bay, he regarded his team, only to be met with questioning looks.

Incredulous, McGrath said, "Had to be underwater demolitions, right? Was that the work of our SEAL teams? Or …?"

Watching the swooping stern of a gray-hulled corvette thrust skyward, then start the slow final plunge to the bay floor, Lawless said, "Could've been stand-off weapons." He regarded Baker. "Tomahawks … or maybe J-DAMs?"

Shaking his head, Baker said, "Rods from God."

Nodding, Dorn said, "I've heard of them. Something about tungsten bolts fired from orbiting military satellites."

Oil slicks dotted the bay where vessels once were. Many more were aflame and going down. A scant few were untouched and attempting to escape the carnage.

The prisoner had taken it all in. He'd had no choice. Baker had held him up to the window. Now, Lei's face was slack and ashen.

Looking Lei in the eye, Baker said, "The *rods* attain such a velocity coming back to earth that when they strike their target they pack the punch of a small tactical nuke." Reverting back to English, he added, "Lei, here, just witnessed thousands of his comrades pay dearly for invading America."

While Baker wanted to watch the few remaining vessels go through their final death throes, a piece of intel Dorn had found in the pocket of the soldier riding shotgun in the lead Humvee needed to be delivered, posthaste, to someone with a better grasp of the language it was written in.

Grabbing up his weapon, Baker shouldered the foragers' packs. "We're oscar mike." Looking from Dorn to Lawless, then finally settling his gaze on McGrath, he went on, saying, "On the way out, make sure you let the commies know who hit them."

As the team filed out of the living room, Baker prodding Lei ahead of him, McGrath deposited a playing card on the face-shot corporal's chest. On the back of the card, hackles up and teeth bared, was a ferocious-looking wolverine.

Chapter 1

Wednesday, July 18, 2012 - 3:00 a.m.

Boise, Idaho

Clad in black fatigues, a sheer black balaclava and four-tube full-color-display NVGs completely obscuring his bearded face, thirty-six-year-old Cade Grayson was first out of the hovering Ghost Hawk. Boots on the ground, the seasoned Army captain and veteran of nearly a hundred combat missions inside Iraq and Afghanistan took a few steps from the helo's open left-side door, quickly dropped to one knee, then aimed the business end of his suppressed M4 carbine the length of the gravel access road.

Behind the former Delta Force shooter, their movements smooth and well-rehearsed, five similarly dressed assaulters spilled from the angular stealth helicopter.

No sooner had the last pair of boots kissed Idaho soil than the door began to close and the bird broke its hover.

Decibel-killing composite rotor blades grabbed air and the matte-black ship climbed to treetop level. Barely audible over the harmonic thrum produced by the whirring rotor disc, twin turbines rose in pitch and Jedi One nosed down and sped off in the direction it had come. Thanks to exhaust routed through a complex web of ceramic-coated pipes, any danger of the ship's thermal signature being detected by enemies who happened to be nearby was greatly mitigated. In a nutshell, the very helicopter used in the storied Bin Laden raid in Abbottabad, Pakistan—the last Gen-5 bird of its breed—was out of sight and undetectable to the human ear in a matter of seconds.

The odor of damp earth and fertilizer hit Cade's nose as a westerly breeze scoured the kerosene-tinged exhaust from the landing zone. Made up of billions of stars, the Milky Way overhead was a luminous smudge arcing across the coal-black night sky.

Cade looked to his right. Kneeling before the twelve-foot-tall fence rising over them all, Chief Special Warfare Operator Adam Cross, a blond-haired blue-eyed Navy SEAL, had already snipped a waist-high vertical seam in the miles-long run of chain-link fence bordering the wide access road.

Gloved hands wrenching the breached fence apart, Fui "Nat" Natanumo, formerly of 7th Group Special Forces and the newest member of the Pale Riders, called the rest of the team over.

As Cade watched the remaining three members of his team assemble before the newly created hole, he heard in his headset confirmation that the other two teams, Bravo and Charlie, were on the ground and advancing on their respective targets.

Ushering the three shooters on his left through the gap, Cade relieved Nat of his job, then motioned for the hulking Fijian and slightly smaller Navy SEAL to fall in behind the others.

Squeezing through the gap after Cross, Cade paused long enough to secure the two halves of fencing with a pair of nylon zip ties.

Spread out before the team was a treeless tract of land a mile deep and nearly a mile and a half wide. During the briefing at Peterson Air Force Base in New District, Colorado (formerly Colorado Springs), the two-star general running the PowerPoint presentation had estimated the rectangular plat to be nearly a thousand acres. Row upon row of green, knee-high plants ran off toward the distant horizon where a series of jagged peaks stabbed toward the heavens.

Whispering, Cross said, "These are potato plants, huh? Not what I envisioned during the briefing."

Navy SEAL Petty Officer First Class William "Griff" Griffin stopped in his tracks and regarded Cross. Voice heavily accented thanks to dividing his formative years between Lubec, Maine and Boston, Massachusetts, he asked, "What's the matter, Surfer Boy? They only grow *kale* in Malibu?"

"Santa Cruz," shot Cross, his NVGs locked on Griff. "And I *despise* kale. Awful texture. Kind of like eating forty-grit sandpaper."

Cade raised a gloved hand to quell the banter. Though it was the middle of the night, thanks to another in a long streak of days in which temperatures had climbed into the hundreds all across the West and Midwest, it was still nearly eighty degrees here in Treasure Valley. Already his Crye Precision top, buried beneath a plate carrier, black fatigue blouse, and chest rig sporting half a dozen spare magazines, was sticking to him like a second skin. Regarding the three wraith-like forms on his left, he motioned for them to move out.

Without a word, Javier "Low Rider" Lopez padded to the strip of dirt between the run of knee-high plants a dozen rows over. Following Lopez, Griff chose a spot between rows nearly equidistant from Cade and the stocky Hispanic.

"I don't like this," grumbled Griff as he gave his suppressed Heckler & Koch MP7A1 a final onceover. "It's *waaaay* too quiet."

Whispering, Cade replied, "Better than taking incoming fire. Or setting down in the middle of a horde of hungry Zs."

"Anvil Actual," Griff whispered, "you're always the voice of reason."

Cade made no reply. Looking to his right, he saw that Nat, Cross, and former SAS sniper Nigel "Axe" Axelrod had all adopted similar spacing. The Brit's balaclava was pulled down beneath his chin. Though Cade's NVGs softened the image, he could still read the pained expression on the younger man's face. Having recently spent a week scouring dozens of refugee camps in England and Scotland for any sign of his wife, Axe had learned from records kept early on that not only had his wife escaped Japan alive, but she had been two months pregnant with their first child—no doubt a secret she intended on divulging in person.

The exuberance felt by Axe had ended abruptly when, like a dagger to the heart, the clerk behind the computer delivering the good news went on to inform him that the military hospital his wife had been brought to for observation had fallen to the zombie scourge sweeping the globe.

The news had crushed the man, aging the thirty-three-year-old a decade in a matter of seconds.

Dark hair now flecked gray, the Brit had returned from the trip withdrawn and stoic. Once jovial and quick with a quip, Axe was now nearly as frugal with his words as Cade.

Cade got it. He had been there. Losing his soulmate had nearly broken him. Losing both a wife and a *child*? He didn't know how that one would go over if he were in Axe's boots. While the notion of eating his Glock would likely ghost across his brain should he ever lose Raven, Cade knew that by taking that way out he would only be helping the enemy. In one press of the trigger his death would tilt the scales in favor of the very ones responsible for all his losses. The *Chinese Communist Party* and the army under their control would be that much closer to seeing their final endgame come to fruition. The burn of justified anger rising up his neck was a stark reminder of his main purpose in life: to do unto the People's Liberation Army what they had done unto Brook and millions upon millions of his fellow Americans.

Stuffing the unbridled fury back into the imaginary vault deep inside his chest, Cade made a mental note to self to pull Axe aside and try and get him to open up. He knew it would be akin to a mime trying to get a clam to talk. But if it helped coax the man from his shell, Cade figured it would be worth a shot. Hell, it might also help him to cope with his own demons.

Sensing that his Pale Rider team was raring to go, Cade held his hand up high, palm forward, then struck out across the field.

Taking point was exactly what Cade's late mentor Mike "Cowboy" Desantos would have done. And while Cade liked nothing about the current hand he'd been dealt, maneuvering across open ground with little concealment and—should they make contact—greatly exposed to enemy fire, fast roping in amongst the vast complex of silos and pre-fab metal buildings breaking the horizon a mile distant was never an option. Though all three birds doing the insertions tonight were stealthy in nature and enjoyed the element of surprise, dropping down in the center of the warren of buildings where rotor and turbine noise would be amplified ten-fold by the close confines had a high probability of drawing immediate fire from the nearby army encampment and was not worth the reward of taking the risky overland approach out of the equation.

Staying a few steps ahead of his team, Cade led them all toward the faint bubble of red-orange light cast from halide bulbs perched atop standards on the target building's far side. Recipient of a coveted LEED Platinum Certification of sustainability, the building, and those surrounding it, were outfitted with an array of solar panels. The kilowatts generated by the roof-mounted panels were more than enough to power the complex's heating, cooling, ventilation, and lighting systems.

***

Ten minutes into the crossing, a door on the distant building hinged outward. Surprised by the squeak of hinges and sudden flare of light, the entire team went to ground, where they remained, pressed against the damp earth, for three long, tense minutes.

Immediately after hitting the deck, Cade had raised his head and watched a man slight in stature close the door behind him and walk to a row of what looked to be portable toilets. The creak of a door opening and subsequent bang of it closing rolled across the open ground, piercing the shroud of silence the team had enjoyed for the duration of their slow and deliberate approach.

Clearly the man was beholden to no kind of noise discipline.

After spending two minutes inside the portable john, and another couple of minutes standing by the fence and speed-smoking a cigarette, the PLA soldier reentered the building.

Once the door had sucked shut, Cade counted slowly in his head. Hitting thirty, he rose up off the ground, verified with a quick glance over each shoulder that his team was formed up, then resumed his steady march across the massive potato farm.

***

Ten minutes after their brief pause, Cade and his Pale Riders were formed up against the twelve-foot-tall run of fence rising over the row of portable toilets.

"Why the honey buckets?" Lopez asked. "Nash indicated the building was dual use."

"For the grunts, is my guess," Cade whispered.

"Wouldn't have the enlisted dirtying up the officers loo," Axe posited.

"Anything's better than squatting over a buried fifty-five-gallon drum," Griff mused. "The reek of burning shit is one thing I can never memory hole."

While Cross snipped a vertical seam in the chain-link, Cade broke radio silence.

"Bravo, Charlie, this is Anvil Actual. We are green for go." He checked the time on his watch, then added, "Two mikes."

After receiving calls of "Good copy" from the other teams, then updating Command back at the Tactical Operation Center of their current status, Cade led his men through the newly created breach, holding one half of the fence back until the five heavily armed black-clad ninjas were standing on the blacktop with him.

While Cross sealed the fence with zip ties, Cade surveyed their surroundings. Everything he saw jived with the overhead photos that had been splashed on the op center's jumbo monitors.

In full daylight, the team would have been cloaked in the shadow of the immense building looming over them. Viewed through his NVGs, it seemed to Cade as if a cruise ship, its hull painted robin's egg blue, was moored in front of them.

JR EPLOT FARMS was emblazoned in red high up on the corner of the forty-foot-tall building.

Sandwiched between the five-foot-tall block letters and metal door the slight man had emerged from was a long row of multi-paned windows. The windows stretched away from the nearby corner, right to left, maybe a hundred feet, until the run was cut short by the first of a pair of massive floor-to-ceiling rolling doors.

At the far end of the building, bathed in the soft orange-red glow coming off the same halide lights the team had spied from across the field, was a myriad of farming equipment. Several wheeled vehicles painted in the green and yellow scheme ubiquitous to John Deere sat idle on the corner of the white cement pad. Rising over the tractors and combines was a pair of hundred-foot-long wheeled conveyor belts. Nearby, partially obscured by the Eplot building, was the motor pool visible on the two-star's satellite imagery. At the moment, due to the poor viewing angle, Cade couldn't tell if the Chinese-made military vehicles present in the photos were still on site. If they were out on patrol, things could get dicey upon their return.

Stay away, Murphy, thought Cade as Axe went to work on the lock with the lock pick gun.

While Cade covered the sliding doors on the team's left flank, Nat shouldered his Mk 46 Mod O lightweight machine gun and aimed its deadly end at the windows above their heads.

Basically a lightened version of the venerable SAW (Squad Automatic Weapon), the Mk 46, made by Fabrique Nationale, was belt fed 5.56mm x 45mm linked rounds and equipped with a foregrip, bi-pod, and holographic sight. With a 200-round ammo belt in the box magazine, the weapon weighed less than twenty pounds. Child's play for the huge Pacific Islander. Certain death for anyone caught in his sights.

There was a soft click, then, one hand gripping the doorknob, Axe turned and faced the team.

"Good to go," he declared, stuffing the pick gun into a cargo pocket.

Cade regarded the ground where the door's kick plate met the poured cement threshold. While there was a rubber sweep, he didn't like what he saw. "Will the probe fit?"

Axe shook his head. "The seal's not hermetic," he answered, "but it's damn close."

Cade met Lopez's expectant gaze. Lopez said, "Split up?"

Nodding, Cade gestured toward Axe and Nat. "Once we're inside, take them and secure the warehouse. I'd bet that's where you'll find our smoker." He made eye contact with Griff, then stabbed a finger at Cross. "We'll go right and clear the upper floor offices. I'll run point."

With the team *stacked* outside the door, weapons held at a low ready and each man with a gloved hand on the shoulder of the shooter ahead of him, Axe yanked the door open.

Chapter 2

Lopez spilled through the door first. Moving between a walk and a run, he rolled left, M4 shouldered and following the sweep of his eyes. Close behind Lopez, Cade looked to be a mirror image of the entry man as he peeled right, the stubby black suppressor trained on the short length of hallway running away from him.

One bulb just inside the door to outside cast its dim yellow light over just a small segment of the thirty-foot-long hallway.

Immediately following Cade through the door, Nat went left, following Lopez into the bowels of the long, shadowy hall.

Griff and Cross flowed through the door next, both going right, closing up quickly with Cade, their suppressed MP7s held at a low ready.

Last in was Axe. He quietly snugged the door closed behind him, shouldered his Heckler & Koch MP5SD, and hustled to catch up with Nat and Lopez.

Eyes probing the gloomy stairwell dead ahead, Cade slowed his pace, raised his carbine to cover the landing above, then pressed his back to the right-side wall.

"Lopez, Anvil. Clear to the landing," Cade whispered into the comms. Keeping the stairwell covered, he waited for a response from Lopez, who was likely already at the distant door and assessing his team's situation.

A beat after Cade and his team had formed up at the base of the stairs, Lopez responded, saying, "Door's unlocked. Utilizing the fiber optic probe. Wait one."

Thirty seconds after entering the massive, darkened warehouse, Lopez had reported back that there was nothing moving inside.

Without another word exchanged between Cade and Lopez, both teams were again on the move.

The old special operator mantra *slow is smooth, smooth is fast* was going through Cade's head as he made the landing. Raising a fist to halt Griff and Cross on the stairs below him, Cade performed a quick turkey peek around the corner. The stairs leading to the door on the second-level landing were lit by starlight filtering in through windows set into the wall high above.

Whispering "Clear," Cade was on the move again, taking the stairs one at a time. The stairs were wooden and well worn. He was careful to step where the treads were nailed to the underlying stringers.

Following Cade's lead, Griff and Cross climbed the stairs, stopping once they were both eye level to the landing.

The door to the second-level suite of offices was a metal item inset with a rectangular window. Reinforced with wire, the window was plastered with all manner of notices germane to agriculture and shipping. Peering through a gap in the papers, Cade saw a long hallway. Set at equal intervals on the left side was a trio of doors. They, too, were steel and featured the same single pane of safety glass.

Cade tried the door. *Unlocked.* Knowing that Lopez's team was likely already beginning their methodical sweep of the warehouse below, he picked up the tempo, pushing through the door solo. Heel and toeing it, he moved swiftly down the hall, stopping briefly before each window to assess what lay inside.

Suite did not apply where these offices were concerned. Like the exposed wood stairs and scuffed linoleum underfoot, the large rectangular rooms were nothing spectacular to look at. All three featured a bank of windows that looked out over the darkened warehouse floor. The furniture in the offices was more Goodwill than Crate and Barrel.

The sickly sweet pong of decaying flesh was coming from the first office. On one of the pair of desks in the room was a large Rubbermaid bin. Two identical bins sat on the floor in front of the desk's kneehole.

A bullet puller and reloading press were clamped to opposing edges of the second desk. Missing was the brass tumbler, primers, bullets, and black powder—all items essential to reloading ammunition.

Standing in the center of the room, totally out of place, was an upright drill press. It was fitted with a tiny bit. Held fast in a clamp directly below the bit was a single bullet.

It was the strangest reloading setup Cade had ever seen.

As he moved on, the sense that something about the whole scene was way off kept gnawing at him.

The second office was stacked floor to ceiling with cardboard boxes. Some were open. Inside one, Cade saw cans of vegetables and boxes of pasta.

Upon opening the door to the third office, Cade was hit in the face by warm air rife with the stench of unwashed bodies. All of the furniture in the room was pushed up against the right-side wall. Four cots were set up in the center of the room. Atop each cot was a sleeping man clad only in boxer briefs. On the floor beside each cot was a rifle, gun belt with holstered pistol, and random personal effects. At the foot of each cot was a neatly folded uniform and pair of smartly polished boots. The uniform near the cot left of the door was different than the others. Whereas the hard epaulets on the others each bore a single gold chevron, the epaulets on the fourth blouse had two.

Private First Class, thought Cade. *The high man on the totem pole.* Which made sense, because whereas the three privates were very young—mid to late teens, the rat-faced individual sporting a thin mustache was early to mid twenties.

Cade guessed the privates were conscripts. Men rounded up in the Motherland and forced to come abroad to prepare their new land for occupation. While they had to be hardy to survive this long in the zombie apocalypse, it didn't mean squat on the field of battle. Facing down fire and returning it in kind wasn't something learned and honed against an undead opponent unable to think or reason.

As Cade's gaze walked from one upturned face to the next, he got the impression that not one of them had ever felt the rasp of a razorblade.

That was all about to change.

Doubling back to the landing, Cade relayed his findings to Griff and Cross and hastily went over what he had planned for the soldiers.

The consensus was that the four sleeping soldiers were the daytime detail. Which led Cade to believe there were at least half as many tasked with babysitting the prisoners throughout the night.

Based on intel provided at the briefing, two more guards would be patrolling the premises in an electric golf cart.

Cade led his team to the door to the third office. After peering inside and confirming the soldiers were still in the same positions they had been when he left them less than a minute ago, he turned the knob.

Certain a muzzle flash from discharging a weapon inside the office would not only light up the entire room but would also spill into the warehouse and compromise the team below, Cade had convinced Griff and Cross to wait outside the door. Back on the landing, convincing them that his plan was solid had taken a three-second-stare followed by the promise that the pair would be weapons hot and covering him the entire time he was alone inside the room.

With Griff and Cross stacked behind him, guns at the ready, Cade pushed the door inward.

No movement. One soldier was snoring steadily. Another grunted and seemed to fumble in the dark for a blanket that wasn't there.

After meeting his team members' expectant gazes and receiving a pair of thumbs-up, Cade swung the M4 around to his left side where it would be easily accessible, drew the Gerber Mark II dagger from its sheath on his hip, and pushed into the room.

Viewed with the color NVGs, the Gerber's black steel blade seemed to shimmer. Eager to see the combat dagger draw blood, Cade moved to the first cot on his right, leaned over, and clamped his free hand over the man's nose and mouth. The snoring ceased, and the body went rigid on the cot.

Before the soldier could wrench himself free from the tight grip of REM sleep, Cade had pressed his knee down on his sternum and cut a wide bloody chasm across his throat. The man put up zero fight. The look on his face when the blade first bit was one of total bewilderment. It gave Cade great satisfaction. For just like the first

Americans to face a dead loved one come back to life, this man had no idea what was happening to him.

One second the almond-shaped eyes had snapped open and fixed the ceiling in the near pitch-black room with a startled stare; the next, warm and sticky blood was pulsing over Cade's hand and pooling in the trough on the cot created by his and the dying man's combined body weight.

The next two PLA soldiers went to their maker in much the same manner. By the time Cade was positioning himself over the fourth soldier, the one senior in rank, the metallic stink of spilt blood was so thick in the air one could almost taste it.

Sheathing the Gerber, Cade unholstered his Glock. Simultaneously, he pressed both a knee on the soldier's chest and the pistol's suppressor to the man's forehead.

Brown eyes snapped open.

It was immediately evident to Cade that, even cloaked in darkness, the private first class knew he was in trouble. Without allowing the communist soldier time to react, Cade said in Mandarin, "Remain silent, or I will kill you."

The soldier's nose crinkled and his face contorted. Cade had seen the same look of revulsion manifest on the faces of people getting their first up close and personal glimpse of the walking dead. He was certain he had worn a similar expression months ago when he had been forced to kill his undead neighbors. Shedding his own normalcy bias that day had been a split-second affair. Same with this man. As soon as he felt the press of cool steel on his forehead, a decision needed to be made. And, fortunately for him, it was the right decision. The *only* decision.

Lifting his hands off the cot and putting them in the air, the man replied in Mandarin, "Who am I surrendering to?"

Cade was about to break it to the man that he was in the presence of the Reaper and his salvation relied on how quickly he provided information regarding the number of troops in the building, as well as how many were garrisoned nearby, when multiple flashes of light from somewhere down below lit up the room. As the sharp reports accompanying the muzzle flashes rattled the windows, the initial short volley was answered by a sustained burst of suppressed return fire.

The follow-on tinkle of brass casings and metal links striking the concrete floor below was quickly drowned out by screams.

As Cade was motioning Griff toward the windows overlooking the warehouse floor, back-to-back gunshots were met by the hollow concussion and brilliant white light that erased every shadow from the room.

NVGs momentarily washed out, Cade pulled the Glock away from the soldier's face. Then, relying on the image in his mind's eye—the last thing he saw before the flashbang stole his vision—he brought the Glock down hard on the side of the PLA soldier's head. Though Cade's vision had yet to return fully, the crunch of bone losing to polymer and the prone man going totally limp suggested the delivered blow had terminated right where he had wanted it to. On the soldier's left temple. The softest part of the skull where there was just enough give to let the blow's kinetic energy pass through and travel, nearly unabated, to the man's *off switch.*

As he rose up off the unmoving body, Cade hoped he hadn't gone too far and killed him. That was supposed to have been saved for *after* all pertinent intel had been extracted.

Leaving Cross to flex cuff the unmoving soldier, Cade moved to the windows. Just as he was forming up next to Griff, the *all clear* call came through his headset. It was Nat, which was odd, since Lopez was the one running the breakaway team.

"Anvil here. Roger that," Cade replied. "Offices are clear. Four tangos down. Give me a SITREP, Nat."

"We made contact immediately upon entry," Nat said. "Lopez put two tangos down just inside the main door. We were spread wide and clearing the room when the smoker pops up in the far corner and squeezes off half a mag. Spray and pray. Fucker's prayer was answered."

Drawing a deep breath, Cade said, "Who got hit?"

"The prisoner the smoker was boinking bought it. Lopez got winged, too."

NVGs back to full functionality, Cade let his gaze roam the warehouse.

"A woman?"

"Negative," replied Nat. "A teenaged boy."

Griff said, "Any port in a storm with these fuckers."

Cade lifted his NVGs and shot Griff a look usually directed at Duncan for using an off-color quip in Raven's presence. But Raven was getting older and quite streetwise, so Cade was a little rusty. Instead of conveying that there was a *time and place* for Griff's observation, his expression came across to the other operator as an *is that the best you got?* challenge. Which Griff ran with, saying: "Short eyes abound when Mullahs and Commies are concerned."

Pounding a fist on the window glass, Cade said to Nat, "Go on." In his head he had an image of the young girl on the PLA general's bed at the OMSI in Portland. It had taken every ounce of restraint on his part to refrain from cutting off the man's flaccid penis and feeding it to one of the Zs clinging to the museum's gate.

Nat said, "The PLA puke put one in the back of the kid's head. Was it accidental? I highly doubt it."

Was a teenaged boy thought Cade as he raised a hand to ward off whatever comment Griff had locked and loaded. "So he's the lone civilian casualty?"

"Affirmative," Nat confirmed. "Two other prisoners caught rounds. Minor GSWs. Both are going to make it."

Cade could see Axe bandaging Lopez's right arm. "How's Low Rider?"

"He's going to make it," Axe said. "However, he will be giving himself stranger wanks for a couple of weeks."

Down below, Lopez was stroking an imaginary boner left-handed.

"His new handle," Griff decreed, "has to be Pee Wee."

After a quick headcount of the prisoners and determining there were twenty-seven, not the fifty or so he'd been led to believe were being held here by the PLA, Cade ordered Nat to have them coalesce near the rolling doors.

Cross called, "This puke is coming to. You want me to give him another love tap?"

"Negative," Cade said. "Drag him downstairs. Make sure his knees hit every stair along the way. If that doesn't bring him around fully, run an ammonia ampule under his nose so he'll be free of cobwebs when me and him resume our chat."

The soldier wasn't a large man. Cade guessed him to be maybe five-five in boots. Couldn't weigh more than a buck fifty wet. No problem for the much larger Cross, so Cade had Griff remain behind. Searching the other offices for intel would go much faster with two of them going at it.

While Griff searched the folded uniforms and personal effects for anything of use, Cade hailed SOCOM Commander, General Don "Smokey" Blake, who was monitoring the mission from the op center, no doubt with a cigar clenched between his teeth.

"Target locked down. One friendly KIA. Twenty-seven recovered." Cade paused for a second to gather his thoughts. It wasn't the first time he'd had someone under his command get injured. Still, it was always a wake-up call. Meeting Griff's gaze, he went on, "I also have one Alpha team shooter wounded. He's stable and ambulatory."

After listening to Smokey relay a SITREP, Cade said, "Copy that. Anvil Actual out."

Griff said, "Helo's inbound?"

Cade nodded. He was looking out the window. Cross had already made it to the warehouse floor. One arm extended, the fingers on that hand encircling the back of the soldier's neck, the SEAL was guiding the PLA soldier past the assembled prisoners.

As if he could somehow see his former captor slipping by in the dark, one of the prisoners, a teenager from the looks of it, launched a sneak attack from behind a stack of pallets. As the teen swung a wild haymaker at the smaller Asian's midsection, a strapping man pushing middle age also lashed out. The older man's balled fist caught the PLA private squarely on the side of the head, sending him sprawling away from Cross and the first attacker.

The scuffle following the ambush soon became a full-blown scrum as the second attacker launched himself at the prone PLA soldier.

By the time Nat could react, both he and Cross were being pushed aside by the follow-on surge of humanity.

As ferocious an assault as he'd ever seen, at least one in which ravenous zombies were not the attackers, Cade witnessed the civilians tear into the PLA soldier. While he had wanted to interrogate and then finish the PLA soldier himself, maybe even give him flying lessons, there was something satisfying about seeing the freed prisoners excise their pound of flesh.

Dozens of kicks and punches landed. When all was said and done—barely ten seconds from first blow to last—the soldier's near-naked body was a mess. A road map's worth of scratches crisscrossed the slight man's upper torso. One of his eyeballs had been gouged from its socket and was missing. The other eye had taken a blow solid enough to break vessels. It was already swelling, the white spotted with blood.

Griff said, "Like a pack of wild hyenas," and shook his head.

Cade was busy breaking open a fresh pack of playing cards bearing the Pale Riders logo. Meanwhile, in his headset, Nat was telling him the PLA soldier was still breathing. As he stuffed the ace of spades into the gaping second mouth on the nearest dead soldier's neck, he said to Nat, "Do your best to keep him alive."

"Little squirt is one tough mofo," Griff noted.

Cade regarded the man. "We'll see about that." As he picked over the pile of stuff Griff had collected from about the room, stuffing a small day planner and the dead soldiers' military identification cards into a pocket, he said, "But first I need to see what's going on in the room with the drill press. Something about that reloading operation isn't sitting right with me."

Nodding in agreement, Griff followed Cade out of the room but not before placing death cards atop the remaining two corpses and snapping a few photographs of their handiwork.

Chapter 3

Upon entering the second office, Griff had immediately torn into three of the boxes, finding them each filled with a myriad of different types of food. One box was full of canned vegetables: water chestnuts, green beans, corn, and green chilies. Another contained cans of Spam and Dennison's chili packed in with a dozen packages of rice noodles. Box number three contained a bonanza of junk food. Chips and crackers shared space with several different types of candy bars. Cartons of American-brand cigarettes were the only constant item included in each box.

Pointing to the symbols written in black ink on each box, Griff said, "Can you read this chicken scratch, Wyatt?"

Cade stopped searching the desk drawers long enough to cast his gaze at the boxes in question. "The one on the left belongs to someone named Wang. It's a real popular surname over there. On the one in the middle, that T-looking symbol with a hook on the bottom is pronounced *Ding*. Looks like Ding had a taste for spiced lips and assholes."

"Nothing wrong with Spam," Griff bristled. "I'd eat it any day over lobster tail."

"That's right. You're the son of a lobsterman."

Griff asked, "So who's the dude with the sweet tooth?"

"That box belongs to someone named Jen." Smile bunching the balaclava, Cade said, "Jen's dead. Grab me a few of his Snickers bars. Won't be needing them where he's going."

The bottom drawer of the desk Cade was rifling through held a bottle of Scotch and box of premium Cuban cigars. They both went into his pack. He had a certain person in mind who would appreciate them.

Leaving all of the food in the second office for the New District citizens soon to be assuming the farming duties, Cade and Griff moved on down the hall.

The door to the first office was locked. Cade fixed the problem with a single kick. As he pushed in the door, the stink of death that had been barely detectable in the hallway hit him full-on in the face. It was coming from the Rubbermaid bins on the desk to his fore. Something inside the bin was producing subtle clicking sounds.

Letting his MP7 dangle on its center point sling, Griff said, "Sounds like someone's raising snapping turtles. I bet they're a delicacy where *Wang, Ding,* and the boys are from."

"Turtle is nothing," Cade said. "Ever been to a wet market where most everything is exotic and still kicking?"

Prying off the lid to the bin on the desk, Griff said, "Been to my fair share of open-air bazaars. Most of the meat is normal; goat, pig, cow. And it's already dead. Just agree on the cut and price, and the butcher starts hacking."

"Wet markets in their part of the world are like the Pike Street market on steroids. We're talking live bats, snakes, centipedes, beaver—"

"Live beaver? Hope it doesn't smell like what's in these bins."

Cade had been inspecting the half-assed reloading operation on the opposite side of the room. Meeting Griff's gaze, he said, "What's in the bins."

"Wing, Ding, and Jen are some sick puppies," said Griff. He had the lids off of all three bins and was staring into the pair on the floor. "These ain't turtles, Wyatt. One of our boys has amassed himself a nice collection of zeke heads. Four in each bin. A couple of them are carved up pretty good." He drew a deep breath through his mouth, paused, and looked at the ceiling. Exhaling, he added, "All of them were kids before …"

While the revelation that the clicking and grinding sounds Cade was hearing was attributable to the constantly moving jaws of a dozen severed zombie heads sent a cold chill running up his spine, that they had been kids before turning made it exponentially worse. And though he had trained himself early on to ignore the noise created by the pistoning jaws of a hungry herd on the move, those same sounds, when amplified by the tight confines of the boxes and echoing off the drop-tile ceiling, was too much.

Without a word, Cade drew the Gerber and went to work silencing the animated heads. When the teeth on the last head, that of a pig-tailed girl who was maybe all of eight years old when Omega brought her back as a flesh-eating ghoul, had made their final skin-crawling *clack*, the former Delta operator fell to his knees in the center of the room. He stayed in that position of supplication for ten long seconds.

Five seconds in, Griff asked, "You praying or puking, boss?"

Cade said nothing.

Griff spent the final five seconds putting the lids back on the boxes. He was standing hands on hips when the row of lights farthest from him snapped on. Then, row by row, like dominoes cascading toward the elevated offices, the rest of the rows of lights on the warehouse ceiling lit up.

Back on his feet, Cade flipped the NVGs away from his eyes. Meeting Griff's questioning gaze, he said, "I was doing one and staving off the other. That sound"—he threw a visible shiver—"It got to me, man." He shook his head. "For the first time in a long time, I almost lost my cookies."

"After getting dipped into a herd a half dozen times to strap a tracker on a zeke, you get used to it." Griff flipped up his NVGs and pulled the lower half of the balaclava under his chin. Smile parting his red beard, he said, "I'm king of the short straw."

Cade approached the drill press. Taking hold of one chrome arm of the tri-spindled handle, he spun it slowly clockwise, running the chuck down toward the press's pitted metal worktable. The bit in the chuck was so small he had missed it earlier.

Griff said, "This is a Frankenstein setup if I ever saw one. It's like half the stuff is still on layaway." He cocked his head. "What do you think the Chicoms were up to? Sure doesn't look like they're putting lead and brass together."

Head adopting a similar tilt, Cade said, "I'm puzzled by it, too. Let me chew on it for a bit."

Griff padded to the corner of the room opposite the door. "You see these?"

Pushed against the wall, a steady humming coming from each, was a small freezer and an even smaller refrigerator. The freezer was the type of upright perfect for an apartment dweller: large enough to store a couple months' worth of meat, yet still small enough to be unobtrusive.

The refrigerator, on the other hand, was the kind of item designed for a college dorm or hotel room.

Griff opened the refrigerator and poked around inside. "Chinese bottled beer and farm-fresh eggs." He hinged up and held two plastic baggies aloft. They both contained substances that were very malleable. One was white and looked like goat cheese. The other was pinkish-white and floating in a hazy viscous liquid. "Tofu? I think," said Griff, shaking the first bag. One eyebrow cocked, he jiggled the contents in the other bag. "Whatever is in this, it sure doesn't look fit for human consumption."

Cade examined the items against the overhead light. While he was doing so, Griff was searching the freezer.

"I think the white stuff is some kind of bean curd. Soybeans were one of Eplot's main crops." When Griff didn't respond, Cade added, "Something about this goo in bag number two is real familiar. I know I've seen it before. Just can't place where."

When Griff finally replied, he was holding a metal canister. It was rimed with frost. Visible underneath the frozen veneer was the unmistakable and universally recognized biohazard symbol. It was red and, though its sharp points were softened thanks to the rapidly melting frost, the image still conveyed a menacing *hands off* kind of vibe.

Nodding at the bag in Cade's hand, Griff said, "I was thinking that one was sushi." He thrust the canister at Cade. "Whatever is in this, we're going to want to handle with kid's gloves."

"Agreed," Cade said. He called Nat and asked him to search for a cooler. Next, he checked the freezer for ice. The ice cube tray was there, but the last person to get ice had put it away empty. Definitely something the old Raven would have done. Not now. Bird was one of the most responsible people he knew. Wise beyond her years. And growing like a weed.

Putting the tray aside, Cade used his dagger to chip some accumulated ice from inside the freezer. He found a small garbage can, emptied the trash, then placed the ice in the plastic liner. The canister and plastic baggies went into the ice-filled liner. He tied a knot and stuffed it all into his pack.

Nat came back over the radio. "Found a cooler. Whatcha got?"

"I'm not sure yet." He paused and regarded Griff. "So let's keep it in-house until we know more."

Griff mouthed, "How's Lopez?"

Cade passed on Griff's question, then listened as Axe delivered the bad news.

Listening in over the shared comms, Griff said, "So he's in shock. Dude just caught a hot round."

"Just a fragment," Cade corrected. What he didn't say was how he found it hard to believe a minor gunshot wound could start his old friend on a downhill slide health-wise. Hell, he'd seen the man suffer an appendix bursting, shrug off the pain for the entire helo ride to Schriever, then return to running ops just a few days after having the offending organ removed.

Nope. Low Rider was tough as nails. Something else was going on here, and Cade had a feeling the items in his pack held the key to it.

Hearing in his headset the call of *airspace clear,* which meant a *helos inbound* warning was imminent, Cade snatched up his rifle and set out to join the rest of the team on the warehouse floor.

Chapter 4

New District of Columbia

Colorado Springs, Colorado

Raven Grayson was torn from a deep sleep by her least favorite ringtone of all those available in her recently acquired iPhone 4—the hottest model out the summer the zombie apocalypse elevated the simple act of surviving just one more day stratospherically above mankind's need for the newest in technological advances.

Placing the smartphone strategically atop a dresser *across* her bedroom from her bed ensured that she wouldn't be able to tap *Snooze* on the glass screen and drift back into some of the best sleep she'd enjoyed since the last Saturday in July 2011—the day the Chinese Communist Party conducted a multi-pronged strike that caught the United States and the world flatfooted.

Perpetrated by an elite cell of the People's Liberation Army, the clandestine operation seeded several cities in the United States with a virus that turned anyone infected into undead ghouls hungering for human flesh. As if the Pearl-Harbor-like sneak attack wasn't bad enough, the insult to that injury came in the form of Chinese warships arriving on America's shores.

Delivered by dozens of People's Liberation Army Navy landing craft, the initial invasion force consisted mostly of PLA special forces teams who snaked inland, spreading like so many tendrils throughout the east and west.

Following a repulsed attack on the United States Marine Corp's Mountain Warfare Training Center at Pickel Meadows, some twenty miles south of Bridgeport, California, the West Coast invasion forces fell back to lick their wounds.

Now, after a purported Chicom spring offensive never materialized, the entire population of Colorado Springs/New District—quickly closing on twenty thousand—were holding their collective breath.

Cursing herself for utilizing her dad's foolproof strategy for waking up on time, she flicked on the lamp on her bedside table, swung her legs off the bed, and stretched her arms high over her head. After stilling the circulating fan at the foot of her bed, she rose and padded across the room toward the slab of metal and glass emitting a noise much too loud for a device so tiny.

Silencing the blaring klaxon-like tone with a stab of a finger, she dropped to the floor and knocked out fifty push-ups. The push-ups were followed by two sets of sit-ups—fifty each. Seventy-five crunches rounded off her morning routine.

She rose and dabbed at the sweat on her brow with a tartan golf towel she'd found at some tony resort during one of her many travels outside the wire. Wetting a travel-size toothbrush with water from her canteen, she quickly brushed her teeth.

Raven's room in the two-story Craftsman in Northern Colorado Springs was identical in size and placement to the one in her old home back in Portland, Oregon.

The seafoam-green paint was where the similarities ended. On one wall, where Lady Gaga and One Direction posters would have been pinned, was a Night of the Living Dead poster. Lara Croft: Tomb Raider—clad in leather and brandishing chrome pistols—took up space above her dresser. Another wall was a shrine to her newest passion: classic rock and roll. Thin strips of green paint struggled to peek around posters of Black Sabbath, Led Zeppelin, The Doors, The Rolling Stones, and Pink Floyd. Had Daymon's connection been able to source a Janis Joplin poster, it would have been displayed prominently on the back of her door. For now, though, a full-size cardboard cutout of a raven-haired Joan Jett was a worthy placeholder.

Eschewing a shower, she dressed in all black. She supposed the choice was partly a byproduct of her current mood, but whenever anyone asked, she just told them, straight-faced, that she was going through a *goth phase*. Far from the truth. While not having to decide on what to wear on any given day—something Sasha always seemed to be obsessing over—was quite liberating, Raven's real reasons were more tactical in nature.

Though it was summer, she always wore long pants and layered her tops, sure to don first something thin and breathable as the base layer. Caught out in the wild and on the run, she reasoned, shedding layers and stowing them for later would be far easier than having to forage afterward for clothes that fit her.

Work smarter, not harder.

Working in the faint light spill from the sixty-watt bulb, she laced on a pair of worn Danner boots just like her dad's. Cracking her neck, she shrugged on the black Kelty backpack she'd purchased at Lola's in town. It weighed north of twenty pounds and contained everything she'd need in the event she had to bugout from home in a hurry or was forced to spend the night outside the wire. She was *never* caught without the pack when away from home.

Be prepared.

Additionally, acquired along with the iPhone in exchange for three cartons of Marlboro cigarettes she'd found at the golf resort was an all-black Benchmade Infidel dagger. The fixed-blade knife rode on her left hip, opposite her holstered Glock 19 semiautomatic pistol.

Rounding off the Johnny-Cash-like ensemble, also black, was her plate carrier/chest rig, the latter carrying a half-dozen spare magazines for her black Colt SBR (short-barreled rifle).

Closing the bedroom door at her back, she called out for Max, the brindle Australian Shepherd that had adopted the Grayson family shortly after the Omega virus had decimated his own.

Raven was halfway down the stairs when she detected the sound of Max's nails clicking on hardwood. As the oak front door came into view, she saw the faintest glimmer of first light peeking around the blackout curtains covering the rebar-reinforced window.

At the bottom of the stairs, she flicked on the foyer light.

The outer edge of the spill fell on Max. The dog was sitting on his haunches in the center of the family room, stub tail going a mile-a-minute, multi-colored gaze locked on his master.

"Hungry?"

Max yawned.

Raven went to the garage and dipped a measuring cup into a half-full bag of Purina dog chow. Dumping the kibble into Max's bowl, she said, "Come on. You need to go potty first."

She walked through the spotless kitchen, unbarred the door to the enclosed backyard, and shooed Max out.

While Max did his business, Raven stowed away in her pack a couple of cereal bars, some carrots from the garden, and a plastic baggie full of Tran's teriyaki-flavored venison jerky.

Calling Max inside, Raven threw the locks and replaced the security bar. "I'm going to work," she said. "Dad should be home before me. You be good, you hear?"

Emitting a low, guttural growl, Max sauntered over to his food bowl and sniffed the kibble.

"I know, I know," said Raven. "You don't like dry food. We've already established that. It's all I got for you. Take it or leave it."

She made her way through the open floor plan, grabbed her house keys off the peg by the front door, and slipped the lanyard over her head. On the way out the door, tugging on a black ball cap and threading her high ponytail through the back opening, she said, "Lola is on the lookout for wet food. If anybody can get ahold of some, she's the one."

Raven closed the door behind her and locked all three deadbolts. Her new all-black Trek Remedy mountain bike sat on the front porch. It was propped against a dozen solar panels waiting to join the dozen Duncan and Wilson had already installed on the roof.

Daymon had come across the competition bike in a shed behind a home outside of Aurora. It was a high-dollar item, complete with carbon-fiber frame, suspension front and back, top-of-the-line Shimano components, Bontrager disc brakes, and more speeds than Raven could ever use.

Daymon had insisted a similar model in a bike shop in Jackson, Wyoming had carried a five-thousand-dollar price tag. Even so, he had traded it to her for a single pound of Tran's peppered jerky. Compared to the old purple tank her dad had scrounged from a store in nearby Yoder, the Remedy was half the weight and ten times the bike.

Navigating by the fading starlight filtering through the oaks lining the street, she rode north, past the home shared by Wilson, Taryn, Sasha, and Peter. *What a crazy place that's become.* Game night was, to use a phrase coined by Taryn, *off the hook*. Which meant games of Axis and Allies or Monopoly—fueled by energy drinks and stale Cheetos—could last all night long.

As she passed the two-story abode, she heard nothing coming from within. Sasha wasn't arguing with *anyone*. Wilson wasn't defending a move or explaining a rule to Peter for the umpteenth time.

Just darkened windows and silence.

Glenda's place was more of the same. Which came as no surprise. With generators outlawed, the new capital was eerily quiet just before dawn. The only people out and about, silent as wraiths as they crisscrossed the city on foot or by bicycle, were wall workers and pikers. Save for the city's first responders, vehicular travel inside the walls was still forbidden from dusk until dawn.

Nearing the two-level Tudor-style house three doors down from Glenda's place, Raven's attention was drawn to a flare of light deep in the bowels of its wraparound porch. Before dying out and being replaced by the bright red cherry at the end of a Cuban cigar, the orange glow briefly illuminated a craggy face she knew all too well.

As she brought the Trek to a complete stop at the end of a cement walk leading to a short stack of stairs, a cloud of blue-gray smoke billowed from the gloom. A beat later, a familiar voice, flavored with a Southern twang, said, "Time to make the donuts?"

Parroting her dad, Raven said, "Nothing in life is free."

Duncan chuckled at that. "From the mouths of babes," he said as his features were again lit up by the flame of the lighter.

Raven said, "Why are you up so early?"

"I don't sleep these days. Melatonin stopped working weeks ago."

She said nothing.

Changing the subject, he said, "Bird of the Apocalypse is a little overdressed, don't you think? Looks like you're going to a funeral."

When Raven didn't respond, he lamented, "It's going to be a hot one today. No central air. No fan in my casa." He took a long drag off the cigar. Blowing a smoke ring, he added, "I think once today really gets rolling, ol' Duncan's going to be sweating like a whore in church."

Raven said, "First off, you *need* to get another saying. I've heard that one a hundred times. Secondly … when is Glenda going to let you back in?"

He drew a deep breath. Exhaling sharply, he said, "Firstly, I'm done future trippin'. One day at a time is new Duncan's approach to life."

"All the while practicing Rule 62, right?"

"That too." He shook his head. "I'm not going to rush the woman. I can't. I owe her amends. Real living amends. Still, I don't know if that's going to be enough to get me back into her good graces." He went silent for a beat. "Sometimes," he added in a funereal voice, "I wish she would have just cut my throat while I slept. Put me out of my damn fool misery."

Raven shook her head. "Don't be so hard on yourself." She made a face. "What's the second thing?"

"It's going to be a hundred or so today. Know how I'm going to be sweating?" Illuminating a smile that didn't match the tone, the lighter flared again.

Raven said, "Like a—"

A cloud of cigar smoke enveloping his bearded face, Duncan interrupted her, saying: "I'll be sweating like a hemophiliac in a knife store. Or a cow in a slaughterhouse. How about sweating like a short nun at a penguin slaughter? Are those fitting? I have more. Shall I go on?"

Chuckling softly, Raven said, "I have to go. *Potvin* gets pissed if the crew isn't loaded on time."

"Piking or policing today?"

"Wherever she puts me," Raven replied. "Pay's the same either way."

"See if you can sweet talk Wendy into letting you pike. Your boots don't get all mucked up. Plus, you don't have to burn your clothes afterwards. Usually don't, anyways."

"The less I have to talk to her, the better." She paused for a tick, thinking. "Hey," she continued, "if my dad isn't home by noon, can you walk Max?"

"Sure thing, Bird. Ain't got nothing else to do but grow older … all alone."

Ignoring the comment, Raven said, "Thank you." She dismounted the bike and delivered the keys to him.

Duncan removed his Stetson. Slipped the lanyard over his head. After stubbing the cigar on his boot sole, he said, "You be careful out there."

Surprising Old Man with a hug and a quick peck on the cheek, Raven said, "Max doesn't like to walk past bars or stores that sell Jack Daniels."

Duncan said nothing. For if he had tried to respond, no doubt he would have started blubbering like a baby. Biting his lip, he watched her return to the sidewalk.

Straddling the Trek, Raven said, "You got this, Uncle D." As she stood on the pedals and started the bike rolling north, she added, "People love you. Don't forget it."

Ensconced in the dark corner of the porch, tears welling in his eyes, Duncan dragged the old .45 from underneath his leg where he had hidden it. Wiping the tears on his sleeve, he decocked the hammer, then slipped the pistol into the holster dangling off the arm of the chair.

Chapter 5

Cade was hitting the Chicom PFC with a barrage of questions when the *helos inbound* call came across the net. Knowing he had five minutes, at best, to gather the team, round up the civilians who wished to be taken to Colorado Springs, and lead them all to the parking lot designated LZ Echo, he gagged the prisoner and, at the top of his voice, let everyone know what he expected from each of them.

Pushing PFC Ding ahead of him, Cade slipped through the yard-wide gap between the massive sliding doors. In tow were the six former prisoners who wanted to get as far away from Idaho as possible. Three were women in their twenties who, after a hard twelve hours spent working the fields, were regularly utilized as *comfort girls* by the day guards who had been watching them toil away under the hot sun.

The other three were orphans of the zombie apocalypse. Unfortunately, Cade had learned, the PLA soldiers did not discriminate on age or gender when it came to having their sexual needs sated.

One of the kids, a fifteen-year-old called Cole, had been the first attacker. He had snatched the Tanto-style knife from Lopez's discarded chest rig. Then, maneuvering under cover of darkness, Cole had lunged at the PLA soldier, targeting the rapist's male anatomy with the Tanto. Instead of hitting his mark—on account of the other prisoners mounting an attack of their own—Cole had buried the razor-sharp blade to the hilt in the Chinese soldier's upper thigh.

"Cole," Cade said as they hustled past the motor pool, "you ever think about trying out for Special Forces?"

"My dad was a Marine," said the kid. "I was hoping to follow in his footsteps."

Didn't look like the son of a Marine, thought Cade. Far from a high-and-tight, the kid's sun-bleached brown hair was shoulder-length, the long unruly bangs framing his deeply tanned face. Dark brown, almost black eyes peered out from the greasy tangle.

Cade said, "You talk about your dad in the past tense. What happened to him?"

Cole straightened up. Then, chest puffed out, he said, "He died in the battle for Fallujah. I had just started the third grade."

It was evident to all present that the act of saying those words stole the wind from the kid's sails. Seeming to deflate, like a pool toy trapped under a sumo wrestler, the teen hung his head and pinched away newly formed tears.

Cade rested a gloved hand on the kid's well-muscled shoulder. "Vigilant Response or Urgent Fury? Do you happen to remember which?"

Meeting Cade's gaze, Cole said, "Urgent Fury. A terrorist tossed a grenade at his feet. He dove on it to save the rest of his fire-team."

"I'm real sorry for your loss," Cade said. "Fallujah was liberated thanks to the actions of your dad and men like him. As a result, a lot of innocent Iraqis, mostly elderly and women and children, made it out of the city alive."

"Your dad was the tip of the spear," Nat added. "Never could have done it without him."

Cross said, "I was spotting from a Force Recon overwatch. Saw some serious fighting on the ground. Tanks and tracks couldn't maneuver very well due to the narrow streets and alleys. There was no other choice but to go in on foot."

The group rounded the corner of a second warehouse due east of the first and were greeted by the sun chinning itself over a nearby mountain range. It was enormous and cast a yellow-orange glow over the vast parking lot.

Shielding his eyes with one hand, Axe recounted how he'd heard from fellow SAS that the fighting was so fast and furious—the Marines' initial push seeing so many friendly casualties—that mates of his in Black Watch Regiment had to be deployed from FOB Dogwood to backstop follow-on quick reaction forces. "Real hard-chargers, those Devil Dogs. Had the tangos legging it at first light. Mates of mine were rounding up squirters all along the road east of Fallujah."

Regarding Cole, Griff said, "What's your last name?"

"Mitchell."

After a brief pause, Griff said, "I met your dad. He was a sergeant, right?"

The *thwop* of rotor blades beating the air broke the still. A murder of crows in a distant tree cawed in displeasure then took flight. The rising sun glinting off their feathers made it seem as if their beating wings were afire.

"Yes," said Cole. "Third Battalion, First Marines."

"If I'm remembering it right," Griff said, "your dad personally led the charge against entrenched fighters. He did so not once, but three times before he dove on that grenade."

"He was awarded the Navy Cross and a Purple Heart. I carried them both with me until …"

"Go on," Nat prodded.

"What happened to the medals?" Cade asked.

"The guy I just stabbed took 'em from me."

"What'd that prick do with them?" Griff asked.

"He made me toss them into the toilet."

Stopping on the edge of the lot, Cade said, "One of the portables back there?"

Cole nodded. "I already looked for them." A tear traced his cheek, splitting a couple of pronounced freckles. "They're gone for good."

Cade said, "Soon there will be plenty of people working these fields. Friendly people." He gestured toward the building Cole had been held in. "I'll have someone get a magnet or metal detector over to the toilets. Come hell or high water, you *will* get those medals back."

Cole was speechless.

Axe asked, "Where's your mum?"

After a long, awkward silence, Cole said, "One night after working the fields, Ding took her somewhere." He shook his head. Wiped away more tears, but this time he didn't try to hide it. "We were planning to escape. Ding couldn't keep his *fucking* hands off of her. Lots of people have gone missing over the last couple of weeks."

Cade said, "All women?"

Cole shook his head. "Most. But not all." As his words trailed off, a thrumming rolled over the field to his fore.

All eyes turned toward the sound. A few seconds later, like a scene straight out of *Apocalypse Now*, a pair of stealth Chinooks, flanked by shark-like attack helicopters, all of them flying fast and low, appeared on the eastern horizon. Painted flat-black and wearing olive-drab markings, the formation stood out starkly against the rising sun.

Only thing missing, Cade thought as the lead Comanche attack helo overflew them all and banked hard before a picket of mature trees, *is a stack of external speakers pumping Wagner and a beachhead with surfable waves.*

Cade said, "Battle damage assessment just came over the net." He regarded his team. "Night Stalkers just got done decimating a company of PLA regulars." He pointed to the north, where a pillar of smoke was just cresting a distant picket of trees. "One Little Bird took fire and made a forced landing."

Concern evident in his voice, Lopez asked, "Casualties?"

Shaking his head, Griff said, "Just you, mi amigo. Bravo and Charlie kicked ass and took names, too. Both objectives are sanitized and sewn up."

Letting his MP7 dangle on its single-point sling, Griff threw up his hands. "Tell me I'm not the only one who isn't dazzled by the direction this campaign is taking. Operation Dust Devil?" He grimaced and shook his head. "Should have been called Operation Happy Meal."

"I get it," Cade agreed. "I'd be happy if it was us smoking the commies instead of the SOAR boys. Bottom line … dead is dead."

Another four helicopters, twin-rotor Chinook CH-47s, also painted SOAR flat-black, came in hot from the west. The inbound

Chinooks' beating rotors quickly rose over and drowned out the soft thwopping and muffled turbine whine coming from the stealth helos.

Face taking on a stony countenance, Lopez regarded Griff. "You were at the briefing. This family-run farm provided the lion's share of spuds that went into Happy Meals the world over." He paused. Glare softening, he added, "You want a repeat of last winter? I don't. By day two of President Clay's rationing program, I was getting real sick of MREs."

Griff chuckled. "Now there's a revelation." Running his gloved fingers through his natty red beard, he went on, saying, "I've been sick of those fucking things since day one in the sandbox." He glanced longingly skyward. "Oh, to be back in Pakiland. Damn, those people know how to season their food."

"Earth to Griff," Cade said, "we're oscar mike in five. Escort Cole and the others to one of the inbound birds. We'll all rally at Jedi One whenever Ari sees fit to rejoin the party." Singling out Cole, Cade went on, "Come see me when you get settled. I'll show you around New District. Maybe even take you to see the Bunker."

Trapping his hair behind his ears, Cole asked, "What's the Bunker?"

"Need to know," Cade said with a grin.

"Is there a barber on base?"

"Let me guess," said Griff. "High and tight?"

Cole nodded. "Ever since my dad was killed, I've kept my hair real short."

Griff offered his hand to the kid.

Instead of returning the gesture, Cole snapped off a crisp salute any drill sergeant would have a hard time critiquing—at least without an ulterior motive.

The inbound birds were bringing the contingent of volunteers willing to sacrifice the relatively comfortable existence of New District for the more spartan quarters and, most certainly, several months of backbreaking labor.

As soon as the Chinooks' rear ramps hit the pavement, crew members wearing flight helmets and brandishing M4 carbines escorted the civilians from the helicopters to pre-determined spots on the lot.

Gesturing for Cole to follow, Griff said, "Let's go get you a seat by a hip window. Always good to see your LZ from the air before you're experiencing it from a prone position with incoming crackling the air all around you."

"Cole isn't a Jarhead yet," Cross shot. "You trying to scare the kid off or something?"

The quip was drowned out by the sudden appearance overhead of Jedi One.

Cole nearly broke his neck trying to get a good look at the stealth helo as it flared hard and settled softly on the lot. Speaking to the action Skipper must have been fortunate enough to have just taken part in, the helo's left-side minigun protruded from the two-by-four port just in front of the open crew compartment door. Though the staff sergeant's face was obscured by the ever-present skeleton mask attached to his black flight helmet, the enthusiastic thumbs-up flashed by the longtime SOAR crew chief all but confirmed Cade's suspicion.

Cade slung his M4 over one shoulder and spun a finger in the air. "Saddle up, fellas!"

Onboard Jedi One, Ding was strapped into the *bitch seat.* Coined long ago by some anonymous operator, the aforementioned seat was located dead center in the row of forward-facing seats. First in and last out was what the unlucky person who found themselves in the seat could expect. The *last out* part was the real reason nobody wanted to sit there. Last out was the person most likely to be exposed to any kind of accurate incoming fire during a hot insertion. Then there was the lack of view, which to most operators—at least those such as Cade who used any time spent in the air to get much-needed shuteye—didn't come anywhere near to trumping the prospect of wading through a hail of enemy lead.

Bookended by Cade and Nat, the heavily bandaged CCP soldier looked more like a school kid serving a punishment for fighting at recess than the brutal pedophile rapist that he was.

While Cross and Griff grabbed the rear-facing seats framing the cockpit pass-through, Axe helped Lopez into the seat next to Nat.

As Axe went to take the seat normally reserved for the right-side door gunner, Nat shot the prisoner a menacing glare. "Bleed on me and you die."

Cade repeating the threat in Mandarin caused the prisoner to sink even deeper into the bitch seat.

Shifting his gaze to Lopez's bandaged right shoulder, the big Fijian said, "Low Rider is one of us. He can bleed wherever he wants to."

Lopez made no response. His eyes had gone glassy.

Seeing Axe plug his comms set into the bulkhead, Cade said, "What's going on with Lopez?"

"He asked me for a sedative. 'Something strong' were his exact words."

Incredulous, Cade asked, "What'd you give him?"

"Bloke's a captain. Since he properly outranks me, I gave him what he asked for."

"So he's stable?"

"Copy that, mate. He'll sleep all the way home. Just like a wee little baby."

"Welcome aboard Night Stalker Airways," said a familiar voice. "I'm Ari, your pilot for the day. Haynes on my left here is the big man on the stick for the first leg of the trip. Please stow your tray tables and return your seats to their upright position." He paused and glanced back into the troop compartment. Below his smoked visor, a wide grin materialized. "Next stop," he went on, "is classified and off the books."

Having heard enough idle chit-chat to last him the rest of the day, Cade closed his eyes and settled in for the ride.

Before Jedi One had reached the wide swath of destruction it and the Comanche gunship escort had wrought on the PLA camp, Cade Grayson was in the middle of a dream featuring his late wife and a tropical island. If he'd been awake and peering groundward, he would have been privy to the zombie horde drawn to the perimeter fence by the impossible-to-miss plumes of roiling black smoke and the wails of dying PLA soldiers.

Ari's request to divert course by a few degrees was drowned out by a combination of turbine noise and the imagined sound of surf crashing onto the conjured-up beach in Cade's head. He also didn't hear Smokey at the op center greenlighting the slight course deviation. For had it registered, Cade would have insisted that getting Lopez to Penrose Hospital to have his wound treated was the more pressing issue.

Chapter 6

When the North Gate finally came into view, the sun was just cresting the high plains far off of Raven's right shoulder. The first thing lit up by the sudden orange flare was a slab-sided dump truck. It was parked with its massive grille aimed for the gate. Brake lights glowing red, it towered over the other vehicles waiting for the gate to open.

Nosed up to the rear of the gore-streaked dump truck—or Dead Sled to those on burial detail—was an equally sullied Chevy Silverado 3500 pickup. The once white work-truck featured a dually rear axle, six-inch lift, and massive wraparound bumpers. The windows were fitted with slat armor—metal plates complete with horizontal viewing ports. The Chevy's wheel wells and undercarriage were protected by a series of segmented wire cages that ran the length of the vehicle. The apparatus was similar in appearance to the Full Hull Protection kit bolted to the outside of the eight-wheeled M1126 Stryker parked opposite the dump truck.

Dressed in dark brown Carhartt overalls, the diminutive head of Task Force North, Wendy Potvin, a fifty-five-year-old former librarian, avid prepper, and lover of post-apocalyptic literature, was busy checking the air pressure of her rig's run-flat tires.

A platform on wheels, its metal floor head-high to the five-foot-three-inch Potvin, was hooked to the modified fifth-wheel coupling in the Chevy's load bed. Three-foot-high walls constructed from diamond plate steel rose up from all sides of the platform. Every foot or so was a port large enough to accept a pike. Overhead was a slab-metal roof that provided the pikers shade while they worked. Access to the highly modified trailer was via the swing-away door and retractable ladder positioned on the right front near the tow vehicle's tailgate.

As Raven locked her bike alongside a handful of others in a bike rack in front of a boarded-over Kinko's copy shop, Potvin's voice carried over to her. "You ready to go, Miss Grayson?" Clearly, Potvin had left her *inside* voice at home.

Flashing a thumbs-up, Raven took a PowerBar from a pocket. As she crossed the road, she scarfed the bar and gulped water from the stalk affixed to the bladder stowed inside her pack.

"Done feeding your face?"

Raven said nothing. She knew from experience that a smartass comment would only get the woman going. Also, more often than not, a wisecrack earned the offending party a ride in the Dead Sled. Not that she was averse to a little hard work. The opposite was true. She just wanted to get the show on the road.

Standing beside the trailer, Raven shot the head of TFN a questioning look.

"It's been a few days," Potvin noted. "You pike or clear last time?"

"Pike."

"Do you have a preference?"

Raven shrugged.

Clearly expecting an answer one way or the other, Potvin asked, "What's your dad up to?"

"If I tell you—" Raven began.

"You'll have to kill me," Potvin finished. "Wouldn't want that. Wouldn't want a possum-playing zombie to bite the kid of a legend, either, so … you'll be piking today."

Raven shifted the carbine from one shoulder to the other. "How long until we're oscar mike?"

Potvin shrugged. "I'm thinking fifteen or twenty. But you know the Army … lots of hurry up and wait."

"So we're going to have an escort?"

Potvin nodded. "Quadrant North is pretty busy right now. Seeing a few glowers, too. They'll stick with us if it's hairy out there. If sailing is smooth, they'll leave us and range further out toward the wastelands. Either way, we'll be fine. Always are."

Cringing inwardly at hearing the kind of talk liable to challenge Mister Murphy—of Murphy's Law fame—to monkey-wrench the entire operation, Raven changed the subject. Looking over both shoulders, she said, "Got anything new for me?"

After determining there were no new arrivals who needed a kick in the pants to get them with the program, Potvin fixed Raven with a perverse grin. "It's your lucky day. Wait right here." She hurried to her truck and came back clutching three books.

Cocking a brow, Potvin said, "*Lucifer's Hammer* by Larry Niven and Jerry Pournelle is about a comet hitting the earth and how society deals with the aftermath." She nodded at a pair of workers just showing up for duty. "Kind of a case study on what's happening here and now. Society pulling itself up by its collective bootstraps. You got brigands and good guys. Lots of similarities to Springs. I mean, New District. I keep forgetting."

With a slight tilt to her head, Raven said, "I'm guilty of that, too. What else you got?"

Though Potvin obviously relished the new job that had gotten her out from behind the checkout desk, the need to expose readers to literature she had cut her teeth on was still strong in her. Smiling wide, she said, "*Fight Club* by Chuck Palahniuk. He's from your neck of the woods. Portland native, I believe. It's got one helluva twist."

Raven cocked a brow. Nothing about the bar of soap on the cover grabbed her. So far, the book cover with the comet streaking across a night sky was the frontrunner.

"Not your cup of tea, eh?" Potvin stuffed book number two into her back pocket.

Raven nodded at the book in Potvin's other hand. "What's that one?"

"*The Road* by Cormac McCarthy." She displayed the book as if she were a bookseller pushing her current favorite read.

Raven inspected the creased cover. A man and young boy trudged a desolate stripe of blacktop crowded by gnarled trees. The duo was shabbily dressed and holding hands. Something about the way the man stared over one shoulder suggested the book was chock-full of nonstop danger.

Fish on, thought Potvin. "I've read it more times than I can count. You want a quick synopsis?"

Though she was already sold by the cover, Raven nodded. "Sure. What's it about?"

"A man and his boy trying to survive after some kind of calamity turns their world upside down."

"Sounds familiar. What kind of calamity?"

"Cormac never really comes out and tells the reader." Potvin riffled the pages with a thumb. "Nuclear war is my guess. Or maybe the Yellowstone super caldera went *kaboom*."

"I'll take it. How much?"

Potvin brightened. Cocking a brow, she said, "Got some of that deer jerky?"

"Nope," Raven lied. "But I can bring you a bag of it next time."

"The old 'I'd gladly pay you Tuesday for a hamburger today' routine, eh?"

The reference didn't register with Raven. She looked to the Dead Sled, then shifted her gaze to the piker platform.

Potvin said, "Wimpy from Popeye. You don't know Popeye? The cartoon?"

"SpongeBob was more my speed."

As more workers arrived and began to assemble near the outbound vehicles, Potvin said, "You kids are missing out on so much." She displayed the book. "This for one bag of jerky?"

Raven stuck her hand out. "I'll bring it next time. You have my word."

Smiling as if she'd just won the lottery, or perhaps traded beads and shells for an island in New York, Potvin grasped Raven's hand and pumped it vigorously. "It's a deal," she said and handed over the well-loved paperback.

***

Raven was leaning against a light pole and already two chapters into the adventure when Potvin cleared her throat and called for the teens and young adults lounging nearby to form a circle around her. Seconds later, Potvin was joined by an African American soldier from the 4th Infantry Division. The tape on the soldier's MultiCam blouse read *Tuttle*. The black chevrons told Raven he was a sergeant.

Without making any kind of small talk, the sergeant quickly ran down the frequency of zombie sightings by zone, then warned that the North and East Zones were seeing a resurgence. "It's a perfect storm," he said. For some reason, he'd been staring Raven in the eye. "The danger of you all running into a herd out near where the two quadrants converge is very high." He handed Potvin a clipboard. After checking the box marked *Departing* and signing on the line beside it, Potvin folded a thick stack of yellow papers in two and trapped them under the chrome clip. The Golden Tickets—the coveted pass given to those who had already demonstrated the ability to survive outside the wire—would be matched with each piece of identification Potvin had collected from the day's crew. The items would be used to ensure everyone who left the wire with Potvin was accounted for upon her return. She would return the identifications and Golden Tickets to her crew once every person had passed a rigorous post-mission inspection.

After the failed assassination attempt on President Valerie Clay, great care was taken to know exactly who was inside the walls at any given time. While miles of razor wire had been strung atop the cement freeway noise abatement panels making up the wall, short of locking down and taking a census of the entire population of the New District of Columbia—a strategy that had been floated by the heads of the growing bureaucracy at the Bureau of Eradication Reclamation and Restoration (pronounced *bear* by the locals)—the only viable way to ensure against the infiltration of spies and would-be-saboteurs was to keep a running log of every person coming and going through the four established gates.

Clearly not a foolproof process. However, since ratcheting up security, the instances of property damage and pro-CCP graffiti had plummeted.

"Grab your gear and mount up," Potvin bellowed. "Get your window seat. First come, first serve."

There was a mad rush for the pile of modified javelins and articles of homemade armor laid out on the sidewalk beside the mobile platform.

Raven dove into another page of her book and let the crew have their pick of weapons and armor. Hanging back would also allow them to grab the coveted seats at the *back of the bus.*

Raven didn't care. She was a *front of the bus* kind of girl. Unlike the others who preferred the rear of the elevated platform, she wanted to be where she could provide security for the most important components of the entire operation: the driver and tow vehicle. Plus, like the seats near the emergency egress doors on a commercial airliner, seats her mom and dad always requested when flying, being near the platform's only door *and* the Chevy's load bed offered multiple avenues of escape should Mister Murphy come a calling.

Keep all your options open.

As the pikers slipped their chosen weapons through the ports from the outside, Raven stowed the book and shouldered her pack. While the pikers formed a line and started up the ladder, she lifted her gaze to the walkway running atop the North Gate.

A couple of dozen kids and teenagers stood shoulder-to-shoulder on the crowded walkway. They wore heavy clothing and helmets. Most had on pieces of makeshift armor: bracers and leg protection fashioned from baseball, football, and hockey gear. All were armed with slingshots of many different designs. Most were the homemade items for sale in Lola's: surgical tubing affixed to crude wooden handles. Others were the type with bent metal tubing, foam grips, and extended forearm braces.

While rocks were plentiful in the nearby green space, half-inch steel ball bearings were the preferred ammo. Having the same diameter as a .50 caliber round, in the hands of a proficient *slinger* with a wrist rocket, the round missiles had no problem penetrating a zombie's cranium.

Knowing what was coming next, Raven made her way to the platform and selected one of the remaining pikes—a relatively short item wrapped with tape and foam to ensure a good grip. She slid her weapon through the open door, then climbed aboard. Finally, doing her duty as the last person to board, she disconnected the ladder and put it on the floor alongside her pack and SBR.

As Raven closed and latched the door, someone out of sight barked an order to the kids on the wall.

At once, the slingers rose up, leaned over the parapet, and let projectiles fly. The action was fast and furious. The *sproing* of taut elastic being released and the static-like *whizz* of ammo rocketing toward flesh and bone went on for close to five minutes.

There was no "stand-down" order shouted. One second the kids were firing down off the wall; the next, they were all turned inward and staring expectantly at the African American soldier standing in front of the Stryker. The soldier lifted a radio to his lips. A beat later, another soldier in the guard tower flashed the rampart kids a thumbs-up.

The go-ahead call started a flurry of activity. The bigger kids hauled up ladders used to access their firing positions. In perfect unison—as if they'd done this many times before—they nosed the ladders over the parapet and lowered them down on the opposite side. Once the ladders were set, a dozen smaller kids scrambled over the parapet and disappeared from sight. Done bracing the ladders for the first wave, the bigger kids legged over the wall and disappeared from sight.

A few seconds after the majority of the kids had vacated the wall, the ladder tenders who had stayed behind started hauling the ladders up.

As the rumble of engines firing rose over the hoots and hollers coming from the kids busy harvesting ears, the gate doors began to part.

Raven craned and saw that the outer doors were already open. A desert-tan bulldozer sat between the two sets of doors, waiting for the outer doors to part.

Taking a cue from the soldier in the tower, the Stryker crept forward, passing through the gate at the posted five-miles-per-hour limit. The dozer's blue-gray exhaust hung low to the ground. The Stryker's eight wheels stirred it up, sending gauze-like eddies wafting away from the armored troop carrier.

The scene outside the wall was not what Raven had been expecting. Of the twenty or so times she had come through the north wall, this was the most carnage she had ever seen. The zombie bodies were stacked three deep atop one another. Many were still moving. An arm snaking from beneath the pile reached for the dozer blade, only to be sheared off cleanly at the elbow.

Like holdout kernels of corn in an air popper, the hollow pops of skulls being crushed beneath the dozer's steadily creeping tonnage intermingled with the sounds of orphans striking it rich.

As the dozer carved a path through the drift of twice-dead zombie corpses, the wall kids were a blur of motion, stabbing and hacking and gleefully thrusting handfuls of severed ears into the air.

Hierarchy on full display, the littler kids collected ears and the bigger, stronger teens moved aside the corpses already harvested of their right ear.

The kids worked in teams, harvesting their bounty from the outside in.

Working ahead of the harvest taking place, a nimble teen girl dressed head-to-toe in a makeshift suit of armor walked a zigzag pattern overtop the corpses. Every couple of steps, she would stop and sweep the corpses all around her with a wand-style Geiger counter. In her wake, a half dozen orange flags protruded from different corpses. They were markers to alert the cleanup crew of the presence of abnormally *hot* specimens.

Turning toward the teenaged boy beside her, Raven said, "Was it this bad yesterday?"

The teen, dressed in armor and wearing a full-face motorcycle helmet complete with mirrored visor, shook his head. Eyes narrowing, he said, "Close. But not this fucking bad. It's been getting worse day by day."

Raven said nothing.

Flipping his visor down, the teen said, "If this is any indication of what's waiting for us outside the RZ, I think I'm going to regret getting out of bed this morning."

If this is the kind of attitude you're bringing outside the wire, thought Raven, *then you're already as good as dead.* She said, "Hold on, the ride's about to get bumpy."

As the dozer peeled away, leaving the path clear for the Chevy, Potvin steered onto the road cutting through the nearby green space and matted the accelerator.

With mature trees flashing by on Raven's right, and the backyards of single-family homes blipping by on her left, she consciously stuffed everything important to her into the imaginary lockbox for safekeeping. Last thing she wanted was for emotion to get in the way of survival. For if there was one thing she had taken away from all the time she'd spent outside the wire with her father, it was that emotion always gets in the way of rational thinking, of sound decision-making.

Allowing that to happen was the quickest way to an early death.

Raven had a strong desire to live. To maybe one day have kids, even if her mom wasn't going to be there to meet them. Granite set to her jaw, she tightened her grip on the metal wall and settled in for the long ride.

Chapter 7

Cade was jarred out of a deep sleep when the helo underneath him suddenly bled airspeed and banked hard to the left. As Brook's smiling face dissolved into blackness, his eyes snapped open. The first thing he did was glance at his Suunto. Seeing he'd been out of it for close to ninety minutes, he shifted his gaze to the window to his left.

Outside the helicopter, the ground below was a dark green blur interspersed by intermittent flashes of fields gone fallow. Now and again, he would catch a glimpse of a two-lane road snaking its way through the rural Utah countryside.

As the pilot on the stick slowed the ship further and began a corkscrew descent, sunlight glittering off a large body of water caused Cade to narrow his eyes and raise a gloved hand to ward off the intrusive rays.

Slipping on a pair of wraparound Oakley sunglasses, Cade looked around the troop compartment. First person to acknowledge him was Nat. The big man was smiling wide. One muscled arm was draped over the prisoner's shoulders. It looked like a big-brother-about-to-deliver-a-noogie kind of scenario. On the prisoner's face was a look of confusion. Clearly he was still thinking about Cade's *flying lessons* comment. *Maybe something was lost in translation*, thought Cade. At any rate, seeing as how Ding was the only prisoner taken alive, nobody was being thrown out of a perfectly good helicopter. At least not until all available intel was wrung from the man.

Heads lolling gently, chins parked on chest rigs bristling with magazines, Cross and Griff were conked out. One would think the extreme high brought on by combat would be better at keeping a person awake than any energy drink or pharmaceutical upper. While part of that was true, the inevitable crash following said combat had the opposite effect. Seasoned operators had learned to embrace either end of the equation. To use it to their advantage. In this case, as it had been ingrained into their DNA during their grueling BUD/S—Basic Underwater Demolitions/SEAL training—they expected the day's activities to be far from over. That at any moment Mister Murphy could throw a CCP scout with a MANPAD missile launcher into the equation. Or a Prairie Fire call for help could come over the net and they'd be diverted and find themselves right back in the thick of battle.

Axe, on the other hand, was wide awake. He was craned around and peering through the window beside the stowed right-side minigun. Detecting movement in his peripheral vision, the Brit met Cade's gaze and flashed a thumbs-up.

Tightening his grip around Ding's neck, Nat said to Cade, "You get some good Zs, Cap?"

Cade's first impression was that the newest Pale Rider was calling him "Cap" on account of his other, recently bestowed nickname. Realizing the staff sergeant didn't even know Daymon, and therefore Nat was just showing respect to the rank, Cade said, "The best kind." Redirecting the conversation, he asked Axe, "How's Lopez? He's not looking so good."

Griff said, "He's taking this Pale Rider thing to heart."

The quip earned Griff a slug on the arm from Cross. "Not cool. Lopez is out of it. If a man can't clap back, you can't break his balls. You know the rules."

"Time and place," Axe reminded. He met Cade's questioning gaze. "Low Rider's vitals are not the best. But he's stable … for now."

The answer didn't sit well with Cade. While he had a good idea of what Ari's cryptic *next stop is classified and off the books* comment was alluding to, he had assumed there was no chance in hell the brief side trip he had mentioned pre-mission would be approved considering Lopez's condition and that they were transporting a prisoner.

As the charred husks of cars and blocks-long runs of concrete pads scorched and devoid of the wooden structures they once supported slid by underneath Jedi One, Cade realized someone at Peterson had given Ari permission to overfly the Eden Compound.

While the side trip wasn't much of a deviation from the straight-line course set between Boise and New District, rescheduling their rendezvous with the refueling tanker—already in the air and en route—would burn precious pounds of hard-to-come-by jet fuel.

After the quick recon of downtown Huntsville and seeing no sign of life in the streets or watercraft scudding the choppy surface of Pineview Reservoir, the helicopter popped up over the picket of pines crowding the city to the east.

"Well, look who's awake," announced Ari over the shipwide comms. "And all bright-eyed and bushy-tailed, too." His helmeted head was turned owl-like, gaze directed toward the troop compartment.

Seeing his reflection in Ari's smoked visor, Cade said, "I see Smokey greenlit the welfare check. Hell must be freezing over."

Ari shook his head then covered the boom mike with one gloved hand. "Not yet. But he's about to." Releasing the mike, he said, "Hitman Actual, Jedi One. How copy?"

Smokey's voice came over the net. "Hitman Actual, good copy Jedi One. Go ahead."

Conspiratorial smile forming beneath the deployed visor, Ari reported spotting a foot mobile mounting a motorcycle. "He's on the state route and heading east," he went on. "Requesting permission to engage in a stand-off pursuit."

"Permission granted," Smokey replied, a tongue-in-cheek tone to his voice. "While you're at it, go ahead and conduct an aerial recon of Bear River."

Covering his boom mike, Cade said to Axe, "Is Lopez going to be okay?"

Downing the last drops of a five-hour energy drink, Axe said, "He'll be coming to real soon. You'll be able to ask him yourself."

Five minutes after the brief radio call to the op center at Peterson, as Ari coaxed the helicopter into another hard banking turn to the left, the Eden compound feeder road presented as a tan blur peeking up through the lush double canopy.

The upthrust treetops quickly gave way to a vast clearing split down the center by a mostly overgrown dirt airstrip. Cade knew at once that something was wrong. First of all, not a single vehicle remained in the motor pool. Daymon's Winnebago, the place where Cade had been forced to put down an undead Brook, was missing. Not having to set eyes on it again was fine by him.

The shiny chrome tanker-trailer full of liquid natural gas, a gift bestowed on the Eden group by the late Alexander Dregan—self-proclaimed Gas Baron of Salt Lake City—was no longer casting its long shadow on the motor pool grounds. Cade shook his head. Dragging that monstrosity out of here and navigating the feeder road with it in tow must have been one hell of an undertaking. Then again, with heating and cooking fuel in high demand, the reward far outweighed the risk.

Sitting all alone underneath the drooping boughs of trees bordering the bare patch of dirt once home to a pair of Humvees and a beat-up Toyota 4Runner captured from the Huntsville marauders, Duncan's DHS Black Hawk was a total loss. Save for the rotor blades, tail assembly, and landing gear, the rest of the navy and gold aircraft was largely indistinguishable. The airframe had been exposed to intense heat, which had caused the cabin superstructure to fold inward on itself.

The turbines were blackened husks of their former selves. They had tumbled from the wreckage and come to rest on the ground beside the craft. The rotor mast and hunk of connected machinery Cade thought might be a transmission of some sort had torn free of their mounts and now listed rearward, at a forty-five-degree angle, supported only by the remains of the tail boom.

Curiously, there was no immediate evidence of an explosion. There were no fuselage parts strewn about the clearing. While the ground around the helicopter was scorched, the grass at the edge of the blackened ring stood tall and proud. All of the evidence made Cade think that whoever was responsible for the Black Hawk's destruction had first siphoned off her jet fuel.

Viewed from the air, the main cabin and cockpit looked like a scorched ball of metal.

Attention focused on the ground below the Ghost Hawk, Ari said, "I'm guessing the H-60 was in one piece when you last saw her."

Replying over the shared comms, Cade said, "Affirmative. There should also be a couple of National Guard Humvees and at least one Toyota SUV down there."

"That's a damn shame," Haynes interjected. "Looks like an A model H-60. Which makes sense, what with the Homeland Security paint." He exhaled sharply, the sound carrying over the comms. "Wow! That old girl didn't deserve to go out like that."

Ari concurred and started the landing gear motoring from the stowed position.

Indicating the tree line concealing the compound's hidden entrance, Cade asked, "Can you put us down between there and the Homeland bird? As close to the center of the clearing as possible?"

Ari said, "Night Stalker Airways at your service," and nosed the Ghost Hawk toward a spot on the dirt strip equidistant from the indicated tree line and immolated chopper.

No sooner had the landing gear locked into position and the Jedi ride was settling on ground Cade never thought he would set foot on again than he was out of his safety harness and standing, hunched over, in the cramped cabin. While the left-side door motored open, he was squeezing past knees and tapping Griff, Cross, and Nat. "Follow me." He met Axe's gaze on the way. "If Lopez comes around while we're still wheels down, give him the option to get some fresh air. Take a piss. Whatever …" He then made eye contact with Ari and Haynes and told them he expected to be boots on the ground for no more than five minutes.

"Copy that," said Skip, who was also out of his seat and waiting patiently for the door to open fully so he could dismount and make way for the hard-charging Pale Riders.

Outside of the bird, head instinctively bowed on account of the whirring blades, Cade asked Skipper to keep the minigun trained on the feeder road. He then intimated to Axe that Lopez was to receive the lion's share of his attention. Lastly, he stabbed a finger at the prisoner. "Knock the commie puke out if he starts giving you any shit," were Cade's parting words to the SAS shooter.

Under the watchful gazes of Haynes and Ari, Cade sent Nat off to check the motor pool area for clues. Once Nat was away, Mk 46 trained on the forest bordering the motor pool, Cade tasked Griff with walking the airstrip. "Look for evidence of a helo landing here," he instructed. "Also, keep an eye out for boot prints and shell casings." While he didn't think Lev and Jamie had been in a firefight with the people responsible for torching the chopper, he couldn't rule it out.

As Cade set off in the opposite direction as Nat, eyes roving the forest ahead for the blind hiding the entrance to the subterranean Eden compound, he heard in his headset a warning from Skip. Turning to his left, Cade caught sight of the small throng of dead emerging from the partially overgrown mouth of the compound's feeder road.

"We've got time until they reach you," Cade noted. "Leave them to us to deal with."

"Copy that," Skipper said dryly.

As Ari came over the net with strict orders for his crew chief to pay extra special attention to Jedi One's tail rotor, Cade caught a whiff of rotten flesh. The sickly sweet pong wasn't coming from the undead. The light breeze was cutting across the clearing in the opposite direction, putting the shamblers downwind from him.

Another fifty yards and Cade was at the spot in the forest he knew all too well. The boughs hung down over the blind Logan "Oops" Winters and Christopher "Lev" Levdahl had erected to conceal the sloping dirt path leading to the compound's steel door.

Memories came flooding back to Cade. In his mind's eye, he saw Duncan's brother Logan training the Barrett .50 caliber sniper rifle on their incoming Black Hawk. Logan's nickname "Oops" scrawled on the bird's nose in chalk by Duncan prior to leaving Camp Williams in Utah had staved off the imminent attack.

The brothers' reunion had been a sight to behold. Cade couldn't remember seeing Duncan happier than he was that day.

The reek of death brought memories of that awful night when Cade had put down his undead wife. While the smell inside the RV had been nothing close to what was now assaulting his nose, being so close to the spot on Earth his beloved Brook had drawn her final breath was dredging up emotions that made every step closer to the blind a monumental task. It was as if each of his Danner boots weighed a ton. Before he even turned the corner, his gut was telling him he wasn't going to want to see the source of the odor.

Cade saw the bare feet first. They were small and talc white, the soles crisscrossed by angry red welts. The ankles were bound with black zip ties that cut deeply into disintegrating flesh. As he cut the corner, his gaze traveled the entire length of the prone corpse. There was not a stitch of clothing.

Jamie, thought Cade, as he dropped to his knees, bile, hot and bitter already tickling the back of his throat. She looked to have been arranged there, on her back, arms crossed and clutching a dead baby to her bosom. The still-attached umbilical cord snaked under the dead woman's pale arms and disappeared into a foot-long gash carved horizontally between her protruding hip bones.

The thirty-something's dark mane had been shorn off. No great care had been taken in the process. Cuts and gouges showed through the short stubble left behind.

There were no bullet holes or signs of blunt force trauma. Cade figured she had bled out after having the child cut from her.

Thankfully, her eyes were closed. Having successfully fought off the urge to vomit, Cade said a quiet prayer and shed a tear for mother and child.

Fearing the corpse could be booby-trapped, Cade let it be, for now. Rising to a combat crouch, he aimed his M4 toward the sloped dirt ramp and set off for the compound entrance.

Eyes scanning the ground for wires or obvious signs the dirt had been disturbed, he rounded the final turn and saw Lev. He was naked and spread-eagled and blocking the metal door. His eyes were open wide and glazed over by death. The thirty-year-old veteran of the war in Iraq had been crucified. Rusty metal railroad stakes pierced the palm of each hand. They were driven deep into the layer of clay above the steel door. Lev's bare feet had been given the same treatment, the stakes driven through flesh and bone and, finally, into the dirt ramp.

Unlike Lev's pregnant wife, his body was riddled with puckered bullet wounds. Clamped in his closed mouth was a playing card. On the card was a black and red cobra. Blood dripping from its fangs, it was coiled and poised to strike. As Cade pinched the card between thumb and forefinger, Griff's voice sounded in his headset. "Wyatt, Griff. A couple of helos made a visit here. Tricycle landing gear. We think they were Harbin Z-9s. Likely PLA Navy birds. Lots of Chicom shell casings in the grass. Found some .223 brass as well. Looks like your friends put up a fight."

Didn't end well, thought Cade. He said, "Nat, Anvil. What'd you find."

There was a second of dead air. When Nat responded, the news wasn't good. Matter-of-factly, he said, "The helo was torched with thermite. Happened some time ago."

That bit of news all but confirmed the Chinese PLA was responsible for yet more carnage. Only this time, his friends had been the ones on the receiving end. Through gritted teeth, he said, "I need one of you to bring me two body bags." He exhaled sharply. Then, shaking his head, he added, "And bring one of Skip's flags."

Chapter 8

"We've got glowers," Raven bellowed, banging a fist on the trailer's sheet-metal roof. She was staring off to the left, gaze locked on a clutch of zombies trudging through knee-high grass, which was slowly overtaking a vacant lot a block away. The fifty-by-a-hundred-foot parcel of land was sandwiched between a two-level Tudor and a boxy glass-and-steel modern cube. A real estate concern had planted their sign on the equally overgrown parking strip paralleling the curb.

There wasn't a stitch of clothing on the Zs. The thing that made them stand out from ordinary first turns was the peculiar skin pallor. Instead of the usual gray tone of the slowly decaying undead, the skin of these three shamblers was mottled with pink and purple splotches.

Having recently spent time following Glenda as she volunteered in the newly expanded Birthing Center at Penrose Hospital, where Raven got to witness live births and hold her fair share of newborn babies, from a distance the Zs' skin tone reminded her of a newborn's prior to their drawing that first, all-important breath.

These were no babies. These things were deadly even if they didn't bite you. A brief encounter with a glower could dose the unfortunate person with enough rads to bring about adverse effects. Prolonged exposure could even lead to radiation poisoning and then a slow and especially gruesome death.

The first stop a mile back saw Raven and the other pikers put down forty-three Zs. The small herd was a mix of first turns and recent turns, with the majority being the former. After Potvin's standard twenty-five-percent cut, the pikers and Dead Sled crew were each left with a pair of ears, or two credits. Not much, considering the dismounts were the ones shouldering most of the risk.

Having received an SOS call while the loaders were still in the middle of their grim task of depositing corpses into the sled, the Stryker escort sped off to render aid to a bus full of survivors stranded on the western fringe of the Red Zone.

Concluding that the bulk of the dead in the area were the ones currently being policed up by the loaders, and that the Dead Sled's armed security detail would be sufficient to deal with any stragglers that might arrive as they were finishing up, Potvin had made the executive decision to range ahead solo.

Now, with the sighting of glowers and the whereabouts of the combined herds still an unknown quantity, the meager thirty credits the job would earn them all didn't seem worth the risk of stopping to cull them and call the coordinates in to the roving team responsible for hot cleanups.

While the entire scenario wasn't sitting easy with Raven, the prospect of the irradiated Zs continuing on toward the northern gate and possibly sickening or killing an unsuspecting survivor was not tenable.

Dragging the two-way radio to her lips, Raven thumbed the Talk button. "Bird to Potvin. How copy?"

After a brief pause, Potvin responded over her own two-way. "I see 'em. How could I miss 'em?"

Raven said, "If you can get us a little closer … do a real slow drive-by, I can put them down and we'll be on our way."

Once the channel opened up, Potvin responded, saying, "It's going to mess with our rendezvous." There was a brief pause. "And with the platform and you all out back, my options are kind of limited as to how close I can get you." Voice taking on a parental tone, she added, "And under no circumstances am I letting you dismount."

"Drive around the block. Stop on the far side of the vacant lot. It'll be a quick thirty credits."

Potvin made no reply.

Raven said, "We *can't* let them scurry back into the woodwork." While she got the gist of her statement, it wasn't original. It was another Duncanism she'd picked up somewhere along the way. *Woodwork,* to her, was a home or business. Most casualties that stemmed from an encounter with a glower didn't occur out in the open. You could just about see the things from a mile away. In this case, it happened to be a city block. The result was the same. The mere sight of them had the hair on Raven's neck standing to attention. One of her frequent nightmares featured her coming face-to-face with a hot Z bearing her mother's likeness.

Slowing the pickup to a crawl, Potvin said, "You get six shots. If that doesn't drop them, we're moving on."

The teen beside Raven, a tall redhead struggling to grow a goatee, whispered, "Take the deal." Clearly, he was thinking about his share of the thirty additional credits. A cut that came with little to no risk for him.

Ignoring the prodding, Raven assessed the situation. As with most of the side streets in New District's outer reaches, the ones here were still littered with moldering corpses, trash, and the occasional fallen tree. Additionally, the garbage and recycling trucks never made it to this neighborhood before the dead began to walk. Still full of rotting garbage, the rolling bins that were to be emptied languished near the curbs both left and right. Adding to the difficulty of maneuvering fifty-plus feet of vehicle and trailer were the curbed automobiles left behind by those fleeing the relentless march of the undead.

Finally, Raven said, "Deal. Six tries. Just get me a little closer." She clipped her radio to the Kelty's shoulder strap and snapped up her SBR. Quickly extending the collapsed stock, she flipped the 3x magnifier in line with the EOTech holographic sight atop the SBR's Picatinny rail. While it wasn't a *reach out and touch someone* rifle like her dad's Remington MSR, the little carbine was accurate out to about seventy-five yards when firing from a steady platform.

As Potvin made the final turn necessary to get the trailer around the block and to the rear of the vacant lot where Raven would have a good angle on the glowers, she inadvertently cut the corner short. When the left-side wheels rode up on the curb, both the Chevy pickup and trailer in tow shimmied and wobbled like ships at sea.

Once the ride settled, Raven laid her Kelty flat on the floor and sat on it cross-legged.

Boughs of mature trees brushed the platform's metal roof as Potvin braked and brought the truck to a halt in the middle of a narrow street.

Off of Raven's left shoulder, maybe half a football field away, the glowers were just getting themselves turned around in the long grass.

Behind Raven, one of the older pikers was taking wagers on whether or not she would drop the glowers within the number of allotted shots. Hearing most of the action going against her ability to do so, Raven felt within her a strong urge to bet on herself. Taking into consideration all of the hardships Duncan had suffered as a result of his gambling addiction, even going so deep into the abyss that he had pissed away a home and sizeable inheritance, Raven kept her mouth shut.

A little miffed at being prejudged—a regular occurrence when dealing with adults inside the walls—she charged her rifle, rested her left-hand palm up atop the trailer's side rail, then hunkered down. Dropping the forestock onto her awaiting palm, she firmed up her grip, snugged the rifle tight against her shoulder, and disengaged the safety.

It took a second or two for her to acquire the targets through the optics. The larger of the three glowers was a balding forty-something male with a pronounced beer gut and decent-sized pair of moobs. Coined by Duncan—*moobs* was short for "man boobs." The day Raven had first heard him say it, she had uttered a silent prayer she would never see him with his shirt off. As it was, the sight of these two cone-shaped purple mounds moving in tiny circles contrary to each other was something she could never unsee.

A multitude of purple-rimmed bite wounds started at the wrist, climbed the glower's flabby right arm, and ended at the upper chest where a rib or some other bone jutted through the skin.

As soon as the Z's slack face filled up the optics, Raven settled the crosshairs on its pug nose, drew a deep breath to steady the gruesome image, then, simultaneously, exhaled slowly and pressed the trigger.

Unfazed by the sight of the glower's nose being literally wiped off its face, she swung the suppressed weapon right by a couple of degrees, targeted a middle-aged female Z, and repeated the process.

Two down, one to go, thought Raven. *And four bullets left to seal the deal.* It looked as if a few of the naysayers looking on were going to be eating crow.

A low murmur rose from the other pikers as Raven adjusted her aim.

Glower number three was about the age Raven was when the dead began to walk. She figured he was maybe eleven or twelve and likely had been close to entering middle school. All put together, the trio reminded her of the family of Zs Max had been running with.

Hoping that was the case with these three, that after she granted them final death they would get to spend eternity together in the same lead-lined grave, she drew a breath and said a silent prayer for them.

The piker who had initiated the wagering was now taking bets on whether the "kid" would score a "hat trick"—whatever the hell that was.

Pushing from her mind the absurd image of a disembodied hand yanking a white rabbit from a black top hat, she caressed the trigger. In the next beat, the small form's head snapped back, and it performed a backward somersault, its bare feet cutting air sullied by a fast-spreading pink mist.

A couple of pikers out of Raven's field of view congratulated her. A few more, the losers among the group, groaned in displeasure.

Raven shook her head. It was against everything she stood for to root against her own team. As far as she was concerned, every single American survivor *was* her team.

As she engaged the safety and rose up from behind the rifle, two things happened, real fast, back to back. First, the pickup's horn sounded. It wasn't a happy "good shooting" type of toot. Besides, only a dumbass would sound a horn unnecessarily outside the wire. At one time, Raven had been that dumbass. And as a result of that transgression, she'd put her dad in grave danger.

On the heels of the horn sounding, without warning, the trailer lurched forward. In just a second or two, as Potvin fed diesel to the

Chevy's 6.6-liter Duramax engine, parked cars a yard to Raven's fore started to whip by.

The pikers who had been standing fell away like dominos. As the upended crewmembers slid toward the rear of the trailer, Potvin cutting a hard right jammed them all together in one corner.

Pikes clattered against their ports. Some slipped free, making a tinny jangling sound as they landed on the street below and skittered away from the wildly listing trailer.

Holding onto the trailer rail with both hands, rifle trapped between her still crossed legs, Raven saw the reason for the sudden departure. Spread out across the road at the end of the block, where Potvin had made the final left turn before stopping in the street, was a sizeable zombie horde. She guessed Potvin had been caught by surprise when the shamblers had emerged from the opposing corner. Though only a few scant seconds had elapsed since the engine roared and the trailer lurched forward, the zombies were still coming, cutting the corner and trampling everything in their path. Shrubs and hedges fell to the staggering juggernaut. A white picket fence was reduced to splinters. There was no way to gauge their numbers. Still, there were enough of them that the garbage cans now in their path were either sent rolling down the street or tipped over, their stinking contents quickly trampled underfoot.

Raven considered herself partly at fault for not seeing the horde first and sounding the alarm. The fact that not a single piker had seen them coming was also troubling.

No time to dwell on that now because no sooner had the trailer begun to right itself than Raven was being pushed hard against the swing-away door. As it flexed under her weight, the redheaded teen slammed into her.

Thankfully, the door latches held. And so did Raven's grip on her rifle, which allowed her to quickly slip an arm through the strap before losing it to the gravitational forces at work.

As Raven wriggled free from the prostrate form pressing against her, Potvin stood on the brakes. The smell of burnt rubber hit Raven's nose, and she was instantly enveloped by a cloud of blue-gray smoke lifting off the road. Knowing what was to come, she rose up, grabbed the leading edge of the roof in a two-handed grip, and brought her knees up to her chest. Quick thinking saved her from being crushed by the fallen pikers who had again been surprised by another of Potvin's unannounced maneuvers.

Affected by the sudden braking, the piker crew was a blur of flailing knees and elbows as bodies barrel-rolled the length of the trailer. There was a loud thud, and air rushed from lungs as the tangle of humanity again met unforgiving metal.

Just when Raven thought the worst of it was over, she detected the ripe stink of rotting flesh, and the truck and trailer began to roll backward. She couldn't see over the cab, so there was no way of telling what had caused the sudden change in direction. Strangely, the motor sounded as if it was still at idle. The rattle-clatter of the diesel powerplant was quickly overtaken by a raspy hissing Raven knew all too well. As the pickup's speed increased, hollow thuds of flesh impacting its metal panels soon drowned out the moans and cries for help coming from injured pikers.

As Raven straightened her legs, searching for somewhere to plant her Danners that would not entail stepping on a face or someone's chest or one of the many arms and legs jutting from the pile, the trailer suddenly went sideways in relation to the pickup.

In the next beat, just as Raven had found her footing, sky traded places with ground.

There was a tremendous *bang* as the trailer slammed down hard onto what had been its right side. The grunts and groans coming from fellow pikers as they were deposited onto unforgiving blacktop quickly gave way to shrill screams. The young man responsible for the majority of the screaming was lying behind Raven. Looking around as she picked herself up, she realized that the trailer had come to rest on one side, trapping most of them within a small, confined space between the trailer's floor and roof. Then she saw that the roof had come down across the man's arm, the sharp metal edge pinning it to the road. Out of sight to her was the man's forearm and hand. Either it had been severed completely and now lay on the street on the other side of the curved roof (the best-case scenario by Raven's estimation), or it was crushed horribly and trapped under all that weight—which was *definitely* a no-win scenario. If a Z got sight of it and took a bite, infection was guaranteed, and the man was doomed.

All around Raven, pikers were rising up. She noted that the overturned trailer's floor and roof were now walls, the former on her left and tracked with mud, the latter to her right and slightly misshapen by the impact with the road. Light spilled in narrow openings front and back. At the moment, the rear egress was unobstructed and clear of Zs. The other option was partially blocked by the trailer hitch snaking up and over the Chevy's tailgate. Though the jury-rigged fifth-wheel was still attached, it was a twisted mess.

After a quick headcount, Raven realized one of the pikers had been thrown out of the trailer as it was tipping over. The remaining ten were crammed in with her like sardines in a can.

"What do we do now?" asked a younger man with a large goose egg on his forehead. "No way we're going to be able to right this thing."

Pointing toward the rectangle of daylight at the rear of the trailer, one teen girl said, "This way is clear."

Shaking her head, Raven looked across the faces of those near to her. Locking eyes with the redheaded kid, she said, "Come with me if you want to live."

Chapter 9

Near Eden, Utah

The only thing Cade dreaded more than setting eyes on his wife's grave was having to face Raven and tell her he hadn't been able to bring Mom home. With Lopez's worsening condition, and the need to bury his friends and their unborn child, there would be no time left to exhume her.

The photos Cade had found in their home during the mission to their old hometown, Portland, Oregon, had had an unintended effect on Raven. Instead of anchoring her to the past, providing good memories to carry her through tough times, the opposite had been true.

Ever since Cade had returned from Operation Clean Slate, Raven's thoughts had become centered mostly on the decades ahead of her—decades broken down into minutes, hours, days, and years, all of which she was destined to trudge through without a mother to confide in.

Hitting Cade especially hard was the fact that, should Raven ever find a life partner in the zombie apocalypse, any eventual offspring they had would never know their grandmother. The stories of survival, specifically the flight from Myrtle Beach to Fort Bragg, would no doubt be recounted over and over to youthful wide-eyed stares. The heroic deeds and the many lives saved by the petite woman who'd never wavered in the face of adversity—even before the crucible of the times had reformed her into the warrior she was when Omega took her—would never be forgotten.

Their home in New District, which Raven had petitioned for and was granted title to, only helped to compound the longing within her. Save for stowing away the pictures of Brook hanging on their walls or moving to an entirely different home (anything besides the Craftsman design that mirrored their old home back in Portland), Cade had no answers. He certainly wasn't ready to allow another woman into his life. Someone who would try to be a mom to Raven but could never succeed in filling Brook's shoes. Not now. Especially not when he was one enemy bullet or zombie bite away from leaving his daughter an orphan.

A tap on the shoulder dragged Cade back to the present. While the Ghost Hawk had just launched from the clearing, the climb to treetop level and subsequent flight following the twists and turns of the feeder road below had lasted less than a minute. Now, as the helicopter leveled off and settled into a steady hover above yet another clearing, Griff was pointing groundward.

"This isn't going to be the quick in and out we were hoping for," he noted. "Zeds all over the place. And the rotten bastards are treading on your hallowed ground."

Careful to not disturb the flag-draped body bags placed crossways on the cabin floor, Cade shifted in his seat and looked out the nearest window. Not visible to him on the previous overflight was the large number of walking corpses lurking near the hidden gate. A scant few were also milling about on the lower third of the gently sloping hill. Based on their stilted movements and general degree of dishevelment, Cade pegged them as first turns. A good thing, he thought, because the ones that had been walking the countryside, exposed to the elements and insects for going on nearly a year now, were much easier to put down than their fresh, recently turned counterparts.

Nearly a year removed from that last Saturday in July, the day Brook and Raven had boarded a jet bound for Myrtle Beach, South Carolina, the day the recently dead began reanimating, the only time first turns ever struck real fear in Cade's heart, the sort of fear that paralyzed most men, was when the hissing abominations were part of one of the many mega-hordes now roaming the country.

The mega-hordes were capable of throwing fire engines off the road, knocking over entire city blocks worth of power poles, and could easily shove two-story homes off their foundations. A man caught in their path didn't stand a chance.

Cade saw that a long run of the barbed wire fence bordering the grassy knoll had been compromised. Four of the wooden fence posts were leaning over, their moss-covered tops aimed away from the road. Great force had churned the soil that had held them upright, bringing large clay-rich mounds of dirt to the surface. Once-taut strands of wire strung between the posts snaked along the ground, now and again disappearing into the long grass.

Dragging his gaze uphill from SR-39, he spotted the row of graves. They were high up on the hill, maybe ten feet or so from the tree line, and arranged perpendicular to the gently arcing stretch of two-lane highway a hundred yards distant.

Last time Cade was here, Brook's grave was a muddy rectangle dotted with bouquets of colorful wildflowers left there by Raven and some of the younger members of the Eden gang.

Now, after the turning of the seasons, the uneven rectangles were all bristling with random clusters of knee-high grass.

Addressing the team over the shipwide comms, Ari said, "I can put her down east of the graves and keep her hot while you work. Since the fence is down," he added, "it's on you and your team, Wyatt, to take care of the welcoming party."

Nothing doing, thought Cade. The team was his responsibility. No way he was going to risk one of them getting bit. He was going this one alone.

After a bit of back and forth, Ari agreed to twenty minutes of loiter time. More than enough for Cade to do what needed doing. As for Brook, returning for her would be a father/daughter outing, which, the longer he thought about it, would be cathartic for both of them.

Meeting his fellow Pale Riders' expectant gazes, Cade said, "I'll deal with the Zs." He pointed out a break in the tree line a few yards beyond Brook's grave. "There's an old observation post in the trees there. It's basically just a patch of flat dirt fronted by a fallen tree. On the ground by the tree is a shovel and pickaxe. Be careful," he stressed, "there's a dirt road that follows a depression behind the hide. Zs have been known to travel the road. With the fence down, there's a good chance some could be lurking about."

An earnest look on his face, Cross said, "Why don't we just take them to Schriever? We can bury them by Desantos. Give Lev the proper sendoff he deserves."

"A twenty-one gun salute," added Axe.

Staring a hole into the prisoner's face, Nat said, "After what those animals did to them … it's the least we can do."

The prisoner's one-eyed gaze jumped from face to face, finally settling on Cade, who was shaking his head vehemently. "I made a promise to Lev and Jamie. Part of a pact, actually. I intend to honor my word." Meeting Ding's angry glare, he growled, "Take this waste of skin with you. Free his hands and make *him* dig the grave. Leave the burying to me." Switching to Mandarin, Cade let Ding know his life depended on how fast he could dig a grave.

As the helo's wheels settled into the spongy ground, Cade cycled a round into his M4 and rose from his seat. Meeting Ari's gaze, he said, "Twenty minutes. Not a second longer. You have my word."

While Cade's previous estimate of five minutes to conduct the welfare check on Lev and Jamie had stretched closer to ten minutes, what with the careful inspection of the compound, which he found completely ransacked, he fully intended this stop to be filed into the *under-promise, over-deliver* column.

The troop compartment door hit the stops, and Cade was out at once. Danners kicking up dirt, he sprinted downhill, rifle tucked tight to his shoulder, suppressor belching plumes of blue-gray gunsmoke. Three ratty first turns were felled by clean double-taps before Cade was out from beneath the whirring rotor blades. By the time he was halfway to the road, he had expended another dozen rounds on kills four through nine.

Leaping over a tangle of fallen bodies, gravity still pulling him downhill, Cade walked a mostly accurate barrage of fire, head-high, across a trio of zombies struggling to rise up from the roadside ditch. As the M4's bolt locked open, he spun the rifle around and brought the collapsed buttstock into the fight.

A young road-worn Z tangled in the barbed wire caught the brunt of the first swipe of the Colt carbine. A number of yellowed teeth dislodged by the strike joined the rancid hunk of bloated tongue already carving an arc across the nearby ditch. Like dice thrown on a craps table, incisors and bicuspids skittered across the near lane. As the excised tongue flopped onto the blacktop, spinning and tumbling as if alive, the teeth ceased their journey, coming to rest a foot shy of the dashed yellow centerline.

Releasing his grip on the carbine, Cade transitioned to his Glock 19. With a round already chambered—the Gold Standard in the zombie apocalypse—he targeted the Zs still congregating near the feeder road gate.

Living up to the nickname bestowed upon him by his late mentor, Desantos, Cade thrust the Glock 19 ahead of him and, holding the polymer 9mm pistol in a two-handed grip, dispatched the three shamblers nearest him with accurate double-taps to the forehead. As he shifted aim to the clutch of monsters nearing the centerline, a child Z loped from behind the slow-moving phalanx. It was a recent turn, the Winnie the Pooh pajamas draping its body relatively clean and mostly devoid of bugs and twigs. Moving much faster than the first turns that had initially concealed it from view, the snarling three-footer reached the white fog line before Cade could line up for a decent headshot. Pressing the trigger three times in rapid succession delivered mixed results.

The first 9mm round entered the Z's right cheek, splitting the mandible bone in two and pulverizing all of the teeth in its path. As the kinetic energy behind the screaming hunk of lead started the Z's slight frame corkscrewing clockwise, the follow-on rounds cleaving the air on a downward angle punched non-lethal holes into the frost-heaved shoulder twenty feet behind their intended target.

The kid zombie went down in a heap, legs twisted, face a mess of mangled flesh.

As Cade fired a single round into the back of its head, he cursed himself for expending four rounds on one threat.

Seeing the next two Zs come upon the twice-dead kid and stumble and pitch forward gave Cade an idea. Pumping four rounds into the pair of fallen first turns and seeing them both go still, face-down, clumped brain matter dribbling onto Pooh's ever-smiling face, he holstered the Glock and took hold of the nearest fence post.

Dropping one knee to the ground, Cade bowed his head, pressed his shoulder to the post's gnarled exterior, and placed both palms against the moss-covered top.

Letting loose a war cry, he shot up from the ground. Danners churning the grass and mud into a morass, he tried standing up the run of fence. Making little progress and just about to go back to the gun, the post suddenly went light in his hands.

In the next beat, Cade heard Nat say, "Hold up for just a second, Boss." Without waiting for a response, the big man, breathing hard and smiling wide, reached long arms across the fallen fence, grabbed twin handfuls of a twice-dead Z's hair, and hauled the corpse across the barbed wire strands. Depositing the dead weight between them, Nat pulled a second stilled corpse from the ditch and dumped it beside the first. "One more," he insisted, "and then we prop this mother up."

Grimacing, Cade said, "I told you *I* would take care of the dead."

"Couldn't let you go it alone, *bruh*. It's not the island way."

Cade said nothing. Adjusting his grip on the fence post, he craned and looked uphill. The prisoner was bent low, shovel a blur, dark rooster tails of dirt arcing over his shoulder.

Griff stood nearby, the flag-draped body bags by his feet, pickaxe propped on one shoulder, watching the gravedigger work.

"Ready," said Nat. "Let's do this."

In his side vision, Cade saw the other man adopt a stance similar to his own. Stacked at Nat's feet, a tidy pile crushing down the grass, were the corpses of the three zombies he had pulled from the ditch.

Working together, the two operators got their posts standing straight.

"A little bit more," Nat urged.

Once they had the posts leaning past ninety degrees, the mossy tops angled more toward the road than the hill at Cade's back, Nat said, "That's good. Hold tight, Boss."

Easy for you to say was what Cade was thinking because just arriving at the far side of the roadside ditch were the ten or so zombies that had been lurking at the feeder road gate.

Finding himself caught between the wall of stench coming off the advancing crowd and the carrion pong of the Zs Nat was busy draping over the fence, Cade cast a furtive glance uphill.

The prisoner was now hard at work with the pickaxe. Cross and Griff stood a short distance away, the latter aiming his MP7 directly at the slight Chicom.

"That should hold," Nat declared. "Let's go."

Cade returned his gaze to the ditch. The first of the Zs were just now stepping off the shoulder and entering the rock-strewn V to his fore. To his immediate right, he was greeted by the rictus grin of a head-shot female zombie. His lethal double-tap had created a second set of eyes directly above the bulging, jaundiced orbs. Grey matter oozing from one ear traced an arc down the curve of its bite-ravaged neck. A lone maggot, white and plump, scudded the length of the gray slab of flesh thrust from its gaping maw.

Tentatively releasing his grip on the post, uncurling his fingers real slow as if the entire run of fence might topple back onto him, might trap him on the ground where he would become a meal of fresh meat for the remaining dead, Cade peered around Four-Eyes.

Nat had positioned the other two Zs in roughly the same manner as the first: upper bodies pressed against the barbed wire strands, knees planted in the churned soil.

While not quite falling under the *work smarter, not harder* heading, Nat's five hundred pounds of carrion counterbalancing the fence looked like it might hold.

Without another word, Cade took hold of his carbine and sprinted back up the hill, the noisy helicopter at his 10 o'clock, the grave-digging detail fifty yards to the right of it.

When Cade and Nat arrived beside the half-finished grave, only a quarter of Ari's allotted time had slipped into the past.

Speaking in Mandarin, Cade ordered the prisoner to drop the pickaxe. Switching back to English, he said to Cross, "Zip his wrists and take him back to the bird. Once you have him strapped in, zip his ankles together real tight." He met the SEAL's gaze. "When you get him squared away, I want a SITREP on Lopez's condition."

"Copy that," said Cross. He handed the flag to Griff, then fished a pair of zip ties from a cargo pocket. Turning the prisoner around, he secured the shorter man's wrists behind his back.

With Griff and Nat standing by, Cade attacked the clay-rich soil with the pickaxe.

Five minutes spent poking and prodding with the axe, then digging the broken-up soil out with the shovel, finished the job. Measuring roughly two feet across, three deep, and six long, the rectangular hole was far from what Cade would have dug had he had the time to do it right.

Tossing the shovel aside, he stole a quick glance down the hill. At the road, the zombies were packed into the ditch shoulder-to-shoulder. As he watched, one of them made it up the steep bank and got both feet planted on the narrow strip of flat earth paralleling the weighted down run of fence. It pressed up hard against the fence, took a couple of futile steps forward, then quickly lost its footing. There was no look of surprise on the creature's face as it fell sideways. Its eyes were still locked on the activity up the hill from it when it began a slow-roll back to where it had started.

Had he not been in the middle of burying two more of his friends, Cade would have found humor in the Z bowling over three other flesh-eaters caught in its path.

After having Griff and Nat help him place the body bags gently atop one another, Cade took the flag from the former and ordered them both back to the waiting bird.

Shaking his head, Nat said, "I'm not leaving you, Wyatt." He scooped up the pickaxe and moved to the back side of the largest of two mounds of dirt.

"Me neither," said Griff. "I get it. You made a blood pact with your friends." He shook his head slowly. "You're not breaking that pact by letting us help you." Dropping to his knees, the SEAL started shoving dirt into the grave with his gloved hands.

Cade sighed and started shoveling.

In just a couple of minutes, the three men had replaced all of the soil.

After spreading the flag out atop the mostly even mound and weighing it down with stones placed at intervals around the perimeter, Cade bowed his head and said a few words to his God. He only asked that his friends be accepted into Heaven. That they would meet their unborn child and find peace together. While he wanted to honor the veteran with a twenty-one gun salute, ammunition was too precious.

As Cade retraced his steps back to the Ghost Hawk, he paused briefly at Brook's grave. He was in the middle of a promise to return and bring her home when he heard in his headset words that he found impossible to believe.

Chapter 10

"This is the only way we survive this," Raven implored. With the raspy moans of the dead growing louder to her fore, she entered the narrow confines between the trailer and the pickup's tailgate. Crabbing past the still-attached and terribly mangled trailer hitch, she stepped onto the pickup's bumper and legged over the tailgate. Once she was in the cramped space on the left side of the load bed—roughly a two-foot-square patch of rippled metal running between the fifth-wheel mount and the inner wheel well—she got herself turned around. Peering over the tailgate, she was saddened to see only four faces staring back at her: the redhead teen calling himself Rusty, a blond kid named Aaron who was about the same age as the redhead, and a man and woman, both in their early twenties and resembling each other enough that they had to be siblings.

The kid with the trapped arm hadn't moved. He was quiet now and all alone on the ground inside the trailer. Though his skin was abnormally pale, he was still showing signs of life. Since there was no blood pooling around the pinched arm, Raven guessed the trailer was acting as a tourniquet. Which was a good thing because she wanted to get the others to safety and check on Potvin before taking the time to assess his unfortunate situation.

She saw that the other pikers had opted to take the path of least resistance, slipping away when she had turned her back to climb into the load bed. Saying a quiet prayer that they be delivered to safety, then a second for the kid with the trapped arm, she helped the ones gathered near the tailgate to clamber aboard.

Raven handed a loosely folded tarp to Rusty. "Cover up and stay down." Turning back toward the cab, she spotted Potvin through the rear window. The former librarian was facing forward, hands clasped atop her head, unmoving. If Raven hadn't known better, she'd have thought Potvin was surrendering to the rapidly approaching herd.

A gentle rap on the sliding rear window failed to get Potvin's attention, so Raven unsheathed the Infidel and jimmied the sliding pane open. Knowing there was no way for Potvin to exit through either door without the dead seeing her, and that the rear slider was way too narrow for the woman to pass through, Raven said in a low voice, "Open the moonroof and climb out. Stay on your stomach. No sudden movements, okay?"

Tearing her eyes from the zombies now filling the street from curb to curb, Potvin met Raven's gaze in the rearview mirror. Nodding slowly, she uncoupled her seatbelt and hit the switch to start the moonroof sliding open.

When the herd's bell cows reached the Chevy's front end, Potvin had already collected her pack, climbed through the open moonroof, and was on her stomach and feeling like the last hors d'oeuvre on the serving tray.

Slithering off the roof was in no way a graceful move. It was more like the kind of head-over-heels tumble that would end up on a bloopers show.

As Potvin was being helped to sit in the load bed, the dead were sluicing around the pickup and causing it to rock side to side. Thanks to Raven's quick thinking, and the fact the bedrails rose above the sightline of even the tallest of the zombies, as the herd surged down the street, they remained oblivious to the fresh meat hiding so near to them.

Briefly swinging her gaze aft, Raven saw the pikers who had decided to not heed her warning. They had exited through the rear of the trailer and were now huddled in the middle of the intersection, maybe a hundred feet distant, their heads panning wildly between the herds converging on them. Clearly, they were undecided on which way to flee. She didn't see the person who had been thrown clear. She could only hope he or she hadn't been too badly injured and was holed up somewhere safe.

Regarding the four heads emerging from underneath the tarp, Potvin said, "Where the hell are the others?"

"They're between a rock and a hard place," Raven stated. "I told them to follow me." She shook her head. "I'm afraid it's too late now."

Potvin inched up and caught sight of the rest of her pikers. They were now on the move, heading south on the nearby cross street. Walking her gaze to the right, she saw that the group of ten or so first turns leading the herd that had caused her to rabbit were just about to reach the intersection.

The color drained from Potvin's face when she looked out over the tailgate and saw that one of her piker crew was still inside the overturned trailer. Craning left, she realized the young man must have had an arm thrust through the viewing port when the trailer tipped. It was now pinned down at the elbow, the end with the hand still attached snaking out from under the edge of the trailer's metal roof. As she looked on, a female first turn dropped to its knees and buried its teeth into the ashen forearm. Its head snapped side to side, a constant motion Potvin had seen before. After a couple seconds of this, the zombie hinged upright, a jiggling hunk of bloody flesh trapped in both hands. Veins and parchment-thin ribbons of dermis danced as the abomination jammed the morsel into its pistoning maw. As yellowed teeth gnashed the meat, blood spattered the road all around the kneeling creature.

"What do we do now?" Aaron stammered. "There's so many of them. We gotta get out of here."

Crawling toward the tailgate, Potvin made it clear that she wasn't leaving anyone behind.

Already monkeying over the tailgate, the SBR now swung around to her back, Raven said, "Stay here. I got this."

By the time Raven reached the man's side, he was conscious and in the process of extricating what was left of his arm. Getting himself into a sitting position, he clutched the stump to his chest. A steady pulsating stream of blood was wetting his shirt. Sweat was collecting on his brow and lip. Every time the dead banged into the thin metal roof at his back, he would flinch, bow his head and whimper.

Knowing she would have to work fast to keep the kid from bleeding out, Raven fished a couple of eighteen-inch zip ties from her pack. She usually reserved these jumbo ties for securing a gate or for wrapping around the knobs of double doors. Nothing like having a Z follow you into a home or business to get the blood pumping.

The jumbo ties would be perfect for this application. Hopefully, they would save his life. "What's your name?" she asked as she quickly fashioned the zip ties into a makeshift tourniquet.

Exhaling sharply, he said, "Connor."

Raven met Connor's shocky, expectant gaze. To distract him while she worked, she said, "You good to walk?"

"I think so." He made a face as she cinched the first tie down until it was nearly breaking the skin of his upper bicep. "Did I get bit? Am I infected?"

Raven looped the second nylon tie over the end of the stump and cinched it down as tightly as she could get it. The bleeding stopped immediately. Wiping her bloody hands on her pants, she said, "I don't think so. I think your arm was pretty much severed before that thing started snacking on it."

"I didn't feel anything biting me," he stated. "Are you sure I'm going to be okay?"

She glanced at the dead streaming past the end of the trailer. "I'm pretty sure both of us won't be *okay* if we don't get a move on."

She helped him to his feet and walked with him to the front of the trailer. Once Potvin had a hold of the man's remaining hand, Raven helped him over with a two-handed push to the seat of his pants.

Awaiting her turn to pass through the breach, Raven stole a quick peek over her shoulder. At the rear of the trailer, a pair of zombies pushed from the steady flow filing by had discovered the narrow opening. The two sets of shark-like eyes never left her as they thrust their arms in her direction. Rotting flesh sloughed from their emaciated bodies as they struggled to occupy the same limited space.

With Potvin and the others calling for her to hurry up, Raven drew her suppressed Glock and went down on one knee. Forgoing a press check, she promptly shot both zombies in the face. As the twice-dead corpses slumped forward, effectively blocking the narrow opening, she holstered the weapon and clasped the hand being offered to her.

Rejoining the others at the front of the load bed, Raven raised her head above the bedrails and did a quick scan of their immediate surroundings.

Peering up from a prone position, Potvin whispered, "Are they leaving?"

Raven shook her head. From two directions, north and east, surged a seemingly never-ending herd of zombies. The former was pouring around the corner a block distant. The latter was coming at them head-on and completely filled up the east/west arterial. Though the flow was parting as it came up against the pickup's front end, a crowd was slowly gathering there.

The young woman started to whimper.

Raven had a niggling feeling some of the zombies had witnessed Potvin's escape from the cab. Putting a finger vertical to her lips, she shot the woman a look that screamed, *Pull yourself together.* Then, regarding Potvin, she said, "There's no end in sight to the herds … in either direction." She covered herself with one corner of the tarp, then pinched the bridge of her nose. "Miss Potvin, by chance, did one of the Zs, at any time, see you inside or outside of the cab?"

Potvin nodded. "Inside. Just a couple of the faster ones that were out ahead of the main group."

Grim set to her jaw, Raven said, "You called an SOS, *right*? To the Stryker commander? Tell me you at least got ahold of the Dead Sled crew."

Potvin drew a deep breath. Shaking her head, she said, "I was relaying the GPS coordinates for glower retrieval when the rotten bastards got the jump on me. I put the radio down right away and scooted. Standard operating procedure: break contact and retreat."

Raven said nothing.

Wearing a sheepish look, Potvin said, "The boulevard we're on adopts an uphill climb after the intersection. Half a block east from the intersection, it takes a shallow turn to the left." Speaking through clenched teeth, she added, "Like I always do, I looked both ways when I crossed the intersection. I *swear* the second herd wasn't there when I did." She regarded the lookalikes. "Did either of you see them?"

The young woman shook her head.

"I was looking the other way," responded the man.

Connor said, "I smelled them about the same time I realized they were coming. I didn't *see* anything. Would have sounded an alarm if I had."

Fixing the blond teen with a look a detective might shoot a perp, Raven said, "What about you, Aaron? You see anything?"

Aaron shook his head. "I was on the opposite side of the trailer." He regarded Rusty. "I was to the right of him."

"See," said Potvin. "The herd had to have come from up around the bend." She shook her head. "What are the odds of circling the block, being ambushed by one herd, and then coming face-to-face with a second?"

Raven made a face. Regarding Potvin, she said, "Since our *bookie* fled with the others, looks like we'll never know the answer to *that* question." Sweat had started to bead on her brow. Sitting here underneath the tarp, dressed in all black, with the sun beating down, was beginning to take a toll. Plus, the stink of carrion was rising to an intolerable level. Wiping her brow, she went on, saying, "None of that matters now. Can't change history. We need to figure out how we're going to get ourselves out of this mess. Where's your radio?"

The color had returned to the older woman's face. Cheeks flushed redder than normal, she said, "I don't know. I didn't see it after I jammed on the brakes. Wasn't even on my mind. I was busy trying to survive … to get the rig stopped so I could get going in reverse. I assume it slid off the seat and is somewhere on the floor."

Assume, thought Raven, *makes an ass out of you and me.*

The male of the lookalike duo said, "What in the hell good is it going to do for us in there?"

A glare from Raven silenced him.

The young woman finally spoke up. Looking at Raven, finger stabbing at the radio clipped to the Kelty's shoulder strap, she said, "Can't you just call for help on *that* radio?"

Potvin said, "I have one, too. Unfortunately, we're out of their effective range."

The woman said, "So call the escort tank back. Or are they out of *effective range*, too?"

"The Stryker commander's radio is encrypted," Potvin responded. "Same with the Dead Sled driver's radio. We're all on the same net. No way we're going to get ahold of anyone without the long-range talkie."

"She's right," Raven said.

Exasperated, the young woman declared, "You've both got guns. Can't we just *shoot* our way out?"

Who did these two bribe to get their Golden Tickets? thought Raven. As she sipped cool water from the Camelbak bladder snugged into her Kelty, she dropped her gaze to the semiautomatic in the holster on Potvin's belt. It looked like a Beretta M9. Standard military issue. Plentiful in the apocalypse. The M9's magazine held fifteen rounds of 9mm. Two spare magazines rode in a Kydex mag carrier on Potvin's opposite hip. After a quick mental tally of her own stock of ammunition, Raven said, "We have about two hundred rounds between us. There's easily ten times more Zs than that in each individual herd."

The young woman went back to whimpering uncontrollably. It spurred her lookalike to pull her in close. As he began to stroke her hair, Raven asked their names.

The man said, "I'm Chris. This is my sister, Tracy." He swallowed hard. "We're going to die here, aren't we?"

Checking the injured man's pulse, Rusty said, "Connor is going to die before any one of us." Regarding Potvin, he asked, "We're not going to get out of here if we don't make that SOS call." He quickly scanned the faces all around him. "So who's going to get the radio from the cab? I'm skinny. I might fit."

Shrugging out of her pack, Raven said, "I'll go. If I shed my chest rig and vest, I'm pretty sure I can make it through the slider." While she had performed the same maneuver once before, she had grown substantially since then, and more than just upward. Now about the same height as her late mother, Raven's hips and chest had also started to fill out.

Gesturing at Potvin with his stump, Connor asked her if she had anything she could give him for the pain.

Grimacing, Potvin said, "Med kit is in the truck, too."

"Wait a sec," Raven said, digging into her pack. She came out with a compact first aid kit. "All I have is grunt candy. I usually split one and take half. How many?"

Potvin made a face. "Four?"

Raven rattled the pills from the canister and capped it. They were white and oblong and stamped with IBU 800.

Accepting the pills, Connor said, "What's *grunt candy*?"

"Eight hundred milligram Ibuprofen. I got the slang name from my dad. He's a grunt."

"Far from it," shot Potvin. "Your dad is a legend."

Thankfully, the sound of dead things caroming off the static truck suddenly increased in volume, going from the occasional *bang* to a full-on sonic tempest. Though it kept Raven from having to address her dad's reputation, the incessant impacts had the Chevy shimmying on its lifted suspension. Raven wasn't too concerned, though. She'd heard it all before. If the truck had been broadside to the flow and not weighted down by the overturned trailer, concern would be warranted. As it stood, once the herd finally moved on, she figured the damage wrought on the pickup's front and sides would end up being mostly cosmetic. Still, from inside the load bed, underneath the tented tarp, it sounded as if a troop of pissed-off baseball-bat-wielding baboons were beating the hell out of the pickup.

Whispering, Potvin said, "How long do you think this will continue?"

Beating Raven to the punch, Rusty said, "Math is my thing. I've been crunching the numbers in my head. At three miles per hour—assuming we don't give them a reason to stop and surround us—it should only take thirty minutes or so for a couple thousand deaders to pass us by."

Only? Raven consulted her watch and noted the time. Keeping her voice low, she said, "Then we better be quiet for the next thirty minutes." She scanned the faces again, ending with Tracy. "The person who gives us up, accident or not, is the first to get fed to the Zs."

Chapter 11

A few miles east of the Eden Compound, lying flat on his stomach near the edge of a water-filled quarry, PLA Special Forces Captain Kai Zhen lifted a pair of liberated Steiner binoculars to his face. As the rubber cups touched the raised pink scar tissue ringing his eyes, he was reminded of the American missile attack that had nearly killed him.

Late October the year prior, Zhen and his Cobra Force had just returned from a mission that saw them infiltrate the National Security Agency in Fort Meade, Maryland. After downloading files containing the whereabouts of secret government redoubts across the country, and then planting in the mainframes malicious code designed to make the United States appear culpable for the release of the Omega virus, Zhen had led his team overland, to a sandy beachhead on the Chesapeake where they ditched their motorcycles and boarded an awaiting motor launch.

The motor launch had spirited Zhen and his team from shore to the destroyer *Lanzhou*. He and his team had transferred to the looming vessel and were just setting foot on her deck when she was struck by a submarine-launched Tomahawk cruise missile.

The initial shockwave had thrown Zhen and three of his men from the deck. The backpack containing the drives full of sensitive information was ripped from Zhen's grip as he hit the cold water. As a pair of enemy Tomahawks struck the multi-role frigate *Yulin*, touching off her magazine and releasing a slick of blazing oil, Zhen had watched in horror as his men, one by one, were consumed by fire.

With the amphibious transport dock *Kunlan Shan* crippled and belching pillars of flame, Zhen swam to a debris field and pulled his battered body onto the largest piece of flotsam he could find. Badly burned about the face and upper body, Zhen had floated on the Chesapeake for hours, surrounded by his countrymen's corpses, their bodies cooking slowly in the licking flames of the slick.

When dawn finally broke, Zhen had located the beachhead and paddled ashore. There he found a handful of survivors still waging a pitched battle against the jiangshi. Though gravely wounded, he had fought tooth-and-nail alongside sailors and officers alike.

Of the sixty-seven men who had survived the missile barrage and made it ashore, only Zhen and a dozen others remained when the jiangshi were finally defeated.

Zhen led the survivors inland. Arriving at a golf course, they commandeered vehicles and supplies. From there, they pushed up the coast, stopping only when Zhen spied a mast-like antenna sprouting from the roof of a garage beside a gleaming white Cape Cod.

The antenna was connected to an operable HAM radio, which Zhen used to contact search and rescue helicopters sent to scour the Chesapeake for survivors.

Upon reaching a nearby high school whose football field Zhen deemed suitable for the pair of inbound Harbins to land, encounters with the insatiable jiangshi had depleted the group's remaining ammo and winnowed their numbers down to nine.

During that twenty-four hours of hell, the human toll had been staggering. In the thousands, Zhen had later learned. At the time, it had been the largest defeat the modern PLA Navy had ever suffered. Those losses, however, were recently eclipsed by a surprise attack on the newly arrived occupation fleet. Moored in Seattle's Elliott Bay to refuel and resupply prior to a mission that would have them steaming north to Alaska via the Inland Passage, save for a few motor launches and tenders, the entire fleet had been decimated.

Those losses had been beyond staggering and had forced the Invasion Council to activate Operation Blanket.

Now, grimace stretching tight the glossy mask Zhen's once chiseled features had become, he shook off the images of the dead and dying and focused his attention toward locating the approaching helicopter. While he could feel in his gut the harmonic thrum of rotors beating the air somewhere to his fore, he couldn't yet see or hear the aircraft responsible.

The Utah countryside was lush and green, with the occasional clearing dotting the valley falling steeply away from Zhen's elevated perch. As he panned the field glasses across the horizon, trying to pick out the aircraft amongst the ground clutter, he forced himself to ignore the disconcerting sensation that grew stronger with each passing second. It was a sensation he was first exposed to months ago in Portland, Oregon. It was akin to being in the path of attenuating shockwaves created by a faraway aerial bombardment, a rumble just outside the range of human hearing.

Zhen had been en route to the site where the leader of a band of rebels responsible for dozens of hit-and-run strikes on PLA patrols was being held. Zhen and his new Cobra Force were transiting an elevated expressway a kilometer north of the museum and had been forced to watch the utter destruction of the large cadre of PLA soldiers garrisoned there.

Somehow the air defenses protecting the site had been nullified. He didn't learn the severity of the damage the occupation had suffered at the hands of the American soldiers until they and their stealth helicopters were long gone.

Walking the museum grounds amid the burned and mangled bodies of his fellow countrymen had been a morbid affair. He had found where the enemy had entered the building: a small ground-level window on the west elevation. He then spent hours studying the building's interior.

Seeing the handiwork of the entry team told him they were formidable opponents. That the death cards left behind weren't emblazoned with the usual snarling wolverine informed him he had new quarry to hunt. An extremely professional adversary adept at employing the same skillsets as Zhen's mostly hand-picked Cobra Force. Efficient, cold-blooded killers trained in the arts of stealth and more than willing to employ violence of action to achieve their objectives.

Acutely aware that the American helicopter's noise signature was greatly diminished thanks to advances in blade design and use of materials and manufacturing techniques yet to be stolen by his country, and that the invisible black devil had been known to seemingly materialize out of thin air, Zhen radioed his men, instructing them to find cover and stay down until he indicated otherwise.

The thirty-nine-year-old PLA lifer had good reason to believe the approaching fifth-generation helicopter was the same type used during the raid on Osama bin Laden's compound in Abbottabad, Pakistan. Though one of the high-tech Ghost Hawks had crashed during the insertion, members of SEAL DEVGRU Red Squadron had destroyed the crippled craft with high-explosives prior to slipping away into the night aboard the remaining stealth helos.

While the Pakistanis had recovered the tail rotor assembly fully intact, the rest of the helo was burned beyond recognition. Sadly, after being allowed to inspect the wreckage at length and in great detail, the engineers at Aviation Industry Corporation of China—the PLA's version of America's Skunk Works—were just beginning to apply their findings to China's advanced prototype helos when the idiot scientists lost control of their America-killing bug. Those fledgling programs died along with a billion of his fellow countrymen.

A quick peek over one shoulder told Zhen that the roll-up door to the bullet-riddled garage remained in the open position. The night prior, a pair of Chinese-made Harbin transport helicopters had deposited his Cobra Force and their motorcycles on this scraggly nub of earth.

At the moment, two of their four dirt bikes were in the middle of a thorough tear-down and entirely useless to the team. Additionally, while the men and machines were hidden from the prying electronic eyes of the American's orbiting military satellites, with the door up and the bikes in the bay and in various stages of repair, they would be fully exposed should the helo's aircrew choose to investigate the long-abandoned quarry.

Zhen lowered the Steiners and brought his radio to the corded tissue that used to be his lips. Speaking Mandarin, he ordered his young staff sergeant, Xian Chun, a fireplug of a man from China's landlocked Hubei province, to call the others inside and close the roll-up door. Tone measured yet firm, he went on, saying, "Sergeant

Chun, prepare the Fei Ying. Have Sergeant Yu tend the door for you. Be ready to engage on my command."

Chun responded with a curt "Affirmative," then signed off.

The FY-6, otherwise known as Flying Eagle, was a handheld man-portable air defense missile. Equipped with an infra-red seeker and high-explosive warhead, in capable hands, the MANPAD could engage aircraft out to six kilometers.

Once Zhen saw the garage door coming down, he plucked the Steiners off the ground and resumed his search. When he finally acquired the helo, it was a tiny black speck skimming the treetops and in an entirely different location than his exceptional hearing had placed it. It was flying right to left, the south by east heading making it appear that it was coming straight for Zhen's position. As he continued to watch, it was evident that the helo was deviating slightly, the heading surely taking it to the den of snakes in Colorado Springs, Colorado.

New District, he thought. The dogs truly think they can rise from the ashes. Such hubris.

Confident his dark camouflage fatigues would mask the subtle movement, he pulled a laminated map of Utah from a cargo pocket. It had been folded so that the immediate area of operation was front and center. He put a finger on the place on the map where he first got eyes on the helicopter. Tracing a line that approximated the helo's heading, he was pleased to see it would likely take them close to the nearby town of Bear River.

Though it pained him to do so, Zhen smiled. He wished he could be a fly on the bulkhead when the aircrew got eyes on the small town. If he were a believer, he would have petitioned God that the operator the people of New District called "Captain America" was aboard the helo, too.

As the helicopter grew larger and its rotor signature rose to a low-decibel hum, Zhen watched it skimming the treetops with his naked eye. When it finally dropped down behind a picket of firs a mile out, Zhen rose, snatched up his QBZ-95 bullpup rifle, and hustled back to the garage.

Entering the building through the bullet-pocked office door, Zhen navigated the moldering furniture scattered about a small waiting room, then entered the garage bay via an interior door.

Hands full, Chun acknowledged his superior with a nod. Balanced on one shoulder and emitting a faint electric hum was the five-foot-long MANPAD launcher.

Wen Bao, the sergeant minding the roll-up door, was from hardy farmer stock. Just six years old when he lost both parents in the Tiananmen Square massacre, he had been a ward of the state until his sixteenth birthday, when he willingly joined the People's Liberation Army. Knowing the manner in which his parents had been killed, under the treads of a Type 59 main battle tank, didn't deter him from having a staunch allegiance to the Motherland. Perhaps it was a bit of brainwashing that had informed his thinking. But if you asked the man why he held no animosity to the state, he would tell you it was his parents' foolish ideology that had left him an orphan.

Sitting on a rolling office chair in the middle of the high-ceilinged double-stall, Second Lieutenant Zi Yong slowly turned a bolt on one of the team's Yamaha YZ 450 dirt bikes.

Seeing Zhen looking his way, Yong said in Mandarin, "Is it your mythical Pale Riders?"

Ignoring the barb, Zhen said, "How long until we ride?"

"I'm a leader, not a mechanic," replied Yong. "Perhaps Bao would like to let go of the chain and get his hands dirty. One hour if he helps. Three if he doesn't."

A hard stare from Zhen silenced the newest addition to the Cobras. While Yong was an exceptional marksman, had a firm grip on tactics, and wasn't afraid to engage the enemy—living or dead—the kid's mouth ran faster than he worked. In fact, if work ethic had been taken into account over family lineage, Yong would have ended up in a PLA infantry unit, not on a Special Warfare team. If Zhen had had any say in the matter, the wiry six-footer from Beijing would have never donned the coveted black beret.

Having been coddled his entire life, the officer's commission handed to him on a silver platter just weeks before the dead began to rise, the twenty-five-year-old son of a long-dead high-ranking party official was, by far, the weakest link on the team. Zhen's every attempt to have Yong moved to another team had been met with stiff resistance on the part of the communist party leaders back home.

Zhen supposed he would be Yong's babysitter until the man either got himself killed, or got them all killed.

"Bao," said Zhen. "Lend the lieutenant a hand." He regarded Chun. "Stow the missile, then top off our tanks. When you're finished, replenish the batteries in all of our gear." He paused and briefly met each man's gaze. Confident they all understood what the coming hours held in store—saddle-sore asses and lack of sleep—he added, "We ride in one hour."

Zhen moved into the office, sat down gingerly on the ugly couch, and closed his eyes. All other senses tuned in to his surroundings, he spent ten minutes meditating on the task at hand. When he opened his eyes, he was refocused and mostly free of the pain that had been his constant companion since late October.

Satisfied that whoever had been aboard the helicopter had more pressing matters to attend to than conduct a flyover of a rust-streaked garage surrounded by dilapidated outbuildings, Zhen shouldered his pack, then strode off to a nearby shed, where he needed to send off a quick message before preparing his Yamaha for travel.

Chapter 12

A little winded from the all-out sprint from Brook's grave to the awaiting Ghost Hawk, Cade ducked his head and climbed aboard. Meeting Lopez's rheumy-eyed gaze, he said, "What the hell are you talking about? You're not going to *die.*"

Axe said, "It *might* be the sedative talking." He made a face. "Doubtful, though. He's quite lucid."

Lopez said, "I swear to God. I *am* dying. I can feel stuff shutting down." He quickly crossed himself, then started to recite the Lord's Prayer.

Eyes locked on Lopez, both Nat and Cross firmed their grips on their weapons and sat up straight in their seats.

In the bitch seat, trying to create some distance between himself and Lopez, Ding strained hard against his safety belt.

Griff popped the top on an energy drink. Though he was within arm's reach from Lopez, he remained his usual nonchalant self. "It's just your imagination fucking with you, Low Rider. Last I checked, you have to get *bit* to get the *Mega.* You, my friend, did … not … get … bit."

Lopez looked to Cade. Sweat was leaching from underneath his helmet and beading on his forehead and lips. Twin runners trickled down his cheeks, wetting the helmet's chinstrap. "I'm burning up, Wyatt." He paused and took a deep breath, then exhaled sharply. "The pain is intense. Comin' in waves." His eyes rolled back in their sockets. When he refocused them on Cade, he said, "I don't want to become a *demonio.* Promise me, Wyatt … promise me, *mi amigo*, if I can't do it myself, you'll do it for me … before I finish the turn."

Speaking through clenched teeth, Cade said, "I haven't forgotten our pact." He looked at the rest of his team, meeting their eyes one at a time, then returned his gaze to Lopez. Tone softening, he went on, saying, "Wouldn't want these yahoos fighting over the chance to put a bullet in you. So I guess we'll have to draw straws to see who gets the honor." The last part was a rare attempt at humor on Cade's part. It was meant to break the sullen mood that had descended on the cabin. Though it was the gallows type of humor the shooters were accustomed to—even expected to hear when under duress—not one of the men averted their eyes from their sickly-looking teammate.

Cade shifted his gaze away from Lopez and regarded the countryside scrolling by outside the speeding helo. Beyond the flitting treetops, about a mile out, he saw the quarry where Duncan's brother, Logan, had been murdered. It gave him solace that he had been able to right that wrong. Make the people responsible pay with their lives. This one, though, was different. If Lopez were indeed infected, to whom would he direct his wrath? Knowing he couldn't kill Ding prior to extracting any and all useful intel from him, he tamped down the rage and went back over in his head all that he could remember from the recent Eplot raid.

Drawing nothing but blanks, Cade decided that taking Lopez for his word was the correct course of action. No sooner had he come to the difficult decision than in his headset he heard Ari say, "Five mikes."

Switching his radio to a channel monitored only by the aircrew, Cade put a hand over his boom mike to keep from having his lips read, then detailed Lopez's condition.

After a brief moment of silence, during which the helo slowed and started a shallow turn to the right, Ari came back saying exactly what Cade had expected him to. While the man on the stick was prone to cracking wise, he was all business as he recited back to Cade the protocols adopted as a result of Omega.

Resting his helmeted head on the bulkhead behind him, Cade snaked a hand in a cargo pocket and withdrew a pair of handcuffs pre-fashioned from zip ties. When he leveled his gaze on Lopez, the man was wearing a look of resignation and already offering up his gloved hands.

Hoping the cuffs would ultimately prove to be an unnecessary precautionary measure, Cade slipped them over Lopez's clenched fists. "I'm sorry, Javier. It's—"

"Protocol," Lopez finished. "Don't forget your promise, Wyatt." Before Cade could respond, Lopez was soliciting Axe for something to ease the building pain.

Not a good sign, thought Cade. If Lopez was infected, he was now entering the stage of the turn every single person went through prior to the onset of first death. Cade had been in the company of more than his fair share of infected in the throes of the turn, including his good friend and mentor Mike Desantos. Some went quickly, some—the slow burns—dragged on for hours. Desantos had been a slow burn and was granted final release by Cade's Gerber. Save for the little terrorist Pug, whose infection Cade had precipitated, witnessing a reanimation was always a haunting experience.

However, if Lopez wasn't really infected and Cade carried out the deed, that would be one hell of a burden to carry for the rest of his days on Earth.

Ari calling "Two mikes out" over the shipwide comms snapped Cade from his morbid train of thought. This was the mark of every flight the SOAR aviator usually reserved for his Night Stalker Airways schtick. This time only silence followed the two-minute warning.

In the midst of deploying the right-side minigun, Skip turned toward the Pale Riders and wagged two fingers at them.

Cade grabbed ahold of Lopez's hand, clenching it tight as he matched his gaze. "You have my word. I'll do it," he promised, throat constricting.

The handshake was not reciprocated. All the fight was leaving Lopez. If he was indeed infected, Omega was winning.

Turning to Axe, Cade gave the go-ahead to further sedate his good friend, adding, "Make sure he's real comfortable."

Without warning, Griff lashed out at Ding, striking the smaller man in the chest with both closed fists. The blow was solid and punctuated by the sound of bones breaking. As the SEAL was working to get unbelted, to get to Ding's neck and finish what he'd started, Nat reached over and forcefully sat Griff back down in his seat. "Let it go, brother. He'll get his."

Veins bulging, Griff gestured toward Lopez. "Tell us what is wrong with him," he demanded, stabbing a finger in Ding's face. "If you don't come clean, I'm going to open the door and throw you out myself."

Granite set to his jaw, Cross said, "Not if I beat you to it."

Face contorted in pain, Ding struggled to draw a breath. At the same time, his one good eye was darting about the cabin. It was evident he didn't quite comprehend the exchange taking place between his captors.

Seeing this, Cade said, "Let me translate," then repeated the threats in Mandarin.

The second Ding regained his wind, he started babbling back at Cade in Mandarin.

Able to understand only a word here and there, Cade said, "Slow down," and patted the air with both hands—universal semaphore for his spoken order.

Ding slumped against his harness, defeated. Then, enunciating slowly, in English, he said, "Jiangshi poison him."

"No shit, Sherlock," bellowed Griff, his face red and spittle flying.

"Tell us something we don't already know," demanded Cross. "*How* did he get poisoned?"

Ding looked to Cade. Pointing at his neck, Ding said something in Mandarin.

Shaking his head, Cade said, "I don't know what that means." He regarded his team, all of whom had been learning Mandarin using the same language program as Cade. Problem was, Cade had been bedridden for days and able to spend hours each day with earbuds plugged into his ears, reciting words and phrases over and over, and was way ahead of the game. Conversely, with the elevated op tempo, the other Pale Riders were learning at a much slower pace, only able to plug in during the limited downtime between missions.

Simultaneously, Cross and Nat shook their heads.

Shrugging, Axe said, "He lost me straightaway, mate."

"I can barely understand his broken *English*," conceded Griff. "The rest of it … I'm not there yet."

Exasperated, Cade pressed a fist to Ding's sternum, causing the man to grimace. Leaning in, Cade said, "What poisoned Lopez?" and pointed at his unconscious friend.

Again gesturing at his neck, Ding repeated what he had said before. But this time, when he was finished, he spit into one hand and offered it for all to see.

All at once, Cade came to understand what the man was getting at. Hanging his head, he said, "The wastes of skin are dosing their ammo with infected tissue. Which explains the half-assed reloading operation back at the Eplot plant." He looked to Griff. "The slop in the plastic bag is salivary glands. I should have put two and two together."

"Same thing that Elvis fucker was doing at Schriever," noted Cross. "Only that mutt was using syringes to inject unsuspecting people with Omega. Started a big outbreak inside the wire."

Cade said, "We really dodged a bullet on that one. Could have easily ended up much worse than it did. The real casualty, though, was peace of mind. Might as well have been a PsyOps campaign. Lost a couple of hundred civilians, if I remember correctly. I know it sure spooked Brook and Raven. Took months to earn back the trust of the survivors still housed at Schriever."

He dug into his pack and came out with the plastic bag. Pointing to his neck, then stabbing a finger at the viscous contents in the bag, he said to Ding, "Jiangshi?"

Ding nodded.

Cade patted his carbine, then made a finger gun and simulated firing it.

Again, Ding nodded. Only this time it was punctuated by a sly grin.

Again, Griff lost it. Though he was still belted in, he landed a flurry of punches to Ding's head and neck before once again being restrained by Nat.

Over the shared comms, Ari said, "Kids, don't make me come back there. Because I *will* pull over." He was craned around and looking back at Cade as he issued the faux threat. When Ari finally turned back to face forward, simultaneously, he spit a string of expletives and the helo lurched and bled a ton of airspeed.

Already privy to what Ari and Haynes were seeing through the cockpit glass, Skipper powered up the electric minigun and pointed its deadly end groundward.

As the rest of the team strained against belts to see out the window nearest to them, Cade pressed his face to his window. Peering groundward at the community of Bear River, he could barely believe what he was seeing.

Hanging by their necks from the limbs of the large oak across the street from the bookstore-cum-courthouse were a number of naked corpses. Had to be at least twenty of them. Men and women. More dead bodies littered the street and nearby intersection. They were uniformly spaced, maybe a yard apart, hands and feet bound with zip ties. Blood pooled around their heads looked to have come from single bullet wounds made at close range, execution-style.

As the Ghost Hawk drew nearer and Ari put her into a steady hover over the town square, Cade realized that the corpses hanging from the massive boughs had been tortured prior to being strung up. Raised welts crisscrossed nearly every inch of skin. Playing cards, no doubt bearing a Cobra, had been affixed to the corpses. One on each. How they were holding on against the rotor blast was a mystery. Cade guessed they'd been nailed there.

A couple of the males had been castrated. No doubt, upon closer inspection, the missing parts would be found in the victims' mouths. Wouldn't be the first time Cade had seen it. The CCP soldiers of the invasion force were savages. They hated Caucasians and African Americans equally. But it was Asian Americans atop their totem pole of hatred. The things they did to those they captured were like nothing Cade had ever seen. Some had been skinned alive. Others were given the Old West wagon-wheel-over-the-campfire treatment: burned to death very slowly.

On one side street below, a pair of bullet-pocked SUVs sat on flat tires in the middle of the road. Both were facing the same direction and separated by less than a car length. Both had BRPD stenciled on their doors. A pair of dark skid marks marred the blacktop behind each rig. Automotive fluids painted the road near each vehicle, too. If Cade were reconstructing what happened here, judging by the silver-dollar-sized engine kill shots puncturing both hoods, and the multiple smaller bullet holes piercing the roof sheet metal, his money would be on this attack having come from above. The pair of two-story storefronts bracketing the block the SUVs sat on created a perfect kill box.

It was apparent the law had been responding to an urgent call, a plea for help likely precipitated by the blood orgy a block away.

Twin blood trails on the road connected the static vehicles to two male corpses sprawled face-up in the nearby intersection. Adding credence to Cade's theory that Bear River had been taken by complete surprise, both dead lawmen had arrived wearing civilian clothes—blue jeans, short-sleeve tee shirts, and tennis shoes. More playing cards littered the ground around their bodies.

The question nagging Cade was where Sheriff MacLeod had been when all of this went down. While he couldn't be certain, none of the dead he'd seen so far resembled the middle-aged woman.

"These people were caught completely flatfooted," observed Cross.

"Agreed," answered Cade. "The tangos took the courthouse first. Considering all the shell casings, must have made a racket coming in."

Nodding, Axe said, "Then they took up station near the egress points and waited for the law to arrive."

"Agreed," Cade repeated. He shook his head. Sheriff MacLeod had seemed so full of hope last time he talked to her. So sad that what had once been a thriving community of hardy survivors was now a scene of utter destruction. Due west of the courthouse, several of the cement noise reduction panels making up the continuous wall surrounding Bear River were now lying flat. He figured that was part of the reason the streets north of the town square were teeming with hundreds of Zs. Some of the walking dead, though, must have been residents of the town.

MacLeod had mentioned that an influx of survivors from Salt Lake had swelled their numbers to nearly five hundred—roughly a two-fold increase, even when accounting for the hundred or so people taken by last winter's flu outbreak.

"Nothing alive moving down there," stated Haynes.

"Copy that," replied Skip. "I'm seeing only rotters. Strange thing, though … there's not a single kid down there. A good thing, I think."

As the helo nosed into a slow orbit of the killing field, Cade concurred, then made a mental note to ask Peter Dregan his thoughts on the matter. Thinking aloud, he said, "Sheriff MacLeod knows this bird is connected to me. So does the majority of the population. Anyone hiding down there should see us as friendly." He consulted his Suunto. "If there's anyone left alive down there, they should have shown their faces and tried to signal us by now."

All the color drained from his tanned face, Cross said, "Looks like three, maybe four hundred Zs packed in near the north wall. My guess is they tried to follow whoever did this as they exited through the North Gate."

Axe said, "Sections of the west wall are down. Wouldn't the Zeds have discovered it and given chase?"

"Though they seem to know to follow the path of least resistance," said Cross, "they're not clever enough to know to double back when they hit an obstacle. Likely, now that we're here, they'll turn around."

Regarding Cade, Nat said, "You think your friends are why the Chicoms paid this place a visit?"

Cade shook his head. "Other way around. No way the Cobras just stumbled upon the compound. It's a needle in one hell of a big haystack." He regarded Lopez, then looked a question at Axe.

Axe placed two fingers on Lopez's sweat-drenched neck. "His pulse is faint and fading fast."

Having slumped in his seat, Ding straightened up and leaned away from Lopez.

Back on topic, Axe said, "This Sheriff MacLeod … did she know about the compound and your connection to it?"

Cade said nothing. He was sitting ramrod straight and peering at the ground, where the hair on the corpses and the death cards tacked to their pale skin were being whipped about by the punishing rotor wash.

Seeing the sudden change in Cade's body language, Axe said, "No need to respond, mate."

Over the comms, Ari asked, "What now, Wyatt?"

"Nothing we can do for these folks," replied Cade.

"There's got to be someone holed up down there," Griff insisted. "Maybe the adults had the kids hide and told them to stay put until someone returned."

Cade nodded. "Maybe so. Short of going down there and searching house-to-house, there's nothing we can do."

Cross said, "We'll be coming back this way on the return leg. Wouldn't hurt to stop back by and do a couple of orbits before pushing south."

Cade said, "Solid plan. If nothing's changed by then, there'll be no need for us to send help."

"Copy that," responded Ari. "Next stop, Bear Lake. ETA: twenty mikes."

Chapter 13

Ten minutes after uttering her thinly veiled threat, Raven had finally gotten Tracy calmed down enough to offer an apology and impress upon her that the statement had been what her father liked to call "gallows humor." It took another ten minutes after that for the twenty-something blonde to stop shaking and acknowledge Raven's explanation and accept the apology.

Now, thirty-eight minutes after Rusty had made his initial thirty-minute proclamation, the sounds of bare feet slapping the road beside the pickup had all but ceased. However, breaking the silence now and again was the subtle squeak of skin dragging against window glass.

Sitting up, Raven made eye contact with Potvin.

"Are they gone?" Potvin whispered.

"They're still out there," Tracy lamented, her voice rising a couple of octaves. "I can still smell them. I can hear them, too." As she began to hyperventilate, her brother drew her in close.

Having uttered only half a dozen words since climbing into the load bed, Aaron looked to Tracy. Whispering, he said, "It's not a herd out there. I can guarantee that. You hear any moans or hissing? Any teeth clacking together? Nails scraping the paint? Shoes scuffing the road?"

"Okay, okay," Chris said. "She gets it. I get it. You don't know what we went through back home."

Raven leaned back, content to just listen.

"I'm the one who should be worried," Connor said, waving his stump at Tracy. "Maybe you should be scared of *me*. One of those things chewed on my arm. If I'm infected—"

Raven cut him off. "You aren't infected," she said. "The trailer roof amputated your arm at the elbow. Your forearm was hanging on by scraps of skin and trailing veins. To become infected, Omega has to get into your bloodstream. No way that could have happened, considering the delivery system was interrupted."

"She's right," confirmed Potvin. Only she left out the part about seeing the undead woman rip the flesh from the kid's arm prior to the appendage becoming completely detached.

Connor laid back down on his side, then drew his legs up to his chest.

Parroting her late mother, Raven said to Connor, "Keep that arm above your head." Addressing Potvin's original question, she added, "I'll take a quick peek. If the herd has moved on, I'm going for the radio."

Nodding, Potvin said, "Make it quick, though. We need to warn the North Gate of what's heading their way." She paused, thinking. "While you're in there, grab my medical kit. Should be under the front seat. On the passenger side."

Busy rooting in her pack, Raven nodded but said nothing. She finally found her iPhone and thumbed it on. It was at ninety-one-percent charge. *More than enough for what I need to do.*

Having had her phone die on her outside of the garage in which the Chinese terrorists were going full tilt on their bomb-building operation, she always made it a point to keep it at a full charge, or at least as close to full as possible.

Using the Infidel's honed tip, she punctured the tarp near her head and cut a hole just large enough to poke her hand through. Sheathing the knife, she tapped the phone's glass screen, peered at it for a second or two, then wormed her hand—phone clutched in it horizontally—through the slit in the tarp.

Aaron asked, "Trying to find a signal?"

Perking up, Tracy said, "How many bars do you have?"

Potvin said, "There is no cell service. *Anywhere.*"

Raven said nothing. She was picturing the phone in her mind's eye, concentrating hard on keeping it level and her arm straight as she slowly rotated her wrist left to right. After completing what she hoped would amount to a complete covert three-hundred-and-sixty-degree sweep of their surroundings, she pulled her arm back inside the tarp.

Clued in to what Raven had been doing, everyone—save for Connor, who was lying prone, eyes closed and sweating profusely—angled in close to get a better viewing angle at the tiny screen.

Craning to see past Raven's arm, Chris said, "What do you see?"

Shuffling over on his hands and knees, Rusty stuck his head between Chris and Tracy and parted the pair with one hand.

Answering Chris, Raven said, "Nothing yet. You need to give me a second to cue it up. But first, I need to make sure the volume is all the way down before I start the footage rolling."

Unable to get close enough to see, Potvin leaned against the mangled fifth wheel. "When the show starts," she whispered, "someone please give me a play-by-play."

Raven nodded, then tapped the Play arrow. At first, as the ninety-second-long video started to play, the picture was a bit jittery. As the back of the cab gave way to the scene on the pickup's right flank, a pale, gaunt face suddenly filled up the screen. It startled Raven, causing her to flinch, and, subconsciously, sent her free hand on a blind search for the cool steel of her SBR.

As the image remained the same, the ghastly pustule-pocked face contorting as if the Z were familiar with the device it was staring at, Aaron whispered, "That thing had to have been a baller. A big man, for sure."

Tracy's gaze swung to the left. Eyes locked on the tarp at the point in space where the recording suggested the shadow of the giant-sized zombie should be, she hissed, "Everyone shut up. If it hears us, it'll pluck one of us out. That'd be a load of horseshit." She stared murder at Aaron. "Is that what you want?"

Shrugging off the attack, Aaron pulled up his shirt. Tucked into his waistband was a boxy black pistol. "I'm ready. Are you?"

Quickly realizing the zombie wasn't actually as tall as the five seconds of lead-in footage made it out to be, that she had been aiming the iPhone down over the bedrail, Raven said to Aaron, "It's one of three rotters on your side. It's normal-sized. So are the rest. So please relax." As the footage rolled on, more details of their surroundings were revealed: single-level and two-story homes lined the south side of the block. When the trailer came into view, it completely blotted out the street and intersection beyond.

As Raven continued narrating what the footage showed, quietly vocalizing for Potvin all that she was seeing on the iPhone's screen, she was heartened to learn that the trailer was still clear of zombies. The pair she had put down with single shots to the face were still tangled together and blocking entry to the trailer's interior.

The final third of the sweep revealed much of the same, down to the type of homes lining the north side of the street and the number of zombies hanging around the Chevy's left side. When the front of the Chevy was revealed, it was a bit blurry due to the rear glass. Though the seatbacks blocked the majority of the hood and view beyond, it was clear a handful of zombies had been intrigued enough with the vehicle to stay behind. They were pressed against the grille, arms draped over the sloping hood. Counting heads, Raven said, "In addition to the three on each side, we have six hanging out up front."

Aaron pointed at an object on the screen. It was deep in the background and moving slowly downhill, through the shadows of the overarching trees, toward the light spill illuminating the nearby intersection. "What's this?" he asked.

"A crawler," said Raven matter-of-factly. "Nothing to worry about."

"No," said Aaron, "behind the crawler."

Raven rolled the footage back to the point where the crawler came into frame. She paused the video and took a quick screenshot. After finding the photo in the photo album, she tapped and pinched and moved the image around until the gently sloping section of street behind the crawler was filling up the screen.

Aaron said, "That's what I'm talking about. Looks like a couple of dirt bikes."

Raven nodded. "I see it."

Tracy said, "Bicycles?"

Raven shook her head. "Off-road motorcycles … dirt bikes," she corrected, handing the iPhone to Potvin. "I see riders in black. What do *you* think?"

Potvin took the phone and scrutinized the image. Finished, she watched the entire ninety-second recording, after which she added, "I see them. What do I think? I think we need to get that radio and call this in."

Putting herself in her dad's boots, Raven shook her head. "Those are what my dad calls Pied Pipers. He's tangled with them before. They're PLA scouts sent out to disable our early-warning sensors. They also try to find the Zs we tag so they can remove their tracking collars."

Potvin lifted off the load bed and made eye contact with Raven. "What are they sticking around for? And what do you propose we do about it?"

"I say we kill them."

"They're armed," noted Tracy.

"So are we," Raven said. "And we have the element of surprise." Regarding Aaron, she asked, "How proficient are you with that Glock?"

Interrupting, Potvin said, "You're not supposed to have that. Your ticket doesn't have the proper endorsement."

Smiling, Aaron said, "I'm not prone to toeing the party line." He looked to Raven. "I'm alright out to thirty feet or so. I've got two spare magazines."

Raven asked, "What are the four tenets of firearm safety?"

As the others looked on, Aaron gave an answer.

"Three out of four," Raven said. "Not bad."

"What one did I miss?"

"Always know what's behind your target. Which means you have to be sure there are no friendlies behind the thing you intend to destroy."

"We're in the RZ," reminded Potvin. "We're supposed to be alone out here."

"The video disagrees," Raven said. Gathering the others close, she laid out the beginnings of a hastily concocted plan.

New District

Duncan thumbed his iPhone to life, tapped the icon to access his music library, then scrolled through the artists until he came to Hank Williams Jr. How Raven had loaded this much music onto such a small device was still a mystery to him. He knew it had to do with copying MP something-or-other files from a computer's hard drive to the phone's onboard memory. Short of the first Leatherman multi-tool he'd bought for himself back in Portland prior to the Y2K fizzle, the tiny phone containing a computer, jukebox, camera, and more games than an old brick-and-mortar coin-op arcade was the coolest thing he'd ever owned.

Just as Hank launched into *There's a Tear in My Beer*, the two-way radio on the table beside Duncan's porch chair emitted its shrill electronic warble. The caller, he estimated, could be one of three people. First on the top of his list was Glenda. If it happened to be her, the news was not likely to be in his favor. His second hunch was that Cade was back from his mission and was being delayed by after-action reports and the like. In which case, a request to feed and walk Max would be the likely reason for the call. Since both tasks were already taken care of, that it could be Captain America did little to move him to want to scoop up the noisy device. Third person who came to mind was Daymon. The man was newly single and restless as hell; always trying to rustle up someone or other to accompany him on a foraging mission outside the wire.

Though Duncan wouldn't mind some company, would actually relish shooting the breeze with someone sharing in his current predicament, he couldn't push aside the notion that his first assumption was flawed. That somehow the love of his life had finally come around to his way of thinking and was calling to tell him all about it.

Hank was just getting to the verse in the song where he was certain the significant other would never come to her senses when Duncan snatched up the Motorola and thumbed the Talk button.

The initial burst of white noise was replaced by a gravelly male voice. *Not my Glenda*, he thought. Keeping pressure on the rubber button, he regarded Max, asleep in a patch of sunlight washing the porch by his boots. "Not Cade, either." Then, with Hank back to lamenting the number of beers he had downed and the multitude of tears he had shed over his loss, Duncan lifted the radio to his mouth and growled, "What do you want, Daymon?"

As soon as the channel opened up, Daymon was back on, saying, "I sure as hell didn't want to be left on hold listening to your sad-ass country and western song."

Thumbing Daymon back into silence, Duncan said, "Get to the point of yer call or I'm turning this thing off and keeping it turned off." Finished saying his piece, he kept the Talk button depressed, which forced Daymon to endure one more tear-jerking Bocephus stanza.

As soon as the channel opened up, Daymon said, "I think Raven is in trouble."

Those six words made Duncan sit up straight. They also made him forget about Glenda and Hank and all of his own troubles.

He said, "Elaborate."

"She went out with a piker crew this morning—"

Interrupting, tone all business, Duncan said, "I want meat, no potatoes."

Reacting to the change in his friend's voice, Max raised his head and fixed Duncan with a contemplative gaze.

Daymon mentioned the side trip to put down the glowers. Then he said, "The driver noted the coordinates for the cleanup crew. That was the last anyone heard from them."

"What about the security detail? The Dead Sled?"

"Stryker peeled off to help some incoming survivors fix their ride. Turned out to be some kids and a couple of teenagers in a school bus. One of those short ones the special education kids used to ride to school in." He paused with the channel open. Finally, he added, "The Stryker commander reported a sizeable herd headed for the North Gate. The cleanup crew lagged behind. Apparently they ended up loitering there to keep from tangling with the herd."

When the channel opened up, Duncan thumbed the Talk button. "So no contact with the Stryker and the Dead Sled crew." He paused for a beat and drew a breath. Exhaling, he asked, "How long are they past due for check-in?"

There was no response. A beat later, though, the sound of tires on pavement drew Duncan's attention to the street, where Daymon was bringing a bright red beach cruiser bicycle to a skidding stop.

Breathless, Daymon said, "Fifteen minutes … give or take." He clipped the two-way radio to the strap of the bulging backpack riding low on his back. He was dressed in worn olive-drab fatigues. Kindness and Mercy, neon-handled machetes, rode on opposite hips. What appeared to be a Beretta semiautomatic pistol was snugged into a black shoulder holster. Scuffed leather boots and a matching olive-green boonie hat rounded out the ensemble.

Duncan said, "How'd you hear about all this? Where'd you get your intel? That ex-girlfriend of yours?"

As Daymon bent over to tie his boots, the slung AR-15 fell from his shoulder. Placing the rifle on the sidewalk, he said, "I plead the Fifth." Looking up, he added, "Doesn't matter. *Time* is all that matters right now."

Duncan rose and stuffed the Colt Model 1911 semi-auto pistol into the holster on his hip. He reached inside the open front door and came away with his go-bag and Saiga shotgun. Shooing Max inside, he put the dog's food and water bowls on the foyer floor and then closed and locked the door.

"I take it I'm driving."

Nodding, Daymon said, "I'm having Whipper stuff a Coyote crate engine into my Bronco. She's all torn apart."

Shouldering his pack, Duncan said, "Purple People Eater, it is. Come on, D. She's in the garage."

As Duncan flung open the garage doors, revealing the front end of his purple dually GMC pickup, he said, "If there's a herd on the way—"

"Herds," Daymon interjected. "Plural. I forgot to mention that two merged into one."

"How many?"

"A lot."

"Elaborate."

Opening the passenger door, Daymon said, "Two … three thousand."

Duncan's door creaked as he opened it. Taking a seat behind the wheel, he said, "And how do you propose we get outside the wire?"

"Again, I'm pleading the Fifth."

"East Gate, I presume."

"They're expecting us."

Duncan fired the motor and started the 4x4 rolling into daylight. "You pullin' a favor, or you puttin' one into the owing one column?"

"The latter," replied Daymon. "Bird's worth it. She's like a kid sister to me."

Turning from the driveway, grille aimed south, Duncan matted the pedal. "Bird of The Apocalypse. What have you gone and gotten yourself into now?"

Chapter 14

Four hundred miles northeast of New District's Red Zone, Jedi One flared hard and ceased all forward movement. Once Ari had the bird in a hover, Haynes brought the Forward Looking Infrared pod online. Instantly, the countryside beyond the Ghost Hawk's nose was replicated on a rectangular portion of the craft's all-glass cockpit.

Ari said, "Zoom in. Normal optics."

Haynes was already manipulating the stick-mounted hat switch with his thumb. "Pushing in. Seventy-five-percent zoom." Once the image on the virtual screen stabilized, he added, "Looks deserted. Nothing moving."

Bracketed between two distant trees was the triangular plat of land home to Bear Lake County Airport. It was surrounded on three sides by a continuous run of twelve-foot-tall razor-wire-topped fence. What looked like canvas panels were secured to the fence on the inside. With the airport situated so close to a well-traveled highway, it was a necessary visual deterrent. It kept the buildup of dead things to a minimum. It also spared the skeleton crew from the disconcerting sensation of always being watched. From having the meat stared from their bones round the clock. Because once the shamblers caught sight of prey, whether they be scruffy first turns or newer specimens, short of putting them down, there was no surefire way to escape their undivided attention.

As it stood, dozens of zombies milled about outside the nearest run of fence. A far cry from the crush of dead present last time Cade had been here.

"Doesn't look like there's been a breach," noted Ari. "Nothing living or dead moving inside the perimeter."

A guard tower rose a dozen feet over the fence at each corner. There was no movement in the towers.

Equidistant between the nearest towers was a canvas-shrouded gate, its doors bowing in under the weight of no less than twenty zombies.

An asphalt feeder road stretched south from the gate and, after a quarter mile or so, came to a T at a two-lane access road. The access road split off west and east. The westbound straightaway linked up with the state road roughly a mile or so from the T. After a short run, the eastbound leg curled north and disappeared behind the fence bordering the airport's eastern flank.

A pair of runways split the airport down the middle. Deep craters peppered the gray stripes of asphalt. Knee-high grass growing in the infields made the landing strips appear much narrower than they were.

Haynes said, "I don't like the looks of those craters. They look fresh."

"Agreed," said Ari. "Let's give it another minute or so. I'll keep her steady. Eyes on the towers. If anyone, be they friend or foe, is still minding the store, that's where you're going to find some of them."

Fifty feet below the hovering Ghost Hawk, its turquoise water choppy and frothed by the helo's rotor wash, was the oblong lake the county and airport had been named after. Formed in a half-graben valley straddling the Utah/Idaho border, the eighteen-mile-long body of fresh water was bracketed on the west by the rambling Wasatch Range and on the east by the craggy Bear River Mountains.

The lush green expanse of Bear Lake Wildlife Refuge extended north from the picket of trees near shore Ari was using to shield Jedi One from prying eyes in or around the airport. The refuge was mostly swampy grassland impeded only where it came up against the two-lane encircling the airport.

In the right seat, holding the helo in a rock-solid hover, Ari was monitoring the electronic intercept screen. If there was any kind of radiation or electronic noise indicative of an active air defense system in the vicinity, the bird's sensors would pick it up. Detecting nothing out of the ordinary, he said, "All quiet out there. Got eyes on anything moving?"

Staring at the FLIR feed, Haynes said, "Nothing moving but the ghosts outside the wire." The "ghosts" he was referring to were walking dead. Their lack of body temperature made them present as gray forms against the colorful backdrop.

Exhaling sharply, Ari said, "Okay. Zoom in and pan the hangars and main building. Eyes peeled for heat sigs. There *was* a skeleton crew here last time we came through. A few MPs, some maintainers, and a second lieutenant. A cadre of about twenty, if memory serves. There's got to be *someone* left alive down there."

Haynes manipulated the hat switch, bringing the FLIR pod left a few degrees. Simultaneously, he zoomed the camera in on the distant airport's infield. After panning left to right and then back again, he said, "Negative. No heat sigs. At least nothing with a pulse. And it looks like those *craters* are just holes. Probably dug with a backhoe."

Tapping the glass where a blob of white pixels stood out starkly against the background, Ari said, "What's this? Kill the thermal and let's see it on optical."

"Copy that," said Haynes. "Switching from thermal to optical." No sooner had the last word crossed his lips than a full-size pickup filled the screen. It was silver and sat in the shadow of a hangar. Its spidered windshield and bullet-riddled front end faced the probing camera lens. The front seats were empty, which was a good thing because anyone sitting there when the damage had occurred would be a goner.

In the troop compartment, eyes glued to the bulkhead-mounted monitor, Cade perked up. "I know that rig!" he exclaimed over the shared comms. "It's Sheriff MacLeod's."

Deeming it safe to proceed, Ari pushed forward on the stick. "Splitting the uprights," he said, threading the helo between the pair of mature trees bookending the picket it had been loitering behind.

Still staring murder at the prisoner, Griff said, "How do you think the sheriff's truck ended up here? More importantly, who shot it up, and where is she now?"

"I have no idea," said Cade. "Don't even want to venture a guess until I get a closer look."

As a wide-open marshy area of the refuge scrolled by under the speeding Ghost Hawk, Ari said, "I'm going to do a quick counterclockwise orbit over the airport. That'll give you a good feel for the grounds. Just let me know where you want to infil."

"We've been here before," Cross reminded. Looking to Cade, he said, "How about round back where you fed Adrian to the hogs."

Pointing at the image framed on the monitor, Cade said, "There's a big barn and greenhouse due west of this squat office building. Put us in near the greenhouse, and we'll sweep south and rally with you on the tarmac in front of the main hangar."

Going off the image splashed on the cockpit monitor, Haynes said, "It was dark when we were here last. But it's all coming back to me now." He pointed out the structures north of the main runway. "Finish the orbit, then go through this breezeway."

"Understood," said Ari. "Thirty seconds out."

Taking the *thirty seconds out* announcement as his cue to spring into action, Skip deployed his helmet's smoked visor, ran the right-side minigun panel open, and then maneuvered the Dillon into place.

Seconds after leaving concealment, the helo was clipping along very near to the ground at seventy knots and fast approaching the southernmost run of fence. Ari said "Brace" over the shared comms and then pulled pitch and banked hard right.

As Cade acted on the advice, his stomach took a tour of his abdomen.

The first leg of the planned orbit was uneventful, taking them over the easternmost tower and along the shorter of three runs of fencing. When the two newer structures and the two-story office building Adrian and her ilk had set up shop in finally came into view, the helicopter was banking hard left over the northernmost guard tower and coming in hot on a westerly heading.

Directly below Cade's window was a fuel bowser. "Bear Lake County Airport" was painted on the tank. Fifty yards west of the bowser, its tricycle landing gear just parting with the ground, was an olive-drab military helicopter. It bore a Chinese flag and markings identifying it as a Peoples Liberation Army Navy asset. The Harbin Z-8 multi-role maritime helicopter, with its slab sides and bulbous, clown-like nose, was just a notch up on the ugly scale from the venerable CH-47 Chinook.

If the Ghost Hawk was a Chevy Corvette, the single-rotor craft Cade was currently staring at was a Chevy Caprice.

Arranged in a semi-circle on the ground near the helicopter's right side was a long row of corpses. Men and women. Cade didn't see any kids. Half of the corpses were clad in civilian attire. The rest wore Air Force ABUs with a subdued tiger-stripe camouflage pattern.

Care had been taken to lay them out neatly, shoulder to shoulder, on a patch of beaten-down grass. Shell casings littering the grass around the corpses glittered under the high sun.

Cade's first impression was that the bodies had been posed for a photo op. At the same time he was taking all this in, Ari was saying, "Harbin, eleven o'clock," and wrenching Jedi One into a tight and rather violent clockwise turn.

"Setting you up, Skip," intoned Haynes.

Ari was back on, saying, "Light 'em up, Skip. Do *not* hit the bowser."

Head and minigun moving in unison, Skip said, "Copy that. Going hot."

Next to Cade, Lopez's limp form was completely at the mercy of gravity. Head lolling around like a kid's toy top, suddenly his arms and legs rose off the seat. The appendages remained weightless and bent at curious angles until the craft bled speed and resumed level flight.

Just as Ari had adopted a hover broadside to the slow-to-launch Harbin, two things happened back to back.

First, the minigun began to whine, and it belched a steady stream of lead at the enemy helicopter. Then, as if the droning noise of three hundred rounds leaving the six-barreled electric Gatling gun had awakened Lopez from his drug-induced slumber, his eyes snapped open. Only there was no life in them. They were glazed over, the pinned black pupils instantly locking onto the nearest meat. Which, as Mister Murphy would have it, just so happened to be Cade.

Mouth agape and teeth bared, the newly reanimated Pale Rider thrust both cuffed hands at Cade's face and angled in for the kill.

Seeing this transpire from across the aisle, simultaneously, Griff and Cross intervened. As if communicating telepathically—not a far stretch considering the years the two had spent training and running ops together—Griff reached for undead Lopez while Cross, drawing from his Secret Service training, put his body between the threat and the principal, who in this case was Cade, *not* Cross's former protectee, New District President Valerie Clay.

Getting a hand on one side of undead Lopez's tactical helmet, Griff redirected the lunging attack toward the prisoner.

With the equal and opposite reaction component of Newton's Law already in full effect, Cross put a splayed-out hand on the zombie's back, the other on the rear of the helmet, then drove the wide-open maw toward Ding's shoulder.

Keeping pressure on the helmet, Griff looked a question Cade's way.

Gerber already free of its scabbard, Cade nodded.

They both knew what had to be done, and Cade was in perfect position to do the deed. Only this wasn't going down the way Cade had expected it to. With Desantos' situation, Cade had been able to say a prayer and a few parting words. However, with the helo starting to move and Skip still engaging the Harbin, there was no time to do anything but insert the Gerber's honed tip between the C1 and C2 cervical vertebrae and thrust upward with enough force to enter the base of the skull and pierce the cerebellum.

As quickly as Lopez's reanimated corpse had gone rigid, it went limp, the jaw releasing the prisoner's shoulder from the crushing bite.

As Cade withdrew the blade, he whispered, "Till Valhalla," into his dead friend's ear.

The minigun abruptly went quiet.

The second or two of silence was punctuated by a thunderclap as the Harbin nosed into the ground behind the main hangar.

Still embracing Lopez, Cade swung his gaze toward the nearest window, where he saw an orange and red ball of flame roil the sky. A plume of thick black smoke came next. It was momentarily dissipated by rotor wash as Ari side-slipped Jedi One away from the crash site.

A long uncomfortable silence ensued.

Peering into the cabin, Ari said, "He turned?"

Cade said nothing. He was angry at himself for letting Lopez turn. For breaking his solemn oath. It was a regret that was going to follow him to the grave.

Axe said, "Lopez is gone. Thanks to Wyatt, he didn't suffer."

He suffered, thought Cade, tears welling in his eyes. *And I am to blame.*

Taking a page from the highly religious Lopez's book, Griff performed the sign of the cross over his chest rig. He glared at Ding. Seeing the blood seeping through the CCP soldier's fatigue blouse, Griff smiled. "Poetic … fucking … justice," he crowed, slapping Ding on the knee. "Couldn't have happened to a more deserving waste of skin."

Nat looked to Cade. "Can we throw him out now?"

Cade shook his head. "I want to interrogate him first." He glanced out the window. Ari's slow clockwise spin had brought the wreckage back around to the Ghost Hawk's left side. The bodies of CCP soldiers thrown from the Harbin littered the asphalt behind the hangar. The burning wreckage had a large patch of the hangar's light blue paint bubbling and peeling and turning black.

"You want to do it here or on the ground?"

After having just experienced Lopez turning inside the helicopter's cramped confines, Cade didn't want to chance the same happening with Ding. Pointing west, he said, "I want to do it on the ground. I want to poke around a bit, too. Look for clues that might tell us what went down here. Think you can infil us near the livestock pens?"

Ari said, "No problem," and aimed the Ghost Hawk for the postage-stamp-sized parcel of grass wedged between a run of livestock pens and rectangle of blacktop crowded with farm equipment.

No sooner had Cade heard the reply in his headset than the prisoner's exposed skin began to pale. Cade watched it happening in real-time, the color first draining from the man's slack countenance, then continuing on down to the extremities. In no time, Ding's forearms were the same color as his hands, which had already gone white thanks to the cuffs pinching off circulation at the wrists.

Though the bite hadn't gone deep enough to sever the carotid and cause catastrophic bleeding, the compress Axe had hastily applied was already thoroughly soaked. Cade figured Ding was one of the small number of infected whose physiology had a particularly difficult time fighting off Omega. After first death, rapid-turns usually began the process of reanimation in a matter of seconds.

Cade feared Ding was on the fast track to passing. With that in mind, he said to Ari, "I need to be boots on the ground … now!" Turning to Axe, he requested an ammonia ampule. Finally, with his gut trying to enter his throat thanks to Ari suddenly dumping altitude, he doled out instructions to the rest of his team.

Chapter 15

Red Zone, New District, Colorado

Raven's hastily concocted plan was very simple. It was also going to prove very dangerous for one of them. So, in keeping with her father's main tenet—never ask someone to do something that you aren't willing to do yourself—she told the others that she would be the one to signal the riders.

The only person to argue was Potvin. "I've done plenty of living," she said. "I couldn't forgive myself if they're the shoot-first-and-ask-questions-later types. Plus, you're the better shot out of all of us. You go down, we'll be massively outgunned."

"She has a point," Aaron said.

"I'm a smaller target," Raven stressed. "Besides, I'm only planning on taking a split-second peek." She looked to Connor. He was propped up on his good arm and keeping pace with the conversation. "I need one of your socks."

Holding the stump aloft, he said, "You're going to have to take it off for me." He grimaced. "Sorry in advance about the smell. Only pair I could find to put on this morning."

"Compared to the things out there," Raven said as she removed Connor's boot and peeled off the sweaty sock, "this thing smells like a rose." Setting the rifle within arm's reach, she pushed the tarp aside and spun around on her knees until she was facing forward.

Thrusting the hand holding the sock into the air, she rose up until just her arm and upper third of her head had crested the pickup's roofline. As she scanned the road ahead, the zombies crowding the pickup keyed in on the movement.

One of the zombies beside the load bed thrust its pale arms in Raven's direction, causing her to nearly jump out of her skin. Though the waggling fingers were nowhere near to touching her, their mere presence had the hairs on her neck standing to attention.

She waved the makeshift surrender flag back and forth for a few seconds. Getting no kind of a reply—No bullets cutting the air near her head. No engines firing to life, followed by mysterious riders screaming down the hill toward the pickup—she dropped back down into the bed and regarded Potvin.

"Well?" Potvin inquired. "What are they up to?"

Glock clasped in a white-knuckled two-handed grip, Aaron said, "Did they see you? Are they coming?"

"They're gone," Raven stated calmly. "Or they were never there in the first place. The video is kind of grainy when you zoom in on it. We could have mistaken shadows for guys on bikes. It could have been an artifact caused by light hitting the lens. My Uncle Duncan says all those photos of UFOs taken over the years were either caused by weather, a bad camera operator, or were experimental aircraft we weren't supposed to be seeing yet." She made a face. "I didn't hear any engine noise. Didn't hear their exhaust, either. All the dirt bikes I've been around are pretty damn noisy."

"The riders *were* there," Tracy insisted.

"They weren't a figment of *my* imagination," Chris assured Raven. "Play the footage again."

Raven shook her head. "That's a waste of time. Doesn't change a thing. It'll just start us arguing." Setting her rifle aside, she looked to Potvin. "I'm going in for your radio."

Aaron said, "Get our tickets, too."

Not a bad idea, thought Raven. She said, "The radio is my prime objective. If I see the tickets, I'll grab them." She regarded Aaron and suggested he put the Glock away. "Too noisy. It'll just draw more rotters."

Nodding, Aaron jammed the pistol into his waistband.

Potvin said, "You've got to grab the tickets. It's the only way I can account for the rest of my crew. I'm responsible for every one of you." She shook her head, tears welling in her eyes. "I feel terrible about what happened."

"Can't change the past," Raven said. Addressing Tracy, she asked, "Do you have a blade?"

Nodding, Tracy produced a folding item. It was good for whittling a sapling, nothing more. Blade deployed, the entire thing was six inches long, at most.

Raven tugged the Infidel from its sheath. Handed it to Tracy hilt first. She regarded Potvin. "You're still the boss of this crew." Meeting the gazes of the others, she said, "Time for all of you to start stabbing eyes and scrambling brains."

By the time Raven was halfway through the rear slider, scissoring her legs and looking like a frogman out of water, Potvin had staked out her position on the load bed's left side and was engaging rotters with a big Bowie-style knife. Tracy, on the other hand, was hanging back and lamenting the discrepancy in length between a pike and the black blade Raven had loaned her.

Taking a cue from Potvin, Aaron stood and made his way to the right side of the load bed. Standing just out of reach of the grabby hands of one of the taller zombies, he withdrew a Ka-Bar fighting knife from a sheath strapped to his leg. With no hesitation and hollering "Oorah" at the top of his voice, he took one of the Z's bony hands in his, yanked the slender twenty-something partially off its feet, and buried the blade in the undead woman's left eye socket, drawing forth a torrent of pus and congealed blood.

Aaron's war cry inspired Chris to bring his convenience-store made-in-China blade into the fray.

Finally, after enduring Potvin's constant pleas for her to "pull her own weight" and seeing Rusty step forward and begin stabbing at the zombies with a humongous blade of his own, Tracy stopped bitching about the difference in standoff distance and put the Infidel to use, plunging its razor-sharp tip cleanly into the eye socket of the geriatric zombie nearest to her.

Hitting the rear seat face-first, Raven curled up into a ball and rolled onto the floor. She ended up wedged in the footwell, face up and staring at the dirty headliner, the transmission hump jamming her in the back.

Beyond her boots, the talc-white hands of the dead were high-fiving the window. The hollow thuds and sharp slaps of clammy flesh striking glass comingled with Potvin's constant shouting and someone's boisterous war cries.

As Raven got herself righted and cast another glance at the window, she was pleasantly surprised to see that the Zs had lost interest in her and had moved on.

Maybe, hopefully, she thought, the dirty work would be done before she was finished here.

She crawled over the seatback and commenced a search of the trash-strewn cab. She found Potvin's medical kit under the seat, right where she said it would be. The radio was underneath a drift of candy wrappers that had accumulated in the passenger-side footwell. If it was still powered on and Potvin had left the volume rolled up past two or three, at the moment, it wasn't broadcasting anything. There were no harried calls for Potvin to check in emanating from the speaker. No communication was happening between the Stryker commander and Dead Sled crew, either. It was as if the missed check-in had gone unnoticed. Either that or the Dead Sled or Stryker—maybe both—had come up against the herd. If true, protocol was to call it in. And if they reported seeing a herd in the thousands on a collision course with New District, defense of the perimeter wall, the North Gate specifically, would be taking any and all focus off of finding a missing piker crew.

Where New District was concerned, the safety of the many *always* outweighed that of the few. So, at the moment, her gut feeling weighing heavily on her assumption, Raven was fairly certain every available resource was being diverted to the wall. No doubt the call to arms would have already gone out in the city, and all of New District's able-bodied citizens would be flocking to the North Gate.

A herd numbering upwards of a thousand—should they all happen to converge on the same section of wall—had a very high probability of stressing the wall to the point of causing a breach. However, should a herd four thousand strong—a surging mass of flesh and bone capable of shoving single-family homes from their foundations and tossing fire engines aside like toys—come up against the wall—the wall most certainly would fail. The loss of life would be staggering.

Already the gate guards and wall watchers would be implementing diversionary tactics. While personal vehicles surged into the neighborhoods north of the wall, their sole mission to locate the herd's lead element and steer it any direction but south, soldiers on the wall would be busy hand-launching surveillance drones to keep tabs of their progress.

If all of this was happening, Raven knew that she and the others were on their own.

Cold ball forming in her gut, she grabbed the med-kit and radio. The clipboard was nearby. It had become wedged in the space between the passenger seat and door panel. Since opening the door to get at it was out of the question, she had to slip off her glove and get her hand in there and snare the papers with her fingers.

She set the stack of papers on the seat and rifled through them. After separating her own Golden Ticket from the rest—the only one bearing the Presidential Seal—she crawled over the seatback.

The one-sided melee was still underway as Raven wormed her way through the slider. Ending up on her knees in the load bed, she braced on the fifth wheel and rose up. A quick scan of the surrounding blocks told her the riders were still nowhere to be seen.

On the pickup's left side, Potvin, Tracy, and Rusty still faced half a dozen Zs. On the ground below their fighting position, a waist-high pile of twice-dead corpses had accumulated.

Rusty had pulled back from the bed rail. He was leaning against the fifth wheel hitch, palms on his knees and gulping air. Blood dripped from the tip of the blade in his hand. A constellation of reddish-black spatters dotted the ribbed metal bed by his boots.

Both of the women's blades were slick with blood. Their hair was damp and matted. Potvin had uncoupled her overall's shoulder straps. The bib was bloodstained and hung loosely down her front. Dark sweat stains ran vertically up the backs of the women's shirts. Seeing this reminded Raven how hot she was, dressed in all black and with the sun beating down on her.

Opposite the trio on the left side, Aaron and Chris were also under siege. The dead were three deep and four wide. Some of the creatures had found their way atop the fallen zombies and were pressing into the side of the truck. Their increased reach was making it hard for Aaron and Chris to maneuver without stepping on Connor or coming up against the twisted fifth wheel apparatus.

Time being of the essence, Raven had them both stand down and step aside. Drawing the suppressed Glock, she immediately started firing into heads from point-blank range, her movements methodical and sure.

Having expended twelve rounds and achieved a perfect one-to-one kill ratio, she swapped for a fresh magazine, holstered the still-smoking Glock, then turned to face the other survivors.

Tracy held the blood-slickened Infidel loosely. Blood spatters dotted her straw-colored hair. Her hands were also bloody and shaking terribly. Catching Raven's eye, she said, "I didn't think I had it in me."

"You rose to the occasion," Raven said, gesturing for the Infidel. "Might want to visit Lola's and find something like it. Anything but that little pocket folder of yours."

Biting her lip, Tracy handed over the knife.

Raven took the Infidel and slid it into its scabbard, blood and all. Time for cleaning and maintaining weapons would have to wait until after the battle.

"You got the radio?" asked Potvin.

Raven dug it out of her cargo pocket and handed it and the Golden Tickets over to Potvin. She placed the med-kit on the bed by the woman's feet.

"It was already powered on. I didn't hear any chatter coming out of it. Nothing at all the entire time I was in there."

Potvin said, "They probably have their hands full dealing with the herd." She thumbed the Talk key and tried hailing the Stryker commander. Nothing. Just dead air. When the attempt to raise the Dead Sled driver went unanswered, she gave voice to what Raven had already assumed.

Arron said, "So if we are on our own, then it's on us to find some wheels. We're what? Ten … twelve miles out?"

Potvin fished a rag from a pocket and started wiping the blood from her hands. "About ten." Finished, she passed the rag to Tracy.

Aaron cleaned his knife off on his pants and returned it to its leather sheath. Staring into Potvin's red-rimmed eyes, he said, "You sure you can't free the truck from the trailer? Maybe drag it until it breaks free?"

Thinking, Potvin glanced at Connor. While the kid's face still maintained some color, he was shaking. The tremors were close together and pretty subtle. This led her to believe he was shocky, not infected with Omega. Returning her gaze to Aaron, she said, "We could try it. It's going to make one hell of a racket."

"You *have* to try it," insisted Chris. "I don't want to have to walk in from here. It's not safe. Too many stragglers."

Again, Raven made a visual sweep of the area. A couple of crawlers were advancing down the hill from the same direction the herd had come. They posed no immediate threat. In addition to the crawlers, a few laggards were just making their way across the intersection. The other points of the compass were clear of dead things. Finally, a quick peek over each bed rail told her that the accumulated corpses were unmoving. They all had been granted a well-deserved second death.

Raven looked a question at Potvin.

"Couldn't hurt to try," the driver conceded. "We need to move Connor to the back seat. If that hitch does come free, no telling what kind of damage it'll do as it swings around back here."

Tracy made a face. "How are we all going to fit inside the truck?"

Raven said, "We're not. We're going to get out and watch from a safe distance. If the trailer comes loose, then we all pile back in."

Potvin said, "Sound plan. Toss your packs inside the cab and get to the curb."

Raven donned her pack and slung her SBR. She shoved Aaron, Tracy, and Chris's packs through the slider. Rusty insisted on keeping his pack, too.

Connor had only the clothes on his back.

By the time Chris and Aaron had helped Connor down from the bed and had gotten him belted in the passenger seat, Potvin was behind the wheel and revving the Chevy's motor.

Chris and Aaron hustled to the curb and stood shoulder to shoulder with Tracy. As the trio was fixated solely on the truck and trailer, Raven alternated attention between monitoring their six and watching Potvin wheel the rig up the block, whipping the trailer back and forth with a series of exaggerated S-turns. This lasted the better part of two minutes. When Potvin finally gave up, stopping the Chevy in the intersection a block distant, the trailer was still on its side and stuck fast in the hitch. The only thing she had to show for her efforts was a whole mess of pulped zombie corpses, a series of black skid marks down the center of the street, and a low-hanging cloud of diesel exhaust that was slow to dissipate.

As Raven covered her face against the noxious fumes, in her head she cursed Whipper for his exemplary welding skills.

The driver's door hinged open, and Potvin hopped to the road. In the next beat, the woman was running down the block toward Raven and the others. In her hand was what looked to be a two-way radio. As she halved the distance, she held the item aloft and bellowed, "Someone calling himself Uncle D is wanting to talk to"—she paused—"Bird of the Apocalypse."

Raven took the radio from Potvin. Looking toward the Chevy, she said, "You're just going to leave Connor in there all alone?"

Potvin planted her hands on her knees. Breathing hard from the sprint, she said, "I'm spent." She flicked her eyes to the radio. "How far away is this Uncle D?"

Incredulous, Raven said, "You didn't ask him?"

Still gulping air, Potvin shook her head.

Regarding Chris and Rusty, Aaron said, "Come on. Let's go get him. They can fill us in when we return."

Watching the trio go, Raven thumbed the Talk button. "This is Bird. Which Uncle *D* am I speaking with?"

"Both," said the voice she easily recognized as belonging to Daymon. In the background, she could hear some kind of country song playing. It was sullen and mournful, which kind of mirrored both Daymon *and* Duncan's moods as of late. "Old as Dirt Uncle D is driving. You have the pleasure of speaking with Youthful and Handsome Uncle D."

"Aren't you going to ask me how *I'm* doing?" Raven radioed. "Maybe question where I'm at? Or why Potvin missed check-in?" A flurry of movement in her side vision signaled the arrival of Chris, Aaron, and Rusty. Instead of Connor moving under his own power, Aaron had him draped over his shoulders, a not-so-textbook fireman's carry. Chris was loaded down with their packs, while Rusty walked behind them, Glock in hand and head on a swivel.

"First off," Daymon answered, "we're talking about Bird of the Apocalypse. Captain America's spawn. A chip off the old *Grayson* family block." He paused for a beat, which allowed Raven to study the faces of the people assembled around her. Clearly, the fact that she was *that* Raven was breaking news to everyone, save for Potvin, who was cracking a sly smile.

"Secondly," Daymon went on, "my sources fed us the GPS coordinates of your last transmission. Which, judging by our current position, should put us about four miles southeast of you."

"Thirdly," said a gravelly voice sprinkled with notes of the South, "Old as Dirt Uncle D knows you're with that old battle-axe, Potvin. She's as tough as a hide left tanning in the sun all summer."

In the background, Raven heard Daymon burst out laughing. Once the laughter ceased, Daymon said, "That old battle-axe is probably listening in. Am I right?"

Raven couldn't have responded if she wanted to. The channel remained open on the other end. After a few seconds of dead air, Duncan said, "If she is listening, I meant every word. It was about the best compliment an old coot like me could bestow on his equal. Back to *thirdly* … Old as Dirt Uncle D has the utmost confidence that you can take care of yourself. With or without Potvin. Hell, you saved the President's life last autumn. Give yourself credit where credit is due. But—" There was another pause. "I found a huge chink in your armor."

The channel opened back up.

Raven risked a peek at the others. On their faces was a smattering of expressions that ranged from disbelief to surprise to awe, the latter gracing Tracy's face.

Scanning her surroundings, Raven thumbed to talk and said, "I have a feeling I know where you're going with this."

"We tried the usual channel on the long-range radio. *No answer.* Tried to ping you with the Thuraya sat-phone. *Nada.*" Duncan paused for a beat but didn't reopen the channel to allow Raven to answer. Instead, he asked, "Your dad was a Boy Scout, right?"

When the channel opened up, Raven replied with a simple, "Yes."

"What would he say if he knew you're outside the wire with just the Motorola two-way? A radio with shitty range?"

"I'm sure I'm going to find out," she replied. "I never keep anything from him. Besides, how am I to learn if I don't make mistakes."

"Mistakes lead to a bite," Duncan reminded. "And we know what that means. Amputation. Or worse."

Changing the subject, Raven said, "Eyes on the road, Duncan. Hands at *ten* and *two*."

"Where are you?" asked Daymon. "I'll plug the cross streets into the navigation computer."

Raven glanced at the nearest set of street signs. She rattled them off, then added, "We're a block west of there. Which is about a block and a half southwest of Potvin's last check-in."

Daymon said, "We're straying pretty far east of the herd. It's about thirty … forty-five minutes or so from reaching the North Gate. Several teams were scrambled and are already trying to divert them. It might screw up our ability to return the way we came. Might even force us all to spend a night outside the wire. "For now," he stressed, "find yourselves a safe spot and hole up there until you hear Old Uncle D's horn."

Raven rolled her eyes. She said, "Will do," then mentioned what was on the footage she had captured with the iPhone.

"Doubt if a PLA scout patrol would chance coming this close to New District," Duncan began.

"But stranger things have happened," finished Daymon. "Listen to Old Man. Get somewhere safe and listen for the tune. Upper level, preferably."

As Raven agreed to heed the advice, Potvin mouthed, "What tune?"

Raven signed off and handed over the radio. "You'll see," she said, eyeballing a nearby Craftsman-style home. It was a two-story with a porch about the size of the one on her place. The front door bore a series of spray-painted symbols—shorthand telling anyone who knew how to read them that the home had already been searched and that two Zs had been put down and removed from within. "That's where we're holing up. Follow me."

Chapter 16

Boots on the ground a mere thirty seconds after the Harbin plowed a deep furrow into the earth and burst into flame, Cade reached down and helped Ding to stand. Though the burning wreckage was a couple hundred feet distant, Cade could feel the heat emanating off of it. Dipping his head, he dragged the prisoner toward the livestock pens.

A dozen yards from the Ghost Hawk, with ammunition inside the Chicom craft just beginning to cook off, Cade shoved the prisoner to the ground and put a knee on his heaving chest.

Semi-lucid thanks to the activated ammonia ampule jammed up his left nostril, Ding looked a question at Cade.

Glowering down at the man, in Mandarin, Cade said, "I'll make this offer to you only once. You tell me all you know about upcoming operations and I will make your death easy. You hold back—" he tapped a finger on the man's sweaty forehead— "I'll let you become *jiangshi.* I've been told the pain of becoming jiangshi is like nothing else. The worst ever." He paused for a beat to let that sink in. "But just to be sure your suffering is like my friend's, I'm going to take your remaining eye. I will then take your ears. Finally, I will take your manhood and feed everything to you." Hoping the prisoner grasped the basics of his offer, Cade lifted his knee off the man's sternum.

As Ding struggled to draw a breath, Cade glanced at the downed Harbin. Though there was an occasional pop of a round cooking off, Cross and Griff were busy dragging limp bodies away from the licking flames.

Beyond the debris field, Cade could see Nat and Axe inspecting the bodies he'd spotted during the harried overflight.

Ding took a few deep breaths, then started speaking rapid-fire Mandarin.

Cade fished his iPhone from a pocket. He snapped a photo of Ding. Then, after starting the voice memo application and urging the prisoner to speak slowly, he placed the smartphone close to the man's pale lips and ordered him to start over.

***

Five minutes after Nat and Axe had slipped around the corner and loped off for the office building, Nat was back on the radio saying that he and Axe had found little of value inside and that they were returning.

"I want you to stop and take a look at the sheriff's rig," Cade instructed.

"Copy that," said Nat. "Looks like the bastards attacked during breakfast. Broken dishes all over the dining area. Blood trails along the main halls. Some were killed inside. The ones outside were probably interrogated in front of a superior before they were executed. That would explain all the shell casings we saw in the grass by the bodies."

So the attackers were infilled at a distant LZ, humped overland, and then struck at first light, Cade thought. Then, after all resistance was put down, the hitters recalled the helo to refuel. It was nearly a carbon copy of the Eplot raid. Which told Cade the dead and dying soldiers were likely Sea Dragon Commandos, a unit similar to US Navy SEALs and US Marine Corp Raiders.

"You find the sheriff?"

"Affirmative," Nat said. "She took one to the back of the head. Still had her badge and Wyoming ID."

"Executed?"

Nat sighed. "Yep. Same with all of the other civilians. Point-blank shots to the head."

"Fuel in the bowser?"

Nat said, "Negative. Bone dry."

Cade said, "Okay. We're oscar mike in five."

"Copy that," responded Nat. "Shouldn't take long to search the sheriff's rig."

"Watch for booby traps," Cade warned. It was something that probably could have gone unsaid. Every one of the Pale Riders was a professional. Still, if something happened to Nat or Axe, considering that he'd already lost Lopez on his watch, Cade would forever question his ability to lead men into battle.

As Cade hauled Ding up off the ground, he looked toward the Ghost Hawk. He could see Ari in the right seat. As expected, since the entire aircrew had been listening in, the aviator was flashing Cade a thumbs-up.

Skip's helmeted head was all that was visible behind the deployed minigun. The crew chief stuck his gloved hand out the weapons port, five fingers splayed, which indicated he had also heard the bad news about the bowser and was remaining aboard the helicopter. The well was dry, so no hot refuel was happening here.

With three minutes to go to launch, Cade walked Ding the rest of the way to the livestock pens. In keeping with his promise, he forced the man to kneel and instructed him to look away. Drawing the Glock, Cade shot the man one time behind the ear.

Cade was feeling zero remorse before, during, or after the deed. In fact, as he hustled over to Jedi One, turbine spooled up and already going light on her landing gear, he smiled and said, "For you, Low Rider. Rest in peace, brother."

As he secured his gear and strapped into the seat by the window, he reminisced over past missions. The successful ones everyone came home from. The ones during which good men had fallen. Fortunately, the losses had been few and far between. Still, every one hurt, this one more so than the others, simply because there was nothing he could have done differently that would have kept the tainted bullet from delivering its deadly payload.

***

Jedi One had been wheels up for fifteen minutes when Ari came on over the comms. "One tanker rendezvous ahead of us," he said. "This tailwind keeps up, we'll all be home in time for dinner."

The moment the words left his mouth, he was full of regret. Meeting Cade's gaze in the mirror above the windscreen, he said, "I'm sorry."

Cade nodded that he understood, then cast his gaze to the floor by his boots, where his eyes fell upon his friend's flag-draped body.

Chapter 17

The elevated front porch of the white and brown two-story Craftsman hadn't seen the business end of a broom since before the Chinese seeded America with Omega. With Connor propped up between Chris and Aaron, the porch was large enough to accommodate everyone underneath its steeply angled roof.

A yellowed copy of the *Colorado Springs Gazette* sat in one corner. The headline screamed *Area Hospitals Overloaded With Infected!*

The ornamental Japanese maples in wood planters flanking the porch had born the brunt of the passage of time and changing of the seasons. Their gnarled trunks and skeletal branches reminded Raven of the weathered corpses sometimes found in vehicles that had run off the road during hasty retreats from fast-falling cities.

Sometimes, in addition to the unlucky occupants—people who had either died quickly from their injuries, or slowly from dehydration—those kind of finds were full of supplies. One would often find batteries bumping up against their expiration dates. Or vacuum-sealed travel snacks high in preservatives and still tasting like they did the day they crossed the convenience store counter.

Striking gold was finding a case of unopened Cokes or carton of cigarettes or chocolate still wrapped in foil—all worth a fortune in trade credits at Lola's.

Sadly, Raven thought, if the markings on the large oak door were to be believed, this home had already been picked through.

Peering at the roof, Tracy said, "Can't we just wait here? There's the stairs down to the walk. Then it's another thirty or forty feet to the street." She craned to see up the street. "And the crawlers are all I see at the moment."

Indicating Connor, Aaron said, "It'll be cooler inside. Better for this guy to be out of the sun."

"Agreed," said Potvin. She tried the knob. It turned.

Grabbing Potvin's hand, Raven said, "You know the rules." If her words were the bark, her glare did the biting.

Potvin nodded. "I've been riding a cushy seat for far too long. Be my guest."

Holding the knob in one hand, Raven pounded a fist on the door. Five hard knocks, then a short pause to listen. Nothing. So she repeated the process, this time with a lot more force behind the raps.

Still nothing.

SBR held at a ready position, she turned the knob, put her Danner on the kick plate, and toed the door inward.

Crossing the threshold, SBR's deadly end leading the way, the first thing she noticed was the stillness inside the place. It was cool and quiet. Like a funeral home. As she drew a breath, she was instantly taken back to her grandma's house in Myrtle Beach. It was the combination of old lady perfume and cigarette smoke, she supposed.

Knickknacks, curios, and figurines adorned nearly every flat surface. Knit doilies prevented the artifacts from scratching the walnut coffee and side tables.

On the coffee table was a glass serving tray. It was in the form of a maple leaf and held some kind of colorful ribbon-shaped candies inextricably intertwined into a single mass.

The television was an old cabinet-style item. It had been knocked over onto its front.

Footprints crisscrossed the powder-blue carpet. They were black with a slight red tint. No doubt tracked blood that had dried long ago. Two different-sized prints were represented. Likely a man and a woman had turned inside the home and spent some time wandering the main floor.

While the others waited on the porch, Raven swept through the downstairs. The kitchen, dining room, and half bathroom took up the rear of the home. When she returned to the living room via a long hall that split the home front to back, Aaron and Chris were in the foyer.

Chris said, "Where do you want Connor?"

"Put him on the couch," Raven ordered. She matched Connor's gaze. His face was a mask of pain, eyes narrowed and blinking nonstop. He looked like a kid trying to stay awake long enough to spot Santa. "Keep that arm elevated, Connor." It was something she'd heard her mom tell her dad to do with the ankle he had injured during a helicopter crash in South Dakota.

If Connor had heard Raven's instruction, he didn't let on.

Once everyone was inside, Potvin closed the door and threw the locks.

Aaron and Chris maneuvered Connor through the maze of furniture in the front sitting room. The plastic on the couch crinkled when the injured man's full weight hit it. As Connor settled in and leaned back, stump elevated over his head, either the endorphins had suddenly stopped flowing, the grunt candy had worn off, or the most logical answer to what happened next: the millions of nerve endings in the stump, all at once, resumed transmitting pain signals. Whatever the case, the scream that issued from the kid's mouth was wholly unexpected and enough to wake the dead.

Potvin started visibly. "You want the zombies to find us?" she hissed. Pulling herself together, she passed her canteen to Tracy. "Try to get him to drink from this." Regarding Raven, she said, "See if you can find anything in the medicine cabinet. Something for his pain. Mouthwash. Aspirin." She glanced at the run of stairs off to the right of the main hall. "I'll check upstairs."

Raven doubted she'd find anything of use in the bathroom. It was the first room she would clean out if she were one of the 4th ID soldiers who had conducted the door-to-door home welfare checks shortly after the fall.

Without a word and trying hard to tune out Connor's whimpering, Raven padded down the hall. After a quick search of the medicine cabinet turned up nothing of use, she moved on to the kitchen, where underneath the sink, mixed in with the cleaning supplies, was a half-full bottle of something called port. She was pretty sure it was some kind of wine. Though she had no idea what it meant, alcohol content was listed on the label. Strangely, the port was the same reddish-brown as the smattering of bloody footprints dried on the vinyl flooring.

Raven met Potvin at the bottom of the stairs, holding the bottle for her to inspect, a curious expression on her face.

"You found some port wine," Potvin stated. "Sandeman Twenty Year Old Tawny, no less." She shook her head. "All I found in the upstairs bathroom was a box of bandages, a couple of tubes of denture cream, and an old-timey water bottle. One of those rubber jobs folks used to fill with hot water and put in bed with them on really cold nights."

Raven didn't know what the woman was going on about. Still, she nodded in agreement.

A long, drawn-out groan spurred Potvin into action. Snatching the bottle by the neck, she hustled over to the injured man, spun the cap off, and forced him to drink. "Make bubbles," she urged.

To Raven, Connor looked like a pet hamster the way he craned and took long gulps from the offered bottle.

"That's it," soothed Potvin. "That should help to dull the pain." She looked to Raven. "The stuff in my med-kit won't cut it. He needs some more grunt candy."

Raven nodded. "How many?"

"Half a dozen."

Rusty returned with a haul of winter coats he'd found in a hall closet. He draped two of them over Connor's lap. The heavy wool pea coat got wrapped around the shivering man's shoulders.

As Raven dug into her pack, searching for the pills, she said, "You don't think that's too many? What with the port and the pills I gave him before. He won't overdose, will he?"

Dumping the pills into her open palm, Potvin said, "If Connor dies from shock, he won't be needing his liver."

Raven said nothing. Not her circus, not her monkeys. She'd done her part. And until the two uncles arrived, she was content with keeping watch on the street in front of the Craftsman.

***

Raven's resolve crumbled five minutes after she turned toward the window. Part of the change in heart was the fact that Connor's intermittent wailing was drawing the dead to the Craftsman. Already four badly decomposed first turns and an especially large and bloated recent turn had wandered in from the west. At the moment, they were milling around in the street, maybe fifty feet from the brick walk connecting the sidewalk to the low stack of stairs leading up to the porch. If they figured out which house the noise was coming from, she feared that the short run of stairs would not be enough to keep the dead from making it onto the porch. She was certain, though, that if they did, the picture window she was standing before would quickly collapse under their weight.

Raven turned away from the window. "Connor," she said, "you like superhero comics?"

Connor drew a deep breath, put the bottle to his lips, and greedily gulped down the remaining inch or so of port. Dragging his forearm across his mouth, he said, "What?"

Speaking slowly, she repeated the question. "Do you like superhero comics?"

The bottle slipped from Connor's hand. It landed on the carpeted floor with a hollow thud. His eyes fluttered once, then fixed on her. "Who doesn't like comics?"

"Marvel or D.C.?" she asked. "What's your favorite universe?" It was the leading question in a conversation she'd had with Peter weeks ago. The topic was the beginning of a long and spirited back and forth that eventually saw Wilson, Taryn, and Sasha all putting in their two cents worth.

Chris quit pacing the room long enough to declare that he was in the Dark Horse camp.

Tracy shook her head. "Boys and their comics. Chris used to try to get me into something called *Umbrella Academy*. A freakin' talking chimpanzee? Give me a break."

Raven said, "Dark Horse is located in Milwaukie, Oregon. Not far from where I lived … back before the rotters started eating people. Their storefront is right across the street from a theater my mom and dad used to take me to."

Connor perked up. At least as much as a person who'd recently lost half of an arm could perk up. Cracking a half-smile, he said, "Marvel for me."

Raven said, "Who's your favorite Marvel character?"

Connor screwed up his face but didn't answer her question. Raven didn't know if the expression and pause was a direct result of the question, or if it was a byproduct of consuming the port. Maybe, she thought, he was all the way drunk and about to start talking gibberish. She'd seen Duncan that way once. It was quite embarrassing. She didn't mention it to him afterward. Strangely, he hadn't brought it up one time since that night at the hotel they all used to call home.

Whatever the case with Connor, he hadn't cried out in a couple of minutes. During the pause, Raven pulled the curtain aside and peeked at the street. The zombies were still congregating at the end of the walk. The monstrous newer turn, as well as one of the first turns—a hunched-over elderly zombie half the newer turn's size and its opposite in the gender department—had found their way onto the Craftsman's unkempt front lawn.

Potvin and the others were now sitting in a semicircle on the carpet. Raven half expected a game of spin the bottle to break out. Instead, Potvin said, "Connor?"

Nothing. No response. The guy's eyes were taking a tour of the back of his skull.

Tracy said, "Connor? Are you okay?" She rose up and leaned in until her mouth was about a foot from his ear. "Who's your favorite *Marvel* superhero?"

Snapping out of his stupor, Connor slurred, "Iron Man. Definitely Tony Stark. But he doesn't drink, does he?"

Rusty chuckled. "Nope. He's sober. You, on the other hand, are not."

Rocking side to side, legs crossed Indian-style, Chris said, "I thought you were going to say Deadpool." He smiled. "Because if you were the Merc with the Mouth, a baby arm would already be sprouting from that stump."

After a second or two lapse, during which it was apparent to everyone looking on that gears were definitely turning in Connor's head, his eyes walked the length of his elevated arm. As his cross-eyed gaze settled on the bloody bandage wrapping the end of the stump, the shocked expression morphed to one of complete surprise. It was as if he'd forgotten the tragedy that had befallen him. A millisecond later, two things happened back to back. First, the look of incredulity was replaced by one of sheer terror. Then, as if channeling his inner Private Wilhelm, Connor screamed at the top of his voice.

Raven hissed, "Pillow!" and jabbed a finger at the love seat.

Quick on the uptake, Aaron snatched the pillow up, rose from the floor, and pressed the overstuffed item hard against Connor's face.

"Don't suffocate him," Potvin warned.

While the pillow did muffle the drawn-out scream, Raven feared it had been applied a little too late. She parted the curtains and took another look at the front yard. Sure enough, Giganto and Hunchback were heading straight for the porch steps. She said, "Take him to the kitchen and try to keep him quiet."

"What are you going to do?" asked Potvin.

Raven looked at her watch. The search of the house and subsequent superhero conversation had burned just north of fifteen minutes. Which meant, best-case scenario, the two uncles were still five or ten minutes out. Long enough for the dynamic undead duo to cause problems for them all.

Hefting the suppressed SBR, Raven said, "I'm going to fix the problem Connor created. Be right back."

With Aaron keeping the pillow in place, Chris and Rusty lifted Connor off the couch. As they carried him to the kitchen, kicking and screaming all the way, Raven threw off the SBR's safety and hustled to open the front door.

A quick turkey peek through the crack between door and jamb told Raven that Giganto was just arriving at the bottom stair. At the start of the walk, Hunchback was making slow progress. It was stopping and starting, just a couple of stunted, shuffling steps separating each action. With every short pause, its head would pan back and forth.

It can't see a thing, Raven thought, elbowing the door out of her way. As she shouldered the SBR and centered the optic's red dot over Giganto's face, preparing to put a dime-sized hole between those wandering eyes, suddenly all that was visible through the square reticle was the front porch of the house directly across the street.

Giganto slamming face-first onto the wooden porch shattered the still air. The bulbs in the porchlight overhead rattled and the boards vibrated underfoot, sending a tremor running up Raven's legs.

Knowing what was to come next, she instinctively leaped backward into the foyer, where her Danners got in the way of each other. Legs entangled, she fell backward, landing hard on her backside, carbine aimed at the ceiling and a lightning bolt of pain assailing her tailbone.

It was clear Giganto had tripped *up* the stairs. Raven had been there and done that. In her haste to set some kind of record ascending the seventeen stairs in her old house, she had slipped and wracked her shin on a tread. Up until now, that had been the worst pain she had ever felt. Now, however, she was nearly incapacitated by the nonstop, eye-watering nerve impulses emanating from the point of impact.

Giganto, on the other hand, was not affected. If he'd broken a shin, or ribs in the fall, he was not suffering repercussions. No adverse reaction. No pain. All gain. The gain component was the freefall forward that had left both mitt-sized hands sweeping the threshold just inches from Raven's boots. The only thing on the Z's mind was a meal of fresh meat. The proof was the focused shark-like gaze and constantly snapping teeth.

Gritting her teeth against the pain, she swept the barrel down and kicked at the zombie's reaching hands. Both movements exasperated her injury. The latter allowed the zombie to get a hand wrapped around her right ankle.

Seeing double, she reacquired Giganto's pale visage and pressed the trigger three times in quick succession.

The sudden tug on her right leg had straightened it out and brought on a fresh tsunami of pain. Aim altered, the first round struck the zombie on the chin, which happened to be several inches too low to do any good. But all was not lost, because the bullet's kinetic energy was sufficient to break the mandible bone, shatter the majority of teeth in the way, and snap the Z's head backward.

Muzzle lift was also working in Raven's favor. Rounds two and three exited the rising suppressor behind a haze of gunsmoke and on an upward trajectory.

The zombie's face collapsed in on itself, and the vice-like grip on Raven's ankle loosened.

Keeping the rifle shouldered, she adjusted her aim and sent a single round screaming downrange at Hunchback. The lead missile hit exactly where she had been aiming: squarely between the zombie's cataract-clouded eyes. Head snapping back, the petite form's slipper-clad feet separated briefly from the brick path.

Coming back to earth was a violent affair. The cringe-inducing *thunk* of Hunchback's cranium losing out to hand-laid brick was nearly as loud as Giganto crashing to the porch.

Raven's spent brass was still caroming about when Aaron and Chris grabbed her by the arms and hauled her to her feet.

"That was too close for comfort," Aaron said.

Being picked up and dragged into the house had caught Raven by surprise. Though the pain was no longer ratcheting up, standing did nothing to ease it. Loathe to be seen as weak, she broke free of their grip and trained the SBR on Hunchback. She was applying pressure to the trigger when she heard the rising howl of a hardworking diesel motor. It was close and rapidly drawing nearer.

She flicked her gaze right, toward the sound. Through the maple's gnarled branches, she detected a flash of purple. Though the vehicle was moving fast and coming out of the shadowed stretch of road where the riders had been, she instantly saw it for what it was. She was opening her mouth to break the good news to the others when the pickup's horn did the talking for her.

Chapter 18

"That's the *tune* we're supposed to be listening for?" Tracy sneered. "Kind of racist, don't you think?"

"It's Dixie," stated Raven. "So what? It came with the truck. And for your information, there's not a racist bone in Duncan's body. Wait until you meet Daymon. Better yet, why don't you ask Daymon to speak to Duncan's character. He'll tell you what I just told you. Sure, he's originally from Texas. He wears a cowboy hat and ostrich boots. He talks with a drawl, too. All that being said, he is not prejudiced."

The GMC Sierra roared down the block toward the Craftsman. A dozen feet short of where a knot of Zs had formed, directly adjacent to where the brick walkway met the sidewalk, the driver locked up the brakes. Tires chirped and the pickup's tail end slithered around as forward momentum was reined in. Too little, too late. Because the rig's bumper and grille guard struck the Zs mid-pack, folding some underneath the front bumper and scattering the rest like so many bowling pins.

Raven stayed on the porch, carbine at a low ready, and waited for someone to hail her on the radio. Instead, inexplicably, Duncan killed his motor, donned the ever-present white Stetson, and exited the pickup.

Potvin said, "What's Mr. Winters doing shutting off the engine? Shouldn't we be loading Connor up and getting a move on?"

Raven said, "I'm sure he has a good reason." As she was speaking, the other door opened, and Daymon emerged. He was wearing a beanie and wraparound sunglasses. The former barely contained his medium-length dreadlocks. Though his eyes were hidden from view, Raven could see that he wasn't interested in her or the others crowding the doorway behind her. He was stalking the Zs on the street in front of the pickup. There were seven that she could see. Two were clearly down for the count, one appendage or another mangled to the point that rising from the road was not possible. Two were just getting to their feet. The three that remained were already up and advancing toward Daymon. *Bad idea.* Because he was brandishing Kindness and Mercy. As he drew within striking distance of the first of the Zs, the machete in his dominant hand cut the air on a level plane, right to left. One second the doddering first turn was hissing and straining to get its gnarled hands on the coveted meat, the next it was deprived of four fingers on its left hand and at least as many inches off the top of its skull.

Light glinted off the long, polished blades as the lanky six-footer worked his way through the Zs. It was kind of mesmerizing watching him slice and dice his way through the ambulatory specimens. When he was finished with the five that presented a clear and present danger to the living, he decapitated the crawlers and placed the heads on the lawn, one on each side of the brick path.

Glancing toward the porch, Duncan tipped his hat. "D here does my light work."

Daymon said nothing. He was busy wiping the blood from his blades. Finished, he sheathed the machetes, put on a smile, and strode up the walkway, nonchalantly, as if he were delivering the mail.

Not a care in the world.

Lots of pep in his step.

Teeth clacked and the eyes in the decapitated heads moved in their sockets, tracking the victor as he stepped around Hunchback and continued up the walk.

Raven slung her SBR. "You guys made great time."

"That we did," Duncan acknowledged. "Ain't going to happen on the return leg."

Raven shot him a questioning look.

"Daymon's *source*"—he made air quotes—"just hit us with a mixed bag of news. Which do you want to hear first? The good or the bad?"

Potvin spoke first. "It's already been one hell of a day. Can't see how it can get much worse. What's the bad?"

Duncan removed his Stetson. Ran a hand through his silver hair. "D's lady friend said the herd gained a few more hundred biters as it passed through the Red Zone."

Potvin shook her head. "What's in the good column?"

"The teams dispatched from the North Gate succeeded in splitting the herd," Duncan said. "They've got about a thousand of them moving east, toward Yoder. If the herd doesn't splinter again, once they draw it out past the suburbs, should be no problem culling the lot of them."

Raven said, "And the other half?"

Daymon said, "There's more bad news." He paused long enough to size up the crowd. Leveling his gaze at Potvin, he went on, saying, "About a thousand made it all the way to the gate. The wall gang is going to be going at them for an hour or two. They'll probably be mopping up stragglers well into the night."

Raven said, "That's only two thousand. What happened to the rest of them?"

Duncan donned his hat. Fixing Raven with a hard stare, he said, "The rest of the herd's been diverted to the I-25. If all goes well, they'll bypass New District and continue on to Pueblo."

Aaron stepped forward. "So we have time to kill."

"That we do," Duncan answered. "And to kill that time, we're going to get elbows deep into a bush fix. Who's with me?"

Gaze narrowing, Raven said, "Bush fix?"

"It's a repair that's done on the fly with the tools and parts at your disposal," Daymon answered. "Like your dad says: improvise, adapt, and overcome. And seeing as how we have time to burn, we're going to go out there and see if we can get that trailer of yours free from the hitch." He pointed to Chris, Aaron, and Rusty. "I need you three to go on a scavenger hunt. You'll be looking for a breaker bar."

Aaron said, "A what?"

Before Daymon could respond, Raven said, "We have an injured person inside the house. His arm from the elbow down is gone."

Daymon said, "Gone? Like *amputated* gone?"

Potvin explained what had happened.

Craning to see over the heads of the people assembled on the porch, Daymon said, "He looks comfortably numb. You sure he didn't get bit?"

Raven shook her head. "Pretty sure the rotter got to the arm *after* it was completely severed. Connor's on like four thousand milligrams of ibuprofen and half a bottle of wine." Saying his name aloud prompted her to introduce the others.

Again, Duncan's hat came off. He nodded and said politely, "Pleasure's all mine."

Gesturing to the three male pikers, Daymon said, "As I was saying … Huey, Dewey, and Louie here are going to go search some garages and basements until they find a long metal bar. Something real sturdy. A weightlifting bar minus the weights would be ideal."

Rusty said, "Would a crowbar do the trick?"

Daymon shook his head. "If Potvin drove around like a maniac and the thing didn't work loose, a crowbar won't do it. We need leverage."

Chris looked to the others. "Let's search the garage out back of here first."

"Don't waste your time," Duncan warned. "I can see plastic on the furniture in there. While the odds are high Granny and Grandpa have an old Aries K or Ford Taurus parked in their garage, I can almost guarantee you they aren't sitting on their own prison-weight pile. Why don't you split up. Each of you pick a garage on this side of the street to search." He grabbed hold of one of Giganto's clammy hands. "First things first. Daymon … help me get this biggun off the porch. He smells like a bag of assholes."

Talking loud to be heard over the steady thunks of the twice-dead corpse's head smacking the porch steps on the way down, Tracy said, "Oh no you don't, Chris. There's safety in numbers. You guys should stick together."

Wiping his hands on his pants, Duncan said, "You fellas do whatever you got to do. Just don't return empty-handed." Next, he addressed Raven and Potvin. "When them boys return, send them down the block. Me and D are going to go and take a look at that trailer. You all hang back and take care of the human slot machine."

Potvin tried hard to suppress a chuckle. Composing herself, she said, "That's not right, Mr. Winters. The kid can't defend himself."

The joke went over Raven's head. Fishing the iPhone from a pocket, she said, "Before anyone goes anywhere near Wendy's truck, I want you two to look at the video I took."

Potvin said, "We're all over the place with what we all think we see on there."

While Raven cued up the short video, Duncan pulled a handkerchief from a pocket. He removed his aviators, gave the lenses a thorough cleaning, then squared them away on his face.

Raven turned the iPhone around and presented it screen-first to Duncan and Daymon.

Daymon leaned in close, studied the jittery image, and came away tight-lipped.

After staring at the tiny screen for a long three-count, Duncan shook his head. "It's shakier than the Zapruder film."

Raven cocked her head. "The what?"

Daymon said, "The only film footage of Kennedy's assassination. You've seen it, right?"

Raven said, "Nope. Portland schools don't dive very deep into history. My dad was pretty pissed to learn they glossed over Pearl Harbor and didn't even mention the Vietnam War. He actually went down to the school and lodged a complaint with my teacher when he found out she made no mention of 9/11 when we were focusing on modern American history."

Duncan said, "That's inexcusable. So is your footage. Why so shaky? Too much coffee?"

Tracy said, "Probably because we were surrounded by walkers."

Raven nodded. "They were pretty agitated. I was worried one of them might get ahold of me."

Duncan took a second look at the footage. Finished, he said, "I guess it could be a couple of riders on dirt bikes. Then again, it could also be shadow and light playing tricks on us." He regarded Raven. "They didn't take a shot at you?"

Shaking her head, Raven recounted the fake surrender plan and divulged that the spot in the road in question was deserted when she did show herself.

Daymon said to Raven, "We better be on high alert, then. When the three amigos return, assuming they found something to use as a lever, you and me will pull overwatch while Duncan cracks the whip."

"I'm more worried about biters than bikers," Duncan said. "Hell, if the Viet Cong couldn't punch my ticket … and the good Lord knows they had plenty of shots at it, no way I'm going to allow a couple of PLA scouts to get under my skin."

Daymon walked his gaze across the faces of those crowding the porch and foyer. Locking eyes with Potvin, he said, "I'm with Old Man. Let's chalk it up to shadows. At least for now. Maybe one of Captain America's intel weenies back at Peterson can make heads or tails of the footage."

"Say the guys do find a *breaker bar* and you two get my truck and trailer separated—what then? We come up against the herd again, whether it's splintered or not, I'm right back to square one." Potvin looked at her boots and shook her head. "I don't even know if my pikers made it to the gate. I definitely don't want to take the chance of losing anyone else."

Hands on hips, Daymon said, "Only good move we have is to lay up here until my source gives us the *all clear*."

Raven said, "You still can't say her name, can you?"

"I don't want to," conceded Daymon. "Pains me to."

Potvin said, "Aww, that's cute. You're still sweet on her. Must be the uniform. Or that she's a nurse."

The return of the three ducks—two of them carrying a long, metal cylinder—mercifully spared Daymon from answering Potvin's question.

As Chris and Aaron angled across the front lawn, coming in from the left, Tracy craned around the porch column. "What is that?" she asked. "Though it's pretty long, doesn't look like any weight bar that I've ever seen."

Rusty sidestepped the pair of dead rotters laid out on the walk and bounded up the steps. "Pretty sure it's a drive shaft. Found it in a garage three houses down. Someone was working on restoring an old pickup."

Setting his end down on the lawn, Aaron said, "Sad the thing is never going to see the road again. The paint was fresh. Chrome recently polished. And they'd crammed an LS3 crate motor under the hood. My guess is they were going to replace the factory driveshaft with something capable of handling all that extra horsepower." He wiped his hands on his pants, leaving the denim smudged with rust and grime. "It's what I would do. That motor is probably putting out five, maybe six hundred horses."

Duncan said, "You a car guy?"

Aaron smiled and nodded.

"Good to know, Matt," replied Duncan. "Why don't you and Chris carry that thing down to Wendy's truck. Could use a little help getting it into place. Hell, maybe I'll just play foreman and watch you all work."

Raven looked to Duncan. "His name is *Aaron*."

Addressing Aaron, Daymon said, "Don't mind him. I think he's got that old timer's disease."

Duncan started across the lawn. Motioning for everyone to follow, he said, "Zombie apocalypse hits and suddenly everyone thinks they're a comedian."

Arriving at Potvin's pickup, Duncan did a quick walk around, paying extra special attention to the trailer hitch and fifth-wheel receiver. Wiping sweat from his brow, he said, "She's tied up and twisted, all right." He looked the block up and down on both sides, then addressed Potvin. "It'll come loose. Of that, I'm certain. But we're going to need to get it at the right angle. I'm going to have you drive your rig onto the sloped lawn in front of the big Tudor on the corner. Once she's in position, we're going to use gravity and a whole lot of muscle. If my spit ballin' calculation is correct, thing should release the trailer."

Daymon said, "Whipper fabricated the trailer?"

Potvin nodded. "Cost me a pretty penny."

"He does good work. Welds are real solid," Daymon said. "You should see my buddy's war wagon. Whipper up-armored it real good. Stroked out the motor, too."

Sounding irritated, Duncan said, "Enough chit chat," and began issuing orders.

Raven and Daymon fanned out. After culling a small group of first turns that were drawn in by the recent engine noise, they went their separate ways.

Raven took up station nearby, her back pressed to the trunk of a gigantic oak whose branches arced out over the easternmost intersection. From her position, not only could she provide overwatch for Duncan and the others as they worked to free the trailer, but she also had clear lines of sight to all four points of the compass.

Daymon retrieved Duncan's Saiga shotgun from the Sierra and hustled down the street. He found concealment behind a row of low shrubs bordering the front lawn of a one-level mid-century ranch-style home whose design looked to have been inspired by the works of Frank Lloyd Wright. From there, without having to worry about constantly checking his six, he could monitor the streets coming in from the north, south, and west.

Standing at the top of the sloping lawn, Duncan directed Potvin as she eased her Chevy up and over the curb. When the trailer got hung up on the curb, he said, "Put her in four-wheel and give her gas."

With all four wheels working in conjunction, a quick stab of the accelerator broke the curb's hold on the trailer.

Hopes dashed that the maneuver would be sufficient to uncouple the pickup and trailer, Duncan backpedaled away from the downslope. Then, pretending he was the one steering the Chevy, he pantomimed which direction he wanted Potvin to turn the wheel as she powered the pickup onto the lawn.

After a little back and forth the Chevy was at the top of the slope, parallel to the sidewalk and listing to the left. There was about a foot or so of daylight between its right front tire and the flat of the overgrown lawn. As the trailer was dragged up the slope, its sharp edges had gouged out clumps of grass, leaving behind deep muddy furrows.

"Perfect," Duncan hollered. "Shut her off and set the brake."

When Potvin opened her door, due to the angle of the pickup in relation to the sidewalk, it was all she could do to keep from sliding off the seat. Eventually, she got her footing on the sidewalk and shut her door. Crabbing away from the listing pickup, she worked her way around the trailer, then joined the others on the flat of the lawn.

Immediately, she stated, "No way you're getting me into the bed to place the lever."

Aaron volunteered and clambered aboard.

With Duncan acting as foreman and Tracy and Potvin steering one end of the driveshaft to Aaron, Rusty and Chris muscled it up and over the bed rail.

It took a good deal of effort on Aaron's part to get his end wedged between the hitch and receiver. Finished, he hopped down to the lawn and took hold of the driveshaft.

The combined weight of four bodies hanging from the driveshaft finally broke the mangled receiver free from the hitch. A keening of metal was followed by a loud bang and the pickup's right front wheel slammed down hard onto the lawn. Freed from the hitch, the trailer went in the opposite direction, its left-side wheels coming down hard on the sidewalk.

For a brief moment, both the trailer and Chevy shimmied on their suspension.

"Mission accomplished," crowed Tracy. She high-fived Potvin and her brother and turned to Rusty, who waved her away. "What's wrong?"

"Aggravated an old injury."

Duncan said, "You can lick your wounds later." He waved Raven over, then plucked his radio from a pocket and instructed Daymon to meet back at the Craftsman.

Potvin said, "Should I pull my truck around?"

Nodding, Duncan said, "Bring her around and park next to mine." Gesturing for Raven to follow, he struck off down the block.

Lagging behind, Raven stopped in the middle of the street and looked to the east. A pair of Zs were trudging her way. They were uphill from the intersection and about to enter the patch of shadow where the riders would have been. Letting the SBR hang from its sling, she took out her iPhone, held it steady as possible, then filmed the zombies. Once the pair had transited the shadow and broke into the sunlit stretch of road, she halted the video. Dropping the iPhone into a pocket, she hurried to catch up with the others.

Chapter 19

The green light to return to New District came mid-afternoon. The "Brady Bunch plus one" as Duncan had taken to calling the disparate group of survivors holed up in the Craftsman had found various ways to pass the time prior to receiving the news from Daymon's so-called *source.*

Raven had remained on the move the entire time. When she wasn't pacing the living room and trying to convince Duncan and Daymon and anyone who would listen that the riders were real and might be outside and watching them, she was upstairs, moving from window to window and glassing the street and distant intersections through her rifle's optics.

Connor, on the other hand, was the direct opposite of Raven. He had remained on the couch, out of it for most of the three hours, stirring only once early on, when the pain had apparently become unbearable. He had screamed himself awake and then moaned and grunted and thrashed about until another healthy dose of grunt candy finally got him calmed down.

Fifteen minutes after coming to, Connor's eyes fluttered and closed, and his breathing fell back into a steady rhythm.

After about the ninety-minute mark, when it was pretty clear to Daymon that the kid on the couch wasn't going to turn zombie on them, he had sheathed Kindness and stopped pacing. Dragging a plastic-covered chair away from the plastic-covered couch, he had taken a seat, stretched his legs out, and pulled the beanie down over his eyes.

Chris and Aaron roamed the home, looking for anything useful to shove into their backpacks.

Potvin had spent most of the wait with her face buried in a first edition copy of George Orwell's *1984*. It was one of many treasures she unearthed during a deep-dive search through a mountain of boxes stashed in one of the upstairs rooms.

After going through papers she found atop an old rolltop desk in another room, she had learned that the home's former occupants had once run a thriving independent bookstore in northern Colorado Springs. An entry in a journal indicated that *Next Chapter Books*, the Carlisles' retirement venture, had been shuttered thanks to the advent of digital media. Which explained the boxes of books, a dozen of which—all first edition classics—were going home with her.

Duncan had spent most of the time in the kitchen, working a *New York Times* crossword puzzle. Occasionally he would poke his head into the living room and bother Rusty, or anyone else within earshot, to help him with a word.

Tracy had stood sentinel by the picture window and watched the world turn through an inch-wide part in the curtains. She had kept a running count on the amount of undead gathering outside the Craftsman. When the call finally came, sixteen zombies were congregated around the pickups parked out front, three were roaming the lawn, and another four had found their way up the brick walk and onto the porch, where they were reacting to every sound coming from within the Carlisles' home.

Now, the female voice emanating from the radio stuffed into Daymon's cargo pocket had the combined weight of the dead on the porch pressing in on the door.

As Daymon started awake and snatched the noisy radio from his pocket, Tracy rushed for the door. Checking the lock on the knob and deadbolt above it for seemingly the hundredth time, she whispered, "Think it's going to hold?"

"I don't know," Duncan called from the kitchen. "But I'm pretty sure it's *locked*." He chuckled and pushed up off the counter he'd been leaning on. Rubbing a kink from his neck, he asked, "What's a three-letter word for vermin?"

Returning from upstairs, Raven said, "Rat."

Shaking his head, Duncan filled the word in. "Why do I even bother?" He folded the puzzle and stuffed it and the pen in a pocket. Following Raven into the living room, he said, "Who's doing the honors? Did you fellas draw straws like Chris proposed?"

"Didn't need to," replied Chris. "Aaron stepped up and volunteered."

Duncan flashed Aaron a thumbs-up. "Good man." Gaze dropping to the Ka-Bar, he said, "You a Marine?"

"I should be. But I'm not." He hung his head.

Tracy said, "What happened?"

Aaron's cheeks flushed red. "I was really overweight coming out of high school. About forty pounds or so. So I entered the Delayed Entry Program. I was supposed to get fit as possible, then report to my recruiter and go through boot camp. That was *supposed* to happen the end of 2011."

Raven said, "Then the crap hit the fan."

Aaron nodded. "That it did."

Duncan looked Aaron up and down. "You sure as hell lost the weight."

Daymon said, "The zombie apocalypse has a way of doing that to a person."

Duncan said, "Well, seeing as how you're not yet a certified crayon eater, I think you're probably going to want to have something a little more lethal than that pig-sticker of yours. You know how to shoot?"

Aaron nodded. "Been hunting all my life. Mostly duck and the occasional pheasant."

"Good," said Duncan. "Means you know your way around a shotgun. I want you to take my boomstick."

"Won't the report bring around more walkers than the ones out front?"

Daymon said, "It will. But if all goes as planned, we'll be long gone by then."

Nodding, Duncan said, "Just like we discussed earlier. You'll go out the back door, fire a round or two into the air, and then wait for the biters to take the bait. When you see the whites of their eyes, shoot a few of the ones out in front. Then, once you have the whole gang's undivided attention, you hightail it around back and meet up with us at the trucks."

Daymon handed over his Motorola. "Keep it on this channel. I already rolled the volume all the way up. Just put it in a pocket and listen for updates."

Hefting the Saiga, its deadly end aimed at the floor, Duncan pointed to the box magazine. "You have one in the pipe and twenty in the magazine. I loaded them flechette, slug, flechette … and so on. Here's the charging handle. And this is the safety. It's semiautomatic. All you have to do is throw the safety and pull the trigger. Right now, the safety is *on*. Understood?"

Aaron pocketed the radio. Taking the shotgun in hand, he said, "Understood. How's the recoil?"

Duncan said, "Not as bad as getting bit by a Z. Therefore, I recommend you don't worry about the recoil. Ride the lightning if you have to." He lifted his Motorola to his lips and made a test call. Hearing his voice coming out loud and clear from the radio in Aaron's pocket, he said a few words of encouragement and sent the kid on his way.

Hearing the back door open and close, Duncan joined Tracy at the picture window.

Two loud booms broke the still.

Potvin said, "And it's on."

Addressing Tracy, Duncan said, "What's happening out there?"

She parted the curtains and stole a quick peek. "The ones on the street are on the move."

"How many? And are they going left or right of the house?"

"About fifteen. They're all angling for the right side of the house." She pointed. "That would be our left."

"How about the ones on the porch?"

Potvin was at the front door with one eye pressed to the peephole. She said, "Still the original four. All but one are turning and going for the stairs."

Thumbing the Talk button, Duncan relayed the information.

As instructed, Aaron made no reply.

Raven moved into the foyer and examined the door. Inset in the door waist-high to her was a brass mail slot. Seeing it gave her an idea. Having Potvin step aside, she drew the Infidel and knelt in front of the slot.

Potvin said, "What in the hell are you doing?"

Raven said nothing. She stuck the knife through the slot, lifted the flap until it went horizontal to the door, then let it slam back down. She repeated the move three more times.

Still peering through the drapes, Tracy said, "It's interested."

Three more shotgun blasts rang out.

"Now it's wavering," noted Tracy.

Out of the blue, Daymon sang, "Should I Stay or Should I Go?" That it was the chorus from a Clash song was lost on everyone but Potvin, who shot him a sly grin as she shook her head.

Holding the flap open with the Infidel, Raven said, "Hey, Prune Face. I'm down here. Want some?" She stuck her free hand through the slot, three knuckles deep, and waggled her fingers.

Tracy said, "That did it. She just dropped to her knees."

Heeding the warning, Raven yanked her fingers from the rectangular slot. Instantly the female zombie's wrinkled face appeared in their place. One moment she was staring it in the face—those beady, roving eyes consuming her—the next the face had changed orientation and the thing was mashing its lips and teeth against the opening.

The stench of decaying human flesh was jump-starting Raven's gag reflex. The clacking of the Z's teeth had the hair on her neck standing at attention.

Realizing that it would be impossible to simultaneously hold the flap open with the Infidel and drive its tip into the thing's eye, she drew the Glock, jammed the suppressor past the blade, and waited for the right firing angle to present itself.

Outside, the Saiga barked twice more. This time the reports had come from the breezeway between the Craftsman and the home east of it. Clearly, Aaron was on the move.

Tracy said, "The porch and walk are now free of geeks."

Duncan didn't bother relaying the information. No need. Aaron's gunfire had told him all he needed to know: The kid was engaging the dead and had succeeded in drawing them around back of the house. Looking to Raven, he said, "Do it now. We need to get a move on."

Raven pursed her lips and whistled. Reacting to the sound, the zombie drew back an inch or so and stared directly into the slot.

She pressed the trigger once. There was a hollow-sounding report, and a nickel-sized hole appeared between the zombie's dead-eyed stare.

Voice rising an octave, Tracy said, "Good shooting, girl." She let go of the curtain. Her pack was already on her back. In her hand was a huge knife she'd taken from a wood block in the Carlisles' kitchen.

Potvin said, "I got the door."

Drawing his .45, Duncan started issuing orders. Regarding Raven, he said, "You take point. Get to the rig and get her started. Be careful. There may still be a Z or two trapped under the front end." He passed her the keys. Meeting Potvin's gaze, he instructed her to watch their left flank. He figured since the Zs were likely going to emerge on the opposite side of the house, that would leave less of a chance for another fly to find itself into the ointment. Plus, Potvin had pulled her Chevy in front of his rig.

Lastly, as previously agreed upon, Chris and Rusty were to haul Connor to Potvin's ride and put him in the load bed.

Acting on a prompt from Duncan, Chris and Rusty each wrapped an arm around Connor's waist. Chris took hold of Connor's good arm and looped it over his neck. Avoiding the bloody stump, Rusty locked his arm around Connor's thigh.

Lifting Connor's hundred and sixty pounds of dead weight off the couch was awkward. Once Chris and Rusty had firmed up their grips and were making their way to the front door, they managed to inject some synchronicity into their movements.

Raven was out the door first. Though her tailbone was still smarting, she stepped over the face-shot Z and bounded down the stairs. Head on a swivel, the SBR keeping pace with her gaze, she sprinted the length of the brick walk, reaching the truck at about the same time Aaron was emerging from between houses. Two quick back-to-back booming reports had drawn her attention to him. He was in a half-crouch and backpedaling along a run of low-fence bordering some long-dead plants that had once been important enough to protect from being trampled. A few yards to Aaron's fore, a tight knot of rotters were doing just that. The fence snapped and folded over under their weight. Puffs of bone-dry dirt erupted underfoot as the sacred ground was tread upon.

The pair of shotgun blasts wrought destruction, in distinctly different ways, on two of the Zs. The first shell contained twenty steel flechettes. As the aerodynamic dart-like projectiles transited the ten feet from the Saiga's muzzle to the zombie's lolling head, they spread out from one another.

The mechanics of it was lost on Raven. It all happened faster than her brain could process. All she saw was gunsmoke and a lick of flame leap from the Saiga's muzzle. If the scene were slowed down, she would have witnessed a swarm of steel the size of a dinner plate erase the Z's face. Dermis, muscle, and underlying tissue would melt away and blossom into a wet, pink mist.

Instead, she saw the head snap back. Watched the limp corpse lift off the lawn and slam into the monster that had been following close on its heels.

Shell number two, definitely a slug, punched a fist-sized hole through another zombie's throat. Unlike the first Z, this rotter was instantly rendered a paraplegic. All at once its limbs stopped working and it crashed vertically into the knee-high grass.

As Raven reached the driver's door, she caught sight of something moving underneath the Sierra. She went to a knee and peered into the gloom. She found herself face to face with what was left of an undead kid. She was ten or so and was impaled on a shroud hanging down from the undercarriage. It was clear she had been dragged the better part of the block. All that remained of one arm was a nub of bloody bone. The other arm was nearly skinned to the bone and making lazy swipes in Raven's direction.

Though the tiny Z wasn't really a threat to her, or anyone for that matter, it was the saddest thing Raven had seen in a long time. There was no ignoring it, either. So before opening the door and climbing in, she unsheathed the Infidel, held the flailing arm at bay, then buried her blade into the thing's eye.

The arm flopped to the street, unmoving. Grabbing the limp appendage, Raven yanked the road-rashed corpse free and pushed it up against the curb.

Leaping into the pickup, Raven shrugged off her pack and tossed it and her SBR onto the backseat. As she jammed the key into the ignition and fired the engine, her eyes took a tour of the mirrors. *Clear on three sides.* The street and intersection beyond Potvin's Chevy was a different story. A crowd of dead had formed and were steadily advancing.

Leaving the door open for Duncan, she vaulted the seatback and opened the driver-side rear door. Sitting with her legs dangling into space, she shouldered the SBR and implored the others to hurry up.

To Aaron's credit, he was holding the line at the edge of the walkway. As Duncan and Daymon led Chris and Rusty to Potvin's rig, the wannabe Marine pumped rounds head-high into the remaining Zs.

Catching Potvin's eye, Raven said, "Coast is clear. They're loading Connor right now."

Potvin didn't need to be told twice. Pack bouncing against her back, she double-timed it across the lawn and sprinted down the sidewalk, arriving at her truck winded and red in the face.

Crossing paths with Potvin, Duncan and Daymon made tracks for the idling Sierra.

Last one off the lawn was Aaron. He took one final shot at the handful of Zs still hunting him, lowered the shotgun, and set off running toward the awaiting vehicles.

Raven had been keeping track of Aaron's shots. She'd counted sixteen before becoming distracted by Chris and Rusty clumsily loading Connor into Potvin's truck. While she knew he'd discharged the shotgun since, it wasn't clear how many times. If he wasn't already out of ammunition, he was dangerously close. "Winchester" was what her dad and warriors like him called it. She called it unacceptable. Some of her worst nightmares centered around her becoming cornered by a pack of hungry Zs and not having any ammo. To date, she had always snapped awake *before* the gnashing teeth found her flesh.

She watched the Chevy fill up with survivors. Heard the *thunks* of the driver's and passenger-side doors closing.

A flurry of motion, Stetson in one hand and wheezing hard, Duncan slipped behind the wheel and slammed his door shut. He was just getting the truck into gear when Daymon opened the passenger door and clambered aboard.

Last one to reach the sidewalk was Aaron. Raven had assumed he would ride with Potvin. Her door was swinging shut when a hand reached inside and stopped it from latching. Before she could bring her rifle to bear on the perceived threat, the door was hinging open and Aaron was clawing his way past her.

Coming to realize he was being pursued by a lone grade-school-aged rotter, and that it was already crossing the sidewalk, Raven reacquired her purchase on the handle and slammed the door shut.

Duncan was following Potvin's lead and committing his pickup to the first leg of the three-point turn necessary to get the Sierra facing east when a gong-like sound reverberated throughout the cab.

Responding to Daymon's questioning look, Raven said, "Aaron picked up a fast mover. That was its little head meeting the outside of my door."

Still trying to catch his breath, Aaron said, "When I turned to make a run for Wendy's truck, the thing was in my way and coming at me. Don't know where it came from. It was like it appeared out of thin air."

Daymon said, "Wasn't on my radar, either." He looked to Duncan. "I have a feeling you're going to be pulling a dent when we get back."

Duncan said, "It'll buff out." He shifted into Reverse and fed the motor fuel. As the pickup's left front tire rolled over the curb, there came a sickening wet *pop*.

They'd all heard the sound before.

They all winced.

Raven threw a hard shiver. In her mind's eye she saw the little Z's head imploding and a miasma of brain tissue and hair and skull painting the hot pavement. No reason to look out the window. She'd seen enough roadkill to last her ten lifetimes.

Without missing a beat, Daymon said, "That one's *not* going to buff out."

Aaron clicked his seatbelt home. "I'll *never* get used to that sound."

Duncan looked to Daymon. "We need to get Potvin on the horn. Tell her what your source told you. I figure if we go back the way we came, at the worst we'll hit the tail end of the eastbound herd and have to deal with a few stragglers. If Lady Luck really takes a liking to us, we'll make the East Gate with no contact at all."

Dragging the radio from a pocket, Daymon said, "That's a lot of *ifs*." He thumbed the Talk button and relayed to Potvin all the information he was privy to, including that they were expected at the East Gate and had already been cleared for immediate entry.

Potvin came back right away. "I've got the injured kid. You sure they'll let us in without putting him through the wringer?"

Daymon said, "Affirmative. We'll *all* be going through the wringer as soon as we're on the inside."

She made no reply. Which made sense because she was busy slaloming her lifted rig through a group of Zs congregated at the intersection.

When the channel opened back up, Daymon said, "You didn't really think you were going to be allowed to move about freely inside the walls without having to drop our trousers and flash the nurse some skin, did you?"

Duncan jinked the Sierra through the scattering dead. When the keen of fingernails raking metal and dull thuds of Zs caroming off the truck's flanks subsided, he said, "I kind of like all the groping. Having been exiled to the ol' no-nookie island, it's the closest I'm going to get to being physical with anyone."

"Gross," Raven said. "*Waaaay* too much information." She draped her arms over the seatback and looked Duncan in the face. "What would Glenda say if she knew you're talking like a weirdo?"

Duncan let loose a trademark cackle. Once he was finished and wiping tears from his eyes, he said, "She knows I'm a weirdo. And you, Bird, should have known I was joking. Now I'm gonna need you to sit down and buckle up. We've got a few miles to go, and there's no telling what's standing in our way."

Chapter 20

Monument, Colorado

Cade had been staring at Lopez's flag-draped body for so long that when he finally looked out the nearby window, for a couple of seconds, stars and bars overlaid the long stretch of I-25 below the speeding helo.

Vehicles cleared off the freeway by reclamation crews cluttered the outer shoulder and inner breakdown lanes. The westering sun reflecting off dirt-streaked auto glass had a mesmerizing effect on Cade. It wasn't until the helicopter bled speed and adopted a heading that had it cutting across the highway that he noticed the scattered groups of southbound zombies shambling I-25's lone northbound lane.

After having been unusually quiet—stoic, actually—for the duration of the nearly three-hour flight from Bear Lake, over the shipwide comms, Ari said, "Skip … I need the left-side gun brought online." There was a hint of stress in his voice. "We're being diverted to provide close air support for a reclamation crew and their security detail. They were reconnoitering a Home Depot and are now on top of the Stryker and surrounded by approximately three hundred zulus. I repeat … three, zero, zero zulus. Quick reaction force is five mikes out. Peterson says the civilian dismounts won't last three mikes."

Skip powered up the minigun, then hit the switch to start the weapon bay door rolling open. Once it was well on its way, he dropped the Dillon down, took hold of its twin grips, and thrust the menacing six-barreled muzzle through the opening.

To allow Skip room to work, Cade clicked out of his safety belt and changed seats. Though he ended up in the bitch seat, maybe a yard removed from the gunner's station, he was still close enough to the windows to see some of what was coming up outside. Unfortunately, due to the angle, he couldn't see the Stryker, nor could he see much of the ground below the helicopter.

"Ten o'clock," Ari said, "Center of the shared parking lot. A hundred yards south of the Walmart. The Stryker and a couple of civilian vehicles. Stryker is high-centered. We have friendlies atop the Stryker. I have eyes on eleven bodies. Do you confirm, Haynes?"

"Roger that," Haynes replied. "I have eyes on eleven civilians. Bringing the FLIR online. Migrating the feed to both monitors."

As the helicopter entered the airspace above the business park, Cade noted that a chain restaurant and wheel and tire store abutted the freeway to the east. He also caught fleeting glimpses of the Walmart and its car-choked parking lot.

Wanting to get a clearer picture of what was happening on the ground, Cade leaned back in his seat and craned to get a look at the monitor. Across from him, Griff and Cross were twisted around, eyes glued to the monitor. In the seats next to Cade, Axe and Nat were already commenting on what they were seeing.

Axe said, "Those blokes on top of the Stryker are in the thick of it."

Agreeing, Nat said, "Looks like they were attempting to exfil the crew when they got stuck."

Sure enough, zombies were crushing in on the multi-wheeled armored vehicle from all sides. The people on top—from the looks of it a mix of men and women—were huddled around the vehicle's top-mounted CROWS weapon system. No doubt, Cade thought, the .50 caliber Ma Deuce had run out of ammunition.

The survivors unlucky enough to have found themselves on the group's periphery were either kicking frantically at the creatures clawing for them or chopping into their midst with the Stryker's onboard hand tools.

As Cade watched the drama taking place below, a survivor wielding a shovel lost purchase on the vehicle and was quickly dragged into the maelstrom of grabbing hands and gnashing teeth.

A feeding frenzy ensued as Ari maneuvered the helicopter counterclockwise over the parking lot, bringing the left-side gun broadside to the surrounded vehicle.

As soon as Cade felt the craft under him repositioning, he swung his gaze to the left-side window. Initially, he saw a large number of zombies moving toward the parking lot from the east. Then, when the Walmart adjacent to the Home Depot was fully framed in the window, he was witness to the steady stream of Zs filing from within the dilapidated structure's darkened main entrance. If something wasn't done to thin the two mini herds out before they converged, he doubted the quick reaction force would make it onto the parking lot, let alone get close enough to the Stryker to effect any kind of rescue.

Ari leveled the helicopter off a hundred yards south of the Stryker and adopted a steady hover. Cade guessed they were a hundred feet or so off the deck. The top of the orange Home Depot sign sliding by below the right-side windows told him he was probably being a little generous.

A dozen opportunist crows were perched atop the sign. They had remained still, their black, beady eyes tracking the helicopter as it slid into position. In the next beat, the murder was taking flight, and the deafening roar of the minigun belching a couple of hundred rounds was assaulting the cabin. Though the burst lasted a fraction of a second, the destruction to the knot of zombies ripping into the survivor was instantaneous and catastrophic.

Mercifully, the man who had been dragged from the armored vehicle was killed instantly.

The twenty or so zombies pulped by the burst wasn't much of a reduction in the overall number of zombies enveloping the Stryker. And there were many more on the way.

Snatching up his M4, Cade started the left-side door motoring open. Before retaking his original seat by the window, he located an anchored safety tether and secured it to his chest rig with the attached carabiner.

Hot air rife with the stink of death and burned jet fuel rushed into the cabin.

There was a clunk when the door hit the extent of its rearward travel.

As Cade sat forward in his seat, rifle butt snugged tight to his shoulder, in his headset he heard Ari apologize to the Stryker commander for not warning him to expect the danger-close incoming fire. Didn't really matter, thought Cade. Considering the number of zombies wedged underneath the Stryker's right-side wheels, there was no danger of it unexpectedly moving. Therefore, barring a random ricochet, the possibility of it being hit by friendly fire was near to zero.

The Stryker commander, call sign Stagecoach Two-One, replied, "Copy that Jedi One." Then, confirming what Cade was seeing, the commander added, "We're going nowhere. But give me a window to get on the public address to warn the people up top."

Having heard Ari's warning acknowledged by the Stryker commander, Skip waited a long five-count before firing two short, controlled bursts into the zombies on the vehicle's right flank. The back-to-back two-hundred-round swarms of lead leveled the majority of zombies assembled there, leaving the lined blacktop covered in shredded torsos, severed limbs, and pooling blood.

Speaking into the shared shipwide comms, Cade announced his intent to engage the Zs advancing from the east. Looking to Nat and Axe, he ordered them to open the right-side door and prepare to engage the Zs exiting the Walmart.

While Skip worked his way through the Dillon's remaining two thousand rounds, leaving a wide swath of unmoving zombies on the ground all around the inert Stryker, Ari had the Ghost Hawk scribing a slow counterclockwise orbit over the parking lot.

Cade pumped rounds from the M4 into the new arrivals. He was changing out his third magazine when he lost his firing angle. He estimated he'd put down twenty-five Zs with ninety rounds. Not a great shot-to-kill ratio by any measure. Especially considering Ari's steady hand on the stick and the relatively short distance from muzzle to target.

As the rambling hills west of I-25 filled up the cockpit glass, Nat and Axe were presented with clear fields of fire. Competing with the minigun in the decibel department, Nat's belt-fed Squad Automatic Weapon spit hundreds of rounds into the advancing throng. It was akin to taking a sledgehammer to the Zs—popping skulls and knocking down bodies in a wide-ranging arc.

While the big guns pulverized the dead, Axe wielded his Remington MSR with methodical precision, gaining an impressive two-to-one kill ratio on the zombies still posing a threat to the survivors.

All at once, the guns went silent.

It was eerily quiet in the cabin, the only sound being the steady muffled *thwop* of the baffled rotors and throaty whine of the turbines.

As the Ghost Hawk broke orbit and side-slipped to the west, Cade continued to watch what was happening on the ground. As the responding Strykers carrying the quick reaction force wove a path through the drifts of twice-dead zombie corpses, Stagecoach One-Two's rear hatch opened, and several camo-clad soldiers scrambled down the ramp. The five troops spread out like the fingers on a hand. *Textbook dismount,* thought Cade. While three of the soldiers engaged the dead with pistols, the other two helped the survivors down from the stricken vehicle. Then, like a well-oiled machine, one of the arriving Strykers rolled up close to Stagecoach Two-One, its rear ramp already coming down and soldiers spilling forth.

In a matter of seconds, the survivors had been transferred to the pair of Strykers, a soldier from the first to roll up had connected a tow cable to Stagecoach Two-One, and the dismounts were beginning to break contact with the advancing dead.

The troops from Stagecoach Two-One clambered back aboard their listing Stryker. The remaining dismounts from the QRF offered covering fire until Two-One's ramp was in the up position, then, firing and moving, they leapfrogged their way back to their Stryker, where they crowded inside with the handful of survivors who wouldn't fit into the tow vehicle.

The lead Stryker slow-rolled forward, stopping only when the cable was stretched tight between the two vehicles. A tick later, diesel exhaust was belching from the Stryker. Stagecoach Two-One didn't budge. As the driver in the tow vehicle coaxed more from the engine, Two-One moved forward a couple of yards, teetered back and forth, then nosed down, its front wheels finally coming back into contact with the gore-slickened asphalt.

If someone would have asked Cade how many Zs would be revealed when the Stryker was pulled free, fifteen, maybe twenty would have been his best guess. And he would have been dead wrong. There looked to be thirty or more. The grotesquely twisted corpses were three or four deep and compressed into a rectangle the size of the Stryker's undercarriage. Arms and legs and hands jutted from the organic mass. A slurry of bodily fluids seeped from all sides. It was as if a small herd had been fed into a car crusher, the finished product deposited on the Home Depot lot.

Skip actuated the cabin doors. In seconds, Cade was spared having to look down upon the scene of utter carnage.

As the Strykers rolled single file down the ramp feeding I-25 southbound, Cade heard in his headset the back and forth between Ari and Stagecoach Two-One's commander. Promises to provide cases of beer to all aboard Jedi One were made. As were many sincere *thank yous* and an offer to put everyone involved in the impromptu rescue mission up for commendations and medals.

As Cade had expected, Ari accepted the beer, even going so far as to request an additional case or two be delivered to the SOAR maintainers at Peterson. Then Ari acknowledged the thanks on behalf of the entire aircrew and customers in transit. Before signing out, he implored the commander to *not* proceed with any kind of formal acknowledgment to higher-ups. Last thing he wanted was to draw any more scrutiny to the Pale Riders than their legendary exploits had already brought on.

The transmission ended, and the helo banked left. Outside Jedi One's mirrored windows, the darkened signs of once high and mighty retail giants scrolled by. The strip malls and dense neighborhoods of Monument quickly gave way to blue sky and distant mountains as Ari pulled pitch and pegged the throttles.

Nat wrapped his gloved hand around his boom mike. Wearing a shit-eating grin and staring at Griff and Cross, he said, "The SEAL twins don't deserve any beer. I don't remember their *pea shooters* making any noise."

Skip was turned around in his seat, the doors and weapon bay door sealed tight. When he retracted his helmet's smoked visor, it was clear he was smiling. Didn't need to see behind the skeleton facemask for confirmation. His eyes said it all.

Being the charitable type, Axe said, "I'll share my allotment with the chaps."

In unison, Cross and Griff flipped the big islander the bird.

Griff said, "If I'd have been on the warehouse floor today with my *pea shooter*, Low Rider might still be with us."

Nodding, Cross said, "You may find yourself in need of some professional overwatch going forward. Maybe you should rethink your position, big fella."

Smile fading, Nat said, "Learn to take a joke, dicks." Offering fist bumps all around, he added, "If you ask me, it's those survivors who need the beer."

"Or a fifth or two of Jameson whiskey," Griff added.

Cade did his best to tune out the banter. With Lopez's corpse literally underfoot, he couldn't bring himself to even feign a smile. Instead, he focused all of his attention on the ground a couple of hundred feet below the helicopter. Some of the landmarks he was seeing told him they were overflying the North Gate neighborhood. When Ari banked the helo a few degrees to the right, Cade knew they were on final approach to Peterson. Then, when the green space northeast of the North Gate came into view, he saw two pickups far off in the distance. One was white, the other purple.

With the Pale Riders looking on, he dug into his pack, fished out the Thuraya sat-phone, and deployed its antenna. Thumbing the Power button, he punched 1 and selected Autodial. There was a hiss of static as the phone contacted a DoD satellite, performed the necessary handshake, and completed the connection. The sat-phone on the other end didn't ring. The call went straight to voicemail. He listened to his daughter's greeting. At the tone, he ended the call in lieu of leaving a message.

No need. Either she was with Duncan in his purple pickup and had missed hearing her phone ring, or she was safe at home with her Thuraya powered off.

Gaze dropping to Lopez's flag-shrouded body, Cade made a decision he'd been putting off since he was forced to end his friend's mortal journey. Speaking into the shared shipwide comms, he voiced his intentions.

There was no pushback. Nobody questioned his decision. In fact, to a man, everyone aboard Jedi One was in complete agreement with the plan.

Chapter 21

As soon as Jedi One was on approach to Peterson and had received clearance to land on the tarmac in front of the commercial aviation hangars recently taken over by the 160th SOAR, Ari switched off the helo's IFF (Identification Friend or Foe) transponder. Simultaneously Haynes did the same to Jedi One's communications suite.

Flying over the Yellow Zone northeast of New District, Ari nudged the stick forward until the helo was gliding just above the tree-lined streets, then leveled off and made a drastic course correction.

The new heading had Jedi One rocketing due south from Peterson at ninety knots and roughly thirty feet off the deck. Seconds after beginning the wholly unauthorized covert mission, Jedi One was not only off radio to anyone trying to hail her, but she was also invisible to Peterson, Schriever, and the nearby Cheyenne Mountain NORAD complex.

Thirty seconds after going dark, the helo was two miles south of Peterson, and Ari was wrenching the stick hard left.

The Gs produced by the near right-angle bank pressed Cade hard into his seat. He saw the high plain change drastically in relation to the horizon. One second, houses and businesses populating a neighborhood southeast of what used to be Colorado Springs were blipping by outside the window; the next, he was seeing the green blur of treetops and the multitudes of black-feathered birds taking flight.

The helo's transition from the high-speed banking turn to level flight started Cade's stomach to churn. He remembered he hadn't eaten for several hours. Nor had he sipped water from his hydration bladder, let alone voided his own bladder since leaving Boise. So many routine things had gone by the wayside as a direct result of the death of his good friend, Javier "Low Rider" Lopez.

Cade looked around the cabin. He wasn't surprised to see that the remaining members of his team had all adopted granite-jawed dispositions. He supposed, could he see his own countenance, it would be a mirror image of those around him.

When the sun had clawed its way over the high plains hours ago, the air crisp and their moods jovial, not a single person aboard Jedi One could have fathomed not being alive to witness it setting behind the distant Rocky Mountains.

Now, to a man, they were all pondering their own mortality. And given the task at hand, it was to be expected.

In six minutes, the Ghost Hawk had devoured the eighteen miles separating New District from the remote corner of Schriever Air Force Base soon to become Lopez's final resting place.

As the helicopter overflew the point where two long runs of razor-wire-topped fencing merged, Ari pulled pitch and made the customary *thirty seconds out* call. After carving a slow counterclockwise arc in the sky above a perfectly graded patch of ochre hardpan, Ari flared hard and brought the helo to a hover.

There was a whine and clunk underfoot as the twin doors opened and the landing gear locked into place.

A dust plume kicked up by the rotor blades rose up off the ground. Once it reached the helo's altitude, it began to roil over on itself around the edges like waves crashing a beach.

Jedi One's descent was slow and methodical. It was as if Ari was reluctant to be wheels down. For by doing so, Lopez's final mission would have concluded.

Not a word was spoken in the cabin as the wheels kissed hallowed ground. The flight crew and customers in back remained tight-lipped, their movements robot-like as they went through the motions of unbuckling safety belts and shuffling gear around in order to make removing Lopez as respectful an operation as possible.

By the time Ari and Haynes had the turbines shut down and the rotors were static overhead, the dust was mostly settled.

Skip removed his helmet. There was a hard set to his jaw as he started the cabin doors rolling open.

A fenced-in dirt parking lot was revealed on Cade's side. It bordered the landing pad to the north. A couple of pickups already parked there were disgorging men clad in camo and carrying rifles.

Over the lot's northern entrance was the type of sign ubiquitous to ranches in the West and Midwest. Painted in white on the slab of wood arcing between sturdy twelve-foot posts were the words *Arlington West.*

Looking beyond the lot, Cade saw more vehicles approaching. They were mostly pickups and arriving from different directions. All of them were trailing low-to-the-ground clouds of ochre dust. Cade wasn't surprised. Most of the fallen requested to be put into the ground by their brothers in arms. People they fought and bled with. Save for Special Operations Commander Smokey Blake, the brass was expected to show their respect and make remembrances from afar.

The vehicles converged and rolled into the lot in an orderly fashion. Men and women exited. Some were carrying weapons. Others came armed with shovels.

Cade shrugged on his pack and secured his M4 to his chest. Without a word, he grabbed hold of one end of the body bag. Enlisting help from Cross, the longest living among the core group of operators he'd been running and gunning with since the CCP unleashed hell on the United States, he started Lopez on his final helo egress.

With Griff, Nat, and Axe in tow, Cade and Cross carried Lopez through the cemetery's lone swinging gate. The solemn procession wound through rows upon rows of graves. Most bore an assortment of hewn marble markers. Most were engraved with Catholic crosses. Stars of David were represented, but they were few and far between. The newer graves, those still awaiting headstones, were marked with simple wooden planks on which names and ranks and dates were printed.

When they reached their final destination, a far corner of the cemetery where Mike Desantos and the first of the tier-one operators to fall in the war against Omega were interred, they let Lopez down gently.

A train of shooters and support people filed through the gate and had fallen in behind. Shovels and pickaxes were handed to Cade and the rest of his Pale Rider team.

In just north of half an hour, the five men had an appropriate grave dug.

Cade and Cross each took an end of the body bag.

Griff and Nat stood by with the flag, ready to drape the black bag once it was settled in the bottom of the yard-deep rectangle.

Flag in place, Cade said, "Until Valhalla, brother," and flashed a crisp salute.

Cross took Cade's place at the head of the grave, said some kind words, then recounted a couple of war stories in which Low Rider featured prominently.

The newer Pale Riders filed by next, each paying their respects in different ways.

Someone had brought a bugle. As the rest of the fifty-strong crowd filed past the grave, the bugler performed a damn fine rendition of *Taps*.

As the mournful notes wafted over the graves of the fallen, Cade, Cross, Griff, Axe, and Nat were joined at the head of the grave by two of Lopez's closest friends. The seven of them lined up shoulder to shoulder, raised an assortment of rifles toward the heavens, placed their fingers on their triggers, and drew back a few pounds of pressure.

When the bugle went silent, the last note drifting into the ether, the seven rifles barked in unison. Finishing off the final salute to their fallen brother, the seven men fired two more closely-spaced volleys.

Heads remained bowed in the assembled crowd as rifles were traded for shovels.

With Cade and the rest of the Pale Riders working together, they shoveled the dirt back into the grave. It took them all of five minutes. When they were finished tamping down the dirt and had placed the temporary marker at the head of the grave, the mourners broke ranks.

As quickly as they had arrived, the soldiers, airmen, and Marines filed out of the cemetery, piled into their vehicles, and drove off to the north—the hasty retreat obscured by a low-hanging wall of dust.

Alcohol was about to be consumed in copious amounts inside FU-BAR—Peterson's only official watering hole. A stool would remain empty at the bar. And as per the warrior code, Herradura tequila, hands down Lopez's favorite, would be poured out in his honor. True stories and a tall tale or two—all featuring the deceased operator—would be recounted. Many tears would be shed. Then jokes would be told, and laughter would rise to the ceiling. Finally, just as the shovelfuls of dirt had obscured the flag atop Lopez's body, the moonless night would envelop the mourners as they staggered back to their billets.

Cade wouldn't be joining his team. He and Alcohol had never gotten along. Besides, he had just lost a man. An old friend. Which meant he had a report to write and intel to deliver to people way above his paygrade.

No doubt he would shed a tear or three. But he'd do it privately and on his own timeline.

As Ari turned away from the grave, he squared up to Cade. "Your boys are itching to get back and get shitty. Wheels up in thirty?"

Cracking his neck, Cade said, "You're going to be two bodies light. I'm walking back to the gate. Need some time to clear my mind. Think about how I'm going to write up this report."

"Tell the truth." Ari paused for a beat. "It's nobody's fault. Well, maybe Murphy's fault. Low Rider knew the risks."

Cade said nothing.

Ari said, "I'll take the heat for us going dark and blowing off the RTB call."

Cade shook his head. "It was my call to bring him here. Any balls are getting busted, they'll be the ones between my legs."

Ari looked to the west. The sun was just slipping below Pike's Peak. Cheyenne Mountain was but a craggy silhouette. Garden of the Gods to the north was afire with the fading rays of day and shining like a gilded throne. Exhaling sharply, Ari said, "It's going to be full dark in ninety minutes or so. You're still going to need to snag a ride from the gate back to Peterson. You sure I can't give you a lift?"

"I'm a big boy. You go on." Cade swapped mags and chambered a round into the M4. Regarding Ari, he said, "Pour a shot for Lopez. Make it Herradura. Order a round for the house … on me. Then get something for you and your crew. Tell the bartender to run a tab. I'll settle up with her later."

"Will do." Ari took a few steps toward the gate, then turned around. "Wyatt."

"What is it?'

"Don't beat yourself up."

Cade made no response. For if he had, it probably would have been a lie. He had a three-mile walk ahead of him. Plenty of time to get right with God.

He waited and watched Jedi One go wheels up and bang away to the west. Once it was a black speck on the horizon, he performed the sign of the cross over his chest, then said a final prayer for his fallen teammate.

***

Cade covered the distance from Arlington West to the main cluster of buildings on the northwest side of the vast base in a little less than an hour. What had started out as a lonely trudge soon became a forced march. Only Cade wasn't being prodded forward by a sense of urgency. Or a Q Course instructor yelling *Faster! Pick up the pace! Don't let up. The enemy will give you zero quarter!*

Though he wouldn't admit it, not even to himself, he was running from the ghosts of dead friends. And the only way he figured he was going to avenge Lopez and the others who had fallen victim to Omega was by learning the true nature of Operation Blanket. Interdicting the enemy before they had a chance to implement whatever it was *had* to be a top priority. And to make it happen, he was either going to have to break a lot of rules and regulations, or his overtures to people in high places were going to need to be as persuasive as hell.

Schriever hadn't changed much since Cade and the family had called it home. Then it had been a sanctuary from the undead. Now, it was a reminder of all he had lost.

Cade's first stop was General Freda Nash's new office. It was in a modern glass and steel building attached to the old 50th Space Wing Headquarters. The airman watching the door, a young Hispanic woman with *Alvarez* on her nametape and sergeant's stripes on her uniform blouse, buzzed him in and asked for credentials.

"I'm just coming back from an op." He raised his arms in mock surrender. "They're back at my place in the ND."

The sergeant smiled warmly. "I know who you are. How can I help you?"

"I need to talk to General Nash." He made a face. "I don't have an appointment."

"Considering your rep," said Alvarez, "I highly doubt she'd send you packing for making a cold call." With a tilt to the head, she went on, "Unfortunately, the general is away until tomorrow. To be honest, she's not here as often as she used to be. Spends most of her time bouncing between Peterson and Cheyenne."

"It was worth a shot," said Cade. Now that the 50th had been incorporated with the 21st at Peterson, it was understandable that she wasn't here. To cover all of his bases, though, he asked the airman for pen and paper. Scribbling a quick note, he sealed it in an envelope and wrote his name on the outside.

"Can you see that this hits Freda's inbox?"

Sergeant Alvarez grinned as she took the envelope.

"What's so funny?"

"I haven't heard anyone call the general by her full name since she got that first star."

Cade looked over his shoulder. *Clear.* Whispering, he said, "Just don't call her Freda Crash." He spilled on Nash's complete destruction of a Humvee. "That was a long time ago and in a different land. What happens in the 'Stan, stays in the 'Stan. You mention it, at the very least, she'll punch you in the arm."

"My lips are sealed," said Alvarez. "And this envelope will remain sealed, too. I'll put it on her desk."

Nodding, Cade said, "Much appreciated." Pausing by the door, he asked if she could call someone to give him a lift to the flight line.

With a nod, she snatched up a radio and ordered a Cushman and driver.

Chapter 22

The two-passenger Cushman was driven by a man in his thirties wearing a Tommy Bahama shirt festooned with palms and surfboards, well-worn khaki cargo shorts, and what looked like spiked golf shoes. If he was active duty military, his blond hair was far from regulation. Unruly curls spilled out from under the black ball cap pulled down low on his head. Thanks to the pair of black Oakley sunglasses wrapping the man's deeply tanned face, Cade couldn't see his eyes. For a split second, Cade thought he was back in the Sandbox. When not away on a mission or getting ready for one, every day was casual Friday for the silent professionals putting it all on the line for God and Country. The skull and crossbones patch on the man's hat further bolstered the theory.

The man stopped the Cushman, set the brake, and stepped out on the side opposite Cade. Spikes clicking on the pavement, he looped around front of the golf cart and extended a hand. He was an inch or two taller than Cade, broad in the shoulders, and possessed one hell of a firm grip.

"Greg Harley," said the man. "Heard a lot about you, Captain Grayson."

"Hopefully more good than bad." He looked the man up and down. "You CIA, Greg?"

"That obvious?"

Cade said nothing. Under normal circumstances, he might have cracked a rare smile and made a joke of the spook's attire. Nothing about what had become a very long and grueling day was anything close to normal.

Reaching for Cade's slung pack, Harley said, "Where to, Captain?"

"Call me Cade. A lift to the flight line, please." He secured his rifle and unslung his pack. "I'll go ahead and hold onto my kit. Thanks, though."

Flashing a thumbs-up, Harley retook his seat behind the wheel. While Cade clambered aboard, the spook filled his lower lip with a big plug of chewing tobacco.

Cade put the pack on his lap, trapped his rifle muzzle down between his legs, and took ahold of the grab bar near his head.

Harley's driving skills were exemplary. Though the cart was far from a racecar, the spook had the tiny rubber tires squealing louder than his shirt's neon-green and burnt-orange print. He kept up a running dialogue and worked the wheel and brake as he snaked the cart between buildings.

"That takedown of the PLA in Portland is legend around here."

Cade said, "It was a joint op. We had a lot of help from outside agencies."

"Dude," said Harley, "don't be so humble. Revel in the fact we have Baby Bird under wraps."

"Moot point," said Cade. "It's been weeks, and that waste of skin is still not talking. Last I heard is that he's far from breaking."

Stopping the Cushman in front of the main hangar, Harley removed his Oakleys. "That's because the *proper* pressure has yet to be applied." As he wiped the mirrored lenses, he said, "Too many shrinking violets in the mix. But that's just one man's opinion."

Cade stepped onto the tarmac. Though it was late afternoon, the cement still radiated heat. Locking eyes with Harley, he said, "Agreed on all points."

"Need me to wait?"

"Negative," said Cade. "Can't go where I need to go in one of these."

"Heading outside the wire, eh? You need a ride to the District?"

Cade shook his head. "I need to get to Peterson."

"No problem," replied Harley. "How long you planning on being in there?"

"A few minutes. Ten at most."

Harley donned his glasses. "Knowing how Whipper likes to hear himself talk, figure you'll be hitting the ten-minute mark well before he cuts to the chase. I'll be back. If I'm not here when you're finished in there … wait inside. I'll honk when I pull up."

Judging by the way the guy drove the Cushman, Cade envisioned the spook rolling up in an exotic sports car. Maybe a Ferrari or Bugatti. Those kinds of rides were out there for the taking if one knew where to look. Saving judgment for when he actually had eyes on Harley's ride, he said, "Appreciate it. I'll try to make this quick."

Harley was back aboard the Cushman and whipping a high-speed U-turn before Cade had a chance to don his pack. By the time Cade had made it to the dented yellow door labeled *Maintenance Department - Command Chief Master Sergeant Whipper,* the clatter of the tiny engine was drowned out by the sounds of maintainers hard at work inside the massive hangar.

Opening the door, Cade said, "Chief Whipper? Anybody home?"

The surly reply was exactly what he'd been expecting; a rare occurrence in a day chock full of the unexpected.

***

Five minutes after touching base with the newly promoted Whipper, Cade was on the tarmac, waiting for Harley, his ruck considerably lighter than it had been when he entered the cramped office. The box of Cuban cigars and bottle of single-malt was received pretty damn well. So well that the slate was clean for all the work Whipper had done on Black Beauty.

Cade heard Harley's ride before he set eyes on it. The engine rumble and accompanying exhaust note suggested the thing was packing at least a V8 under the hood.

Instead of emerging from between the nearby buildings via the cart path, the noisy rig appeared at the north end of the hangar. Instead of coming in hot, like Harley had with the cart, he rounded the corner at a slow-roll and with all of the vehicle's lights ablaze. It was the kind of entrance one might expect to see in front of a Zagatrated Hollywood eatery with a sidewalk full of TMZ paparazzi and a starry-eyed pack of celebrity watchers crowding the velvet rope.

The thing was painted a foreign camo scheme and sat higher than Black Beauty. Bracketed by a massive wraparound grille guard was a Mercedes Benz logo. It was the size of a dinner plate and backlit with the same blue light as the HID lamps housed in the quad headlights.

As the Benz pickup got closer, Cade saw that it was a 6x6, with a single axle up front and two dually axles out back. The rear fenders had been flared to accommodate the jumbo off-road tires—likely the same run-flat rubber his F-650 rolled on. The wheels were Beadlock items and appeared to be the type—similar to a Humvee—that could inflate and deflate on the fly. And like the F-650, the Benz had bulletproof glass all the way around. It was also skirted with similar diamond plate steel.

Clearly this was another of Whipper's creations. The man was an artist who could have had a car building show on cable television had the CCP not released Omega.

Cade approached the passenger side and climbed aboard. Expecting another experience like the one he'd had aboard the Cushman, he belted in and located all available grab handles. As for Harley, he saw that the man had swapped the spikes for a worn pair of Army-issue jungle boots. The spook had also gunned up. A Beretta pistol rode in a leather shoulder holster. On the seat next to him was a suppressed and fully kitted-out AR-style carbine.

Wearing a wide grin, the spook said, "I'll have you there in five mikes. Promise."

"I'm in no rush," Cade said. "But knock yourself out." In a way, he kind of wanted to see what the rig was capable of. On the other hand, if they came upon a herd, what with their propensity to follow roads, it could end in disaster.

Harley had made it this long in the zombie apocalypse; no reason to think today was going to be the day. No sooner had Cade thought it than Lopez was on his mind. He had been jovial and joking with the team the entire day—all the way up until he had the epiphany that he was dying. Even then, the man had retained the stiff upper lip. Not once did he bitch about the stinking demonios or complain about the heat or gripe about Ari's flying. Though he had led the Pale Riders on many missions, on this one, he had accepted his role as a team member, not the team leader. If the saying *Easy Does It* needed a face, Lopez was the man.

Harley observed all posted speed limits while on the base and its feeder road. At the northwest corner of the base, he slalomed the German-made behemoth through the maze of staggered Jersey barriers. Reaching the gate, he ran his window down and spoke with the guard.

After the guard waved them through without requiring credentials, Cade cast a sidelong glance at Harley. "Looks like you're big man on campus."

"I don't have any creds to show. Just how I roll."

"Guard didn't want to see mine?"

"There you go, Humble Pie." Harley turned left at the T with the state road. Once he had them hurtling along at twenty above the speed limit, a feat achieved in a handful of seconds, he said, "Everyone knows who you are. They talk about the Pale Riders in hushed tones. Hell, your daughter is a celebrity in her own right. That thing with the president. How she cracked the case like a little Nancy Drew." He shook his head. "Damn … that apple didn't fall far from the Grayson tree."

As the long row of mass graves blipped by on the left, Cade said, "She gets it all from her mom."

Harley said, "Real sorry for your loss."

What don't you know about me, thought Cade. He said, "She's in a better place."

Steering around what looked like a coyote lying dead on the centerline, Harley said, "They released those first batches way too soon. Better odds playing Russian Roulette with a semiauto than trusting the antiserum." He went quiet and gazed at the golf course abutting the road. It was totally overgrown. A number of zombies mired in a muddy water feature turned their heads and watched the vehicle as it passed them by.

Breaking the awkward silence, Cade said, "Are the scientists seeing any progress with subsequent batches?"

"The pointy heads have made some headway in stability and storage," Harley replied. "Still, they're having trouble cracking the ninety percent efficacy barrier. If you ask me, I don't see them ever producing a perfect batch of antiserum. It's the damn rapid mutation that's the problem. Almost as if Omega knows we're gunning for it."

Cade nodded but said nothing. He'd already heard it all. And he agreed with the spook. Mother Nature *was* a fickle bitch. He went back to scanning the road ahead. So far, he'd seen quite a few Zs patrolling the neighborhoods sliding by off his right shoulder. More than usual.

A short distance past the golf course, where the road dove into a series of swooping curves, Harley's reflexes were tested.

Following the centerline, four abreast and six deep, was a motley group of first turns.

Harley failed the test. Grinning, he tightened his grip on the wheel. "Don't fret," he said. "This is nothing."

The racket of cold bodies impacting the grille guard and bumper was far from *nothing*. A flurry of loud bangs was followed immediately by hollow thunks as bodies were sucked underneath the bumper. The Mercedes' long-travel suspension kept the ride smooth as its six tires chewed up and spit out the fallen zombies.

Arms and legs flailed as more bodies were sent airborne.

Cade craned and looked out the back window. Bodies and parts thereof were scattered across both lanes. A couple of the Zs thrown into the air were coming back to earth amid the slurry. A lone Z clipped by the bumper was struggling to stand, only to have its horribly mangled leg collapse and send it crashing back to the road.

All put together, the scene reminded Cade of the aftermath of a jihadi suicide-vest attack. Only thing missing was the crowd that always seemed to magically appear and, under the guise of policing up the human detritus, proceed to pilfer anything of value.

Pounding a palm on the steering wheel, Harley said, "She's a beast … ain't she. Aussie Defense Force contracted with Daimler to have these made especially for their SF guys. She's basically a stretched G-Wagen, but with quite a few mods. Not only did they want IED survivability, but word is they also included the ability to survive a frontal collision with a full-grown male kangaroo. Damn things get to be huge. I guess the roads in the Outback are thick with them. Almost as choked with them as ours are with Zs."

He slowed to half the posted speed limit and turned onto a road bordering Peterson's eastern perimeter. Nearby was the row of hangars used by the 160th. The doors were parted on the largest among them. Jedi One was inside and lit up by overhead lights. Panels stood open. Red toolboxes on rollers were positioned at various intervals around the helo.

Cade could see maintainers moving about the static aircraft. Two were on their knees near the ship's angular nose and working on the FLIR pod. Another maintainer was up on a ladder and running his gloved hands along one of the drooping rotor blades.

Off in the distance, beyond the hangars, a light gray Air Force KC-130 refueling bird was taxiing on the main runway. Cade tracked it for a couple of seconds before returning his attention back to the road.

Harley slowed to negotiate a sharp left-hand turn. Straightening the wheel, he said, "You should know, Grayson, when I saw your monster of a rig, I had to have one of my own … or something similar."

"Love at first sight, eh?"

"Yes, sir. I saw your Ford when it was in Whipper's shop. I have a connection in Australia."

Incredulous, Cade said, "You had this shipped over from Australia?"

Nodding, Harley said, "My buddy pulled some strings and got this thing loaded onto a bird coming out of Swan Island. The DEVGRU guys hitching a ride back to CONUS didn't say boo about it."

"What's happening down under with Omega? Are they getting a handle on it?"

Harley shook his head. "Still a long ways to go. Especially in the coastal cities. But the Aborigines"—he slapped his palm on the wheel—"those folks are really taking it to the biters. They've formed hunter-killer teams with edged weapons and didgeridoos. They go ripping around in panel vans, jump out when they see a pack of shamblers, and lure them in with that mournful-sounding instrument.

Blood-effin-bath. It's truly a sight to behold. The Maori"—he shook his head—"they may have a reputation as the OGs of warriors, but they've got nothing on the indigenous Aussies."

Harley clammed up as Peterson's rear gate came into view. It was a dozen feet tall and fronted by a maze of cement Jersey barriers. Though not quite as fortified as the entrances to New District or Schriever, it was still a pretty intimidating sight to behold. The rolling gate and hurricane fencing were topped with double strands of coiled razor wire. The gate and outer run of fence were clad with rust-streaked corrugated metal. A guard tower rose up behind the twin runs of fencing. In the no-man's-land between the inner and outer fence sat a brick and glass guard house. It was no bigger than a Dutch Brothers drive-through coffee stand and was manned by three Marines wearing MultiCam fatigues.

Harley threaded his rig through the barriers and stopped a yard shy of the final row of barriers.

The outer gate rolled open, and a clean-shaven twenty-something stepped from the guard house, carbine at a low-ready. Hand raised and wearing a serious expression, he walked out onto the road and took up station behind a Jersey barrier.

As Harley negotiated the last of the barriers, he powered his window down, then slow-rolled the last couple of yards, stopping broadside to the young Marine.

Speaking to Cade out of the side of his mouth, Harley said, "I'm gray at the moment. No creds. You're going to have to get us through."

Cade leaned across the cabin. Making eye contact with the Marine, he said, "I don't have creds on me." He explained that he'd just returned from an op and had business at Schriever. Following that, he vouched for the spook and indicated Harley would be on base for, at most, five minutes.

The Marine, a lance corporal whose nametape read *Storm*, matched Cade's gaze. After a couple seconds scrutiny, he said, "I know you, Captain Grayson," and quickly threw a textbook salute. "You're good to go on ahead, sir."

Cade returned the salute. Said, "At ease, Storm," and sat back in his seat.

Displaying a little more pep in his step, the Marine returned to the guardhouse, opened both gates, then waved them through.

Harley waved as he rolled past the guard house. "That was easy." Powering his window up, he said, "You're going to the Bunker, right?"

Cade nodded. As Harley pulled into the lot, Cade unbuckled and gathered his gear.

Stopping behind the F-650, Harley said, "Lord knows I tried to find one as nice as yours. Nothing doing. Didn't want a former tow truck with a billion miles on the odometer."

Cade elbowed open his door. "So you went with a used and abused former military rig. Makes sense to me. What with all the weight the term *military-grade* carries."

The men had a laugh at that. The DoD and its counterparts in other nations usually listened to the bean counters instead of the men and women who would actually use the items in the field. The result: more often than not, durability took a backseat to unit cost.

Patting the dash, Harley said, "Greta's never let me down."

Cade thanked the spook for the lift, stepped onto the lot, then stood there in the warm night air, watching the exotic rig until its taillights were just twin red pinpoints in the distance.

Chapter 23

Cade hadn't lingered in the lot while Harley drove off for any other reason than he was dreading all that he had to do once inside the Bunker. All alone with the ghosts of his past, there would be nothing to distract him. No inane banter to take his mind off of yet another senseless loss.

Lugging his kit, he scaled the short stack of stairs leading to the nondescript steel door at the rear of the hangar. Pressing his hand to the biometric pad gained him access. The lights in the corridor were dimmed to their lowest setting.

He pulled the door closed behind him, then paused for a second, luxuriating in the conditioned air while his eyesight adjusted to the low light.

The steel door to the Bunker was at the end of a long hall. Placing his hand on a biometric pad identical to the first opened the door. Entering the Bunker, he hit the light switches, bringing two dozen fluorescent tubes online. Save for the massive table and dozen or so chairs positioned around it, the team room was empty. Which made sense. Everyone not currently on an operation or preparing for an impending mission was at FU-BAR, toasting Lopez and numbing out to the fact that they could very well be next. To a person, dying from Omega and then reanimating was a fate worse than being stuck in Purgatory for all of eternity.

Commingling with the sweet smell of gun oil was the lingering odor of a recently smoked cigar.

Smokey was the culprit. When the four-star wasn't actively puffing on a Cuban Cohiba, one was either protruding from a pocket or trapped between his teeth. The man was nearly a decade and a half older and reminded Cade of a character in a comic book his grandfather had once given him. It was all there: the ubiquitous cigar, perpetual five o' clock shadow, Sergeant Rock physique, and an unflinching can-do attitude. Only thing missing was the M1 helmet with straps dangling. In its place was Blake's cover of choice: the beret he'd earned decades ago. And it was always canted just so, leaving one eye in perpetual shadow.

To say Smokey was *old school* would be the understatement of the century. No different from Desantos, General Blake was firmly set in his ways. And everyone who knew the man understood that it was his way or the highway.

Cade spent the first hour or so cleaning his weapons. Writing the after-action report took the better part of another hour. Finding the words to justify the side trip to Arlington West, all while keeping the others out from under the bus, stretched the limits of his writing prowess. Finished, he wrote a note to Nash and sealed it in a separate envelope. It was identical to the first and bore her name on the outside. The ask was going to be a heavy lift. Even for a person as connected as Nash.

He figured the odds of her going to bat for him were about as high as his favorite Trail Blazer, Clyde Drexler, making a full-court buzzer-beater for the win. If the ask bore fruit, it was worth taking the shot.

He heard Desantos in his head. *You'll never know if you don't ask.* Sage words, indeed.

The intel collected on the Idaho raid, as well as the personal effects Griff and Nat had taken off the dead PLA soldiers who'd been thrown from the crash at Bear Lake, went into a cardboard box. The smartphone Nat had found in MacLeod's rig and the sealed envelope meant for Nash went on top.

As Cade was stowing his gear in the Pale Riders' fenced-in storage compartment, he heard footfalls echoing in the corridor. There was no care taken to be stealthy. He knew at once who was about to come through the door.

Taking a seat at the massive team table while waiting for the human tornado to make his entrance, he studied the stack of intricately carved skulls on the wood near his crossed forearms.

There was a beep outside the door as the biometric scanner confirmed the person's identity. It was followed by a mechanical whirring and audible click as the deadbolts retracted into their housings.

Cade rose, pushed his chair in, then stood at rigid attention, saluting as he did so.

The door made no sound as it swung inward.

Though the leader of United States Special Operations Command was only an inch or so taller than Cade, the man filled up the doorway. His entry was much quieter than his initial approach. He was dressed in MultiCam ACUs, the pant legs tucked into coyote-brown desert combat boots and bloused nicely.

Seeing Cade, Blake said, "At ease, Captain Grayson."

Cade relaxed but remained standing.

Blake closed and locked the door. He slung his M4 on a peg on the wall and dropped his beret on the table. He said nothing throughout all of this. He also remained tight-lipped—literally and figuratively—while he lit the Cohiba clenched between his teeth. He puffed and puffed on the stub until a bright red cherry appeared.

Attempting to break what he perceived as ice, Cade said, "They say those things will kill you."

"Not as fast as a round tainted with the China virus."

Cade said nothing to that.

Looking up, face shrouded by a rising cloud of cigar smoke, Blake said, "Too soon?"

"I should have seen something like this coming."

"Bullshit," said Blake. "That's like saying Cowboy should have known zombie kids are fast movers. That he should have known a tiny bite on the wrist would be the battlefield wound that put him in the ground. Lopez had no idea today would be his last. Hell, none of us know when the Reaper is going to come a callin'. And we sure as shit don't know how he's going to cut us down." He dragged an ashtray closer to him and stubbed out the cigar. Gesturing with the stunted Cohiba, he went on, saying, "The PLA are ruthless bastards. They have zero boundaries. Children, women, men … so long as they get what they want out of them … it's game on. All the organ harvesting that went on before all this." He arched a brow. "Think about how many millions of little girls were victim to their One Child policy. Sucked out of the womb without thought. They're as cold and sterile as the instruments they use to snuff out all those embryos. Human life means *nothing* to those godless heathens."

Blake stood and began to pace the room. His tanned face was flushed, the red creeping up from his collar.

Cade started to reply but was quickly cut off.

"The Chinese people are as much a victim to Omega as we are. The CCP doesn't care one wit about the rest that they see as peasants. The upper-echelon party apparatchiks are in their bunkers. They're going to ride this train all the way to the station and then come out playing the victim."

"What's the station?"

"The cure." He gestured at the open box. "One look at that tells me all I need to know. The canister with the biohazard symbol." He snatched up a folded sheet of paper.

Cade said, "I read a little Mandarin. Still, a lot of those characters mean nothing to me. If it's another shopping list, it's different than the ones Alamo picked up in Seattle and Portland."

"You think they're getting close?"

Cade nodded. "They've had plenty of time to work on it."

Blake stopped pacing. Planting both palms on the table, he stared Cade in the eyes. "I'll be damned if I'm going to sit back and let them beat us to the punch. No way. Not on American soil. Not when our scientists keep hitting the wall with each new batch."

Cade looked a question at the four-star.

Pounding a fist on the table, Blake said, "I'll get this intel to the people who need to see it. In the meantime, you need to take a couple of days off. Stand down. Go home and spend some time with that firecracker daughter of yours. Take your time and mourn Lopez. I get what you did earlier. Diverting to Schriever. It's what Low Rider would have wanted. Nobody wants to be seen like that. As one of those things."

"I screwed up and let him reanimate." Cade paused. "He didn't get bit. I guess I was holding out for a miracle."

"That's neither here nor there. Bottom line is you followed through when it really counted. And you'd do the same for me, right?"

Cade nodded.

Smokey snatched up the Cohiba. "I'd reciprocate if the tables were turned, Wyatt." Chomping down on the cigar, he said, "Lopez is where he needs to be. Where he wanted to be if Omega got him. He'll rest for all time in the same soil as Desantos and all the others who've made the same ultimate sacrifice."

A sense of relief washed over Cade. Everything Blake was saying was spot on. It was as if he'd tapped into his head and could read his mind.

Blake relit his cigar and took a long drag. Exhaling, he told Cade about the combined herds. Though he was privy to Raven's involvement, he left those details for Cade to mine. Finally, making a shooing motion, he said, "Now scoot. It'll be dark soon."

Cade didn't need to be told twice. He was grateful the ass chewing he'd been expecting never came. And though he didn't know how he was going to be able to wind down after operating on such a high tempo for weeks on end, he thanked the general for the time off, grabbed up his M4, and shouldered his pack.

Cade left Blake all alone in the Bunker. He threw his gear in the F-650 and climbed in.

The guards waved him through the gate with no fanfare.

Due to the large number of zombies wandering the Red and Yellow Zones, and the piker crews actively hunting them, the short drive to New District's East Gate was an hour-long endeavor.

All of the stopping and starting gave Cade plenty of time to think about how he was going to break it to Raven that her mom was not coming home any time soon.

When he finally rolled up to the East Gate, stars were visible in the night sky to the west, and all of New District was blacked out. His temperature was checked by a guard with a handheld scanner. The guard then took his credentials and disappeared into a trailer.

As Cade waited for the guard to return, he watched a second guard inspect the Ford's undercarriage for bombs. After the assassination attempt on the president, new entrance policies had been adopted. He was glad to see, even after all this time, that those policies were being adhered to religiously.

Consulting his Suunto every couple of minutes, Cade grew anxious. He hadn't spoken to Raven all day, and he had a lot he wanted to say to her. It was getting close to the time she normally turned in.

Five minutes after the guard had entered the trailer, the door opened, and he emerged. He returned the credentials and then spent a couple of minutes detailing Raven's involvement with the converging herds.

"Thanks for the heads up," Cade replied. "Now I have a favor to ask of you."

The guard took a step closer to the idling Ford. Ear cocked, he leaned in. "What is it, Captain?"

"I need you to call inside and get me past quarantine. I've been gone *all* day. On a very long mission during which I lost a man." He put on a sad face. Though it felt unnatural, he continued to frown as he said, "After learning all that my daughter's endured while I've been outside the wire, what with her recently losing her mom … I don't want her to be alone one second longer than she has to."

The sergeant nodded. Without comment, he took a square of paper from a pocket. It was safety orange and laminated. He stepped up onto the Ford's running board, reached across the hood, and slipped the item underneath the wiper blade.

Chapter 24

Cade pulled up real slow in front of his home, extinguished Black Beauty's running lights, and killed her engine.

As he clicked out of his seatbelt, he noticed that someone had gone and put a sofa and loveseat on the front lawn. It was a matching pair. Shiny metal frames and saddle-brown leather. Very little padding, if any at all. The Scandinavian style Cade had forbidden Raven from bringing into their Craftsman. What with all of the abandoned homes in North New District, furniture was real easy to come by. At present, their home was decorated with period furniture that matched the millwork. No doubt Raven's tastes would change and, one of these days, assuming the younger guys hadn't tired of her using them for their muscle, he'd come home from a mission and find that, yet again, she had changed everything out. This was one glaring aspect in which Raven was totally different from her mother. Cade attributed her penchant for rummaging around in vacant homes and businesses to all the downtime. Life in the apocalypse was long stretches of boredom interspersed with flurries of adrenaline-producing action that usually had one's life hanging in the balance.

He got it.

There certainly were worse habits he could think of her adopting.

No sooner had the engine gone quiet than, all at once, seven heads turned in his direction. Most of the old gang was here.

Duncan was currently engaging in one of those bad habits Cade prayed Raven would never dabble in. He was sitting all by himself on the loveseat, cigarette dangling from his lips, stocking feet propped up on what looked to be a safe. Likely a contributing factor to Duncan having the entire loveseat to himself was that his ratty ostrich-skin boots were sitting on the grass next to him.

The sofa was a twelve-foot-long item. It looked like it could accommodate a whole bunch of hipsters in skinny jeans. At present, it was sagging under the weight of Wilson, Taryn, Sasha, Peter, and Daymon, the latter of whom was busy putting a fresh edge on one of his machetes.

Raven had the stoop to herself. She was sitting on the second step from the bottom and drinking sun tea out of a mason jar. Her Danners and socks were on the walk by her feet.

If Cade didn't know any better, judging by the group's relaxed attitude, he would have thought the zombie apocalypse was over. Truth be told, the Yellow and Red Zones in every direction were teeming with flesh-eaters.

He sat in the truck for a full minute listening to Bob Marley trying to convince him everything was going to be all right. While the Wailers wove their music around the late reggae star's final refrain, all Cade could think about was how he was going to break the awful news about Jamie and Lev and their unborn child. At least with most everyone who knew them present on the lawn, he'd get it over with in a hurry. Wouldn't have to go around and knock on doors like a notification officer. Yanking the bandage off real quick was always less painful than trying to peel it off slowly. No matter how he went about delivering the news, it pained him to know that he was about to sadden and anger a whole lot of people.

Cade pocketed his keys and collected his weapon and ruck. He elbowed open the door and stepped to the warm pavement, where he lingered for a few seconds, steeling himself for the task at hand.

Everyone was still seated when he strode up the walk.

Duncan stubbed his cigarette out. "Why the long face?" he asked. "One of those days?"

Cade said nothing as he made his way to a spot on the lawn equidistant to Raven, Duncan, and the five on the couch. He set his gear on the grass and crouched down so that he was eye level with everyone.

Though it was growing darker by the second, he could still see the whites of their eyes.

Exhaling sharply, he said, "I have terrible news to share."

Daymon stopped what he was doing and put the whetstone and machete off to the side.

Sasha went quiet and gave Cade her undivided attention.

Removing his arm from around Taryn's shoulders, Wilson scooted forward until his backside was barely in contact with the couch.

Peter pinned his blond hair behind his ears and fixed his blue eyes on Cade.

Raven rose up off the stair and set the half-full jar of tea on the porch rail.

Sliding his feet off the safe, Duncan drawled, "Why don't you take a load off before you do."

Cade sat down on the safe. Eyes downcast, he said, "Jamie and Lev are gone."

Eyes welling with tears, Raven said, "Gone? As in dead?"

Choked by emotion, Cade simply nodded.

Raven exhaled sharply. "What about their baby?"

Cade met her gaze. "They're all gone. Eden is destroyed."

Letting herself down slowly, Raven retook her place on the step. "How? Why?"

As Sasha rose and moved to Raven's side, Wilson blurted, "Who do we need to kill?"

Duncan removed his Stetson. Shooting Wilson a hard stare, he said, "Stand down, son. Let the man say his piece."

Drawing a deep breath, Cade said, "I'm not going into specifics on how they died. I will say it was the work of the PLA. It wasn't quick. They made sure our friends suffered."

Peter said, "My father called them monsters before they attacked us with their bioweapon. He said they did bad stuff all over the world. All in the name of Communism."

Wilson said, "All that aside, they need to pay for what they did."

"The PLA aren't to be messed with," Cade asserted. "Some of them are inept. Most of the scouts we're encountering are well trained. And they're now using our military equipment." After a short pause, during which he walked his gaze over the others, he went on, saying, "I lost a good man today. A real professional. As good as they come. He was shot by one of those PLA soldiers. The wound was a through and through. Not life-threatening. Axe patched him up, and he was good to go."

Daymon said, "He go into shock? Have a seizure or something?"

Cade shook his head. "He was fine at first. Then he spiked a fever." He got up and paced the lawn, trying to find a way to say the next piece.

Duncan said it for him. "Those slimy bastards are tainting their ammo, ain't they?"

Cade nodded. "For now, we need to keep this to ourselves. Keep it close to the vest until my bosses figure out exactly how they want to inform the public."

Duncan smacked his hat down on the love seat. Once all eyes were on him, he said, "First good ol' Tricky Dick visits their Motherland and gives those godless commies validation on the world stage. Hell, they used proxies to kill us on battlefields from Korea to Vietnam. Blood on the latter still wasn't dry when our elites started cozying up to them. Then Billy Blue Dress signed a free trade agreement with them, thus cementing their presence on the world stage. And *then*, lest we forget, just before the shitbirds unleashed their virus on the world"—he stuck a finger in the air to make sure he had everyone's undivided attention—"our former Commander-in-Chief turned a blind eye on their Confucius Centers, all their damn thieving of our military secrets and intellectual property. And that's just the tip of the iceberg."

Raven raised her hand.

Meeting her gaze, Cade said, "What is it?"

Pinching tears from her eyes, Raven told on herself. She left nothing out. In finishing, she cued up the footage she had caught with her phone and handed the device to her father.

All eyes were on Cade as he tapped the screen. He watched the footage twice, grunted, then handed the phone back.

Lighting another cigarette, Duncan said, "We all have our own opinions as to what's on that video. Mine is … and this is no slam on Bird's camera skills—she was going through a lot at the time—but that there, it's more Blair Witch than Zapruder. Personally, I think it's two dudes on steel horses. Some of us, though, see Bigfoot. Others don't know what they see and remain noncommittal. I ain't pointing fingers at anyone. We could *all* be wrong. It's not like it's real film we're looking at. Who knows? It could just be a glitch in the software. If that's a thing." He looked at Cade. "What's your take?"

"I'm sort of in the noncommittal camp. How's that for waffling? Seriously, though. While I want to see what Duncan sees—mainly so I can justify donning some NVGs and going out right now to hunt them down and make them pay for what they did—I need confirmation." He singled out Raven. "Did you show this to anyone else?"

"Just Daymon's ex. While we were waiting at the East Gate for the ambulance to come get Connor, she uploaded it to her laptop. Said it would get to the right people. Analysts, I assume."

Cade said, "Good job, Bird. Gets you off the hook for going outside the wire without a long-range radio. From now on, I recommend you take the Thuraya, too." Starting with Wilson. he let his gaze jump from face to face. Locking eyes with Raven, he went on, saying, "For now, I think we should act on the assumption that those were PLA scouts."

Shooing smoke from the cigarette away from the others, Duncan said, "Dollars to doughnuts they were responsible for the herds converging where they did. One of them probably drew a group of biters in from Monument. The other could have collected a following of them east of Springs. Maybe started around Yoder and made a few sprints through the little towns between here and there."

"Doubtful," said Cade. "The numbers don't pan out. The Pied Pipers don't traffic in numbers south of ten thousand. The pair Skipper and Axe killed in Vegas had a few hundred thousand on the hook. Thank God they weren't successful in showing them to our doorstep." He shook his head. "These walls won't last a minute against those kinds of numbers."

"No matter what," Daymon said, "we can't let ourselves be cowed into staying inside the wire. Poisoned bullets or a bite from a rotter, it's all the same. Bottom line … we gotta keep on living."

"Agreed," said Duncan. "This is our country."

Cade said, "We're taking it back. Make no mistake. The wheels are turning." He regarded Raven. "I'm hungry and tired, and I've been holding a piss since I left Peterson an hour ago."

Knees popping as he stood, Duncan said, "Let's leave these two be." He looked the others over as he put on his Stetson. "Who wants to come over and shoot the shit? I've got an unopened bottle of Jack you all can have. Lord knows I can't have it."

Wilson said, "How about I walk you home and take that off your hands for you. Then, if you want, you can come to our place and play Monopoly."

Duncan considered it for a second. "How about we play Spades? A credit a point?" He looked to Daymon. "What do you think? Partner up with me?"

Daymon rose from the couch. Sheathing the machete, he said, "Since I'm broke as a joke, I'm down." He looked the others over. "Y'all take IOUs?"

Peter said, "My father always liked to say, 'Know your opponent.'" He rose, big smile on his face. "I'm in."

Sasha declined. "I'm no good at games. I'm going home."

"Me too," said Taryn. "I think it's a setup. The old guys are going to clean the youngsters out."

Duncan looked to Daymon. "They're onto us."

Addressing Wilson, Peter said, "Me and you. What do you say?"

"As long as Old Man comes through with the bottle … *and* … he agrees to stay on the wagon—I'm in."

Peter said, "One more thing, Duncan."

Duncan snatched up his boots. Shooting Peter a pained look, he said, "Another demand? Better not be that I provide the Coca Cola to go along with the Jack."

Serious tone to his voice, Peter said, "I only ask that you do not smoke around me. Those things killed my father."

Finished slipping on his boots, Duncan said, "I'll cover D's IOUs. The other stuff … I don't take orders from terrorists. Or kids, for that matter. But I will do my best to refrain from both vices as long as humanly possible. If my resolve crumbles, I'll be lighting a coffin nail before booze crosses my lips. I'm on a pretty long dry spell—"

"In more ways than one," Daymon quipped.

"The quittin' has to be my decision. I have to do it for *me*." He looked toward the stairs. "That being said … I really do need to get back in Glenda's good graces. Maybe some of you can put in a good word for me. Let her know I'm still sober and that I'm fighting the good fight."

Raven said, "If I see her, I'll be sure to mention it."

Picking up where he left off, Peter said, "If you must smoke at our house, you must do so outside."

Nodding, Duncan said, "Deal. And since I just remembered you and Sasha are minors and can't drink inside the walls—which I think is complete bullcrap—I'll dip into my secret stash and bring along some Cokes."

Holding the door for Raven, his gear clearly weighing him down, Cade said, "I don't care what you all do. Smoke. Don't smoke. Get drunk. Stay sober. But whatever you decide, please do it elsewhere." He paused for a second while Raven crossed the threshold. Once she was inside the house and out of earshot, he ordered Wilson to make sure the safe and furniture went home with them.

Closing the screen door, something lying on the porch caught Cade's eye. Lighting it up with his Scorpion tac-light revealed that it was a fully articulated prosthetic arm. It was fitted with a hook on one end and a series of straps on the other. It was one of the newer models, the light playing off the carbon fiber.

Making a mental note to ask about it later, he killed the light and closed the doors behind him.

Inside the Grayson home, Cade saw that Raven had already run his pack and helmet upstairs. Returning to the main floor, she led him down the hall and into the kitchen, where she had the small table set for dinner. In the center of the table, bracketed by plates and service for three, was a single lit candle. The flickering light it cast off caused their shadows on the walls to stretch and shrink, undulating like a pair of shapeshifting monsters.

"I see you set a place for your mother."

Raven nodded. "You're home safe and sound. Have to keep with tradition."

"I'm appreciative of the gesture, Bird. But I don't know if I have it in me to lift a fork. If I'm lucky, I'll get in a quick shower and have enough energy to eat a Snickers before crawling into bed." He went quiet for a long ten-count. When he spoke again, it was a near whisper. "I buried Jamie and Lev on the hill next to your mother. I'm real sorry I couldn't bring her home with me. That'll have to be something we do on our own. When things return to normal. Or as close to normal as possible. Once we kill or drive all the Communists from our soil, I promise I will beg or borrow a helicopter and aircrew and make it happen."

"That could have gone unsaid. You always do what you say you're going to do, Dad. There are two Is in integrity."

"I will—" he began.

"I did," she finished.

Grabbing a pot off the stove, she approached the table, ladle in hand.

"What is it? Smells good."

"Chili. It's from a can, though." She shrugged. "At least it's Dennison's. Lola hasn't had it on her shelves for weeks."

In Mandarin, he said, "My favorite." He took a seat, unfolded his napkin, and spread it out on his lap.

She scooped chili from the pot. In passable Mandarin, she answered, "One or two?"

Cade smiled and held up a finger. "One scoop is enough. Might shock my system if I have any more than that."

She ladled out the chili. Doling out some homemade biscuits, in Mandarin, she said, "Milk or?" Switching to English, she conceded she didn't know how to say apple juice, let alone sparkling cider.

Cade said, "Mandarin is a tough nut to crack. But you're doing great for having just gotten started. Be forewarned, though. Learning a new language is nothing like shooting. Practice does *not* make perfect."

"I know, right? I've been putting a lot of hours into it the last couple of weeks. Pretty much been using your phone every time you leave the house."

"I know you have. I checked the phone's usage meter." He lifted his glass. "What kind of cider? Martinelli's?"

"Only the best." She retrieved the bottle from the refrigerator and poured them each a glass.

"Lola never fails to impress." He lifted his glass. "A toast."

Raven took her seat.

Cade said, "To Brook."

"To Mom."

They ate in silence.

Finished, Cade said, "I hate to eat and run. But if I don't, this plate is going to become my pillow."

"We don't want that," she said. "I'll clean up. But before you go, did you come across any peanut butter cups?"

"Just a few Snickers I took off a guy who is no longer alive to enjoy them. They're pretty fresh. Want one?"

She curled her lip.

"Beggars can't be choosers."

She stuck her hand out.

Cade rose, folded his napkin, and placed it on his plate. He dug a couple of candy bars from a pocket and handed them over. Kissing Raven on the top of the head, he said, "I settled the rest of my debt with Whipper. Turns out Cuban cigars are worth their weight in gold."

"I wanted to take care of the rest."

Cade smiled. "It's done." Changing the subject, he said, "What's with the artificial limb on the porch?"

She started to unwrap a Snickers. "The Connor guy I mentioned. He lost part of his arm."

"That's a pretty significant detail to omit from your daily SITREP."

"I didn't want to have to answer Sasha's stupid questions. What did it look like? Did he bleed a lot? Did he pass out? You know how she can be." She made a face. "Plus, we were about to eat dinner."

"You fixed the tourniquet?"

She nodded. "Stopped the bleeding right away. You taught me well."

"Where is he now?"

"The gate guard called an ambulance. Ambulance took him to Penrose. Last I heard, he was no longer in shock. Glenda said the doctors cleaned up the wound and did whatever they do after an amputation."

Cade said, "He's in good hands there." After a long pause, he asked, "You sweet on him?" and cracked a smile.

Raven said, "No way, *Dad*." The color on her cheeks told a different story. "He's too much like Wilson for my taste. And he's a lot older than me."

While it was the duty of all dads the world over to probe further in matters such as these, Cade was out of gas. Instead of commenting on the kind gesture, he said, "You did good today. Pulled your weight, and then some. You're more like your mother than you'll ever know." He tousled her hair, then trudged back down the hall, the prospect of scaling the stairs stealing the last of the wind from his sails.

Chapter 25

Cade awoke to the smell of something good cooking downstairs. Smelled to him like pancakes. Only these weren't ordinary buttermilk flapjacks. He drew in a deep breath. *Banana!*

Banana pancakes, maple syrup, and half a rasher of bacon was another traditional meal Brook always served on day one after he returned from deployment as an Army Ranger in the 75th. Later, when he was a member of the Unit and they were living near Bragg, he got to enjoy the meal after every operation.

Excited to sink his teeth into the fluffy goodness, he threw off the thin sheet and swung his legs off the bed. As he stood, his thirty-six-year-old knees reminded him of his age. Skiing had put some wear and tear on them during his formative years. The majority of damage had been done over the decade-plus he'd spent soldiering in the United States Army.

As he stretched to limber up, the scar tissue on his back reminded him of all the times he'd caught a bullet or fragments thereof. *Getting older sucks*, he thought as he stepped into a faded pair of Levi's. He laced on his Danners, then pulled on a Black Sabbath tee shirt Raven had picked up for him at Lola's.

He looped a belt around his waist and attached the drop-leg holster to it. Snugging his Glock into the formed Kydex holster, he threw on a ball cap and made his way downstairs.

"Made you your favorite," Raven said, greeting him with a hug. "Only Lola didn't have the real thing. Had to settle for a flavored extract. I'm amazed she had it."

"A for effort, Bird. I have a feeling it's going to be a long time before we see a fresh banana." He sat at the table. Already his salivary glands were ramping up. His stomach growling reminded him that the chili and biscuit he'd eaten the night before had been wholly inadequate in replenishing all the calories he had burned during the operation, digging the grave, and on the long walk from Arlington West to Nash's office.

"How many?" Raven asked.

"As many as you can fit on my plate."

There was hot coffee in a mug in front of his empty plate.

"Two of my favorite meals in a row," he noted. "And you scrounged up some"—he sniffed the steam wafting from the inky black goodness in the mug—"fairly fresh coffee." Eyes narrowed, he said, "You're buttering me up. What do you want? It's got to be a *huge* ask."

She shook her head and transferred a stack of pancakes from a spatula to his plate. "Nothing at the moment. Let's just add any accrued credit to my *ask* bank."

"Duly noted." He looked the table over. "Syrup?"

After rifling through a cupboard, she brought a brown plastic bottle and set it on the table. "It's Log Cabin. A couple months past its prime. It was all Lola had."

"What?" Cade said, putting on a faux frown. "No maple syrup fresh from the spigot?"

"Beggars can't be choosers."

"Touché." He plowed through the stack. Swallowing, he said, "Remember how your mom used to be real picky about her bananas?"

Raven made a face. "One brown spot and she couldn't look at it."

"But she always waited until they were nearly black and attracting a squadron of fruit flies before doing anything about them."

Raven snickered. "She was always saying she was going to freeze them and use them later to make banana bread."

"But never did." He shook his head. "I remember taking two dozen frozen black bananas out to the compost. She never even missed them."

Raven went quiet.

Cade said, "I sure miss her."

Raven said nothing. As she got up and cleared their plates, Cade noticed the tears forming in her eyes. He was about to take the plates and comfort her when the Thuraya charging on the kitchen counter emitted its usual annoying electronic warble.

Raven dumped the plates on the counter and scooped up the phone. Glancing at the screen, she said, "It's Freda Nash."

Cade traded a clean napkin for the phone. He said, "Looks like you've been cutting onions. Better wipe your eyes."

He thumbed the Talk button and initiated the conversation by announcing himself.

Raven dabbed at her eyes but didn't take them off her dad as he listened long and hard to the woman who her own mother had cultivated a strong resentment toward. For a call from Nash almost always preceded her father announcing yet another trip downrange—an order that Brook always accepted, but not without experiencing a certain measure of dread.

The call lasted five minutes, during which Cade grunted a couple of times, said "Yes" between two long pauses, then, finally, ended the call with a confident-sounding, "Not yet. But I will by day's end."

Raven looked a question at her dad.

Cade grimaced. "It's a need-to-know thing."

"If I tell you, I have to kill you. I get it. When will you be back?"

"Tonight. I'm on a mandatory two-day stand down. That's set in stone by Smokey. He rarely changes his mind. The man never second-guesses himself. Sees it as a weakness in others who do."

"When?"

"I have to meet someone at the Capitol Building." He checked his Suunto. "And I have ten minutes to get there."

"Love you."

Giving her a one-armed hug, he said, "Love you too." He donned his ball cap, snatched his keys off the counter and, on the way out the door, grabbed his backup short-barreled Colt Commando rifle from the cubby underneath the stairs.

The drive from North District to the recently anointed United States Capitol Building took less than five minutes. Cade slowed at the intersection with Vermijo, turned left off of Tejon, then squeezed the F-650 into one of the nose-in spots out front of the granite two-story building. Situated in the center of Alamo Park, the massive multi-windowed affair was surrounded by beds full of colorful flowers and a sea of well-manicured grass.

A domed clock tower rose up from the center of what was recently the Colorado Springs Pioneer Museum. Not only was the historic building serving as the seat of power for the struggling nation, but it also was home to her founding documents—irreplaceable items whose rescue Cade had had a hand in.

The stalls and trailers belonging to vendors who had set up shop on the museum grounds after the walls went up around Springs were now clustered around Lola's double-wide, which had been moved a block east and now sat in the shadow of the perimeter wall.

A stone's throw from the hustle and bustle of the mercantile district was the Bureau of Eradication, Reclamation, and Restoration. A line of people emerged from the cement building's wide double-doors, snaked down the short stack of stairs, and then stretched along the sidewalk before disappearing around the far corner. Most of the people were sitting on lawn chairs and fanning themselves with whatever they had available. Some waved limp magazines or squares of cardboard in front of their faces.

Cade guessed he was looking at fifty or sixty bodies, all languishing under the noon sun. Likely half as many—the lucky ones—were already inside the building and awaiting their turn to be called to the information window. He'd been there and done that. However, unlike the rides at Disneyland, where Cade and Brook had taken Raven when she was little, getting to the front of this line rarely delivered a satisfying experience.

With work hard to come by and food even more scarce, the bureaucrats in the BERR building had their hands full trying to placate the growing population. If Eplot Farms gave up their current crops and then continued to produce at even a fraction of their pre-apocalypse potential, in the coming days, the citizens of New District would all be benefitting from the steady stream of fresh produce.

As Cade stepped from his truck, he was approached by an unsmiling man wearing dark glasses and dressed in way too much clothing for a sunny day in July. The imprint of some kind of personal defense weapon, likely an H&K MP5 or MP7, was clearly evident beneath his windbreaker. Further evidence that this six-foot-four behemoth was a member of President Clay's protective detail was the flesh-colored comms bud in his right ear.

"Captain Cade Grayson?"

Cade nodded and produced his military identification.

After a thorough examination of the credentials, the agent said, "I'll need to relieve you of your rifle and sidearm."

Without protest, Cade handed over his weapons.

"I'm sorry, sir," said the agent who hadn't bothered to provide a name, "but I'm going to have to take the dagger, too."

"Understood," said Cade. "You want my multi-tool?"

"Yes, please," replied the agent. "Anything else I need to know about? You'll be going through a magnetometer shortly."

"Just my keys."

"I'll hold them for you."

Cade handed them over. "If you take her for a spin, be sure to top off the tank."

Pocketing the keys, the agent glanced at the F-650. "Tempting," he said. "She's a beast."

Under close scrutiny of the similarly attired African American agent fronting a pair of giant-sized oak doors, Cade scaled the half dozen steps.

Agent number two was unsmiling and all business. He gave Cade a quick pat-down and then opened the door for him.

The Capitol's foyer was adorned with copious amounts of marble and polished wood. The furniture pushed up against the walls to the left and right was of the same style that would have been in use a century ago, back when the building was still hosting trials, and lawyers and judges walked the halls.

A dozen wooden chairs with pioneer-themed scenes carved into their legs and arms formed a chute leading to the magnetometer.

Nodding, the female agent standing on the opposite side said, "Captain Grayson. Welcome. Please put your hands over your head and come on through."

The machine made no sound as Cade walked through.

The agent glanced at her counterpart at the door. Leaning in close to Cade, she said, "Big fan of your work."

Nodding, Cade said, "Back at you." Smiling, he asked, "Where to?"

Giving the African American agent the word to seal the building, the female agent said, "Follow me."

The room housing the founding documents—the Declaration of Independence, Constitution, and Bill of Rights—was maybe one-tenth the size of the vast Rotunda for the Charters of Freedom inside the National Archives Building in Washington D.C., where the documents were last on permanent display.

Judging by the chair rails decorating three of the room's four walls, the low boxed-beam ceiling overhead, and the single, narrow door at the rear of the room, Cade figured he was standing in what was once a courtroom. The door opposite him led to what he guessed was once the judge's chambers.

Heavy curtains over the windows blocked out all natural light. To keep the documents from further degrading, the lights overhead were, at most, forty-watt items.

President Valerie Clay stood, head bowed, before the hermetically-sealed case containing the Declaration of Independence. She was dressed in her usual Indiana-Jones-esque attire: low-heeled boots, khaki pants, leather bomber jacket. In lieu of the fictional adventurer's high-crowned wide-brimmed sable fedora, the president wore a navy ball cap, her dark hair in a high ponytail and sticking out the back. Without taking her eyes off the document, she said, "What do you think the men who signed this would say if they were alive today?"

"Madame President. First off, I want to thank you for meeting with me. I was expecting, at most, a phone call from one of your aides." He made his way to the row of cases. Standing shoulder to shoulder with the president, eyes roaming the faded signatures, he said, "I think they'd be speechless."

"Because of the zombies? Or because we've been invaded?"

"Because, knowing what we know about communism, we allowed the CCP to worm its way into every level of our society. Academics. The once *free* press. Entertainment. Social media. Commerce and industry. Government. Wasn't there a senator from California whose longtime personal driver was a card-carrying member of the CCP?"

Clay exhaled sharply. "The Intel Committee didn't even slap her on the wrist. I'm privy to all of it now that I'm president. It was worse than I'd like to admit. Both sides of the aisle were compromised. Some had fallen victim to honeypot schemes. Blackmail is one hell of an effective tool. Others employed family members as bag men and enriched themselves during the entire time they were posing as public servants. Board seats and lucrative contracts were passed out like candy to family and friends. Oftentimes the company whose seat was offered turned out to have had direct ties to the PLA. The CCP's tendrils stretched deep and wide. If they wouldn't have had the containment breach at their Wuhan lab, I believe, in a decade, maybe fifteen years, they would have taken us over completely. Would have mined our corporations of all useful technology. Patents meant nothing to them. In no time, they would have been making all of the high-tech items we were producing. They'd be dominating in the field of artificial intelligence and cloud computing." She went quiet and stared Cade in the face.

"Scary thing," Cade replied, "is that they were doing it all from within. If they'd had enough time, it would never have gone kinetic. They'd have us underneath their boot heel all without ever firing a shot." He paused and stared at the Constitution. Let his gaze roam the opening lines atop the yellowed parchment, then went on, saying, "Communism is a cancer. It gets a foothold and metastasizes. Once you've reached that point, save for military intervention, there's nothing *We the People* can do about it. Especially so if Odero's wish to strip us of our Second Amendment rights would have come to fruition."

Clay had been nodding agreeably. She said, "I was *very* vocal about not letting them into the WTO. When my spineless colleagues started eating at the trough of special interests, began taking tax-payer-funded junkets over there, and posing for photo ops with upper echelon party officials and apparatchiks, I knew it was already too late. The writing was on the wall. My floor speeches weren't getting through to them. Calling them out in the media didn't faze them. They were all getting drunk on power and influence."

Cade said, "They got to see how the elites over there operate. There is zero pushback from the people. With help from our big-tech overlords, their Internet is controlled entirely by the Communist party."

Clay said, "Power corrupts; absolute power corrupts absolutely. China didn't deserve to be given developing nation status. They were a first-world power on their way to having the largest economy in the world. With their third-world policies and the way they treat ethnic minorities, you'd think the same crowd who's always meddling in Africa, Haiti, Libya, etcetera … would have been up in arms. Instead, those arms were wrapped firmly around Dear Leader's ample midsection."

"The virus's release changed the timeline drastically," Cade noted. "Accelerated their pace of operations to the point that the soft coup had to go kinetic."

"And now they're here." Clay made a face. "But not for long. We've been hitting them pretty hard the last few weeks. Operation tempo has been off the charts. Now with the successful ops that saw us claw back our farmland, we have them where we were mid-winter: hungry and backed into a corner."

Cade said, "That's when a wild animal is most dangerous. When you're dealing with an army of men, that danger grows exponentially. Some intel we gathered from Eplot Farms leads me to believe they're already testing a cure. Other evidence tells me they're testing it on human subjects."

Clay said, "You called for this meeting. What do you want?"

Speaking in hushed tones, Cade laid it all out. When he was finished, Clay said, "I'll allow it. One condition, though."

Cade looked a question at the Commander-in-Chief.

"No matter what you learn, I can't afford you the same leeway as I did last time." She stared at him for a long three-count. "Can you live with that?"

Cade nodded. "Agreed." He checked his watch. "I'm stood down until tomorrow midnight. Can I get started at midnight plus one?"

"I'm overriding the stand-down. We'll go now. I'll give you a ride. Does that work? Or do you need to make arrangements to have someone watch Raven?" Realizing what she had just said, she smiled and added, "That girl of yours doesn't need anyone to watch her." She laughed. "I pity the sitter who tries."

Cade said, "No time like the present, Madame President. One of your men has my keys. I need to get in my truck to grab my *tools*."

Addressing the agent standing in the doorway, Clay said, "Find Captain Grayson's keys and get his tools from his vehicle."

"Pelican case in the back seat," Cade called.

The agent nodded and strode from the room.

Chapter 26

President Clay's agent had just left to fetch the Pelican case when a trio of agents slipped into the room. They formed a ring around Clay and escorted her through what Cade had assumed used to be the judge's chambers. As he followed in their footsteps, he learned the cramped space was now being utilized as a pass-through between two larger rooms.

The second room was double the size of the first. Head-high glass cases were spaced evenly about the room. The cases held artifacts and newspaper clippings that told the story of how Colorado Springs came to be. In the left rear corner of the room was an emergency exit. The door was inset with a square, wire-reinforced window. Through the window, Cade could see the presidential limousine known affectionately as "The Beast." Black paint and chrome gleaming under the sun, it sat at the curb, bookended by a pair of like-colored Chevrolet Suburbans. A third black Suburban was parked on the street, broadside to the limo, its bulk providing an extra layer of protection. A half dozen agents, suppressed MP7s on full display, stood vigil around the static SUVs.

As soon as the president and her detail emerged, three more agents converged on her, adding more bulk and firepower to the human barrier already moving in perfect synchronicity with the petite woman.

At first glimpse, the limousine appeared to be a typical four-door luxury sedan. Hidden underneath the outer sheet metal were the IED-proofed underpinnings of a heavy-duty GMC TopKick truck. With its Whipple supercharged engine, off-road-capable running gear complete with run-flat tires, five-inch-thick bullet-proof glass, and titanium armor plating, The Beast could go anywhere and survive just about anything a bad actor could throw at her.

After Clay was ensconced safely inside her ride, a lone agent returned and escorted Cade from the emergency exit, led him around the vehicle's boxy rear end, then quickly ushered him inside.

The door shut behind Cade, and he found himself in a cocoon of complete silence. Though the limousine was roughly the same dimension as the F-650, its interior was more spacious than Cade had expected it to be. Disappointing to Cade was the fact that the once luxurious interior was showing substantial wear and tear. Which he quickly forgave, considering the entire United States was also showing substantial wear and tear.

He sat on the forward-facing bench seat opposite the president and watched the trio of black Suburbans line up just outside his window. He remained tight-lipped while she talked into a sat-phone. She was still conversing when the lead Suburban sped away. She didn't bat an eye when her driver pulled smartly from the curb and accelerated briskly to match the Suburban's pace.

Surprisingly, considering how much get-up-and-go the president's limousine had exhibited as it made its move, the engine noise was nearly nonexistent. Which was a far cry different from the F-650. A prolonged stint running full out in that *beast* usually resulted in a short-lived case of tinnitus.

Once Clay finished her call and had tucked the phone away, she turned to face Cade.

"I have several meetings today at Peterson. But for security reasons we'll go straight to Schriever first." She paused for a beat. "Remember, you're to take him to the edge of the precipice, no further."

He met her gaze. She was actually real easy on the eyes. In fact, though she was already north of forty by a year or two, the woman reminded him of Brook. The dark hair, big brown eyes, tanned skin, and physical stature were all spot on. The attitude was similar as well. Being ever the hard-charger, Clay had already burned through two vice presidents and was currently hunting for a replacement for the Ohio senator who'd just stepped down, citing "emotional distress" as his reason for doing so.

After staring at Clay for a bit too long, he said, "Copy that, Madame President. I will not let you down."

She smiled, revealing perfectly straight teeth. "You have yet to do so, Captain Grayson." She looked out her window. "And we are here."

Expecting the four-vehicle convoy to be nosing up to the East Gate, where he presumed they would pick up a Stryker escort, Cade shifted his gaze forward. Instead of seeing brake lights flaring on the back of the lead Suburban, he saw the president's V-22 Osprey—call sign Marine One—filling up The Beast's windshield. The hulking tilt-rotor aircraft was painted the same matte-black worn by Jedi One and all the other 160th SOAR birds. Its markings—fin flash, serial numbers, flags, and roundels—were all subdued, a dark shade of gray that helped them to blend in with the main body color.

Surrounding the bird was an impressive ring of security that consisted of hurricane fencing, Jersey barriers, and bollard posts. A Stryker sat on the street broadside to the landing pad. A platoon of Marines in full battle rattle stood at attention beside the wheeled armored vehicle.

Inside the wire, the bird's crew chief was underneath one of the vertical nacelles, apparently giving it a last-minute once-over.

As The Beast came to a halt parallel to the pad's lone gate, the lead Suburban made a quick J-turn that placed it as a barrier to any threat that might come at them from the south. The trailing vehicles pulled around and completed what was essentially a three-sided armored corral around the already sufficiently armored limousine.

The same agent who had ushered Cade inside the limousine appeared outside his door.

Their movements and tactics a mirror image of the transfer from the Capitol to The Beast, the president's detail escorted them to Marine One, where the crew chief took over, leading them up the rear ramp and to a pair of padded fold-down seats.

The crew chief, whose nametape read *Martin*, provided the president with a helmet and headset. He helped her with the chin strap and safety belt, then raised his voice and asked if she was comfortable.

Flashing a thumbs-up, the president motioned for the agent guarding the ramp to come aboard.

As a second agent secured Cade's weapons and Pelican case full of "tools," the crew chief provided Cade with a helmet and headset. After that, Cade was left to his own devices, which was no problem because this was close to his hundredth ride aboard an Osprey.

Cade donned the helmet and headset, then plugged the headset jack into the receptacle above his head. Seeing the president drag a phone from her coat, he did the same.

Once the bird had launched and the vibration caused by the transition from vertical to level flight had ceased, Cade thumbed the Thuraya to life and banged out a text to Raven. Without divulging any classified information, he filled her in on where he was going and when he expected to return. Next, he spent a couple of minutes trading texts with Nash.

Not only had Nash come through with his first ask—getting him a face-to-face meeting with the president—but she had also agreed to provide the specific items he had requested in his note to her. Nash had also taken the initiative and rushed the recently gathered intel to the analysts, who, amazingly, in less than twenty-four hours, had pored over everything and provided a full report of their findings. The canister with the biohazard sticker had been empty. Swabs taken from its interior surfaces had come back negative for anything biological in nature.

A linguist had concluded that Ding's final words recorded on Cade's iPhone had amounted to nothing more than babbling about how he was only following orders and that he had expected the Geneva Convention to be adhered to. Cade smiled at that revelation.

Cherry on the sundae was that they had also been able to crack the passcode on Sheriff McLeod's phone.

As Cade read Nash's rather detailed description of the video footage and looked at dozens of stills pulled off the device, his jaw tightened, and the fury that'd been simmering since he buried Lopez began to rise to the surface.

To confuse anyone tracking the president's movements, as soon as Marine One crossed over the east wall, the Marine aviator banked the bird hard right. Maintaining low-level flight, they sprinted five miles south. Once the noisy aircraft was well past the South Gate and out of earshot of any enemy spotters who might be lurking there, the pilot nosed the bird around to the east.

The first leg of what would be a circuitous route that would ultimately deliver Cade to Schriever, then Clay to Peterson, took them over a series of connected subdivisions. The land had not been divided up in grids like Cade's hometown. Below, there was no rhyme or reason as to how the streets were laid out. It didn't seem to be dictated by the lay of the land. It was basically a crazy patchwork carved out of the ochre-colored high plain. The drab scenery was dotted with multi-family homes complete with colorful tile roofs and algae-choked swimming pools.

The streets were filled with roving packs of zombies. *Lots of right ears to be had down there.* He filed that tidbit away for future reference. Only explanation he could think of for the large concentration was the combination of cul-de-sacs and total absence of extended straightaways. If he had to venture a guess, a small horde had likely found its way into the neighborhood. Over time, as the lead pack split up and continued on divergent tangents, the horde splintered into the small herds he was looking at now.

Ten minutes after launching from New District, Marine One was crossing over the southwestern edge of Schriever Air Force Base. It was moving so fast that Cade caught only a fleeting glimpse of Arlington West, during which he concluded there was no kind of symmetry to how the headstones were aligned. It was unacceptable. Somebody was going to have to come in with surveyor's equipment and square the place away.

Seconds later, a low rumble transited Marine One. On the heels of the familiar sound, the bird slowed considerably, and the engine nacelle on Cade's side began its slow sweep from horizontal to vertical. In no time, the nacelle was locked in the upright position, the huge propellers having effectively become rotors, and Marine One was engaged in a slow and steady descent.

As the ground crept steadily nearer, the crew chief unbuckled and rose up off his seat. Holding up a finger, he said, "One minute out."

Thirty seconds into the approach, with the base's running track, pair of opposing baseball diamonds, and meticulously manicured nine-hole golf course presenting on the Osprey's left side, the pilot spun her on axis, a full one-eighty, stopping only when the landing pad and adjacent building was dead ahead. Nosed in next to the single-story structure was a one-of-a-kind vehicle. Its presence alone meant that Nash had reneged on one of Cade's most important demands: That he be allowed to work alone.

The pilot brought them down expertly on the center of the circular cement pad. There was no bounce after the tires kissed terra firma. The Osprey didn't roll forward an inch. It was as solid a landing as Cade had ever experienced. Only person capable of besting it was Ari. But he would have to be under enemy fire to do so. Because that was when the Night Stalker shined the brightest.

Cade unbuckled, stowed the helmet and headset, then policed up his gear. As he passed by the president, all weighted down and lugging the Pelican case, she said at the top of her voice, "Looks like Harley's already here. I think you two are going to hit it off nicely."

Off Cade's right shoulder, there was movement and twin slivers of daylight lanced into the fuselage as the crew chief started the ramp motoring down. "I spotted his ride," Cade said. "Can't miss that exotic beast. I met him yesterday. Guy's got personality to match that Mercedes of his." He crammed his ball cap down on his head.

"I figured you two alphas would have clicked."

"I gotta be honest with you, Madame President, the guy is real hard to read." He watched the ramp come into contact with the cement pad, then lock into place. Shaking his head, he added, "I'm still on the fence about him. Not really feeling anything either way."

"Give him a chance," she begged. "I think you may have just found the Yin to your Yang."

Opting to keep to himself what he really thought about the matter—that the spook seemed more Austin Powers than James Bond—Cade instead thanked the president for the lift.

"Any time," she said, flashing a half-smile. "I'm in the market for a VP. Everybody knows you. Everybody respects you. Some even fear you. And nobody has a bad word to say about you. That's a whole lot of upside."

Cade shook his head. Thinking *Hell no, they don't know the real me*, he flashed a smile, planted a hand atop his hat, and hustled down the ramp.

Before he was clear of the wind-whipped grass encircling the landing pad, over the roar of the whirling blades he detected the wail of a guitar solo coming from the building to his fore. It was faint at first, then grew louder as he put more distance between himself and Marine One.

He reached the door as Marine One was lifting skyward. Reaching for the knob, the door sucked inward. Filling up the doorway, dressed in nearly the same outfit as the day before, was his newly anointed *Yin*, Greg Harley.

The big man wore a wide smile. Yellow shooter's muffs covered his ears. On his hands were elbow-length black gloves made of thick rubber. When he made a wide, sweeping motion, inviting Cade to come inside, the gloves shed droplets of water.

Shouting to be heard over the heavy metal emanating from within the building, Harley said, "Good to see you, Captain Grayson." He glanced at the stainless steel Rolex Submariner on his right wrist. "You missed the trailers." Then, acknowledging Cade's Sabbath shirt, he made crude devil horns with both gloved hands. "Saw Sabbath in '92. Dehumanizer tour. Dio's no Ozzy. That's for damn sure." He handed Cade a set of shooter's muffs. "Unless you want the true SlipKnot front row experience, I'd suggest you wear these."

Donning the muffs, Cade said, "I'm only here for the main attraction," and crossed the threshold, the cool conditioned air pricking his skin.

Chapter 27

The base detention facility would be considered utilitarian by anyone's standards. There was a building similar to it in just about every small town all across America. They were occupied by police departments or the county sheriff. This squat bunker-like building was where Cade had interrogated Pug prior to sending him to Hell.

A waist-high counter fitted with floor-to-ceiling ballistic glass stood between the cramped lobby and open-concept office reserved for the base MPs. The office was home to a trio of desks, each with a computer and monitor and rolling chair parked in the knee well. The young airman behind the glass was the only person Cade could see.

The office was accessed via a lone door on the left-hand side of the partition.

The airman buzzed them in. He was wearing ear protection and made no attempt to communicate with either Harley or Cade as they filed through.

Harley led Cade through the workspace and unlocked a steel door with a key card. "After you, Captain."

Knowing his way to the cells and interview rooms, Cade pushed past the agent, hung a right, and then continued down a long, narrow hall.

As they neared the far corner of the building, the music grew exponentially louder. Cade got his first glimpse of Baby Bird on the monitor above the door to Interview Room 3. General Sun Jinlong, thirty-three-year-old former leader of the Continental Assimilation Force, was clothed only in a pair of government-issue boxers and sitting on a steel chair. The chair was bolted to the gray cement floor. A gray steel table, also bolted to the floor, sat horizontal to the prisoner.

On a table in one corner of the room was a pile of wet towels. Different-sized buckets sat on the floor nearby. Beside the table was a water cooler, the bottle nearly half full. Though there was some standing water on the floor below the table, the area around the prisoner's bare feet was mostly dry.

A pair of concert speakers were suspended on chains snaking through holes punched in the drop-down ceiling tiles. As Corey Taylor's vocals gave way to a breakdown featuring a subdued drumbeat and steady *thwap*, *thwap* of Paul Gray slapping his bass, the bare paper cones in the speakers pulsed and quivered.

Hunched over, manacled hands pressed against his ears, the general's body convulsed in near synchronicity with the heavy metal beat. The color image piped to the monitor was crisp and clear. There were no obvious signs the man had been beaten. He also appeared to have all of his original fingernails.

Maybe it was due to the fact the monitor was no bigger than the one mated to your average computer, but the man seemed much smaller than Cade remembered.

When Cade had snatched the man up at the museum in Portland, Oregon, the son of the current Chinese president had been so sure of himself. Caught naked and facing the deadly end of a suppressed MP7, the man had maintained the bearing of an aristocrat. Even aboard the extraction bird, he had continued to exude an air of invincibility. That attitude had persisted up until the moment Cade shoved his interrogator from the helicopter. Being forced to watch the dead tear the mortally wounded interrogator limb from limb had had a profound effect on Jinlong. And though he sang like a canary all the way back to Colorado Springs, over time, nearly everything he had divulged that night had turned out to be bad intel. Either his own father had been keeping him in the dark about the spring offensive being a feint, the museum and nearby convention center were being prepped for more than just the western headquarters of the occupation, or the man was one hell of a good liar. No matter the case, before the day was done, Cade was going to get to the bottom of it all.

Stabbing a thumb at the floor, Cade mouthed, "Turn it down."

Harley ducked into the interview room next door. A beat later, Cade could hear himself think again.

Harley returned a few seconds later carrying a large vinyl pouch. It was emblazoned with the words TOP SECRET and sealed with red-and-yellow-striped tape.

"You must have some heavy pull, Grayson. First, I get a call from General Nash informing me I'm to wrap up my session and prepare to receive a visitor. Then, not five minutes later, an airman comes ripping up on a Cushman and delivers this." He offered the pouch to Cade. "Then imagine my surprise when said visitor arrives aboard Marine One. All without a Secret Service advance detail paying the area a visit. Highly unusual."

"This has been in the works for less than twenty-four hours. We're acting on brand new intel. I would have expected Nash to have already read you in on it. If it's any consolation, I didn't know of your involvement until we were on final approach and I saw your rig." He gave the spook the Cliff's Notes version of the Eplot raid and all that had followed after. Only thing he left out was the murder of his friends and ransacking of the Eden compound.

Harley nodded. He was used to the Seventh Floor machinations at Langley. The compartmentalization. The cliques. How slowly fully processed and confirmed intel trickled down from the director and his minions to the rank and file. How sometimes it got buried altogether. Especially if one of the lifers was implicated. He was also aware that most of the old government, from the top down, had operated in much the same manner. Sadly, the legacy players who remained from those agencies and institutions, the ones who had survived the outbreak and follow-on invasion, they were all still so set in their ways that the old status quo had gone mostly unchanged.

Knowing what the pouch contained, Cade set the Pelican case down on the floor, unholstered his Glock, then slipped the Gerber from its sheath. Trading the weapons to the spook for the pouch, Cade set the pouch atop the Pelican case, then hefted it all off the floor.

Stowing the weapons in a nearby lockbox, Harley said, "You going to play good cop or bad cop?"

"No playing. I'm going to *be* worse cop. And I'm going in solo." Nodding at the door, he added, "I'll also need you to turn off the camera."

Obviously expecting to be continuing his efforts, not be pushed to the curb, Harley stood and stared at Cade.

Ignoring the heavy load, Cade said, "Yesterday, you told me this ongoing interrogation was a dry well. Your exact words were 'the *proper* pressure has yet to be applied.' Had I known you were the point person, I would have picked your brain instead of inserting myself into the equation. I had to call in a couple of favors to make it happen. But it's too late now. Know that this is in no way to be construed as me going behind your back." He looked at the ceiling tiles, thinking.

Harley raised his hands in mock surrender. "No worries, Captain. No blood, no foul. I just hope they didn't tie your hands like they did mine. This little prick needs some extra encouragement. Humiliation doesn't work. He's too vain."

Cade didn't go into the limitations put on him by President Clay. Instead, to ascertain how tight the spook's hands had been tied, he said, "Aside from the waterboarding and aural manipulation, what other techniques have you employed?"

Stripping off the rubber gloves, Harley said, "Mostly white. All of it having to do with depriving him of comfort. I keep him blindfolded most of the day. In between playing *Spit It Out* at maximum volume, I harass him verbally." He planted his hands on his hips and shook his head. "I'm forbidden from laying hands on him. Hell, this is a spa compared to *the* spa."

Cade said, "Gitmo?"

Harley nodded. "I spent a couple turns around the sun constantly going in and out of there."

"You Special Activities?"

Harley smiled. "I am now. Prior to 2005, I was in Fifth Group." He paused. "I'm no Cade Grayson, but I can hold my own." Adopting a more serious tone, he said, "I was tip of the spear in 2001. My ODA helped liberate Mazir. Later on, I spent time running ops with SAD in Iraq."

"So you were one of the horse soldiers of Task Force Dagger fame."

Harley said nothing.

Cade said, "You can neither confirm nor deny. I get it."

With a wink and a nod, Harley grabbed the knob and opened the door. Craning around the jamb, the spook said, "Sun … a dear old friend of yours has come to visit."

This got Jinlong's attention. Slowly, he placed his hands palm down on the table, lifted his gaze to match Cade's, and then cracked a wicked smile. The whole sequence made Cade think of that possessed doll in the B-grade eighties horror movie. All that was missing was the red mane and ridiculously large butcher knife. While he couldn't remember the title of the movie, he recalled the doll's name.

He got the impression *Chucky* was on the verge of some kind of mental breakdown. However, when in perfect English and with perfect syntax, Jinlong said, "You healed up quite nicely," the affect had left his face. There was no detectable stress in his voice, either. Schooled at Columbia University, before that last day in Saturday when the dead started to rise, the man had been a fixture at all the best parties in New York, Chicago, Los Angeles, and D.C. To say he was spliced into the mainline of power running through all of those cities would be a vast understatement.

Responding to the question, Cade said, "Good thing I wasn't dinged with a tainted round."

"Indeed," responded Jinlong, the smile returning. "At the time, that tactic was still in its infancy. No doubt it has been perfected by now."

In his head, Cade saw Lopez's slack face. One fragment was all it took. One fucking minor wound did him in. That was pretty damn *perfect* by anyone's account. Jaw clenched, he dragged a heavy oak chair across the room and positioned himself at the table across from the prisoner.

Refraining from making eye contact with the man across the table, Cade broke the seal and pulled from the pouch a thin manila envelope and a rugged military-issue Panasonic laptop. The envelope went on the table to his right. He flipped up the laptop's slim screen and pressed the Power button.

While the hard drive chirped and clicked and the screen flickered to life, Cade scooted the Pelican case along the floor with his foot until it was out of the way. As he did so, in his peripheral vision, he saw Jinlong tracking his every movement.

"What's in the box?"

Cade said, "Jumper cables … and a few other *tools*."

"Perhaps a cordless drill is hiding in there? Or, *maybe*, a reciprocating saw?"

False bravado, Cade thought. He made no immediate reply. Opening the folder so that only he could see its contents, he removed the lists taken from the dead PLA soldiers. He set the creased sheets of paper in front of the laptop. Finally, looking up and making eye contact, he said, "These are shopping lists. Why send regular army cadre out on scavenger hunts?" Before Jinlong could answer, Cade had pulled an eight-by-ten photograph from the folder and placed it on the table, in front of the open laptop, where Jinlong had to look at it. It was a headshot of a forty-something man. Perched on his head was a beret. The upper part of the man's dress uniform was awash in ribbons and medals. Eyes black as coal, he had that clenched-jaw thousand-yard stare going on.

"Captain Kai Zhen. He and his team killed a whole bunch of Americans. I know it was Zhen because a friend's phone had footage of him executing civilians. They killed all of the adults but spared the kids. For some reason, they took the kids with them." He paused and stared at the photo. "Why the kids and what part does Zhen play in all of this?"

"You barely missed meeting him." Jinlong steepled his fingers and smiled. "It seems that twice in one day, you were lucky."

Cade leaned away from the computer, put his hands on his lap, and said, "How's that?"

"In certain circles, Zhen is known as *Sishèn*. In English, he is called the Grim Reaper. If you and he had collided, you would have not been the one to walk away. You almost had him in your nation's former capital. He escaped minutes ahead of you and then went on to survive the Tomahawk barrage on the Chesapeake. He is a survivor."

"The kids?"

Jinlong smiled. It was that of a possessed Cheshire Cat.

Without warning, Cade swung a roundhouse right. It came from below the table's edge, cut a wide arc through the air, then caught Jinlong squarely on the left ear. To keep from rupturing the man's eardrum, Cade left his fingers splayed out. Still, the sneak attack knocked the smaller man halfway off his chair.

Jinlong's smile dissolved like a sand mandala in a gale. Blinking rapidly, he said, "Like I told the spook: Zhen is spearheading the offensive."

Cade had been staring at the prisoner's face, keeping watch for any micro-expressions. Tells that the man was not being truthful. Seeing a slight eye tick, Cade landed another blow, only this time it came in faster than the first, and from the left.

"I'm not Harley. I don't have to play by the same rules." He paused and took a deep breath. "You're lying to me," he went on. "If it continues, there will be severe consequences. What is Operation Blanket?"

Jinlong licked his lips. It was clear he was deliberating. Doing a cost-benefit analysis on the spot. After a few seconds of silence, he said, "The *shopping lists* are compiled of the items the scientists require to continue their work toward producing a cure for your so-called Omega virus."

Again Cade had been searching the man's face for any tell he was lying. This time the man had looked up and to his right as he answered. Whereas the tick was but a ripple on the pond of truth, the breaking of eye contact, combined with the direction his eyes had swept, was a full-on tsunami of deception.

Withholding any kind of physical response, Cade said, "You're still lying. To save us both the wasted time and you the pain I could bring if I opened my box and went to work on you with my tools, I'm going to show you exactly where you stand. Reveal to you irrefutable evidence of how shitty the cards you're holding really are. Spoiler alert: I'm holding the ace-high royal flush. You've got a pair of deuces. Jack high—at best."

Jinlong said nothing. He was busy opening and closing his mouth. Clearly, his bell had been rung by the blows to the head.

Turning the Panasonic around, Cade rose and moved to Jinlong's side of the table. Standing, he adjusted the screen so the glare from the overhead lights didn't interfere with the static beginning frame of the video clip he had just pulled up. Finished, he crouched next to the chair. Careful to remain outside of the cuffed prisoner's limited reach, Cade tapped the keys necessary to start the footage running.

The video was shot from a high-rise building in downtown Seattle. The Space Needle was to the left. Behind it, sparkling in the summer sun, was Elliott Bay. It was dotted with dozens of surface vessels in all different sizes and configurations.

Cade said, "This was filmed July the fourth. Our Independence Day. And that's a sizeable portion of your three combined fleets."

When the person filming from the overwatch position consulted their wristwatch, the camera inadvertently panned groundward. The two-second deviation revealed knots of zombies moving about the streets several stories below the spotter's perch. As the camera lens swept up and around, picked up on the periphery and bracketed by the Space Needle and water beyond was a sea of cement bristling with cranes. Lashed to the dock, each within easy reach of a crane of its own, was a trio of transport ships. Intermodal shipping containers, stacked three high and four deep to the dock's edge, were being transferred onto the transports' rust-streaked decks.

In the foreground, trucks motored from ship to ship, delivering personnel and offloading supplies at each stop.

Cade said, "Those are your people. They're resupplying your fleet with stolen goods."

Jinlong sat up straight. Looking in Cade's direction, he said, "Goods made in China and bought by you with money borrowed from China. Kind of ironic, don't you think?"

It took all Cade had in him to resist tearing the fucker's tongue from his throat. Instead, knowing what was about to happen, he reigned in the anger and stared at Jinlong. No way he wanted to miss the man's reaction to what was about to befall the fleet.

Out of nowhere, unseen projectiles bombarded the vessels. The battleships and cruisers offshore caught the opening salvo. Some were split in two and sank immediately. Others exploded and keeled over. The largest of the lot were struck but failed to sink. Their resistance to joining the rest in their watery graves lasted only as long as it took for the initial fires to reach their magazines.

The secondary explosions were biblical, the shockwaves and ensuing wall of flying debris sufficient to scythe through any smaller vessels anchored nearby.

Cade let the footage run for ninety seconds, then paused it with the image of the fleet's flagship dead center on the screen. All that was visible of the once-mighty vessel was about thirty or forty feet of its angular prow. It was jutting skyward and seconds from being lost from view forever. Strung from the bow, colorful semaphore contrasted sharply against the frothed water. Two sailors, their images blurred by motion, were in the process of abandoning ship.

Gesturing at the screen, Cade said, "That was Thor's Hammer."

"Kinetic space weapons are nothing new," Jinlong sneered. "And those are all acceptable losses. Losses that will not go unavenged."

Cade turned the laptop around so that the screen was facing him. He hovered the arrow over a file labeled *OPERATION RESILIENT EAGLE* and clicked it open. Inside was a list of video files. Sensing Jinlong's eyes on him, he clicked on the file labeled *DOOLITTLE* and started the footage rolling.

Turning the computer back toward Jinlong, Cade said, "Pearl Harbor. Honolulu, Hawaii. One week ago."

The footage was captured by a drone circling high over Battleship Row. Once home to the United States' Pacific Fleet, consisting of dozens of U.S. Navy surface ships, including Arleigh-Burke-class destroyers and a large contingent of Los-Angeles-class and Virginia-class nuclear submarines, Pearl's blue-green waters were now occupied by dozens of Chinese warships.

Opposite the ships of the PLA Navy's East fleet was the Arizona Memorial. Dwarfed by the enemy warships, the white marble viewing platform seemed to be hovering over the rusting hulk of the once-proud battleship. Cavernous circular housings where the main guns used to reside were clearly visible just underneath the calm surface. So too was the entire outline of what remained of the ship's top deck. Speaking to the quality of the drone's camera, in addition to revealing the underwater details in great clarity, it also picked up on the surface the rainbow shimmer of oil that had been leaking steadily from the ship since the day she was sunk.

Cade was standing up now and observing Jinlong as he watched the drone footage. The screen had the slight Asian's undivided attention.

A roar emanated from the speakers. It originated from something somewhere off-screen. It rose in volume for a split second, then was drowned out by a series of booms as the interloping fleet was rocked by explosions. Smoke roiled from the larger vessels at anchor in Battleship Row. A beat later, a second salvo rained down on the smaller corvettes and cruisers. On the heels of that came a third barrage that rocked the oilers and cargo ships, splitting their hulls and setting a majority of them on fire. Then, just like they had on that fateful December day in 1941, the attackers' aircraft winged over Pearl, screaming in from the east and dropping more munitions on the already crippled fleet.

It was over inside of two minutes. Half the fleet was at the bottom in the first minute. A matter of seconds later, the remainder was on their way to their final watery resting places.

As the drone that had captured it all was repositioning to a lower altitude in order to get an accurate battle damage assessment, its optics caught a flight of F-22 Raptors flash in from the right and dump their ordnance on the scores of tiny figures scurrying away from the growing conflagration.

Cade stopped the video. Closing the file, he said, "That doesn't leave the Motherland with much of a surface fleet. Hours after that attack, ninety percent of your submarine force suffered the same fate."

Retaining the air of invincibility, Jinlong said, "We have millions more survivors than you. Our dry docks are operational. Keels have already been laid and materials assembled. We will make your Greatest Generation's Liberty Ship operation look like child's play. Come the new year, we will be assembling the fleet that will put the stake in your country's heart. This time next year, America will cease to exist. I may not be alive to see it, but mark my words, the Chinese flag *will* fly over your new capital."

Face devoid of emotion, Cade said, "I had a feeling that would be your reply." He pulled up some stills of the shipbuilding facilities. They were taken by a passing KH-11 satellite. Even from space, it was clear all of the massive dry docks were submerged, never to rise again thanks to explosives planted below the waterline by industrious teams of Navy SEALs.

"All the keels your people laid are now underwater," Cade said. "Your dry docks have more holes in them than a colander. Though you can't see the damage in these stills, our boots on the ground, working with a lot of C4, rendered all of your assembled materials useless."

If the first two revelations hadn't let the wind from Jinlong's sails—at least outwardly, where Cade could see it—this one did the trick.

"What is Operation Blanket?"

The general hung his head but said nothing.

Cade said, "Nobody is coming to get you." He clicked on another video file. Started the footage running.

Jinlong stared at the screen. Perked up at once.

"I figured you'd recognize the compound. Keep watching. We know the location of every one of them. Their coordinates are logged. Should Thor's Hammer not decimate your family, should the strike somehow fail to erase your entire lineage from the face of the earth—kids and all—the SEAL teams who destroyed your shipbuilding facilities, well, they're eagerly awaiting the call to finish the job."

Defeated, Jinlong dropped his gaze to the table.

Cade took hold of his chin and yanked his head up. Staring daggers into the prisoner's eyes, he said, "Omega took my wife. Took more people I loved than I can count on one hand. I wish I was with those SEALs. I'd love nothing more than to personally take from you what you've taken from me. Taken from us. Every one of those pipe hitters on the ground in your country has lost their entire families to

Omega. Now, last chance to tell me the truth. The whole truth and nothing but the truth."

As Jinlong began to speak, Cade focused his entire attention on looking for deception. Through the entire confession, he detected none.

"We're done here," Cade said. "I can't wait to attend your execution."

Without another word, he policed up the pictures and laptop, stacked it all atop the Pelican case, then called for Harley to open the door.

Chapter 28

No sooner had Cade called to be let out of the interview room than Harley was opening the door and stepping aside. It was almost as if the man had been pressing his ear to the other side of the door. Shooting holes into Cade's premise was the half-eaten package of Nacho Cheese Doritos clutched in the CIA man's hand. Kind of hard to eavesdrop while chomping on corn chips.

Licking his fingers, Harley said, "You weren't in there very long. What'd you extract from him?"

Cade set the Pelican case on the floor and closed the door behind him. Gunning up, he said, "Everything I needed to know."

Incredulous, Harley said, "What's in that box of yours? Black Widow spiders? A couple of rattlesnakes?"

Smiling, Cade said, "Nope." He popped the top on the Pelican case. Inside was an assortment of tools, jumper cables, several cans of aerosolized liquid tire sealer, a multitude of automotive lubricants in all different-sized containers, Maglite flashlight, wool blanket, bottled water, and an assortment of MREs. "The box was just for show." Adopting a more serious tone, he went on, saying, "Clay forbid me from putting the screws to him. I did slap him around a little to soften him up. Ultimately, what did the trick was the threat of DEVGRU shooters snuffing out his entire family line."

Harley stomped his feet and spun a tight circle.

To Cade, the unexpected outburst looked like a drunken clown trying to perform a Cherokee war dance.

Harley said, "I need to add that to my repertoire. Torture them with their own imagination. Priceless, Captain Grayson. Consider me in awe."

Cade lifted the case off the floor. Looking to edge past the spook, he said, "Be my guest. But do it later because I do need to get going."

Harley remained in Cade's path. "C'mon, man. What'd Baby Bird regurgitate?"

Cade said, "Need to know. Sorry."

Harley nodded. "Understood. Where's your ride?"

"Back in the District."

"Can I give you a lift? Or do you have Marine One on speed dial?"

Cade said, "I didn't ask for the ride. It was wholly unexpected."

"Come on," Harley pressed. "Let me give you a lift. Sergeant Croswell can hold the fort down. Baby Bird is going nowhere. I'll turn on some mood music and leave the two of them alone." He looked over his shoulder, then added, "If I'm seen at the gate with you riding shotgun in my rig, my stock with the single ladies will go through the roof. Hell, last night at FU-BAR, demand for Señor Gregory was lukewarm, at best. Getting laid in the District is nearly an impossible task. With the ratio of men to women survivors who have been showing up lately, the place has become a sausage fest."

Smiling inwardly, Cade said, "First, I need to brief General Nash. Can you stand by?"

Throwing his hands up, Harley said, "As long as it takes. Thanks to you, my job here is done. At least until the next VIP comes through the door."

"What are you going to do with all the downtime?"

Harley feigned like he was stepping up to the tee and lining up a golf shot. On the front end of the exaggerated practice swing, he said, "Work on my handicap." After the follow-through, he held the pose—arms up, imaginary club still gripped tight—and added, "Eat your heart out, Tiger Woods."

Cade really didn't get the allure of golf. He'd heard it described as a "good walk spoiled." Made sense to him. Chasing a tiny white ball all over hell and gone wasn't his idea of fun. But he did get the gist of what a handicap was. And seeing as how the course looked as if it had seen regular upkeep, he figured Harley's handicap had to be commensurate with his prowess as a groundskeeper. Still, Cade wasn't in the least bit curious to know the specifics.

Time was of the essence and slipping away at a mighty clip.

Accepting the ride, Cade said, "I needed to be oscar mike five minutes ago. And this Pelican case isn't getting any lighter."

Tossing a ring full of keys atop the case, Harley said, "Give me thirty seconds to tuck Baby Bird in for the night. I'll catch up with you at my rig."

The drive from the detention facility to the glass and steel building housing the offices of the 75th Space Wing was a short one. Leaving his rifle and Pelican case in Harley's care, Cade trapped the laptop and folder under one arm, then shouldered open the Mercedes' armored door.

He entered the building through the front doors. Airman Alvarez looked up from whatever she had been doing. She smiled when she saw him.

"I hear Nash is in this time."

"That she is," confirmed Alvarez, hand going for the phone.

Cade put a hand up. "Don't bother. She's expecting me." A lie. He didn't want his visit to be able to be verified by the call log.

Smile fading, Alvarez handed Cade a clipboard and pen. "Better sign in."

Smiling, Cade said, "Pretend I was never here," and strolled past Alvarez's post. Though he could feel her eyes on him, he didn't turn around. Just kept on walking.

Acting on Harley's insistence that he "take his time," he did just that. He needed a couple of minutes free from the spook's nonstop commentary to formulate how he was going to break the horrific news to Nash. Whether he'd soft-peddle the intel or just lay it all out on the table. No matter the approach he chose, what Jinlong had divulged could never be shared by electronic means. Nor could it be put into written word. Information this sensitive had to be delivered mouth to ear between people with only the highest clearances. For if it passed by the wrong ears or got in front of the wrong eyes, the panic it would whip up among New District's already twitchy population could start a mass exodus. Not only that, should word spread among the growing populations of the six other fledgling cities spread out across the West and Midwest, the president's dream of reconstituting the United States could be dealt a deathblow—both literally and figuratively.

Navigating the warren of hallways from memory, Cade found Nash's office. Though a shade was drawn down over the window glass, a thin sliver of light shone around its edges. He knocked lightly on the wood frame, took a step back, then removed his ball cap.

The door sucked inward, and General Freda Nash invited him in. She was a head shorter than him, but she carried herself as if she had no idea. Her hair was cut into a short bob. Once dark as a raven's feathers, it was now streaked with gray. No doubt the drastic change was a byproduct of a war being fought on multiple fronts.

Cade nodded. "General Nash."

She nodded at him. Her eyes were glassy. She said, "I'm so sorry to hear about Lopez. He was a favorite of mine. Always so sweet."

Looking her in the eye, Cade said, "We all have one with our name on it. Happened to be his time." Getting a bit misty-eyed, he paused and pinched the tears away. "He had a proper sendoff. Twenty-one gun salute. And I hear they poured a lot of tequila out for him."

"No doubt Low Rider is smiling down on us as we speak." She pointed to the chair squared up before her desk. All business, she said, "Have a seat, Wyatt."

He placed the laptop and folder on her blotter, then sat on the offered chair.

Nash remained on her feet. She said, "Did you color inside the lines?"

"Mostly. I slapped him around a bit."

"Did he break?"

Cade nodded.

"Please tell me he spilled something other than the spring offensive mantra of his." She paused for a beat, then said, "Did he know anything about Operation Blanket?"

"He broke. At first, he fed me a line about it having to do with some kind of a cure for Omega. He was lying."

Tapping a finger on the desk blotter, she said, "Go on."

"Turns out they're working on a bioweapon. Operation Blanket is what they're calling the distribution phase."

"What are they planning?"

"He doesn't know the details. Our op in Portland disrupted a meeting between the lead scientist and Captain Zhen. Zhen was there to finalize plans for a mission he was to head up. A mission back to mainland China. I also brought up the empty biohazard canister we took from the Eplot raid." He shook his head. "Jinlong didn't know a thing about it."

"So if Blanket is a go," she said, "that must mean the mission to the Motherland was a success."

Cade nodded. "Zhen and his Cobras were to be choppered to the lab in Wuhan. Same lab Omega escaped from. But Omega wasn't the only program they were working on. They had two other weapons on the shelves. Both flu based. Both are highly contagious and airborne. One is a slow burn. They were going to introduce it to our population. The theory was it would spread rapidly, and our hospitals would quickly become overwhelmed. We'd run out of beds. Then our hospitals and care centers would run out of protective gear. To combat all of this, we would lock the country down. That would eventually bring us to our knees economically."

Nash uncrossed her arms. Face a mask of concern, she asked, "And the second weapon? How is it different?"

"It's very deadly but not yet perfected. The objective was to bring the samples here—"

"Where they could replicate one or the other," Nash interrupted. "I'd bet the house it's the latter. And that means if they're going ahead with Blanket—which is one hell of a sick name for the op, especially considering how smallpox was introduced to the Native Americans—then the mission was successful."

Cade said, "That wasn't lost on me. The fact they're enacting Blanket tells me that they have a stockpile ready for delivery and are operational, or they're real close and will be pulling the trigger real soon."

Nash pounded her fist on the desk. "If only your team would have infilled at OMSI thirty minutes later. You would have rolled them all up in one fell swoop."

"But we didn't," Cade stressed. "It's never that easy."

She crossed her arms. "So Zhen is also involved in Operation Blanket?"

Cade nodded. "I showed Jinlong the footage your guys extracted from Sheriff MacLeod's phone. He fingered Zhen as the executioner." In his mind's eye, Cade saw the horrific scene playing out. Nearly two dozen Bear River survivors kneeling on the centerline of the town's main drag. They were blindfolded, arms flex-cuffed behind their backs. Though the sheriff had been a block or so away, filming the atrocity from a less than optimal angle, it was clear to Cade that the main antagonist was, in fact, the Cobra squad commander. Treating the prisoners as if they were dogs, Zhen walked the line, calmly firing a pistol from point-blank range into the back of each of their heads. Face flushed red, Cade said, "I don't know how Bear Lake fits in with Blanket. You'd think at the time MacLeod shot that, Zhen and company were still putting the pieces in place."

Nash made a face. "How does what Zhen did at Bear River fit in with the activity at the Bear Lake airport? What was the helicopter doing there? Why wasn't Zhen among the dead? Why kill everyone there, including the sheriff?"

"I don't know. What I do know," Cade stressed, "is that once the weapon is perfected—"

Nash said, "By perfected, you mean aerosolized?"

"That I don't know for sure," Cade acknowledged. "And neither does Jinlong. His tells are very easy to read. Ask the right questions, his face answers before he can formulate the lie."

"So what do you think?" she asked, face full of concern. "What's your takeaway?"

"I took *perfected* to mean they want to get the bug to a point where it's as nasty as possible. Very virulent and with a high mortality rate."

Nash tapped a beat on the table blotter. "So why not use the folks as guinea pigs instead of killing them?"

Cade said, "Zhen wasn't wearing a mask in the footage from Bear River. Means he wasn't handling dangerous biological material. Then there's the dead PLA soldiers at Bear Lake. None of them were masked up. Tells me it's highly likely they weren't transporting the weapon in the downed Harbin. All put together, I think they're getting close but aren't quite there yet."

Nash shook her head. "Too many unanswered questions. I don't like it." Drawing a deep breath, she said, "Let's talk dispersal."

"Aerosol delivery makes the most sense," Cade proffered. "Less moving parts. That way, they only have to be exposed to the bug one time."

"So what's the delivery method?"

"I'm thinking drones," Cade replied. "The operator would be able to do his thing while maintaining a nice standoff distance."

Nash looked at the ceiling. After a moment of contemplation, she leveled her gaze at Cade. "A few days ago they were still working those shopping lists, right?"

Cade nodded. "No reason to be carrying them around if they weren't still actively searching for items on those lists."

Nash cocked her head. "Which could mean they're still trying to get a handle on how they're going to transport the weapon without getting their own people sick."

Sounding hopeful, Cade said, "Then we may still have time to catch them prepping for the attack."

"Question is, where are they staging? Likely they'll choose somewhere near the targets, but still far away enough they can work without drawing attention to their operation. And I'd bet they would need a lab to prep the agent."

"Do you have a map?"

Nash pulled a map of the United States from her filing cabinet. Spreading it out on her desk, she said, "We know New District has got to be their main target. It's the most populated of the upstart communities. Do you think they're targeting the others?"

"I would if I were them," Cade said, matter-of-factly. "I'd hit Bastion as well."

Nash drew in a deep breath. Exhaling, she said, "I'll get the analysts working up probable locations close to target cities."

"What's the satellite situation?" Cade asked.

She shook her head. "Not good. All available birds are providing overwatch out over the Pacific and South China Sea. Our Pacific Fleet … or what's left of it, is busy chasing down the squirters from the Pearl attack."

"If we're going in blind," Cade stressed, "we're going to need as many teams as you can round up."

"We're kind of stretched thin in that department, too." Nash lifted her gaze from the map. "Smokey has a couple of ODAs out replacing sensors in the gap between Fountain and Pueblo. Another is pulling security for the Eplot operation. Keating has all but two of his SEAL teams pulling security for the crews out reconning the Gulf Coast refineries."

"We'll just have to make do with what we have on hand," Cade said. "Time is *not* on our side."

"Agreed," said Nash. "I'll get Lee and Smokey on a conference call and bring them up to speed."

"What about my team?" Cade asked. "They're still serving Smokey's mandatory forty-eight-hour stand-down."

She said, "Put them on rapid-ready status. I'll start getting SOAR assets lined up. Call me direct if anything else strikes you."

Cade rose. "Thanks again for setting up the meeting with POTUS."

"How'd it go?"

"I was amazed you managed to wrangle me the face time with her. And with such short notice. To be honest, your call caught me flat-footed." He tapped his chest. "Not sure how the concert shirt went over with her."

"Doubt if she even noticed your attire. That woman is being pulled in a thousand different directions."

"She mentioned her VP issue," Cade divulged. "Hinted I might be in the running."

"She told me. Said you blanched at the prospect. I guess you're the one who needs to work on your tells."

"Politics is not my wheelhouse. You should know that by now."

"That I do." She rapped her knuckles on the blotter.

Taking that as a sign they were done here, Cade said, "I'll be standing by."

Rising from her chair, Nash asked if he needed a ride.

"Thanks, but no. Greg Harley is going to run me back to the District."

"God speed, then. Keep in touch, Wyatt."

Chapter 29

New District - Two Days Later

Head up, gaze locked on the bars of midmorning light painting the living room wall, Raven struggled to knock down the last of her daily push-ups. Having recently upped her regimen from fifty to seventy-five, the final ten or so were still especially taxing. Which had been the case when she transitioned from twenty-five to fifty a day. But she knew it would get easier the longer she stuck with it. Whether it be gaining upper body strength, learning a new language, or honing her firearms proficiency—hard work paid huge dividends. It was a good lesson learned from her father. Never the quitter, arms quivering, she persevered, pushing through the last five, teeth gritted and snarling out the count.

Finished, a satisfying burn radiating from deep within her arm and chest muscles, she rolled over onto her back and powered through a hundred sit-ups. No problem at all on this front. Raven had developed a firm set of abs and, according to Sasha, was on her way to getting "ripped"—whatever that meant.

The sit-ups took her all of three minutes. As she lay there on her back to cool down, her mind raced over the events of the last few days. That the riders had, in fact, been there on the road the other day wasn't as troubling to her as the revelation their ammunition may have been tainted with the zombie virus. While getting shot was a survivable affair—her father being the actual living proof of that—the CCP scumbags had just turned all of that upside down. A big part of knowing each bullet could lead to becoming a zombie—a consequence worse than death—was the fear it instilled. Which her father had said was likely the main reason the PLA soldiers were adopting the new tactic. Let the masses know that not only could a zombie bite transfer Omega, but now, so could every one of the enemy invaders. And seeing as how there was no way to know how many of their troops were using the tainted bullets, her father had stressed to her that going forward, she was to act as if they all were.

Remembering the food cooking on the stove, she popped up off the floor and dashed into the kitchen.

Upstairs in the Grayson home, Cade stood underneath the showerhead and let the weak, tepid stream splash his newly clean-shaven face. Having slept in, a first for him in a long while, he felt a little groggy. It was as if he'd been drugged, his brain wrapped in gauze.

Turning the knob from Hot to Cold, he spun a half-circle and let the ice-cold water patter against his neck and back for a full minute. It was just what he needed. When he cut the water off, his head was clear of cobwebs.

It had been two days since the meeting with the president. He was beginning to grow impatient. Right there and then, he decided, reaching for the towel, that if he didn't receive the call before noon, he was going to drive to Peterson and start rattling cages.

Parting the curtain, the unease of not knowing where the mission stood but a dull ache in the back of his head, he stepped from the shower. Instantly, the smell of something cooking downstairs hit his nose. While he couldn't determine what was about to hit his belly, where breakfast in the zombie apocalypse was concerned, Raven did not disappoint.

He toweled off and dressed quickly in MultiCam fatigue pants and black tee. He laced up his Danner boots and strapped on his Glock and Gerber. Snatching the Thuraya sat-phone off his nightstand, he double-checked the volume level, then stowed it away in a cargo pocket.

"What's for breakfast?" he called, clomping down the stairs two at a time.

"Brunch," she corrected. "Something special coming up. Give me five."

Perfect, he thought, dropping to his knees. He spent the five minutes knocking out his own daily regimen of push-ups and sit-ups.

Raven was just placing plates on the small table when Cade entered the kitchen. She was moving much better than she had been the day before. He said, "How's the tailbone?"

Grimacing, she said, "Better. The Motrin helps to keep the pain down. I'll live."

"Don't overdo it with those things. A little goes a long way for someone of your size."

"Quarter of a pill every four hours. With food, of course. Speaking of food," she said with a smile, "yours is on the table and getting cold."

Taking a seat and arranging a napkin on his lap, he looked down at his plate. Staring up at him was thinly sliced pan-fried Spam, a biscuit left over from dinner the night before, and eggs. Only the eggs weren't the usual powdered variety that, when reconstituted and cooked, ended up a barely edible yellow goop on the plate. On the contrary, these eggs were the real deal. And they were cooked sunny side up—just how he liked them. He grabbed his fork and stabbed one. Like lava from a miniature volcano, the yolk, bright yellow and viscous, came sluicing out. Incredulous, he asked, "Where did you find fresh eggs?"

"Lola's." She smiled. "I'm a *preferred* customer. She sets some things aside for me. From now on, I'll be getting a dozen a week."

Cade set his fork and knife down. "Lola has *laying* hens?"

"A whole coop full of them. It's pretty ingenious how she set it up. She's strung chicken wire between the back of her store and the outer wall. Used sheets of wood for the roof and walls. They seem happy in there. She's also got roosters and is hoping to get eggs incubating." She smiled and rubbed her hands together. "I'm on the shortlist for baby chicks."

Cade picked up his service and wolfed down one of the eggs. Wiping his lips, he said in Mandarin, "Where did she get chickens?"

Answering in Mandarin, Raven said, "From a woman." Switching to English, she added, "She said a newcomer was pulling a trailer full of them. You should see Lola's. She's now got *two* double-wide trailers. And they're both packed to the ceiling with everything you can think of."

After savoring the second egg, eating it in four separate bites, each morsel bookended by a square of Spam, he said, "Does she have any Snickers bars?"

Raven took a drink of powdered milk. Shaking her head, she said, "All sold out. Candy bars are high up on her procurement list. Right up there with cigarettes, batteries, and ammunition." She took a folded sheet of paper from off the windowsill. "Here's her newest list. That pocket of Zs you mentioned yesterday. Think there are some homes on those cul-de-sacs that aren't already pillaged?"

He pushed his plate away. It was all he could do to keep from picking it up and licking it clean. Looking across the table, he said, "I'm certain the 4th ID cleared them of Zs. Whether they've been ransacked, no way to tell from the air. Marine One was moving at a pretty good pace. There were *hundreds* of Zs, though. Just go there for the ears. Anything else you come across is gravy."

Pouting, Raven said, "You're not coming? We haven't had a father/daughter outing in almost a month."

"I'm on rapid recall. So I can't stray far from home. Until we have a clearer picture of some *things* that are going on, Command wants me tethered to the Thuraya."

Raven cleared their plates. Returning to the table, she said, "Can you tell your only daughter what's going on? The redacted version, at least?"

"I can't, sweetie. I would if I could." Switching gears, he said, "Nash had her people take another look at your video. They applied every technique in the book. But since the footage was so jittery, and the riders were in the shade, they couldn't glean anything new. That being said, when you do go back out, forget everything I said about assuming. It's fine this time around. In fact, I encourage it. Assume there are Chinese scouts operating in the area. Keep your head on a swivel and your eyes and ears open."

"What I find strange is that none of us heard them." She paused, thinking. "Then again, the Zs knew we were there and were smacking into Wendy's truck. Fingernails scraping the fenders." She threw a hard shiver. "You know … that high-pitched sound you can't unhear."

Cade nodded in agreement. That cringe-inducing nails-on-a-chalkboard sound was second only to that of a skull popping. He said, "Even if Wendy's truck hadn't been under assault, it's highly likely you wouldn't have heard their motorcycles. For one, they were blocks away. I've seen one of those bikes up close. They muffle the exhaust. Makes it real hard to hear even if it's right on top of you."

"If I do decide to go outside the wire," she said, "I'll be with Daymon and Duncan. Should be easy to get one of them to drive if I offer to pay for the gas."

Cade was about to make a quip about there not being enough ears in the world for him to put up with the Odd Couple's constant bickering when the Thuraya came to life. Snatching the phone from his pocket, he viewed its illuminated screen. *Nash.*

Raven said, "Is this the one?"

Cade nodded. Activating the call, he said, "This is Cade."

Nash announced herself, then said, "You better be sitting down."

Cade knew a response was not necessary. He spent a couple of minutes listening and taking notes as Nash rattled off times, locations, and who was going where.

After questioning her thinking on a couple of points and formally adding his thoughts on the matter, he ended the call and tucked the notes and phone away in a pocket.

"You're leaving?"

"Ask me in Mandarin."

Raven complied.

"Yes, I am," he replied in Mandarin. Switching to English, he said, "When I get back, I expect you to be able to recite the Pledge of Allegiance in Mandarin."

Not quite sure if he was joking or not, she stood and hugged him real tight. Pulling back, she assured him that her sat-phone and long-range radio were both fully charged and that from now on, she would be taking them everywhere she went.

"Getting stuck outside the wire without them was a lesson you won't soon forget."

She made a face. "Won't happen again," she promised.

Cade said, "I'll have mine on me. If you get into any trouble, anything at all, I want you to call me right away. If I don't answer, it's because I can't, not that I'm ignoring the call. That happens, you call General Nash. She'll know what to do." He kissed her on the cheek. "And remember, I don't want you doing anything I wouldn't do."

Smiling, she said, "Me? Daddy's little girl." She shook her head. "Never."

Cade scooped his keys off the counter and thanked Raven for the stellar meal. On the heels of that, he added, "And make sure Duncan is taking good care of Max. I kind of miss that rascal."

"Duncan or Max?"

Cade shook his head. Had to hand it to his girl. She was developing a pretty good sense of humor. Which he found quite impressive, seeing as how much adversity she had faced over so short a time. Answering her quip, he said, "I meant Max. But you might as well go ahead and give Old Man a scratch behind the ears. Tell him it's from me."

Handing him a biscuit for the road, she said, "Stay frosty out there."

He grabbed his pack off the hook in the hall, then retrieved his M4 from the under-stair cubby. Gripping the doorknob, he turned to face her. "You too, Bird. Love you."

Raven locked the door behind her father, then peeled back the blackout curtain and watched him load his gear in Black Beauty and get behind the wheel. As she dropped the curtain, the noise of the big V-10 firing reached her ears. She was lacing her boots before the rumble of the retreating vehicle had fully dissipated.

Gathering her gear and rifle, she called Duncan on the Thuraya. When he didn't pick up, she left him a message, telling him she had an offer he couldn't refuse and that she was coming over.

At the East Gate, precipitated by Nash's advance call, the guards waved Cade around a line of vehicles waiting to be allowed outside the wire. In his side vision, he detected a couple of angry glares. In the rearview mirror, he spotted someone in a jacked-up pickup flipping him the bird. *Things never change.*

As the gate parted to allow the F-650 passage, two Marines in full battle rattle walked ahead of it, their weapons sweeping the handful of twice-dead zombie corpses waiting to be policed up by the teens and young adults pulling wall duty.

The recent culling of the combined herds had had a severe impact on overnight accumulation, the headcount plunging from a couple of hundred to fifty or less.

There were very few ears to go around.

Cade saw that the midmorning accumulation had also cratered. As he drove through the gate, the cleanup crew was hard at work to the left and right, collecting ears and dragging bodies. Today's noon bounty looked to be, at most, around two dozen.

Once the Marines moved off to the side of the road, one of them raised a gloved hand and waved Cade on. Tromping the pedal, he thanked them with a single toot of his horn.

Cade was rolling up to Peterson five minutes after leaving the East Gate behind. The entry had been fortified with a new layer of Jersey barriers since he'd been here last. To the right of the rolling gate was a Stryker armored vehicle. The commander, a red-faced soldier who looked to be in his late twenties, protruded from the open cupola hatch.

The gate guard, a young female airman, walked the thirty feet from the guard shack. Though her pace was leisurely, everything about her body language screamed high alert. As she drew to within spitting range of Black Beauty, she wrinkled her nose at the sight of the blood- and detritus-streaked front bumper and grille guard.

Asking for his credentials, she stepped back from the driver's door and gave them a thorough looking over. While that was going on, a second airman walked around the pickup, inspecting the undercarriage with a mirror on a six-foot pole.

Finished, the female airman handed back his credentials. "You're good to go, Captain."

Though he knew the answer, Cade asked, "Why the extra security layer?"

"We received a credible terrorist threat."

Pocketing his identification, Cade said, "Better to be safe than sorry. Stay frosty."

"Thank you, sir. You too."

Driving onto base, Cade glanced down the flight line. More than a dozen black aircraft sat nose to tail before the trio of hangars used by Task Force 160. Front and center was Jedi One. Behind the Ghost Hawk sat the pair of Stealth Chinooks. Next was a half dozen CH-47 Chinooks, which were less angular than the stealth models. Bringing up the rear was a number of V-22 Ospreys, the massive rotors atop their upturned nacelles casting long shadows across the tarmac.

At first blush, it looked like the makings of a scene straight out of Black Hawk Down, but as he drove around back and parked the F-650 amongst the multitude of other personal vehicles, he began to suspect that instead of one combined assault on the target General Nash had pointed to as being the most likely to bear fruit, her briefing was going to reveal a day filled with a whole bunch of small, surgical strikes, each carried out by a single team.

The Bunker was so crowded with operators that Cade had to wend his way past bodies to get to the Pale Riders' team cage.

The massive table in the center of the room was covered with so much gear and ammunition that the carved inlay was entirely concealed from view. Smokey's ashtray sat on the table, too. The man was nowhere to be found.

The entire team had beaten Cade to the cage. To a man, they were clad in tan desert camouflage fatigues. Axe was busy stowing his long gun in its custom Pelican case. Nearby, Nat was perched on the front of a folding chair and running a towel over his weapon. Huddled together in a corner, Griff and Cross stopped loading magazines long enough to acknowledge Cade with a thumbs-up.

All of his men radiated a cool energy, their every movement precise and measured. The jovial atmosphere that usually preceded every foray into harm's way was nowhere to be found.

It was clear Lopez's death had left a void, not only in the team room but also in every one of their hearts.

Clearing his throat, Cade said, "Lopez left each one of you something in his will. Each item was small and of a personal nature. You'll find them in your top cubby."

Finished burying Lopez, Cade had ended up here, every nerve in his body numbed by grief, and had read the fallen man's death letter. After locating the items Low Rider had bequeathed to his teammates, Cade had sat down and cleaned and oiled his weapons. He had also topped off his magazines and stuffed them into his chest rig. Now, all he needed to do was replace batteries, throw on his desert fatigues, and then don his armor and chest rig.

Scanning faces, he added, "Briefing in ten. A couple of you need to spend five of that trimming your beards. All of you need to dig out your M50 masks and give them a thorough looking over. We'll be needing them where we're going." The latter instruction could have gone unsaid. The men were professionals. He was just doing what he had learned from Cowboy—dotting i's and crossing t's.

Ignoring the grumbling, mostly coming from Griff, whose beard was an unruly thicket, Cade grabbed his kit and headed for the flight line.

Chapter 30

Peterson Air Force Base

Cade and his team stowed their gear and weapons aboard Jedi One, then commandeered a pair of Cushman carts from the 160th SOAR hangar and ripped over to the steel and glass building housing the 21st Space Wing.

The team surrendered their sidearms and edged weapons to an MP at the door. After passing through magnetometers, they grabbed bottled waters off a nearby table and hustled down the main hallway, four abreast, like a herd of wildebeest just escaped from the zoo.

Making the tactical operations center with ten minutes to spare, the entire team grabbed folding chairs stacked near the door and positioned themselves, backs to the wall, behind a long table at the rear of the massive low-ceilinged room.

Due to dozens of computers humming away on desks occupied by uniformed airmen, the phalanx of oversized flat-panel monitors on the walls fronting the room, and the multitude of aviators and operators packed in like sardines, it was nearly as hot inside as it was outside. And that was saying something, seeing as how the noontime temperature was already flirting with ninety degrees.

Cade scooted his chair closer to the table, opened the briefing folder Smokey had handed him on the way in, and started reading.

The first paragraph confirmed Cade's suspicion that the various teams would be going in several different directions. Operation Rising Storm would have a shotgun start.

Nearly thirty labs with biosafety ratings of three and above dotted the nine states closest to New District. Special attention was given to identifying the labs in the six states abutting Colorado, assigning highest priority to those nearest the new capital.

Thumbing through the packet, he learned that Green Beret A-Teams from Group 19 out of Camp Williams in Draper, Utah were to secure the four Bio Safety Level 3 labs in greater Salt Lake City. The teams were already being choppered down the Wasatch front in a pair of CH-47 Chinooks. They were to be infilled south of Salt Lake City, where they would split up and ride silenced Kawasaki dirt bikes onward to their respective targets.

The staged Ospreys would launch first, each bird carrying a SEAL team tasked with securing one of five targets in Arizona and Montana, with Team 6 drawing the Rocky Mountain Laboratories BSL-4 facility in Hamilton, Montana.

Though the tiltrotor Ospreys were much faster than the stealth helos, necessary calculations had been made to ensure the first wave of assaults took place simultaneously.

While the SEALs were en route aboard Ospreys, ODAs from 10th Group would be transported north from New District aboard the pair of Stealth Chinooks. One team was assigned the BSL-3 lab in Denver. The second team was scheduled to arrive simultaneously in Fort Collins to secure the state's only other Level 3 lab.

Lastly, Cade pored over the page listing the labs to which his team had been assigned. Instantly he saw that his earlier protestations during the phone conversation with Nash had been ignored. Instead of first killing two birds with one stone—the pair of BSL-3 labs in Albuquerque, New Mexico—she had given Los Alamos National Laboratories top billing. It had big-name recognition. Cade understood her thinking. And that was exactly why he had argued against it being the first on the list. It was too obvious. Plus, it wasn't even a Level 4 lab.

Swallowing the bitter pill, he turned his attention to the admiral approaching the podium at the front of the room. After the SEAL commander concluded his briefing, Smokey would be stepping up to brief the teams under his command. Which was a good thing because by then Cade figured he would be a little less hot under the collar and slightly more receptive to his commander's point of view.

***

Admiral Keating's briefing to his SEALs lasted all of ten minutes. Eschewing the PowerPoint crap so many of the higher-ups favored, he had basically gone over the team assignments and then capped it all off with a Sun Tzu quote.

Once the SEALs and Osprey aircrews had filed out of the room, Smokey stowed his unlit stogie in a pocket and strode to the lectern.

After looking the remaining teams over, he said, "My gut tells me the bastards are staging out of one of your targets. You're all professionals. You don't need me to wax inspirational. That being said, let's snuff them out before they have a chance to go operational. Dismissed."

160th SOAR Flight Line

The Ospreys were spooled up and about to launch by the time Cade and the rest of the Pale Riders rolled onto the tarmac aboard their Cushman carts.

Ari and Haynes were aboard the Ghost Hawk, no doubt going over call signs and refueling schedules. Skip, helmet visor down and with the grinning-skull mask obscuring the rest of his face, was busy giving his bird her usual pre-flight inspection.

Without warning, the roar of ten Rolls-Royce turboshaft engines rose in unison. With the mechanical cacophony reaching an ear-splitting crescendo, the five birds lifted straight up from the sun-scorched tarmac. Then, as if performing some kind of aerial ballet, beginning with the lead ship, twin nacelles tilted forward, massive rotor blades bit the hot high-plains air, and, one by one, each bird picked up enough forward momentum to begin to transition from vertical to level flight.

One moment the five marvels of human engineering were seemingly defying all the rules of physics; the next, the thunderous display was over, the Ospreys but black specks on the eastern horizon.

Since the mission timeline dictated that Jedi One was to be next to last to launch, Cade took the time scribbling out *the* letter. Finished, he ran it to one of the maintainers in the SOAR hangar, leaving the man with explicit instructions on what to do with it should he not return from the mission. He was going to tackle writing the death letter this morning, but that had been derailed by Nash's unexpected call. Like stuffing all his emotions and thoughts into the imaginary lockbox in his heart, it was one of the rituals he never failed to complete. It was also the hardest of them to do.

Walking back to the awaiting helo, he said a prayer that Raven would never have to read those heartfelt words.

He was almost to Jedi One when, with a whoosh and subtly rising whine, the turbines aboard the pair of Stealth Chinooks bound for Denver and Fort Collins flared to life. By the time he was clambering aboard the Ghost Hawk, the rotors atop the hulking stealth helos were a blur of motion. While he was taking his seat and didn't witness the first helo launch, the sudden rise of the tell-tale harmonic vibration produced by the baffled rotors told him it was happening.

Peering out the left-side window, he witnessed the twin-rotor bird skimming the tarmac nearby. Then, conducting a maneuver belying its size, it popped up over the fencing on Peterson's northeast corner, made a shallow left turn, and thundered off north by east, a diagonal tack that would see it to Fort Collins.

Seconds later, the Stealth Chinook bound for Denver launched. It skimmed the tarmac in the wake of the first. Once it cleared the base perimeter, it nosed hard around and shot off on a north by west heading.

Once silence had returned to the tarmac, Nat said, "Who's the baby-faced newbie?" He reached across the troop compartment and ran his gloved hand over Griff's clean-shaven face.

Snapped out of his catnap, Griff lashed out. Grabbing Nat's wrist in a vice-like grip, he said, "His name's gonna be *whoopass* if you pull that crap again."

Axe said, "So why'd you go the Brazilian route, mate? Wouldn't just a wee trim of the whiskers have sorted things?"

Releasing Nat's hand, Griff said, "Damn mask is like one of those alien face-huggers. No matter what I did, I couldn't get it to seal around my beard. And I did try a *wee trim*, first. Just made me look like a retarded lumberjack. So I went with this." He looked around the cabin and made a show of stroking his bare chin. "You bastards should be thanking me. Very few people have seen this *beeeautiful* mug."

Axe said, "Thanks for the visual, mate. But what makes you think a face-hugger would French kiss you?"

Piling on, Nat said, "I know, right. Tell us the truth, Griff. When's the last time you pulled a honey from the FU-BAR?"

Shooting the pair a squinty-eyed glare, Griff buckled in and bit his tongue. It wasn't lost on him that he was sitting in the bitch seat. But for now, he was going to roll with it.

There was a whine, and the auxiliary power unit fired Jedi One's turbines. Glancing into the cabin, Ari said, "Two mikes to launch. Buckle up, ladies and gents. Since this is a short hop, there will be no inflight service."

Cross shook his head. "Not cool, dude. I was hoping a pretty blonde stewardess would be pelting me with peanuts."

Skip turned away from his right-side window. Grinning at Cross from behind the skull mask, he said, "If you like, I can open an MRE and pelt you with Smarties."

"You're too scary," quipped Cross. "But if Baby Face does the pelting …"

Griff had had it. "Fuck off, Cross. The old William will be back before you know it. I can already feel the five o'clock shadow pushing through."

Though a curtain of silence descended over the cabin, the spirited banter seemed to have buoyed the team's collective mood. And while nobody said it aloud, it was clear to everyone aboard, at least for this mission, that Griff had just taken Lopez's place as the butt of everyone's jokes.

Grateful for the brief respite, Cade made himself as comfortable as one could on a helo flying nap of earth, pulled the set of laminated floorplans from his pack, and began to commit them to memory.

On a low ridge three-quarters of a mile northeast of Peterson, Xehua Peng set his binoculars aside and slipped the encrypted Inmarsat phone from his breast pocket. It was his only lifeline to his superiors. Save for the rifle on the ground next to him, and the pistol in the drop holster on his right leg, the sat-phone was the only piece of equipment he kept on his person at all times. Without fail. Charged to capacity.

He punched in the unlock code, then dialed a number from memory. While he waited for the phone to complete the electronic handshake with a Chinese satellite orbiting somewhere high overhead, his mind retraced the steps that had him dressed as a bush in a foreign land and spying on one of their most important airfields.

Exactly one year ago today, he had been celebrating his twenty-fourth birthday all alone at a chain restaurant in suburban Houston. Answering the call from his party handler—a staunch loyalist posing as a diplomat working out of the Houston consulate—the last thing Peng had expected to hear was that he was being activated.

He was told to cut all ties and go underground. It was time to put to the test his two years of service in the People's Liberation Army, an additional two as a junior agent in the Ministry of State Security—the Chinese equivalent to the Central Intelligence Agency—and an additional two years as an undergrad at Rice University, where, until that day, his sole job had been to siphon from the NanoEngineering program every bit of intel he could get his hands on.

Never in Peng's wildest imagination could he have predicted that the call he received that last Saturday in July 2011 would see him transition from stealing intellectual property to spying on government buildings, hospitals, and sprawling military bases. Nor could he fathom that the reason for the spying was a hastily planned invasion and, up to now, a year-long occupation.

The only thing to hit Peng harder than the revelation that the invasion he would be participating in was not of Taiwan, but of the United States, was confirmation of the accidental release of a deadly virus in his homeland. Up until then, he had interpreted the news about the infection as American propaganda meant to weaken China. To give the American president a leg up in an already strained relationship. To widen a rift precipitated by U.S. saber-rattling over islands being created in the South China Sea—a body of water China claimed dominion over and had always seen as vital to her national security.

Shortly after Peng's going operational, when America had been weakened to the point it was deemed safe for the occupation to commence, the pride he had felt was tempered by word that every countermeasure his country had enacted to stop the virus's spread in the Motherland had ended in failure. Not only was America overrun with flesh-eating jiangshi, but so was all of China.

Now, a year later, and with millions of his countrymen back home on the brink of starvation, their very lives hinging on the outcome of a military operation taking place half a world away, it looked to Peng as if several weeks of round-the-clock surveillance was about to pay off.

Once the connection was finally made, a familiar voice said, "Go."

Skipping formalities, Peng consulted his logbook and read off all of his observations, beginning with the arrival of dozens of civilian vehicles at the area of the base known to cater to special operations aviation and ground assets and finishing with all he had witnessed take place on the tarmac over the last ninety minutes or so. He included the types of aircraft involved, number and makeup of personnel that had boarded each aircraft, exact times of departure down to the second, and the direction of travel each aircraft maintained after takeoff. It was all there, and he felt a sense of great worth knowing that, in his own way, he was finally contributing to the fight.

Peng was certain his ancestors were smiling down at him.

Ending the call, he dialed a second number. While he waited for the connection to be made, he checked his surroundings for the pack of jiangshi he knew were roaming the area. Though the stink of death had hit his nose periodically while he was giving the goings on to his fore his undivided attention, at the moment, the only thing moving on the graded and surveyed parcel of sunbaked ground spread out behind him was a lone tumbleweed. He shifted his gaze to the row of homes a few blocks west of him. Seeing no tell-tale flashes of movement, he looked over his left shoulder.

Nothing there. Usually a gathering place for the dead, the sidewalks in front of the coin-op laundromat and adjacent convenience store were deserted.

He shifted his gaze back to his six and watched the tumbleweed until it came to rest against a nearby sign announcing the site as the future home of *Silver Creek Estates.*

Satisfied he was alone and undetected, Peng turned his attention to the phone and typed out a lengthy SMS message, detailing to a third party everything he had just relayed verbally to the others integral to the overall mission.

Chapter 31

New District - South Gate

Duncan brought his purple GMC pickup to a slow-rolling stop twenty feet shy of the South Gate guardhouse. Giving Daymon the side eye, he said, "This isn't going to work." He looked at his watch. "And I certainly don't want to sit out here baking in the sun until the next egress window."

"Glass half full," said Daymon. "You radiate negativity, you attract negativity."

"I'm supposed to take advice from the philosopher who put the capital S in surly?"

Raven planted her elbows on the seatback in front of her. Thrusting her Golden Ticket in Daymon's direction, she said, "Make sure it's on top, with the presidential seal in clear view."

In a child-like voice, Daymon said, "Make sure it's on top with the *Raven is a superstar* seal in clear view." Flashing a mischievous grin, he snatched the sheet from her, put it atop the others as instructed, and started his window running down.

Breaking eye contact with the approaching Marine, Duncan said, "Little lady sure likes to throw her weight around."

"Just like her dad, Captain America."

"My dad says to exploit every possible advantage to its fullest. That's exactly what I'm doing." She shot Daymon a questioning look. "Why are you always busting my dad's balls?"

Duncan guffawed. "From the mouths of babes."

Daymon said, "Have you heard how me and your dad met?"

"I know you were on *marijuana*." Raven smiled as if she'd just divulged a monumental secret.

"That was the old me," Daymon assured. "I was napping—"

Interrupting, Duncan said, "Bullshit. You were high as a kite. Admit it."

"Guilty as charged. However, I did learn a valuable lesson that day." He turned to face the backseat. "It was real early in all this shit they call the zombie apocalypse. I was returning from trying to find my moms. Big failure that road trip was. I didn't get very far down the Wasatch front before I was turned back by the biters. There were sooo many of them streaming south from Salt Lake City. A bunch of undead stormin' Mormons." He raised his hands in mock surrender. "I'm not bagging on them or their religion. My adoptive parents were Mormon. I was raised in the church. They're real nice people. Just not my thing as an adult."

"Your point is?" Duncan drawled. Then, speaking low and out of one side of his mouth, he added, "Mister pisses napalm and eats concertina wire for breakfast is fast approaching." He smiled and tipped his hat to the Marine, who was still a few yards distant.

"I awoke staring down the barrel of your father's gun."

Raven said, "That's why you don't like him?"

"I dig your dad. I owe him a lot. And I also learned the meaning of 'stay frosty' from him that day. Nothing like the prospect of eating a nine-millimeter round to wake a fella up."

Mouth forming a silent O, Raven sat up straight. It was clear to Daymon and Duncan that the proverbial lightbulb had just gone off in her head. "Oh," she said, "busting balls is the same as teasing?"

"Bingo," said Daymon. "Calling him Captain America is both a tease and a term of endearment. Kind of like calling him a booger face and patriot in the same breath."

Squaring up to the driver's door, the Marine stared into the pickup. "You missed the noon window."

"Stuck in rush hour traffic," Duncan quipped. "Can you make an exception?"

The Marine, whose nametape read *Lincoln*, put a two-way radio to his mouth and engaged in a brief conversation with someone out of sight. Finished, he asked, "Just the three of you?"

"Yes, sir," Duncan replied. "Two peons and one member of royalty." He took their passes from Daymon and handed them out the window. "I was hoping you could show a little mercy and allow us to pass."

The Marine scanned the top page, then quickly thumbed through the others. Removing his cover, he stared into the backseat. "Miss Grayson." Handing back the tickets, he nodded at Duncan. "Y'all are good to go."

Duncan thanked the man. Returning the tickets to Daymon and Raven, he said, "Nothing like hanging with Bird of the Apocalypse to grease the skids of bureaucracy."

***

Twenty minutes after passing through the South Gate, they were five miles east of New District, the GMC parked on a two-lane access road fronting the entrance to the subdivision Cade had marked on the map.

Three-dimensional bronze letters spelling out *Liberty Heights* were affixed at eye level to the stucco wall. The wall looked to be about ten feet tall and was a light shade of brown. Parked on the dead grass fronting the wall was a Mountain Metro city bus. Its tires were flat, the rusty steel wheels sunken into the high-plain soil. A mountain of furniture, most of it broken, covered the grassy curb opposite the inert bus.

It was evident to Duncan the road leading into the walled community had at one time been blockaded. The condition of the bus suggested the blockade had been short-lived. Why the blockade had been taken down was a mystery.

Just inside the entrance, the road widened and split off in opposite directions.

Folding the map, Raven said, "This is the place. I'm sure of it." She nudged Duncan's shoulder. "What do you think? Left or right?"

Duncan said, "Flip a coin."

"Who carries money these days?" replied Daymon.

Fishing an Alcoholics Anonymous coin from his pocket, Duncan said, "I do. And this'll do the trick. The Serenity Prayer we'll designate as heads. Twenty-four hours will be tails. Heads we go right. Tails, left."

Raven said, "Got it. I'll call it in the air."

As Duncan tossed the coin, Raven chose tails.

Duncan caught the coin in his palm midflight and slapped it down on the back of his hand. He stole a quick peek, then showed it to Daymon. "Tails it is."

Raven said, "Settled. We go left."

Duncan said, "Keep your eyes peeled, boys and girls. If we come up on a herd, and it's blocking forward travel, we'll have to backtrack and find a way to get it to splinter. After that, you know the drill."

The "drill" was a choreographed maneuver that had proven successful for the trio dozens of times over. Duncan was always tasked with driving whenever the team was faced with large, mobile groups of dead. And in this scenario, Daymon was always the designated culler. While the former firefighter whittled away at the dead with Kindness and Mercy, Raven would bat cleanup, following in his wake to collect and bag the ears.

Raven and Daymon always got an adrenaline spike from the process.

Aside from a couple of close calls, Duncan was always bored to tears. Deep down, he wanted in on the action. To really earn his keep. But Father Time was creeping up on him. So he stiffened his upper lip and accepted his new lot in life.

Craning left and right, Daymon said, "I'm seeing nothing. Place looks like a ghost town."

Duncan said, "Only one way to find out," and let off the brake and wheeled the pickup left. A block in, he noted that all of the homes were crowded close together and had very small parcels of brown grass for front lawns. It was clear a homeowner's association had been calling the shots on all things aesthetic. Not one of the homes was more than two stories. All of the homes were painted in one of three different earth-tone schemes and roofed with red mission-style clay tiles.

Duncan drove on, following Sage Grouse Lane at slow speed as it looped clockwise through the entire subdivision. At about the halfway point, maybe half a mile in, they came upon the small community's northern entrance. It was blocked by a number of vehicles, an oversized box truck chief among them. On the truck's slab side, emblazoned in red, were the words *DOCUSHRED - Sensitive Document Shredding Services.*

The truck had Georgia plates, which struck Duncan as odd. Who'd driven that thing all the way to Colorado? And why the big gas-guzzling truck when there were so many other vehicles for the taking?

Just past the blocked northern entry, Sage Grouse Lane transitioned to Plover Lane. Then, maybe a hundred feet further, where Plover took a hard dive to the south, the gray asphalt and white cement sidewalks flanking it were sullied with dark reddish-black splotches of dried blood. Scraps of fabric and tufts of hair were fused to some of the pools.

Discarded shoes were piled high near the left-side curb. They were all different sizes, with boots and sneakers and dress shoes all mixed in together.

Though Duncan was loath to say it aloud, the evidence suggested someone had beat them here. The lack of bodies meant it was the work of a professional outfit. He was beginning to think that certain "someone" was none other than Wendy Potvin. If so, the odds of this excursion paying out were dropping faster than the level of gas in his tank.

Daymon slipped one of his machetes from its sheath and started to tap it against his open palm. Once they had covered another zombie-free block and were nearing the mouth to a deep cul-de-sac close to the southern entrance, he wondered aloud where all the Zs were hiding.

Raven said, "My dad saw this place from the air. There were lots of rotters here a few days ago."

Knowing from personal experience how hard it was to pick out granular details on a single low altitude flyby, Duncan said, "He meant well, Bird. It'll be alright. We still have Plan B." Inwardly, though, he feared that Fort Kit Carson's kill and clear teams were about to make a liar out of him.

Sounding dejected, Raven said, "I thought it was solid intel. Sorry, guys."

Waxing optimistic, Duncan said, "Let's not call it yet." He steered right, drove into the cul-de-sac, then pulled hard to the curb in front of a brown and gray two-story with an attached two-car garage.

Raven asked, "Why stop here?" She walked her gaze around the cul-de-sac. "All the front doors have the markings. Means they've already been entered and searched."

Duncan threw the transmission into Park and killed the engine. "I'm aware. But for shits and giggles, let's check out a couple. See if the Big Green Machine left behind any of those things on Lola's want list."

Shrugging, Daymon said, "We're here. I'm down."

Duncan elbowed open his door. Turning back around, he said, "Raven?"

Recalling the bottle of port wine she'd found stashed away in the Craftsman north of New District, she said, "Couldn't hurt. But we'll need to post a lookout."

Duncan said, "We take turns. Anything we find, we split up equally."

"Deal," Raven said, "I'll take first shift."

Arriving on the porch, the group formed a tight knot, Duncan in the lead. Spray-painted door or not, he always followed protocol. He banged a fist on the door, then listened hard for the obligatory ten-count. When nothing responded to the noise, he tried the knob. *Unlocked.* Which was par for the course. These homes were cleared by soldiers with orders. And according to Cade, those orders dictated that upon leaving, they were to leave doors closed and unlocked.

While Duncan and Daymon were inside, Raven waited on the porch, her little Colt SBR at the ready and listening hard for raspy moans and the scuff of shuffling feet.

Two minutes after entering the home, hopes high, Duncan exited empty-handed. "Nothing spectacular. Just some leather furniture and the usual large consumer electronics."

With more than ninety percent of the population either dead or turned zombie and roaming the country, household items that used to be large expenditures for the average person were now so abundant that every survivor in New District with a place to call their own had accumulated everything they needed. And it wasn't off-brand entry-level stuff, either. It was all of the expensive brand name items people used to covet, but only a select few could afford.

One stroll down the aisles at Lola's was all it took to drive home that, even during the zombie apocalypse, the age-old law of supply and demand was alive and well.

Daymon strolled onto the porch a couple of minutes after Duncan. He was packing a lava lamp and a Technics turntable.

Duncan shook his head. Chuckling, he said, "You opening a disco, mi amigo?"

"If I am, you won't be on the VIP list. You'll just have to listen to my *jams* from the street."

Plodding down the stairs, Duncan said, "The ladies don't want none of this grizzled carcass anyway."

Raven said, "I'm going to pretend I didn't hear that. Because what I didn't hear, I won't have to report back to Glenda."

Changing the subject, Duncan pointed to the home directly across the cul-de-sac. "I have a good feeling about that one. Let's go do a little breaking and entering."

Duncan was the last to make it up the stairs. By the time he was on the porch, the door was hanging wide open. Raven had already knocked and listened. Daymon was standing in the doorway and looking at his watch.

"What took you so long?"

"I'm dragging ass. Hell, I'm nearly double your age. And little whippersnapper here, I got her lapped by a huge margin."

Though the short walk and scaling of two flights of stairs had left Duncan a little winded, he still lobbied Daymon to let him go inside with Raven.

"Suit yourself," Daymon said. "But you two better make it quick. There's a deader coming." He pointed toward the mouth of the cul-de-sac. "And it's pretty fresh. Look at it move. All smooth and with a pep in its step. Total opposite of Old Man."

Ignoring the ribbing, Duncan said, "Pretty lifelike from this distance, don't you think?"

"*Too* lifelike," said Raven as she disappeared through the door.

***

Five minutes after going in, Raven and Duncan emerged with nothing to show for their efforts.

Frowning, Duncan said, "I was wrong. Nothing worthwhile in the garage. Kitchen was cleaned out. Not even a bottle of cooking sherry."

That earned him a sidelong glare from Raven.

Throwing up his hands, he said, "Not for me. For trade at Lola's. It falls under the booze category."

Daymon said, "Spray paint don't lie."

"We can kill this rotter and split the ear three ways," joked Duncan.

Shaking his head, Daymon said, "Not worth the effort to meet it halfway down the street, let alone expend the energy to split its dome." He paused and looked the other two square in the face. "Want to hear Plan C?"

Duncan grunted. Most of Daymon's plans usually involved some bending of the truth and a lot of embellishment. He was known to understate danger while accentuating the positive.

Duncan looked a question at Raven.

She nodded. "Doesn't hurt to listen."

"What are you thinking, " Duncan growled.

Daymon spent a couple of minutes detailing his plan. When he finally went silent, Duncan and Raven stared at him for a long ten-count.

Breaking the silence, Daymon said, "One of you mimes better say something."

Raven said, "First off, we're not authorized to go to Pueblo."

"And it'll burn another four gallons of gas," Duncan lamented. "Better be more than one ear to go around."

Daymon addressed Raven's concern first. "That presidential seal on your Golden Ticket lets you do just about anything you want. I was there when the president presented it to you. I heard her say as much with my own two ears."

"But … Pueblo? That's a long ways away."

Daymon said, "At the top end, it's an hour drive."

Duncan said, "I thought that raging fire ate up most of Pueblo."

Shrugging, Daymon said, "Not north of town. There were quite a few places where the fire didn't jump the river."

Not fully convinced, Duncan said, "So you've been there?"

"More than once." Daymon smiled wide. "I have a special place I like to visit."

"It won't be a waste of my gas?"

Daymon said, "I think you'll be pleasantly surprised."

Duncan looked to Raven. "What would your father say?"

Smiling, she said, "When he left this morning, he said 'don't do anything I wouldn't do.'"

Daymon said, "Your dad never backs down from a challenge. That's another reason I call him Captain America."

Rattling his keys, Duncan said, "Let's go. We're burning daylight."

Chapter 32

After sweeping around New District's eastern flank, Jedi One sprinted south, cutting the airspace over Fort Kit Carson at five hundred feet AGL and scooting along at one hundred and seventy knots.

As the helo passed close by Cheyenne Mountain and the cabin grew dark, Cade's attention was drawn to the Colorado landscape flitting by outside his window.

He saw a train moving south, its cars carrying coal destined for the Ray Nixon coal-fired electric plant. Though the undertaking was called "ambitious and risky" by the handwringers in New District's burgeoning bureaucratic ranks, thanks to a team of volunteers, the plant was just days from returning to limited service.

The same soldiers out of Kit Carson who had worked so hard at getting the trains running again had done a fine job of clearing Interstate 25 between New District and Fountain. The thirty-mile stretch between Fountain and Pueblo was still a work in progress with only a single lane of travel opened up in either direction.

Usually swollen by runoff from frequent seasonal thunderstorms, Fountain Creek was but a silver strand trickling from the distant wooded foothills.

The flight path followed Fountain Valley until it opened up north of Pueblo. Along the way, Cade got a bird's eye view of the cities of Stratmoor, Security, Widefield, and Fountain. While the cities were not teeming with Zs, small packs of them roamed the streets.

Five miles out, Pueblo presented on the horizon as a patch of black in a sea of ochre dotted here and there with green spaces. A year earlier, nearly two-thirds of Pueblo had been ravaged by fire. As the helo got within a mile, two things were evident to all aboard. First, it became clear that it was the northern third of the city that had been spared from the worst of the conflagration. But unlike the smaller cities they had recently overflown, Pueblo *was* teeming with undead. As Ari committed the helo to a shallow turn to the right that took it directly over the downtown core, the Zs on the ground froze in place and directed all of their attention skyward.

Leaving a glittering Lake Pueblo and its zombie- and tent-choked shores behind, the Ghost Hawk cut a straight line over south-central Colorado. The terrain varied from knife-edged mountains sprinkled with pines and low scrub to wide-open swaths of high desert scored with shallow arroyos and slot canyons.

Crossing over into northern New Mexico, the landscape was more desert than alpine. So as not to stir up the local population, the small settlement of Taos was given wide berth. From Taos to their primary target, Ari kept Jedi One flying low to the ground, dipping into arroyos or taking advantage of low hills to mask her approach.

After transiting three hundred and fifty miles through Colorado and New Mexico airspace, with everyone aboard Jedi One either catching some shuteye or refraining from small talk, Ari patched in to the shipwide comms. "Ten mikes out," he called, his tone all business.

For Cade, the sudden announcement emanating in his headset was a welcome intrusion. It had jogged his mind from a ninety-minute tug of war he'd been waging over what, if anything, he could have done differently to alter the outcome of the Eplot mission. Losing Low Rider had hit him nearly as hard as Mike's passing. That the common denominator had been his Gerber finishing what Omega had started was not lost on him.

Across from Cade, Skip was giving the ground below the speeding helo his undivided attention. To Cade's right, still strapped into the bitch seat, Griff had removed his yellow-tinted glasses and was busy rubbing sleep from his eyes. On the opposite side of the cabin, Nat and Axe were both staring out their respective windows.

Cross was in the rear-facing seat directly beneath the monitor. Unlike his fellow SEAL, he was wide awake and nodded at Cade when the two men made eye contact.

The big islander turned away from the window and looked to Cade. "Not much ground clutter for this bird to hide behind."

Nat had a point. Aside from the occasional outbuilding or copse of trees standing in the way, nearly every possible approach to the Los Alamos National Laboratories was across open ground and impeded by hurricane fencing. None of it was optimal for a daytime raid. Which was why the plan was for them to recon the building from a standoff distance, utilizing the full capabilities of the helo's optics suite to gather as much intel as possible prior to commencing the assault.

Calling "Thirty seconds out," Ari dropped them to treetop level behind a copse of maple trees, side-slipped the helo until he found a break in the upper branches, then commenced a steady hover.

The facility was a series of mostly interconnected buildings, the tallest of which was a three-story steel and glass affair that rose up from the center of the cluster. The surrounding buildings were mostly windowless and topped with school-bus-sized ventilation units. The squat bunker-type eyesores were connected by gangways supporting long runs of shared piping.

Viewed from the west, the main structure looked as if a kid had built the fairly symmetrical structure out of gray building blocks.

Ari said, "Bring up the image. Zoom in to one-fifty."

Haynes said, "Roger that. One-fifty coming up."

A second later, a much larger version of what Cade was seeing with his naked eye appeared on the monitor above Cross. Acres of parking surrounded the installation. The lot abutting the west elevation was ringed by fencing and low shrubs already dead from lack of water. Sunlight glinted off the glass and chrome of a handful of dirt-streaked vehicles that looked to have been abandoned in the first days of the apocalypse.

Roaming the lined blacktop inside the fence were a number of Zs that most definitely had been there since the first days. Time and elements had reduced their clothing to scraps of fabric barely hanging on to their emaciated frames. One middle-aged rotter was entirely naked. Bald and of Asian descent, it had been morbidly obese in the past life. Though exposure had reduced its fat rolls to dried sheets of unmoving dermis, the Z still looked a lot like a super-pale version of Buddha. Knotted tightly around its thick neck was a noose fashioned out of red nylon rope. With each stilted step the thing took, the trailing length of rope would jerk and hop and dance across the ground like a downed powerline.

Stating the obvious, Axe said, "Suicide fail."

Griff said, "Betcha big boy Buddha broke the rope before the rope broke his neck."

Smiling, Nat said, "That's a lot of Bs, frogman."

Cutting the banter session off at the knees, Cade said, "Real quiet out there. Let's see what shows up on thermal."

Ari said, "Switch to thermal."

"Roger that," replied Haynes. "Going thermal."

The image on the screen in back switched from a true representation of what the human eye would see to one in which the buildings and vehicles and Zs all were rendered as multi-colored silhouettes. To the untrained eye, it came across as a bad acid trip. Cade saw it for what it was: a dry hole. The boxy ventilation and cooling apparatus beside the target building radiated roughly the same heat signatures as the inert vehicles. Another tell was that the dozen or so exhaust fans atop the HVAC equipment were still.

If someone had been using the facility in any capacity, they were now long gone. Still, Cade's orders were to get eyes on the building's interior and assess the condition of the lab's specialized equipment.

Ari said, "Want me to find another picket of trees and take a thermal scan from the east?"

"Negative," Cade said. "No reason to. Proceed to the LZ."

Ari said, "Affirmative," and the helo rose up over the trees.

Stoic and tight-lipped, the Pale Rider team unbuckled and began to don packs and ready their weapons.

Running open the left-side gun hatch, Skip dropped the Dillon down from its stowed position, powered it up, and aimed its deadly end at the target building.

Cade said, "Mask up. Everyone stay frosty. Let's get this one checked off the list and be on our way."

As he snugged on the M50 mask, in his headset Ari was sharing that the SEAL teams were beginning to assault the Midwest targets. Also passed up from Salt Lake City was news that both labs there had been breached and confirmed unoccupied and unused.

So much for synchronized assaults, thought Cade. It was to be expected. An operation this wide-ranging hadn't been undertaken since the first days of the Omega outbreak. Everyone was a little rusty.

I-25 South

Plan C was unfolding exactly as Daymon had promised, then I-25 abruptly choked down from two open lanes to one. It happened six miles north of Pueblo and wouldn't have been an issue if care had been taken to see that the vehicles pushed off the road had been deposited on one side or the other. Instead, the people tasked with the job had really botched it. Not only did the single lane meander left and right with no kind of predictability, but it did so through a veritable chute of stalled-out vehicles so narrow that in spots Duncan was forced to slow to a walking speed and pull in the mirrors to keep from losing them.

Then there was the problem of the Sierra's wide rear fenders. After traveling two miles at a fraction of the posted limit, both sides of Duncan's truck had taken a beating.

As if the physical damage to the pickup wasn't enough, it seemed as if the cleanup crews had intentionally left behind more than a few rotters. Nothing better to get the heartrate up than the occasional pustule-riddled arm reaching out from a static vehicle's open window. On a couple of occasions, Duncan's reaction time had been insufficient to prevent a collision between a flailing arm and the pickup's grille guard.

Nearly as unsettling as the unexpected *bang* and follow-on *crunch* of phalanges and metacarpals being pulverized was catching a fleeting close-up glimpse of an ashen face—darting tongue and all—mashing against clouded auto glass.

A few minutes of this had everyone on edge.

Duncan had been strangling the steering wheel so hard his knuckles were white as barnacles. Out of the blue, he said, "Who do you guys think cleared the stretch of I-25 between New District and when this damn Chinese finger trap began? Anybody want to venture a guess?"

Raven said, "The Army?"

"Ding, ding, ding," said Duncan. "Correctamundo, little lady. Now riddle me this. Who do you think is responsible for this"—he gestured at the road ahead—"this cluster … eff-word?"

"Good catch," said Daymon. "Wouldn't want Raven to hear a word she's already heard a million times over. I bet she's even said it herself once or twice."

Duncan jinked the pickup right to keep his folded back mirror from splitting the skull of a Z poking its head through an open window. Straightening the wheel, he looked at Raven side-eyed. "You dropped an eff bomb? Our precious little angel?"

Smiling, Raven said, "Who'd you hear that from, Daymon?"

"Your father."

"Doubtful," Raven said, crossing her arms. "He doesn't air family issues in public."

Flashing a *gotcha* smile, Daymon said, "We have confirmation."

Still fuming, Duncan said, "At this point, she could spew Carlin's seven words for all I care. This is pissin' me off. It's got to be the work of a civilian contract crew. And on display here is taxation without representation."

"Not exactly," Raven corrected. "Taxation without representation is when—"

"I don't care," Duncan shot. "When we get home, I'm going to go straight to the bureau building and lodge a complaint with Chief Riggleman. Ask her whose idea it was to award this job to Helen Keller and Stevie Wonder."

"I'm just glad it's your rig that's getting beat up and not mine," Daymon said. "If this was mine, I'd throw it in the gutter and go buy another." He looked back at Raven. "Know who sang that, Bird?"

"What I know," Duncan said, "is that I would rather be pushed in this than seen driving that Ford of yours." Glancing at Raven, he went on, saying, "You know what *Ford* stands for, right?"

"Nope," she said, "but you better be nice; Black Beauty is a *Ford*."

Unable to restrain himself from twisting the verbal dagger he'd just stuck into Daymon's back, Duncan smiled wide and said, "Fix. Or. Repair. Daily. If we would have taken that baby Bronco of his, we may have had an easier go at this stretch, but it's pretty damn likely we'd have been pushing her at some point."

Tiring of the car talk, Raven said, "So who sang the *throw it in the gutter* song?"

Daymon said, "Eazy mother-effin E. Song is called *Boyz in the Hood.* And goes a little something like this." Looking out the window, he rapped a few verses of the Compton rapper's first big solo hit.

"Don't quit yer day job," grumbled Duncan.

Unimpressed, Raven said, "How much further?"

Still bobbing his head to a beat heard only by him, Daymon said, "We're real close. Another mile or so. You'll know we're almost there when you see the U-Haul storage place just off to the left of the freeway. That's not the place, though. It's been thoroughly picked over. You're going to take Exit 101 and then turn left."

Duncan shot Daymon a skeptical look. "And this honey hole of yours is how far from the exit?"

"A chip shot," Daymon assured him.

Chapter 33

Los Alamos National Laboratories

Jedi One came screaming in over the southern edge of the installation making sixty knots and so low to the ground that Cade expected to hear the coiled concertina atop the perimeter fence rake the fuselage. At the last moment, with the structure central to the facility looming in their path, Ari maneuvered around the glass and steel building, flared to bleed airspeed, then side-slipped the rapidly slowing helo toward the target building.

When the ship finally adopted a steady hover, some twenty feet above the three-story bio lab wing, both cabin doors were already in the full open position and Skip and Nat were kicking a pair of fast ropes into space.

Pale Riders were spilling from both sides of the Ghost Hawk before the ropes had fully uncoiled.

Cade hit the rooftop first, gloves warm from friction with the fast rope and his senses heightened from the sudden adrenaline dump. With Nat already riding the rope to the rooftop, Cade vacated the big islander's landing spot.

Griff was boots on the roof a second after Cade. He stood aside, dropped to one knee, and trained his suppressed MP7A1 at the nearby stairwell door. No sooner had Cross and Axe joined the rest of the team on the roof than Jedi One was spinning a tight one-eighty and speeding away to the east, the ends of the fast ropes real close to dragging the ground.

Cade looked at his Suunto. *Perfect. Less than thirty seconds on target.*

If anyone were inside, even if they had detected the helo's baffled rotor noise, it was such a unique sound that it was highly unlikely they would attribute it to a helicopter.

By the time Ari radioed that Jedi One was in the pre-determined overwatch position, the Pale Rider team had slalomed through the stacks of air-scrubbing apparatus and were assembled beside the rooftop door.

Cade quickly doled out tasks. Captain or not. Team leader or not. He considered running point his responsibility. He didn't delegate. Nor did he ask any member of his team to do something he wasn't prepared to do. It was his own unwritten code. One constant component of all he had learned from the many men he had had the honor of serving under.

Stepping forward, Axe inspected the bottom of the door.

Cade asked, "Can you scope it?"

"Too tight a seal," Axe replied. Stowing the small monitor and fiber optic probe in a pocket, he brought out the pick gun and went to work on the lock.

While the SAS shooter worked at defeating the tumblers, Cade flipped his NVGs down and powered them on. Seeing Axe flash the thumbs-up, Cade formed up in front of the door, just outside of its sweep, and shouldered his suppressed SBR.

Once the rest of the team was stacked up to the right of the door, Griff in the lead and awaiting the signal to yank it open, Cade initiated the entry with a nod.

Griff pulled on the knob and pressed his body hard to the exterior wall.

As the door began its right to left swing, Cade went into a combat crouch. Simultaneously, every muscle in his body tensed and his senses came alive.

Slow is smooth, smooth is fast was his mantra as he stepped toward the entry. When the door reached the midpoint in its sweep, the light from outside penetrating only as far as the handrail just inside the landing, he was crossing the threshold and cutting the corner right to left.

Calling out "Clear" softly into his boom mike, he lowered his carbine, stepped to the handrail, and looked into the dark abyss.

Rendered in full color was a deep chasm surrounded on all sides by three levels of concrete stairs. Each stair run consisted of seventeen steps that arrived at a six-foot-by-four-foot landing. The schematics Cade had memorized showed six separate runs that switched back on one another. Every other landing was fronted by a steel door. The door at the very bottom would be on the wall opposite to the one containing the door to his back. It opened up onto a long hallway running the entire length of the bio lab workspace.

The stairwell to the team's fore was cramped. A single handrail was all that graced the windowless poured-cement walls.

As Cade moved out, SBR's business end sweeping the stairs ahead, his sudden intrusion sent dust motes scudding the air in front of his face.

Their every footfall echoing in the enclosed space, the team made the bottom landing in a matter of seconds.

Arriving at the ground-level door ahead of the others, Cade cocked an ear and listened hard.

Nothing.

He drew in a deep breath. There was no detectable stench of decaying flesh. Nor did he smell the nauseating stink the PLA's version of the MRE gave off.

A good thing. On both counts. The former more so than the latter.

Using hand signals, Cade instructed Axe to inspect the door.

After running a hand along the bottom of the door, Axe shook his head.

Cade motioned for him to proceed with the pick gun.

Once Axe had the lock picked, the team employed the same tactics and stealthy precision to open the door and push on into the hallway.

Cade looked left and right, then left again before announcing the hallway was clear.

The pale yellow walls and white tile floor were awash in natural light filtering in through the windows at each end of the long hallway. The floor under Cade's boots was covered by a thin layer of dust. Whether it was a year's worth or not, he had no way of gauging.

What he did know was that nothing, living or undead—not even a mouse—had treaded down the hallway in a very long time.

Lifting up his NVGs, Cade told the others to stay put, then made his way to the door to the bio lab's security checkpoint.

Stopping before the steel door, he cupped his hands around his face and peered through the slit-style window. Though the glass was tinted green and wire reinforced, he could see a layer of dust on the floor just inside the door. It, too, was untracked. To the right of the door, behind a low wall featuring a sliding glass window, was a guard post. It was spartanly appointed. Just a desk and rolling chair and a lone filing cabinet. Everything on the desk, from the pens on the blotter to the curled-up stack of papers trapped to a clipboard, wore the same thin coating of dust.

Summoning Axe, Cade had him pop the lock.

The door opened into a long hall that ended at the door to one of the lab's two negative pressure airlocks.

Leaving Nat alone to cover the door and hallway with the squad automatic weapon, Cade set off to the left, the rest of the Pale Riders in tow.

The door to the pass-through was unlocked. After a bit of manipulation, they got it to open. Cade led the team through the airlock. It was roughly ten feet from door to door, the floor, walls, and ceiling all white and pristine.

Reaching the second door, Cade peered through the window. The room was a massive rectangle with high ceilings and no windows to outside. Stainless steel tables and biomedical equipment dominated the center of the room. There were what looked to be DNA sequencers on one table. On another, row upon row of centrifuges sat idle. Shelves on one wall were crammed with books and three-ring binders bulging with papers.

Since field-of-view was cut down to eighty percent with the mask, Cade pressed the shield to the window and craned left and right. Nothing moving inside. The floors were shiny and white, not a speck of dust to be seen. His first impression was that the cleanroom was currently unoccupied. Moreover, there didn't appear to be any equipment missing. There were no bolts protruding from machine-sized footprints on the floor devoid of the usual wear caused by foot traffic. There were no disconnected ventilation hoses or power cords dangling from the ceiling. The place appeared to have been abandoned during the first days of the outbreak. Which made sense because the response to Omega's rapid spread had been marshaled out of the CDC in Atlanta. Initially, the west and southwest had gone largely ignored.

While Cade's gut and eyes were telling him their work here was done, he needed to expel all doubt to the contrary. To do that, they would have to enter the lab.

Cade and Axe tackled the interior door. There was a hiss as the seal was broken.

Cade motioned for Griff and Cross to enter and range off to his right.

Taking Axe with him, Cade entered and went in the opposite direction.

SBR held at the ready, suppressor following wherever his eyes tracked, Cade padded to the end of the room, where he paused to inspect a glassed-in area. Left turned inside out, the fingers curled into harmless claws, three pair of black rubber gloves drooped from a trio of gloveboxes. Behind the glass was a trio of tables. Test tubes and vials and shallow specimen dishes left atop the tables suggested some kind of work had been ongoing when the lab was vacated. That no care had been taken to police up the workstations pointed to a hasty exit. Maybe the scientists and lab technicians had been whisked away to the CDC aboard military birds. Then again, perhaps they had dropped everything and fled home to save their own lives and reunite with loved ones.

There was no way to know. Back then, the mundane task of record-keeping had taken a backseat to survival. Everyone's awakening to the horror that the recent dead were rising was a unique experience. Some fell victim to normalcy bias. Those people quickly fell victim to the undead hordes.

These people had been armed with the knowledge of what Omega truly was. Therefore, Cade figured, one way or another, most of them had made it out of here alive. Where they were now was anybody's guess.

Cade said, "Griff, Anvil Actual. All clear on my side. How copy?"

"Good copy," Griff radioed back. "We got nothing moving over here."

"Roger that," Cade replied. "Any signs of recent activity?"

"Negative," Griff confirmed. "Quiet as King Tut's tomb."

"Copy that," Cade announced. "Rally back at the airlock."

"Roger that," Griff replied. "On our way."

Silently lamenting the fact that Nash hadn't given the Albuquerque labs priority over Los Alamos, Cade radioed Jedi One and requested an immediate exfil. Next, he hopped frequencies and hailed the tactical operations center at Peterson.

The airman, a Captain Jensen monitoring the net at the op center, handed the call off to Nash straightaway.

In bullet-point fashion, Cade relayed the facts to Nash, then waited for her response.

Nash didn't apologize. Nor did she acknowledge her misread. Instead, all business, she reminded him that Operation Blanket was still a threat to them all. Finishing up the call, maybe to ease Cade's mind since he was outside the wire and away from Raven, or maybe just because she felt the need to provide him the 40,000-foot-view of the ongoing operation that only she was privy to, she told him that Smokey had all of his remaining alpha teams deployed in concentric rings around New District. RQ-9 Reaper drones were also up and providing around-the-clock surveillance over the city. She concluded her oration by letting him know that President Clay had given Harley free reign over the prisoners.

While it was good to know extreme measures were being taken to ensure the safety of the thousands of civilians inside the walls, it would all be for naught if the remaining facilities were found to be deserted. With each new dry hole the teams uncovered, the odds rose exponentially that they would find themselves back at square one—playing defense and at a severe disadvantage.

Exiting the airlock, Cade was stopped by Nat. Instead of speaking, Nat nodded toward the door at the west end of the hallway. Backlit by the afternoon sun was a lone zombie.

Cade said, "The one with the noose?"

Nat nodded. "It was the only one I saw out and about on that side of the building."

Striking off for the door, Cade said, "I'll handle it."

Arriving at the end of the hall and seeing that the Z was indeed alone, Cade took stock of the door. It was a steel item with the same slit-style window as the guard station. Trouble was, the door opened outward.

Like a switch had been flipped, the zombie went from pawing listlessly at the window to body-slamming continuously headlong into the door.

Cade depressed the panic bar with his hip, dropped his shoulder to the door, and placed both hands on the window. When the Z drew back to mount another attack, Cade ran the door open, all of his weight behind the effort.

The door's sharp vertical edge caught the Z square on. The impact pulverized its nose, opened a vertical, foot-long fissure in its distended gut, and sent it sprawling backward.

As the zombie toppled like a felled tree, the energy from the blow sent it spinning away from the door. The thing made no attempt to break its fall. It face planted just outside the reach of the door's return sweep.

Seeing Jedi One's shadow darken the parking lot to his fore, Cade drew his Gerber and dropped down hard on the Z's back. Planting one knee at the base of its spine, he snatched up the rope and wound it around his free hand. Once there was only a foot or so of rope remaining between his hand and the crudely fashioned noose, he leaned backward until the rope was taut and the Z's back was arched to the point bones were beginning to crackle and pop.

Keeping the Z in the forced yoga pose, Cade buried the dagger into its right temple and wiggled it back and forth, scrambling the brain and stilling the snarling beast. Keeping tension on the rope, he wrenched the dagger free, introduced the serrated edge of the blade to the Z's Adam's apple, and sawed furiously.

Finished, Cade tossed the severed head aside and rose up off the headless corpse. When he turned back toward the building, his team was filling up the doorway, looks of incredulity parked on all of their faces.

As Jedi One settled on the blacktop a couple of hundred feet away, Cade locked eyes with Griff.

"What the fuck was that?" mouthed Griff.

Though Cade heard nothing in his headset, he did read the man's lips.

Responding, Cade said, "Practice."

Picking up just the single word, Ari said, "I hear practice leads to perfection, Anvil. But right now, it's go time. We have a tanker rendezvous to make."

Cade said, "Copy that," and directed his team to the awaiting helo.

Wearing questioning looks, the Pale Riders filed past their leader—a man who had just committed before their eyes an act that demanded explanation.

Chapter 34

Pueblo, Colorado

Arriving at a spot on I-25, where, miraculously, the inept civilian road crew had managed to clear both lanes running up to Exit 101, Duncan braked hard near the bottom of the ramp and brought the pickup to a complete stop.

Though the ramp had been cleared of vehicles, upwards of thirty zombies ambled downhill, all eyes focused on the idling pickup.

The majority of the zombies had been touched by fire postmortem. The specimens most affected, the ones that had burns covering eighty and ninety percent of their bodies, looked like things from a nightmare. They were hairless and entirely naked, all of the dangling fleshy parts burned away. As they stalked down the ramp, corded muscle could be seen moving beneath blackened dermis shot through with cracks and fissures.

As soon as Duncan set the emergency brake, Raven appeared between the front seats. Hooking her elbows over the seatbacks, she craned to see out over the hood. The mere sight of the rictus grins of the immolated creatures sent a shudder through her body. Those contrasting teeth and jaundiced eyes really set them apart in a crowd. Then there were the ones with empty eye sockets, the blind followers of the pack that frequently turned up in her nightmares. Give her a ratty old first turn any day. Those no longer triggered a response. She'd put down so many of the creaky bags of bones that once the count had topped a thousand she had stopped keeping track.

Raven swung her gaze to the nearby embankment. Rising over the crest was a pair of signs. The Dunkin' Donuts and McDonald's restaurants the signs once advertised were blackened piles of rubble. During their approach to the overpass, Daymon had been explaining how Cesar Chavez Boulevard was the demarcation line for the northern edge of the burn.

Gesturing at the dead things, she said, "Anyone else see a problem here?"

Duncan said, "Beside the fact they're blocking the road?"

Daymon said, "No ears."

Raven said, "Exactly. Which means there's no reward for putting them down." Frowning at Daymon, she said, "Tell me there's another way around."

Daymon nodded. Hooking a thumb over his shoulder, he instructed Duncan to get back on the freeway. "You'll want to go under the overpass and then make a hard right and drive up the freeway on-ramp. It'll be clear of vehicles. At least it was last time I passed through. I have no idea about biters, though."

Duncan reversed clear of the off-ramp divider. It was one of those collapsible water-filled jobs meant to compress upon impact. Spinning the steering wheel, he got them back to moving south on I-25. Keeping to the slow lane, he drove under the overpass. Coming back into the light of day, he slowed and scoped out the ramp.

Daymon's promise about it being free of stalls rang true. As Duncan made the sharp hairpin turn to access the ramp, he saw a contingent of dead whose numbers rivaled the herd they were trying to avoid.

"It's my fault," Daymon admitted. "Last time I came this way I ventured a few blocks into the burn. Did a little prospecting north of Chavez." He gestured at the zombies cresting the top of the ramp. "They were probably the ones following me on my way out."

Duncan said, "Once they get eyes on a fella, nearly impossible to shake them. My guess is they didn't see you get back onto I-25. If they had, by now they'd be someone else's problem."

Raven said, "Maybe we can backtrack. Head north and find an alternate route to D's honeypot."

"Honey hole," Duncan corrected. "Daymon no longer has a honeypot."

Daymon shot Duncan a sidelong glare. "Maybe I do. Maybe I don't."

Muttering something under his breath, Duncan started the pickup rolling up the on-ramp.

Raven sat back in her seat and buckled her lap belt. Voice rising an octave, she said, "You sure about this, Duncan?"

On Raven's mind was the time Black Beauty's tire had started to go flat. It happened somewhere on SR-39 between Eden and Randolph. They had pulled over right away. She was peeing by the side of the road while her father crawled underneath the truck to inspect the tire.

A large herd of first turns had gotten the drop on them.

Though they had survived the ordeal, the shard of antler that had become embedded in the tire was the reason she had splurged and had Whipper fit the Ford with the run-flat radials.

Duncan's pickup did not have run-flat tires. Which was a major problem. Because she didn't see how he was going to avoid plowing through the zombies congregating at the top of the ramp. And going by past experience, should some of the zombies go underneath the pickup, any one of their femurs could splinter and ruin everyone's day.

"No problem," Duncan replied.

"Just don't get a flat tire," she implored.

Punching open the glove box, Daymon said, "You have a can of liquid flat repair in here, right?"

Duncan said, "Nope. Used it. Been meaning to go to Lola's and resupply."

Incredulous, Raven asked, "When's the last time you checked the spare?"

"Start of summer."

Hands going for her SBR, Raven said, "No wonder Glenda's had it with you."

Tightening his grip on the steering wheel, Duncan said, "And here I thought me and you were thick as thieves. Best buds. Pals. *Amigos*."

Raven was too busy focusing on the threat to reply.

While they had been discussing their options at the bottom of the ramp, the dead had been arriving at the top of the ramp. By the time the pickup was at the ramp's midpoint and building speed, the dead were packed shoulder to shoulder across the boulevard, with more arriving by the second.

Duncan didn't remind his passengers to buckle up. Nor did he advise them to hang on. As if he had a death wish, when the Sierra was a couple of truck lengths from the top of the ramp, he tromped the brakes and wrenched the wheel hard over to the right.

The sudden maneuver caused the pickup to list to the left and its right-side tires to lift off the road. With gray smoke billowing from the wheel wells, Duncan counter-steered, bringing the wheels back to earth and saving the truck from rolling over.

While the forced power slide was far from a thing of beauty, it was highly effective. Instead of plowing through the phalanx of zombies head-on, the lifted pickup—most of its forward momentum spent—plowed into them broadside.

A fusillade of loud bangs rang through the cab, and most of the dead making up the front row were lifted off their feet and sent flying. The ferociousness of the impact started a ripple of kinetic energy running through their ranks. Duncan was just getting the pickup moving again when the entire lot began to collapse outward.

Cupping his ear, Daymon said, "You hear that?"

Eyes going wide, Raven said, "A tire's losing air?"

Daymon said, "Naw. I was just pulling your leg."

Raven hauled off and punched Daymon on the arm. "How much further, jerk?"

Duncan pointed to a sign coming up fast on the right. "Looks like Daymon's idea of a chip shot is a mile and a half."

Rubbing his arm, Daymon said, "That it is. You like the clue I ever so subtly dropped?"

Duncan said, "That clue was about as subtle as the hurt I just put on the deaders back there."

Reading the sign, Raven said, "We're going to the Walking Stick Golf Course?" She crossed her arms. "What's there?"

Daymon said, "Lots of overlooked homes."

Raven said, "What's so special about them?"

Duncan said, "Homes on golf courses cost many times more than the average home. It's a prestige thing."

Daymon smiled at Raven. "Who golfs?"

Brows knitted, she said, "Old businessmen?"

Daymon said, "Yep. And what do old businessmen all have in common? Beside screwing the little guy, that is."

Duncan cackled. "I thought you were going to say, 'screwing the secretary.'"

Brow furrowed, Raven said, "Old businessmen are rich."

"Correctamundo," Daymon said. "They *were* rich. Past tense. You know all the real expensive stuff in the back of the Costco mailer? The two-thousand-dollar espresso machines and the five-thousand-dollar video golf trainers? Those are trinkets to people who could afford homes on the golf course."

"In layman's terms," Duncan added, "they had *all* the toys. Which reminds me of an old saying: He who dies with the most toys wins."

Smiling, Daymon said, "They're our toys now."

A few blocks east of I-25, Cesar Chavez was bordered on the left by an open swath of scrub-dotted range cut through by Fountain Creek. Though the creek was unimpressive, the flood plain was vast, with dried-up vein-like tributaries snaking far and wide.

Flashing by outside Daymon's window was Pueblo Mall. It sat on a large, flat parcel of land and, amazingly, was untouched by fire. It was anchored by a Dillard's on one end and a Hobby Lobby on the other. Daymon surmised it must have been open when the apocalypse reached the final fever pitch just before President Odero declared martial law and ordered the nationwide shutdown.

The parking lot was nearly full; two, maybe three hundred dust-streaked cars, SUVs, and pickups languished under the blazing sun. Proof that old habits died hard, or at least lived on in small part in the brains of the undead, there were easily twice as many walking corpses patrolling the mall's perimeter. God only knew how many, acting on snippets of memory, had managed to get inside the mall.

The thought alone reminded Daymon of a zombie movie in which a group of survivors holed up in a large indoor mall. He wondered if the director had survived long enough to see fiction become reality.

Surrounding Pueblo Mall on three sides was a wasteland of charred tree trunks and the skeletal remains of burned-out buildings.

On the mall's west flank, beyond a dirt embankment, I-25 carved a right to left arc.

Duncan kept the gas pedal matted until the truck was barreling along at nearly twice the speed limit. He wanted to put as much distance between them and the dead prior to making the left turn he knew was coming up. While they would definitely be out of sight by then, given that sound traveled far and wide in the high desert, he also wanted to be out of earshot.

The road feeding the golf course came up fast. The only way to get to it was from Cesar Chavez westbound. Slowing, Duncan eased the pickup left and, to keep from having to take the distant overpass and backtrack, he crossed the median illegally.

Coming out of the sweeping U-turn, he hung a right and sped down Desert Flower Boulevard.

Half a mile north of Cesar Chavez, after a couple of gentle curves, Desert Flower became Walking Stick Boulevard.

Colorado State University Pueblo campus rambled off to the east. It consisted of several multi-story buildings and what looked to be a sports complex. It appeared deserted.

Walking Stick Boulevard meandered along the edge of the college campus for half a mile before choking down to a wide and unmarked lane that cut through a pair of low stucco walls. The walls were painted a shade of pink that fell somewhere between salmon and Pepto Bismol. A sign advertising Walking Stick Golf Course was affixed to the wall on the right. Twin pickets of mature trees rose up behind the walls. A gentle breeze shook the dry leaves.

The pristine blacktop, smooth and flat, wound past a bone-dry putting green before ending at a closed gate secured with a combination lock. Beyond the gate were the Walking Stick clubhouse and a mostly empty parking lot that looked as if it could accommodate upwards of a hundred vehicles.

The Mountain-style clubhouse, with its red steel roof, exposed wooden beams, and rough-hewn stone exterior, was on the left side of the parking lot. Golf carts were parked on a cement apron beside the front doors. A length of chain was threaded through the dual door pulls and secured with a fist-sized padlock. Beyond the twenty or so carts was a pair of putting greens.

The tee box for the first hole sat adjacent to the practice area. A sign rose up like a periscope from the waist-high grass. On the sign was the hole handicap, its slope rating, yardage from the tee box, and a tiny overhead of the hole depicting bunker placement and where the green sat in relation to the tee box.

Nosed up to the Walking Stick pro shop's mirrored windows was a pair of Ford E-Series vans. They were both white and wrapped with colorful graphics featuring one of the course's signature holes. In the background was a jagged mountain range. In the foreground, a pair of golfers were on the green, one crouched down and studying his line, the other standing by the cup and tending the pin. Frozen mid-flap, the yellow flag atop the pin bore the course's name and stylized cactus logo.

Daymon clicked out of his seatbelt. "I'll get the gate."

Duncan hooked a thumb over his shoulder. "Bolt cutters are in the bed."

Tapping a finger on his temple, Daymon said, "No need. I have the combination."

"It's your lock, eh? Pretty smart."

Scooching forward on her seat, Raven said, "At least we know nobody has come in this way."

As he stepped to the road, Daymon said, "It's my first layer of defense."

Duncan watched from the cab as Daymon removed the lock and walked the gate open. He drove through and waited while Daymon reversed the process. Once Daymon was back inside the truck, Duncan pointed to a trio of mansions ringing a distant cul-de-sac.

Starting the Sierra rolling forward, he asked, "Is that your honey hole?"

Daymon shook his head. "Nothing but dead bodies in there. Kids and adults. House on the left is shot up pretty good." He paused and tucked a dreadlock behind his ear. Continuing, he said, "My guess is that a couple of families banded together. Joined forces to ride this thing out. When it came time to guard their castle, they lost."

Raven said, "Marauders?"

Daymon gestured toward the clubhouse. "Yep," he said, "bodies were pretty dried out. Makes me think it went down months ago. Whoever did the killing carted off everything of value."

Following Daymon's direction, Duncan wheeled left. "You'd a thunk the marauders would have put down roots. Made one of these McMansions home." He chuckled. "I guess fairway views aren't for everyone."

Raven asked, "That your chain and lock on the clubhouse doors?"

"Not mine," Daymon said. "Nothing but deaders inside the clubhouse. The restaurant is picked clean."

Exasperation evident in his tone, Duncan said, "So where's the dang honey hole? All I see is tall grass and golf carts. Is there really one here? Or is this another one of your vision quests?"

"I'm not imagining things." Daymon pointed to the pair of vans. "Take the cart path left of those shuttle vans. It wends around past the cart pool we saw from the entrance."

Duncan drove onto the cart path. Looping around front of the clubhouse, he squeezed his rig past the static golf carts, kept to the path, and continued following it as it split the pair of putting greens. Arriving at a T in the cart path, he quipped, "We flipping a coin here?"

Pointing across the hood, Daymon said, "We're going there. Those four homes up against the first hole green are my honey hole. Aside from taking this approach, they're only accessed by the last cul-de-sac in the subdivision. So far, they've remained untouched by looters."

"Hate to drive across a golf course," Duncan muttered as he let his foot off the brake. "Just doesn't feel right."

Having died long ago, the grass on the greens was brown and still relatively short. The grass on the fairways was a different story. It had grown out of control and came up to the bottom of the pickup's front bumper. A swishing sound arose as the Sierra cut a laser-straight path toward the faraway green.

Daymon said, "Third house on the right. I always park behind the shed. Hides my rig pretty good. This purple thing, though … maybe, maybe not."

Chapter 35

Cade felt Jedi One decelerate and glanced up from the floorplans he'd been studying. Gazing out his window, he saw the aerial refueling KC-130 Hercules banking away and beginning a steep climb into the westering sun.

He watched the bird until it locked into a new heading. About the same time Jedi One would be closing with the first target in Albuquerque, the retreating Herc would be busy refueling the aviation assets returning from their unsuccessful missions in Arizona.

Now, twenty minutes south of Los Alamos, with the knowledge that only two targets remained, the first of which he would have eyes on in just under ten minutes, Cade confronted the elephant in the crowded troop compartment.

"I saw the looks on your faces back there," he said, gaze moving from man to man. "I owe you all an apology. I saw red back there." He stared at the floor by his boots. "Scratch that. I saw Zhen in that thing. I saw the bastard who shot Lopez. And the commie scientists who unleashed Omega on the world. The virus that took out our families. Our fellow Americans. Crushed my country." He pounded a fist on his chest rig. "I let the demon out of the box. For that, I am sorry. It won't happen again."

A heavy silence fell over the cabin.

Ten long seconds ticked into the past before the first person spoke.

It was Griff. He said, "It wasn't the act that unhinged my jaw, Boss. It was the emotion attached to it." He noted the helmeted heads bobbing all around him. "I don't think I've ever seen you release the beast. You're all business all of the time. Even when you fed Alamo's torturer to the Zs in Portland … that was a means to an end type of thing. Hell, it got Baby Bird to spill about the spring offensive. Why the offensive didn't happen is neither here nor there. As far as I'm concerned, what happens in Los Alamos, stays in Los Alamos."

Cross said, "I totally get it. Mum's the word, brother."

Matter-of-factly, Nat said, "May sound strange, but I nearly popped wood seeing the helo in Bear Lake break up and catch fire and start spitting out dead commies. That Z back there, you did him a favor. You released his soul from Purgatory. Allowed him to rejoin his ancestors in the afterlife."

Axe said, "He was dead, mate. Twice-dead to be precise. That's all there is to it. Case closed."

Skip started the left-side gun-port door running open. To Cade, he said, "I was watching." He nodded toward the cockpit. "We all saw what you did. We discussed it. And we all decided that if Smokey or Nash or anyone else *ever* brings it up, we're all taking the Sergeant Shultz defense."

Cade was about to respond when, in his headset, he heard Ari deliver the five-minute warning.

***

When the one-minute call sounded over the shipwide comms, Jedi One was one mile out and approaching the first target from the west. With the sun at her six and the desert floor a tan blur less than fifty feet below, unless one knew exactly where to look, picking up the sleek bird on approach with the human eye would be next to impossible.

A half-mile from the target building, Ari flared the Ghost Hawk and adopted a steady hover. The desert floor here was peppered with rock and scrub brush and home to the occasional cactus.

Dead ahead, the joint civil-military installation housing both Kirtland Air Force Base and Albuquerque International Sunport stretched away to the east. In the background, the Sandia Mountains presented as a dark brown smudge on the eastern horizon.

The airport's shared main runway ran away diagonally from the nearby perimeter fence. Beyond the runway, parked on the tarmac fronting the glass and steel concourse, was a smattering of civilian jet liners. They were an explosion of color in a sea of earth tones. International and domestic carriers were represented. Articulated skybridges connected the jets to the airport.

Due to its close proximity to a city with a population of nearly one million people, the airport had fallen to the Zs just two days into the outbreak.

The 58th Special Operations Wing based at Kirtland had remained until the last possible minute, filling their Ospreys, Pave Hawks, and C-130s with those who'd been stranded at the airport. The perimeter fence had been breached, and Zs poured onto the runway as the last of their fixed-wing aircraft were clawing their way into the night sky.

Kirtland was but one of many airbases around the country whose location had proven to be its ultimate undoing.

A year later, the entire complex still belonged to the dead. They wandered the tarmacs and runways. Several of the ground-level doors below the concourse stood open, giving zombies free reign over the airport's lower levels, where baggage handling and customs enforcement once took place.

Addressing Ari, Cade said, "This is a no go. Too many Zs."

Agreeing, Ari said, "I'll relocate us north of the complex. Hope the last airman to leave turned out the lights and locked the gates."

In one smooth maneuver, the helicopter spun on axis, went nose down, and sped off to the north. A few seconds later, after looping around the airport, Ari had Jedi One parked in a steady hover a dozen feet above a rundown two-story apartment building in Albuquerque's International District.

From this vantage, the airport looked very utilitarian. The hangars were all battleship gray and devoid of the colorful signs that adorned the commercial carriers' hangars. The cement tarmac, on which sat a handful of smaller aircraft abandoned by the 58th, bore a minimal amount of markings. There were no train-like baggage cars piled high with suitcases going nowhere. Following rules and regs to the end, the last airmen to leave Kirtland had parked their fuel bowsers and support vehicles in a uniform row beside the building housing the maintainers' shops.

Matching the map in his mind's eye with the scene outside his window, Cade picked the multi-story Tangent Biomedical building out of the cluster of structures on Kirtland's northeast corner. From this distance, the details were a bit fuzzy.

Haynes said, "Target building is coming up on the display."

As Cade swung his gaze to the troop compartment monitor, the Tangent building filled up the screen. The exterior was a near carbon copy of the Los Alamos facility down to the boxy air-scrubbing equipment on the roof, bus-sized HVAC units on the ground next to the building, and even the materials used in the bunker-like structure's construction. That was where the similarities ended. Whereas Los Alamos was surrounded entirely by twelve-foot-tall razor-wire-topped fencing, Tangent was not. With the combination of the airport's perimeter fencing, Kirtland's base security force, and the TSA's own officers patrolling the airport round the clock, no extra care had been taken to protect the BSL-3 lab from outside threats.

That had been a mistake. Not only was the parking lot and loading dock area behind the facility occupied by a large number of what looked to be first turns, but the building had also been torched. Windows at the ground level were spidered and bowing inward. Speaking to some kind of explosion, the glass on the upper-level windows had been blown out of their frames. The shards littering the cement glittered in the afternoon sun.

The ensuing fire had consumed the entire second and third floors, leaving the cement exterior around each individual window streaked with soot.

Though Cade knew what the image on the screen meant, he confirmed it with a quick look at the Tangent building floorplans. Looking up from the plans, he said, "Labs were on the third floor. Any heat signatures?"

"I scanned it with the FLIR on approach," replied Haynes. "No heat sigs. No hot spots. The fire damage is old news."

Shaking his head, Cade said, "We're done here."

"And then there was one," Griff said. "What are the odds the last one turns out to be *the* one?"

As the helicopter broke hover and began to swing around to the left, Nat said, "Maybe they're not prepping the weapon in a static lab. Breaking Bad ring any bells?"

Cade and Cross shook their heads.

Axe said, "My bell is silent."

Nat said, "Breaking Bad was about a high school chemistry teacher who's diagnosed with cancer. To leave his family flush with cash after he's gone, he starts cooking and selling meth."

Griff's eyes went wide. "If I'm remembering it right, Walter White started cooking in an RV. A Winnebago or something similar. You think the Chicoms are prepping their weapon in a rolling lab?"

Shrugging, Nat said, "Maybe. That would explain all the dry holes. If you were setting up a mobile lab, you'd need the stuff on those shopping lists."

Cade said, "I'm not sold. Touring Yosemite in an RV is one thing. Safely handling germs in one is an entirely different ballgame. Let's shelve that until we've exhausted all other options."

Nodding, Nat said, "Just spit-balling, Wyatt."

Interrupting the back and forth, Skip held up two fingers indicating the University of New Mexico campus was fast approaching.

Over the shipwide comms, Ari said, "Haynes is going to pick up Building 55 on approach. As soon as he's locked on, I'll swing wide to the south. Circling back around, I'll come in out of the sun and find a suitable spot for you fellas to do your standoff recon."

Cade said, "Roger that."

After crossing over the airport east to west, the helo took a turn to the north and skimmed over a golf course.

Cade was eyeing a pair of Zs trooping across an overgrown fairway when movement in a dormant water feature caught his eye. Trapped in the brackish water, most of them in it up to the waist, was a dozen or so zombies. They were watching the helo with rapt attention, their flailing arms frothing the water. As the lone ship banked directly over their craning heads, they all thrust their arms skyward.

Coming in low and slow, Ari parked the Ghost Hawk at treetop level over a park bordering the university's western entrance. He said, "Migrating image to cabin monitor."

Peering out his window, Cade watched ducks scudding the brown water of the pond in the center of the park. A walking path wove between the trunks of mature trees as it wound around the pond's rocky shore.

The six-story cement building splashed on the monitor. It was rectangular and roughly twice the size of the Tangent building. With yard-long horizontal slits for windows and no visible HVAC units on the roof, it looked more like a prison than a place where students studied microbiology, gene splicing, and deadly viruses.

The main entrance was at the building's southeastern corner. It was a three-story cube constructed with steel girders and clad with green glass panels. It struck Cade as an architectural afterthought. Something tacked on to appease some kind of aesthetics code.

Now, with Building 55's unimpressive western elevation filling up the monitor, Cade's interest was piqued by a pair of impressions in the wide grassy expanse bumping up to the building's south side.

On the edge of his seat, eyes glued to the monitor, Cade said, "Zoom in on the grassy area in the breezeway."

The camera pushed in until the swath of grass was the only thing visible on the monitor.

Cade said, "There. Magnify, please."

As the patches of beaten-down grass took over the entire screen, Griff said what Cade was thinking: "I've seen those imprints before."

Axe was nodding vigorously as Nat spoke up. "Same ones we saw on the grass outside Wyatt's old compound."

Seeing the same thing on the cockpit monitor, Ari said, "Tricycle landing gear. I think a pair of Harbins loitered here."

Cade said, "Agreed. Question is: Where are they now?"

"Did the eggheads stay behind?" Cross wondered aloud. "If so, did some PLA troops remain behind to protect them?"

Ari said, "Haynes was running a thermal scan on approach. It came up blank. If anyone is in there, they aren't running any machines."

Cade didn't like how this was unfolding. "The vents emitting anything?"

"Hard to tell," Haynes answered. "Since the building is certified green, all of the systems are subterranean. Solar panels on the roof are kicking off a lot of residual heat. If there is any exhaust being vented, I can't single it out."

Cade said, "Can you put us on the roof without deploying the fast ropes?"

"It's doable," Ari said. "But it'll be a tight fit."

"Alright," Cade said. "Let's see if anyone's home."

Feeling the helo begin to move forward and grab some altitude, Cade snugged his mask tight and gave his SBR a once-over. As Skip started the right-side door sliding open, the helo was nose down and rising to the level of the target building's roof.

By the time the Ghost Hawk was clearing the southside parapet, the entire team was gunned up and wearing their game faces.

As Ari flared Jedi One and started her on final descent, in the troop compartment the team was already out of their safety harnesses and crowding the open door.

Since Ari was unable to put the ship down safely among the sea of glass panels, the insertion was conducted wheels up. Which meant there was no room for error.

Averting his eyes from the glare coming off the solar panels, Cade held his rifle tight to his chest and stepped from the hovering helo. The drop was five feet at most. Landing cat-like between rows of panels, he immediately took a knee and scanned a quick three-sixty. Seeing nothing lurking beneath the multiple rows of south-facing panels, he called "Clear" and turned to watch the rest of his team exit the helo.

Axe dropped to the roof ahead of Cross and Griff. The three were moving to meet up with Cade when Nat took the plunge. Catching a hip on the top edge of one panel sent the operator off balance, causing him to land with a forward lean, all of his weight absorbed by his toes.

Cade watched Nat crumble to the roof. That the Green Beret didn't pop right back up and declare himself "good to go" was a tell

Cade couldn't ignore. Just about anything a team member did wrong on a mission or during training was fair game for good-natured ribbing. Some things—such as a propensity for air sickness or constant bitching about something that everyone accepted as normal—could earn one an unwanted nickname, regardless of one's stellar track record up to that point.

Moving to the fallen man's side, Cade said, "Anything broken?"

Grimacing at Cade through his fogged-up mask, Nat said, "A few toes, I think." He reached out a gloved hand. "Help me stand. I'll fight through it."

That's all Cade needed to hear. So as not to suffer a hernia, he enlisted the SEALs to help.

Working together, the trio got the big operator on his feet.

Cade said, "Good to go?"

Sweat beading on his forehead, Nat nodded. "Put me on our six. I'll keep up."

"Negative. I'll take point. You'll be on *my* six," Cade insisted. Before moving out, he tasked Cross with bringing up the rear.

Chapter 36

The rooftop door was equidistant to all four corners of the rectangular roof. In keeping with the prison theme, it was a windowless slab of steel at the bottom of a short run of stairs.

Ushering Axe forward, Cade made room for the Brit to work.

After scoping the door, Axe rose up. To Cade, he said, "Stairwell is illuminated. The door opens into an alcove. There's nothing on the landing. No moving shadows that I could see. No telling what we're going to find once we're boots on the stairwell."

That was going to have to be good enough intel to go on. It was all they had. If there were dead things occupying the stairwell, their raspy moans would give them away the second the first footfall echoed in the enclosed space.

Having the element of surprise over any PLA soldiers who may be in the building was critical. That being the case, the usual bang-on-the-door-and-wait routine was out of the question.

Getting the go-ahead from Cade, Axe popped the pair of locks with the pick gun and moved aside.

Cade pushed the door inward and crept onto the cement landing. Suppressor sweeping right to left, he cut the corner slowly.

Unlike the Los Alamos Laboratory, this dimly lit stairwell did not descend in one continuous run. It was two and a half flights of cement stairs that ended at a door identical to the first. Though the light cast from the emergency bulbs was dim, deploying NVGs wouldn't be necessary.

It was clear to Cade that the rooftop stairwell was to be accessed only by authorized personnel. It was spartan and secured by heavy-duty deadbolts top and bottom. Though the floorplans didn't convey detail such as types of doors or number of steps in each individual run, Cade had a hunch the stairwells to the other floors, those accessible by students and instructors, were going to be vastly different.

As Axe scoped the interior door, Cade stood over him in order to see what was happening on the six-by-four-inch screen. He could see, like the door to the roof, that this one was recessed in an alcove deep enough to accommodate the door's full sweep. The door opened into a hallway that ran away to the left and the right—east and west, respectively.

So far, everything jived with the floorplan Cade had committed to memory.

Whispering, Axe said, "Movement."

Gazing down on the small screen, Cade saw the creatures' shadows merge on the carpeted hallway. A second later, their physical bodies crossed paths just outside the alcove. He couldn't make out much detail from the brief glimpse. Still, based on their stilted movements, he had no doubt they were Zs. Likely first turns. They weren't alone. As he continued to watch, another zombie entered the picture. It paused before the door, scuffed tennis shoes less than a yard from the tiny lens at the end of the slender probe.

Cade said softly, "Adjust the angle."

Axe manipulated the stalk in tiny increments until the Z was framed fully on the screen.

"Looks like a college-aged kid," Axe noted. "Gaunt face. Shriveled neck. Sunken eyes."

Cade said, "First turn. Same as the other two." He looked Nat over. "How are the wheels?"

Having popped a handful of grunt candy, Nat was beginning to feel a little less pain. Whether it was from the swelling crushing the nerve endings in his toes or from the Motrin beginning to kick in, he wasn't certain. He was just grateful the lightning bolts of pain that had come with each step were beginning to ebb.

"I'll keep up," he answered truthfully.

Meeting Nat's gaze, Cade said, "Me, you, and Axe will sweep left. Cross and Griff will go right. Weapons hot, but let's try to keep the gunfire to a minimum. Once the hall is clear of tangos, we rally at the northeast stairs."

In his head, Cade saw their path to target as a red line snaking across an imagined set of floor plans. The red line proceeded laser-straight from his current position, culminating at the corner of the building, the northeast stairwell on the left. Picking back up on the second floor, the imaginary red line doubled back to the bio lab and a number of rooms associated with it.

If things got hairy and the front entrance was not accessible, there were two other ways to egress the building. The first was via the emergency stairway affixed to the wall north of the main entrance. Though it wasn't inside the building, it was encased in the same green glass as the front entrance.

The other exit was on the ground floor. It was accessible through the northwest stairwell and opened up to a wheelchair ramp.

When the Z loitering the hall before the rooftop stairwell door lost interest and had moved off to the right, Axe withdrew the scope. Leaving the device assembled and powered on, he crammed the whole thing into a cargo pocket. Working quietly, he defeated the lock with the pick gun. Finished, he stowed the pick gun in a pocket and snatched up his suppressed M4.

With Nat and Axe on his six, Cade pushed the door open, shouldered his SBR, and slipped left.

Cross and Griff padded off to the right and made contact straight away. Having detected the door opening at its back, Tennis Shoe Z was already mid-turn when the pair of rounds fired from Cross's MP7 punched a fist-sized hole between its sunken eyes.

With one eye dangling by a bloody tendril and the remains of its decayed nose hurtling toward the nearby wall, Tennis Shoe suddenly went boneless and crashed to the carpeted floor.

"Tango down," was just crossing Cross's lips when muffled reports from Griff's chattering MP7 drowned him out.

Meanwhile, entering the hall and finding just the one Z blocking the hallway to his fore, Cade let his rifle hang on its sling, snatched the Gerber from the sheath on his thigh, and rushed to close the distance.

The waifish first turn was beginning to react to the sound of the stairway door opening when the volley of suppressed gunshots sounded at Cade's back.

So much for keeping the gunfire to a minimum. The old adage *When you're a hammer, everything is a nail,* certainly applied to Cross and Griff.

Not too concerned that the suppressed gunfire could be heard several floors down and on the other side of the building, Cade wrapped his fingers around the Z's skinny neck, windmilled his knife hand in from the right, and drove the dagger into the thing's right temple. Easing the limp form to the floor, he checked his six only to see the entire team stacked up behind him, waiting.

Without a word, Cade struck off down the hall. He ignored the closed doors. The doors that were hanging open got his utmost respect. Prior to crossing the plane, he would perform a quick turkey peek and announce to the others what he was seeing.

A minute after exiting the rooftop stairwell, the team was standing before the northeast stairway. Someone had jammed folded-over magazines underneath each door, trapping them wide open.

Cade caught the stink of death drifting up from below. He also detected faint scuffing noises. They, too, were rising up from deep within the stairwell.

"Dead things on the stairs," he announced. Worried Nat was going to have issues navigating the four runs of stairs, let alone doing so while engaging a cluster of Zs, Cade moved to the rail and stared into space. He saw shadows rippling across the stairs two floors down.

Regarding the team, he carved an imaginary letter Z in the air before them. Patting his chest, he pointed to the stairs going down, then made a walking motion with his fingers.

Zs on the stairs.

I'm going alone.

Four heads nodded in unison.

Knowing his role, Cross moved off the landing and set up to watch their six from the confluence of two long hallways.

Gerber in hand, Cade descended the stairs, two at a time. Finding the fifth-floor landing clear and the double doors closed, he pushed down to the fourth floor, where he found the doors propped open and a lone Z occupying the landing. It was standing still on the threshold to the left-side door and facing away from him. Though he couldn't see its eyes, Cade guessed it was in the semi-catatonic state that Zs sometimes fell into when alone for long stretches with no stimuli.

Setting foot on the landing, he took one long stride forward and introduced his Danner to the thing's narrow ass. As the creature struck the hallway floor face first, arms and legs akimbo, Cade bent down and removed the folded magazines propping the doors open.

He watched the zombie struggle to rise from the floor, moving on only when the doors had clicked shut.

Descending to the second-floor landing, Cade saw that the left-side door was being held open by a corpse. The adult male looked to have been in his mid to late thirties. Cause of death was a single gunshot wound to the forehead. The entry wound was dime-sized and elongated, the surrounding skin in tatters.

Small caliber weapon. It looked as if the man had turned his head prior to being shot.

The man's hair was blood-soaked. Blood had pooled underneath his head. It was tacky to the touch.

While there was no evidence the man was infected with Omega prior to being executed, there was a strange rash on his bare chest. It climbed from his beltline to his neck, which was swollen and mottled with purple splotches.

It was here that Cade encountered the source of the scuffling sounds. Twitching snout red with blood, a rat the size of a small dog was atop the corpse and staring up at him. The rodent had already consumed the eyes, lips, and earlobes. From the looks of it, the opportunist vermin had just started to eat the dead man's bloated tongue.

The rat froze mid-chew and watched Cade until he was one stride away from the landing. The second his Danner hit the landing, the rat leaped off the corpse and disappeared through the open door. That it fled into the building, instead of down the stairs, told Cade there were likely no Zs in the immediate vicinity. At least not in the hallway right outside the doors. It was also a pretty good indicator that not only was the pair of helicopters long gone but so was the rest of the personnel.

A quick turkey peek through the left-side door confirmed his hunch.

Backing away from the corpse, he radioed a SITREP to the team and called them down.

While he waited, his eyes never left the corpse. There was nothing normal about the swelling and uneven red splotches. It definitely wasn't attributed to typical postmortem decomposition. Suddenly he was thankful for his mask's ability to filter out microscopic airborne pathogens.

Cade stopped the team short of the landing and posited his theory on what had happened here.

The entire team agreed the man had been infected with some kind of exotic disease. There was also complete agreement he was a test subject and that he had made it here on his feet. Nobody argued the fact that the gunshot wound to the head was the definite cause of death.

There were mixed feelings on why he had been executed. Everyone, save for Cade and Cross, theorized that the man had fled his captors and that the execution had been to send a message to other captives who may have been planning an escape.

Cade said, "The blood on the landing is from the head wound. If he'd died instantly, his heart would have stopped. It takes a beating heart to expel this much blood. Tells me he got shot somewhere else, made it here alive, and then bled out."

Cross nodded. "I concur. That's a tiny entry wound. I'm not moving his head, but I'd bet the house the bullet's still in there." He scanned the landing. "I don't see a shell casing."

Axe said, "If the bloke was shot somewhere else, why didn't the shooter make sure the deed was done before moving on?"

"Would you want to touch that body?" Griff said. "Fumble around that sausage neck for a pulse? I sure as hell wouldn't. I would have double-tapped him in the first place."

Gaze locked on the open doorway, Nat asked, "So where's the biter did that to his face?"

Cade said, "That's the work of one helluva big rat." Leaving the corpse blocking the door, he entered the hall through the other.

At once, he noticed blood droplets on the gunmetal gray carpet. He had missed them during his initial peek into the hall.

Pointing them out to the team, he continued following the line on the map in his head.

Unlike the stairwells and other floors in the building, the level containing the BSL-3 lab was fully illuminated. It was so bright that Cade's eyes were still adjusting when he halted where the long hall came to a T. The blood droplets on the carpet went left and continued on down the hall.

Cade crouched down, shouldered his SBR, and pushed on, following the blood trail until he reached the lab.

The lab was an open affair fronted by wire-reinforced glass. Though it was half the size of the Los Alamos facility, it housed nearly as much equipment. Clearly, square footage was at a premium.

Seeing nothing moving behind the glass, he rose and padded down the hall. Making it to the halfway point, it became evident the lab had been in use recently. He had been instructed to scrutinize the glove boxes. They were instrumental in safely dividing the agent and prepping it for distribution.

The lab was a mess. Half-open boxes of supplies sat on the floor. Beakers and glass tubes were scattered about a central table. Some of the tubes were on their sides, broken and leaking an unidentifiable liquid. Whatever it was, Cade had no desire to get anywhere near it.

Another table held multiple centrifuges. They were all bristling with stoppered test tubes and in constant motion.

The gloves in the nearby glove box were turned inside out. Suggesting the work here was done, the box was empty, and the hermetically sealed door had been left hanging open.

On the floor nearby was a mound of discarded surgical gowns. A small wastebasket was brimming with used surgical gloves.

Having seen enough to know that the third time was indeed the charm, Cade moved on down the hall, heel and toeing it toward a door hanging open a few yards distant.

The map in his head indicated the door was to the first of three conference rooms.

Peeking around the door, he saw the room had been used but was now unoccupied.

Sending Griff and Cross ahead to check the other two conference rooms, Cade slipped through the open door.

There was plenty of evidence the room had been used as a place to eat. Paper plates, some of them still containing food, sat on a long table in the center of the room. On the table was a petri dish doubling as an ashtray.

A fifty-five-gallon garbage can in the corner was overflowing with cardboard macaroni and cheese boxes, opened sardine tins, empty liquor bottles, and a whole mess of the unmistakable pea-green Chinese MRE wrappers.

From the hall, Nat said, "I've never known the enemy to be fans of mac and cheese."

"Me neither," Cade acknowledged. "The rest of the stuff jives. And there's a lot of it. They were here for days, maybe a week or more."

As Cross and Griff returned, Axe wondered aloud how much of a head start the enemy had on them.

Cade looked a question at the returning operators.

Griff said, "They were sleeping in the next room. Table and chairs all pushed against the wall. Left a bunch of sleeping bags behind."

Cade said, "PLA issue?"

Shaking his head, "Griff said, "High-dollar items. Marmot, North Face, Kelty."

Cross said, "Found two more bodies in the third room. Man and woman. Both mid-forties. Wedding bands are similar styles. They'd been done like the guy in the hall. Only they didn't get up and wander away."

Axe said, "I wonder what compelled the bloke to chase after his would-be killers."

"We'll never know," Nat said soberly.

"How's your toes?" Cade asked.

Nat grimaced. "The less stairs I have to negotiate, the better."

"Better pop some more eight hundreds," Griff said. "Because I am not up to carrying your big ass."

After radioing the op center and passing along a SITREP, Cade went quiet and listened as Nash relayed new orders. Filing it all away, he switched channels and filled Ari in.

Holding Jedi One in a hover above the pond to the west, Ari said, "Copy that. Five minutes out."

Cade looked the team over. "It's a no-brainer these pukes are going to hit New District." Parroting Axe, he said, "Anyone care to venture a guess as to how much of a head start they have on us?"

Cross said, "Find me a glass thermometer, and I can determine time of death to within fifteen minutes."

After snapping photos of the lab and all three rooms, Cade led the team back to the northeast stairway, where they paused to let Cross put the thermometer taken from the lab to use.

Producing a throwaway pocketknife, Cross flicked it open, kneeled before the corpse, and plunged the four-inch blade into the man's lower right abdomen. He withdrew the knife at once and tossed it into the hallway, where it skittered across the carpet.

The thermometer was close to eighteen inches in length and nearly as big around as a Sharpie pen. The end containing the mercury was slightly tapered.

Cross wet the tapered end with the man's blood, then plunged the thermometer into the hole he had cut. He pushed firmly until he was satisfied with its placement, then backed away.

"What now?" Nat asked.

Griff said, "We wait and see what the liver's internal temperature is. I saw this on an episode of CSI."

Craning to see past Nat, Axe asked, "Where'd you learn this little trick of yours, Adam?"

Smiling, Cross said, "Probably the same episode of CSI Griff watched."

Cade shook his head. "You're serious?"

"As a heart attack," answered Cross. "Take it or leave it."

After about a minute, the mercury stopped rising.

Griff crouched down by the body, tilted his head, and scrutinized the thermometer. "Ninety-seven degrees," he declared.

"What do you think the temp is in here?" Cross said to nobody in particular. "About normal room temp?"

"Roger that," answered Cade.

Cross said, "Human body cools about one-point-five degrees an hour under normal circumstances. Best estimate is that this guy's been dead for ninety minutes, give or take."

Cade shook his head. "Too much of a head start." He stepped into the hall and called it in to the op center. Finished, he asked Ari for a SITREP.

The news wasn't good. A small herd of Zs had wandered in from a nearby soccer pitch. A large contingent of the herd had splintered off and now stood between the building's entrance and the LZ the enemy choppers had used. The same LZ Cade had chosen for their extraction.

Breaking the news to the team, he started down the stairwell, SBR shouldered, head on a swivel.

The team didn't encounter any Zs between the second and first floor. The doors from the stairwell to the lobby were closed. Peering through the window, Cade spotted three first turns standing in the lobby. They were about a dozen yards away and between him and where he needed to be. After issuing orders, he pushed through the right-side door, snugged his rifle tight to his shoulder, and started pressing the trigger.

Team in tow, Cade slalomed through the lobby. Passing between the trio of face-shot Zs sprawled out near the entrance, he spotted behind a planter the festering corpses of a pair of twenty-somethings. The man was semi-spooning the woman. It was clear to Cade he was looking at a murder-suicide. It wasn't the first he'd come across.

She had taken one to the back of the head. Then the male had laid down behind her and sucked on the barrel of the little snub-nosed .38 still clutched in his withered hand.

The lobby furniture was jumbled haphazardly next to the front doors.

Thankful he wasn't the one who had to deal with moving the makeshift barrier, Cade pushed through the front doors, curled to his right, and took a knee at the top of a low stack of stairs. Making room for Nat to work, the rest of the team did the same.

Mk 46 shouldered and hot, Nat settled the EOTech's red pip on the Zs nearest to him and pressed the trigger. His body juddered from the recoil as the squad automatic weapon spit controlled three- and four-round bursts downrange. One by one, the Zs fell to the hot cement walk, brain tissue dribbling from ruptured skulls.

Having cleared a path for the team to get to the breezeway, Nat hobbled down the stairs and took point. Firing and moving, he led the team to the LZ, where they all crouched on a patch of grass darkened by Jedi One's rapidly expanding shadow.

Chapter 37

Duncan had jockeyed the Sierra around until all but its bumper and about a foot of its right rear quarter was concealed behind a fence meant to protect the nearby mansion from errantly hit golf balls.

The home was one of three near-identical structures looming over the green to the first hole—a near straight three-hundred-and-fifty-yard par 4. It was a ten-thousand-square-foot three-story affair with more pitches to the roofline than there were holes on the course. The black steel roof and earth tone paint scheme helped it to blend in nicely with the copse of pines growing up around it.

Pointing to a lone Z ambling toward the pickup, Duncan said, "That was quick. How's the rest of the neighborhood? More biters where he came from?"

"Unfortunately, yes," replied Daymon. "Don't worry about Bernie, though. He's a *fixture* around here."

Elbowing open his door, Duncan said, "You named your watch-rotter Bernie?"

"The lady whose name I won't utter named him," Daymon said. "She showed me this place. We were pretending we were on vacation from all this bullshit. Bernie was the first to crash the party. So he got staked down."

Duncan snugged his Stetson on. Scooped the Saiga off the floorboard. Looking at Daymon, he asked, "Why Bernie?"

Smiling, Daymon said, "She took inspiration from *Weekend at Bernie's*. The flick with the two junior executives who go to the boss's mansion for the weekend. They get there and find him dead. Instead of calling the meat wagon, they decide to make the most of the weekend. They dress him up and take him out and about."

Incredulous, Duncan said, "Not only did you get close enough to tie the tether to its ankle, but you took the time to dress him in Tommy Bahama and khakis and then lace tennis shoes on his dead feet?" He paused and shook his head. "Is this how the boss man in the movie dressed?"

"The two dudes dressed him in vacation attire." He shrugged. "I guess I was showing off. Proving to the woman I thought I loved that I fear nothing. Which is a load of crap. I'm afraid of heights. I'm also not a fan of tight spaces. And … I have recurring nightmares I'm going to be a Bernie one day."

"You shush," Duncan commanded. "Quit that talk. You do go and get bit, I'm going to put you in a pink tutu and set you on your way. Forever roaming the countryside as Daymon ballerina."

Raven hooked an elbow over the seat. "Never heard of the movie. And you don't have the legs to pull off a tutu. But you know what?"

Exhaling sharply, Daymon said, "Shoot."

"My mom said you should never name a zombie," Raven continued. "She said it humanizes them. Makes it hard to forget them."

Throwing his hands up, Daymon said, "I didn't name him."

Shooting Daymon and Raven a stern glare, Duncan said, "Enough chit-chat. We're burning daylight. Let's go see if D's honey hole is as good as he's built it up to be."

Approaching the mansion single file, they gave Bernie a wide berth.

In the lead, Daymon made his way to a sliding glass door. It was at ground level and fronted by a large cement pad home to a full ensemble of outdoor furniture that had seen better days and a pair of empty planters. Condition of the accoutrements notwithstanding, the patio had a stellar view of the green, the approach from the fairway, and the distant clubhouse. Back before the event that created Bernie and billions more like him, this would have been the perfect place to sip a lemonade in the shade of the tall trees and enjoy the action on the green.

Pausing at the slider, Daymon bent over and inspected the frame beside the door pull. Rising, he said, "Hasn't been opened since the last time I was here."

Duncan said, "The old strip of clear tape trick?"

Daymon nodded. Machete in one hand, Beretta semiauto pistol in the other, he instructed them to stay put while he walked the perimeter to get a look at the other doors and ground-level windows.

***

Daymon was gone for a few minutes. When he returned, he was wearing a smile and flashed a thumbs-up. "Both vehicles are still in the driveway. No breaches. I took a quick look at the homes on either side as well as the one across the cul-de-sac." He shook his head. "Nothing out of the ordinary. That's the good news."

Adjusting his glasses, Duncan said, "The bad?"

"The biters heard your noisy rig. I spotted six or seven of them coming down Augusta."

"What are we waiting for?" Raven stepped to the door. Taught to trust her training, instincts, and what her eyes, ears, and gut told her, she banged hard on the glass.

"Unless someone slipped through the mail slot," Daymon said, "the place is uninhabited."

Raven said nothing. She was standing to the side of the door, SBR at the ready, waiting. If something were in there and slammed into the glass, the drapes would move first, allowing her half a second or so to slip her finger onto the trigger and eliminate the threat.

Stepping forward, Daymon hauled the door open.

Hot air rife with the stench of death hit them all in the face.

Daymon held the drapes aside and ushered them inside what he described as one of three guest bedrooms. As he closed and locked the door behind them, he made a point to warn them not to go anywhere near the bathroom.

Raven was stunned by the size of the bedroom. Five or six the size of hers in New District would easily fit inside the rectangular space. And from the looks of it, the en suite bathroom Daymon had warned her to avoid was easily four times the size of the largest of the two bathrooms in her new home.

Curiosity building, she said, "What's in there?"

Shaking his head vehemently, Daymon said, "You don't want to know."

Duncan dabbed at his forehead with a kerchief taken from his pocket. "C'mon, Daymon … in her thirteenth year on earth, this little lady has seen more than most adults saw during their entire miserable lives in the old world." He looked to Raven. "It's your choice. Nobody's going to stop you from going in there."

She looked to Daymon. "Tell me first."

"The owner and his extended family are dead in the shower."

Duncan said, "Must be a big shower. Suicide?"

Daymon said, "Sort of. I think someone went out and brought Omega back to the house with them. Infected the rest of the family. Dad was last to go. I'm no crime scene expert, but best I can tell, the patriarch lived long enough to put them all down. He then fed himself a bullet. It's real messy."

Raven made a face. "How many?"

Daymon said, "Seven. Four are little kids. Best I can tell it went down early spring." He pointed at the ceiling. "There's a calendar upstairs. Last day to get crossed out was March fourth."

Duncan said, "What makes this place a honey hole? Is there a full pantry upstairs? A massive safe brimming with guns and ammo?"

Daymon said, "Nope to both. Nothing worth seeing upstairs." He nodded toward the only other door in the room. "Follow me."

Daymon led them through the lower-level game room, pausing long enough to gesture at a wide door and describe the home theater behind it.

Near the front of the house, a flight of stairs took them down to a door leading into a huge mudroom and pantry. All kinds of food filled the shelves. The cans and glass bottles were arranged neatly so that the labels faced out. Stacked on the floor were twelve packs and full cases of beer and soda. There was evaporated milk and boxes of dried pasta. One shelf was dedicated to candy bars, the colorful boxes stacked three high and four deep. Another shelf held all Asian-style food and sauces. One shelf at eye level was stocked solely with Mexican staples.

"It's a start," Duncan drawled. "What else?"

Daymon said nothing as he flung open the door at the far end of the mudroom.

Before the door had reached the end of its sweep, Duncan was formed up next to Daymon and thumbing on his miniature tactical flashlight.

Duncan whistled. The garage was stuffed to the rafters with all kinds of food, most of it still sealed in boxes as if it had just come from the factory.

There was more beer and soda stacked chest-high by one wall. Cases of wine and cartons of cigarettes were stuffed underneath an immaculately clean workbench. Atop the bench was a pair of Rubbermaid bins. They were filled to the top with sealed packages of batteries—all of the normal sizes represented.

Duncan said, "It's like I walked into a Quickie Mart."

"Exactly." Daymon smiled and hooked a thumb toward the garage doors. "The panel van outside in the driveway is chock full, too."

Raven said, "Where did all this stuff come from?"

Daymon said, "Going by the papers I found in the upstairs office, the family owned a bunch of convenience stores in town."

Duncan said, "How'd they get it here before their stores were sacked? Lots of desperate folks runnin' around and acting crazy those first few days."

Daymon tapped his head with one finger. "The guy was smart. He probably saw that footage of the Chinese government welding their own citizens inside their apartments. Those measures they took the first day or so to stop the spread on their own soil were pretty drastic. Speaking for myself, I didn't snap out of the fog until all the cannibalism talk hit the local news. The guy chomping the other guy's face down there in Florida was the last straw for me. By then, all I could do was try to go and save my moms."

"What were you going to do with all this?" asked Duncan, making a broad sweeping gesture with one arm.

"I'm opening my own store. A Daymon Mart to counter Lola's. Between this and the stuff in the garage next door."

Eyes going wide, Raven said, "Next door?"

Daymon nodded. "Both garages. The owners must have bugged out shortly after the fall. That or they're vacation homes. This guy also owned a couple of restaurants: a Dairy Queen in Fountain and an Outback in Pueblo."

"How were you going to get it all home?" asked Duncan. "In your Bronco? It'd probably take you at least a hundred round trips to get half of it home."

Brow arched, Raven said, "That's where you come into play, Uncle D. You get to drive the van."

Daymon said, "She's a quick study." Entering the garage, he tore into a package of teriyaki-flavored beef jerky. Passing the bag around, he suggested they eat a proper meal before loading up the Sierra.

***

Forty-five minutes after Duncan had hijacked Daymon's *proper meal* idea, the three of them were upstairs and sitting at one end of a massive oak table.

On the tabletop between them were the remnants of a canned ham. A bowl with gold accents held the runny, jiggling remains of a can of jellied cranberry sauce. There were green beans and candied yams—also from a can.

Still somewhat fresh, Twinkies had capped off the impromptu feast.

Raven looked incredibly small sitting in the throne-like chair at the head of the table. Regarding Duncan, she said, "We should probably start loading up your truck." Hearing her dad in her head saying *Work smarter, not harder*, she suggested he back the truck up to the slider to make loading easier.

Loosening his belt a notch, Duncan said, "Good thinking." He jabbed his fork toward the front of the house. "Who's going to deal with our solicitors?"

Raven cocked her head.

Daymon said, "There Old Man goes again with the big words of his." He met Raven's questioning gaze. "Jehovah Witnesses, Mormons, Green Peace signature gatherers, Girl Scouts selling Thin Mints … those are *solicitors*. The things at the top of the steps out there are all mine."

Duncan said, "You got a death wish or something?"

Daymon rose from the table. "That's the pot calling the kettle black. You've been begging to get in the mix since Glenda kicked you to the curb." He grimaced. "I hate to be the bearer of bad news, friend, but you've lost a step."

Instead of replying to Daymon's unsolicited observation, Duncan rose from the table and turned toward the great room. It had a cathedral ceiling and was fronted by massive floor-to-ceiling windows that faced the golf course. Raising a hand in the air, he said, "You two hear that?"

Whispering, Raven said, "Hear what?"

Daymon shook his head and stalked over to the window. Brows furrowed, he stared off into the distance.

Duncan formed up next to Daymon. Craning to see through the pines, he said, "A helicopter's approaching from the east." He shook his head. "It's not a Huey. And I'm pretty sure it's not a Black Hawk or Chinook."

Raven said, "Jedi One?"

"No," said Duncan. He patted his chest. "You feel that one in here, and by the time you get a handle on where it's coming from, the damn thing is right on top of you. By then, it's too late. Your dad or some other pipe hitter is about to punch your ticket." Cocking an ear, he added, "Sounds like a Dauphin. Which is a Coast Guard bird. If so, they're a long way from the nearest coast."

Daymon took a knee in front of the window. "I think I see it. Look above the clubhouse. It's not white and orange, though. The thing is dog shit brown. And damn if it isn't slowing and descending."

Bracing himself on an overstuffed armchair, Duncan dropped down to his knees. He shuffled over to Daymon, both knees popping and emitting a sound not unlike sandpaper dragged over a two-by-four.

Pointing toward the distant tee box, Daymon said, "See it? Looks like a military chopper. It's not one of ours. I'm pretty sure of that."

Raven dropped to her knees then laid down on her stomach, her nose nearly pressing the glass. Seeing a trio of doors open on the helicopter's smooth underbelly and the landing gear emerge, she said, "I've never seen one like it."

"I got eyes on," Duncan said just as the helo was settling in front of the clubhouse. "It's a Harbin Z-9WA. Newest variant. It can carry a variety of missiles. Maximum altitude is just shy of fifteen thousand feet. Top speed is one hundred and sixty knots. Which is about two hundred miles an hour, in case you were wondering. It's usually deployed from a PLA Navy surface ship. And the *asshole* is putting her down on top of the practice green."

Raven said, "What are they doing here?" She turned to face him. "And how do you know all of that?"

"How? I was still getting Aviation Week magazine when the virus hit. To answer the why: I have no idea. The Harbin is a ship-based asset. Could be a forced landing. Maybe they experienced a mechanical issue. After all, a helo *is* a million different parts all trying to vibrate loose."

Daymon said, "It's screwing with my mission. That's what it's doing here." He rose up off the floor and stalked off toward the foyer.

Struggling to stand, Duncan asked a retreating Daymon what he had in mind.

"There's a spotting scope upstairs," Daymon called back. "The view is way better from up there, too."

"If the scope is in the sun," Duncan called, "make sure you pull it back into the room a bit. Wouldn't want them catching a light glint off the lens."

Raven popped up off the floor. To Duncan, she said, "I'm going to the truck to get your Steiners. Where do you keep them?"

"In the center console. Truck's locked. Better take my keys." He fished them from his pocket. As Raven snatched them up, he reminded her about Bernie and stressed that he may no longer be alone.

Patting the suppressor on her SBR, she said, "I think I can hold my own."

"That I don't disagree with." He found the helicopter through the trees. "They're shutting her down. Means they're planning on staying for a spell. It'd be a disaster if they heard you shooting that thing and came to investigate."

Raven said, "I'll use my blade."

Duncan didn't like that she was going it alone. Then again, it really wasn't his place to micromanage the Bird of the Apocalypse. So, instead of interjecting any more unsolicited advice, he just implored her to hurry back.

***

Like one of those so-called helicopter parents everyone was talking about before being one became tantamount to not only the child's safety but also the entire family unit's survival, Duncan stood by the window and watched Raven poke her head out the slider. The girl looked both ways. Then, upon seeing that Bernie was still alone, she emerged fully, closing the slider at her back.

Wasting no time, she crouched down and hustled to the pickup.

Duncan noted how the entire time she kept her profile low, head on a swivel, and the pickup and blind between her and the noisy helicopter.

Sounding like a proud grandfather, Duncan said, "Good job, Bird."

Raven dipped into the pickup and reemerged with the Steiners in hand. It was a ten-second in and out. No wasted energy. No fumbling around.

After craning around the pickup's rear quarter to sneak a quick peek at the helicopter, she retraced her steps to the slider.

When Raven reentered the great room, binoculars in hand, Duncan said, "Looked a lot like your dad out there. Cold as ice. Sneaking and peeking like a little ninja."

Duncan mentioning her dad caused Raven to wonder where he was and what he was doing. With this in mind, she said, "Thanks. I'd appreciate it if you don't bring him up while he's downrange. I don't like to think about him when he's away. Sometimes my mind makes up stuff. The worst kind of stuff. Glass half-empty stuff."

"I'm sorry, Bird. And I get it. I really do," he replied. "Let's go upstairs and see what the commies are up to.

Chapter 38

Captain Kai Zhen was unbuckled and out of his seat before the Harbin pilot had the bird's turbines at idle. He looked into the rear area and saw that the hooded and bound captives were all still lying on the floor where he had placed them. Only the oldest was moving, which was to be expected. Not only had the kids' lunch of macaroni and cheese been tainted with the new weapon, it had also been laced with a mild sedative.

Weighing nearly twice as much as the second oldest sibling, sixteen-year-old Bryce had been last to succumb. Now, nearly three hours later, his metabolism having processed the drug faster than the others, he was first to come to.

"Where am I?" he asked, voice a bit raspy. "Where's my family?"

The answer was delivered by Second Lieutenant Zi Yong. It came in the form of an open-handed slap to the head. Then, in broken English, he hissed, "No speaking. You do not ask. Only answer."

Zhen was by the left-side door and waiting for the crew chief to open it for him. Smiling at the captive, he said, "If you play by our rules for a while longer, Bryce … this day may turn in your favor."

Wisely, Bryce made no comment.

Zhen addressed Yong in Mandarin. "Unload the bikes, then fetch the charger and fuel and come find me."

Looking sidelong at the captives, Yong held up his hand. In Mandarin, he said, "I touched him. Do you have sanitizer?"

"I believe the scientists' every word, and so should you," Zhen shot. "They are not yet contagious." He checked his watch. "They won't begin shedding the virus for another three or four hours. Maybe longer for the oldest." As he smiled at the thought of all the death soon to visited upon the stalwart Americans, the scar on his deeply tanned face turned white. "And by then," he continued, "they will be inside the vipers' nest. In twelve hours, the Americans will be fighting disease and death, and we will be well on our way to our next target."

"A night operation, yes?"

Zhen nodded. "Though our numbers are few, we will have the advantage."

The door opened, and the crew chief pulled a lightweight aluminum ramp from the cabin floor. He positioned the ramp in the open door and then clambered aboard to unload the pair of dirt bikes.

Glancing out the door, Zhen saw that the crew chief had succeeded in getting the camouflage netting draped over the helicopter's rotor blades. How the diminutive fireplug of a man continued to do so alone and with such efficiency never ceased to amaze Zhen. Furthermore, he did so without complaint.

Everyone eventually finds their calling, Zhen thought as he watched the man muscle one of the bikes from the helo. It was clear that the son of a Cold-War-era T-80 battle tank commander had definitely found his.

Upstairs in the mansion some four hundred yards away, Steiners pressed to his face, Duncan had watched the crew chief toss lines over the helicopter's static rotor blades and then draw the connected camouflage netting across the rotor and out over the tail boom.

Though it was north of eighty degrees in the sun, and the crew chief was dressed in a one-piece jumpsuit and still wearing a flight helmet, Duncan doubted he had broken a sweat. It was a great demonstration of working smarter, not harder.

Next to Duncan, Raven had been watching through the spotting scope.

Having been happy to relinquish the spotting scope, Daymon was sitting on the carpeted floor and giving his Beretta a going over with a toothbrush liberated from the master bathroom.

When the crew chief wheeled a second dirt bike down the ramp, Raven said, "What do you think they're doing with those?"

As two men in matching camouflage uniforms exited the Harbin, Duncan said, "Nothing good. That's for sure."

With the sliding door fully open and light flooding the helo's interior, Raven was able to pick out more detail. On the floor by the rear wall were a number of small human forms. When one of them hinged up into a seated position and pressed its back against the padded wall the motorcycles had been leaning against, Raven's jaw dropped open.

She said, "I see a kid. He or she is hooded and flex-cuffed."

"There's more than one," Duncan noted.

Raven said, "I count four kids and one adult."

Matching her gaze, Duncan said, "My gut tells me that's a teenager." He lifted the Steiners and bracketed the soldiers. He watched them conversing. After only a few seconds, it was clear the shorter of the two, who was also older and had a hard set to his jaw and the eyes of a cold-blooded killer, was the one in charge. The leader gestured at something out of sight as he spoke. Try as he might, Duncan couldn't read the man's lips. Not a single word. Which made him think the men were not speaking English.

"You speak Mandarin, right, Bird?"

"Some," Raven replied.

"Can you read their lips?"

"I tried. Couldn't make out a single word," she conceded. "They're talking way too fast. I'm still at the '*ordering from a menu*' or '*asking where the bathroom is*' stage. At least that's what my dad calls it."

Duncan said nothing. He had just watched the crew chief and the subordinate soldier walk off toward the clubhouse and was wondering what they were up to.

The crew chief was lugging a red gas can in one hand and had what looked to be a portable battery charger in the other. Since those type of chargers could also jumpstart a vehicle with a totally dead battery, Duncan decided that their mission had something to do with procuring a vehicle.

While Duncan waited for the two to show their faces again, he kept his binoculars trained on the leader. He noted how the man moved like a big cat. Like a predator. There was no wasted motion. Just like Cade Grayson. A minute of this, and Duncan was pretty sure the soldier, who wore no rank or insignia on his fatigues, was Chinese special forces. There were Tiger Teams, and then there were the Cobras. Perhaps the man was the leader of a Cobra squad, the PLA's answer to the U.S. Army's Delta Force.

The pink scars on the man's face suggested he had seen his share of action. That he had survived told Duncan the man was someone he didn't want to tangle with. Just looking at him produced an uneasy feeling that lingered as he watched a pilot emerge and urinate on the practice green.

Duncan's question was answered when the Walking Stick shuttle vans came barreling down the cart path. They followed nearly the same route he had taken earlier, splitting the practice greens and driving onto the fairway. However, instead of charging toward the first hole's distant green, both vans cut sharp U-turns and parked near the women's tee box.

The soldier driving the lead van exited, suppressed bullpup in hand, and stalked back toward the clubhouse. He was rounding the Harbin's tail rotor when a zombie appeared from behind the clubhouse. As the soldier stopped to shoulder the weapon, more creatures emerged. Following in lockstep with the first, lips pulled back over yellowed teeth, they quickly fanned out.

Duncan lost count at fifteen.

The soldier leaned into his weapon and pressed the trigger. Though Duncan couldn't hear the reports, he saw the man's body judder, gunsmoke belch from the suppressor, and shell casings arcing from the ejection port.

When the firing ceased, Scarface beckoned the shooter over. There was now an urgency to Scarface's movement as the two men held a lengthy conversation. When the two parted, Scarface went to the helicopter, removed the hoods from the captives, and led them, one at a time, out onto the vacant practice green.

Duncan noted that the younger kids were moving sluggishly. The lanky one whom he had pegged as a teenager was, in fact, a fifteen- or sixteen-year-old male. The moment the hood had come off, the teen's head swung back and forth, looking a lot like an owl searching out prey, a slow pan belied only by his darting eyes. He was scanning his surroundings. It was obvious he was wondering where in the hell he was.

While this was happening, the subordinate had opened the rear of the first van and had hauled out two rows of seats. He then returned to the helicopter and wheeled one of the motorcycles over to the tee box. Once the crew chief had put the ramp in place, the two men loaded the bike into the back of the van.

Holstering his cleaned and oiled Beretta, Daymon said, "SITREP?"

Raven described everything she had witnessed. When she was finished, Duncan added his own observations.

Directing his question at no one in particular, Daymon said, "What do you think it all means?"

Duncan said, "Maybe they're running into Pueblo to look for parts to fix the helicopter."

"That would explain why they took the kids out," Raven theorized. "Giving them a chance to get some fresh air. Stretch their legs."

Shaking his head, Daymon said, "Pueblo Memorial Airport is about six miles east of here. It's largely untouched. The Air Force foraging teams even left behind a few bowsers full of fuel. One would think that if these guys had mechanical problems, they would have set their helo down there."

Duncan agreed with Daymon. Speaking to Raven's theory, he said, "I've heard what they do to kids, to captured soldiers. Cade's said before that *nothing* is off-limits. As far as they're concerned, the Geneva Convention is something you wipe your ass with." He paused, thinking. "If they're going to get parts, why the second van?"

Back to watching through the spotting scope, Raven drew a deep breath. Exhaling sharply, she said, "Just got your answer to that question. They're leading the kids to the van."

Daymon was up and standing beside Raven. Though he could see with his naked eye what was transpiring near the tee box, he said, "Which van?"

Duncan said, "The one they put the motorcycle in."

Daymon addressed Raven. "Remember your outing with Potvin?"

Nodding, Raven said, "I won't forget it anytime soon. But what's that have to do with this?"

Daymon said, "The Stryker left Potvin and you all out there by yourselves. Why was that?"

Raven said, "They left us to help some survivors whose van broke down."

"Who were the survivors?"

Duncan had been hanging on to Daymon's every word. Frustrated at how the younger man was dripping out information, making a game of it, he interrupted, saying, "Cut the crap and spit it out already. What are the commies planning?"

"I honestly don't know," Daymon said. "Just noting similarities."

Raven watched the soldier with the scar stop the teenager outside the van and lead him away. Fearing the worst, she drew a deep breath and held it in. But instead of putting a gun to the kid's head and executing him, the soldier put his hands on the teen's shoulders, locked eyes with him, and began to speak.

Though the teen was flex-cuffed, the two held a rather animated conversation. A few seconds later, looking totally defeated, the teen bowed his head.

Without uttering another word, the soldier with the scar loaded the teen into the van with the others, climbed into the passenger seat, and motioned for the other soldier to drive.

Seeing the van speed off toward the clubhouse and disappear from view, Raven released the breath she had been holding.

Rising up from behind the spotting scope, Duncan said, "I don't get it."

Raven took the Thuraya from her pack and powered it on. As she started banging out a text message, she said, "Let's see what my dad thinks."

Though the erratic driving was throwing Bryce around, he fixed his eyes on the van's headliner. He was awash in emotion. Agonizing over how much he should tell his younger siblings, he kept his eyes locked on a small tear in the vinyl and forced himself to weigh what his gut was telling him against what the soldier calling himself Zhen had just divulged.

Was the occupation truly over? Zhen had indicated his forces were on the verge of defeat. That they were being forced into a tactical retreat, whatever that meant.

The main thing nagging Bryce was the true whereabouts of his parents and uncle. He had last seen them three days ago at the medical facility he and his siblings were just evacuated from. A facility whose location had been kept from them all until just now.

While he wanted further proof that the helicopter transporting the rest of his family, along with several of Zhen's men, had really suffered a mechanical failure and crashed—killing all aboard—he didn't want to risk drawing the driver's ire. And right now, as Zhen had stressed just after informing him he and his siblings were being released, he was the man of the house. The oldest. The only one who could drive them all north—to safety.

"A walled-in city" was how Zhen had described the new Capital. It was sixty miles away, and Bryce had four other family members to worry about.

Getting them to safety was number one, he decided. The rest would have to wait.

The van was coasting to a stop near an overpass when twelve-year-old Brian came to. As he craned around, a blank look on his face, the three-year-old twins, Brie and Bristol, started to come out of their stupor. Then the sight of his other little sister, ten-year-old Bailey, fixing him with a questioning look started a new wave of worry in his stomach. It was compounded by the realization that the twins' car seats were in the Suburban, which was sitting useless somewhere outside of Taos. The bandits had come out of nowhere, firing their weapons into the tires. As his dad was surrendering, he had pointed out the spidered window glass and announced to everyone in a reassuring tone that they were all lucky to be alive and that God had been looking over them.

The first trip in the helicopter—also the first time Bryce had ever been hooded and flex-cuffed—was an experience he would never forget. It was also the first time he'd seen his parents and his Uncle Jack show any real fear. Word stealing fear. Sure, the meat bags could strike a nerve when they vastly outnumbered a person, but the effect these foreign occupiers had on all of them was not even close. They were nice one moment, brutal and unfeeling the next.

Dad had said they were just trying to keep everyone "on their toes." That they were maintaining the "upper hand."

Uncle Jack called it "good cop, bad cop."

Having been brutalized by some of the soldiers, Mom simply turned inward and stopped talking altogether.

Whatever the strategy, it had worked. It had broken the adults. And up until this very moment, with the driver of the van about to hand it over and just let them all go, it was a mystery to Bryce why they had been brought here in the first place.

When the driver's seat was turned over with an unsmiling Zhen still in the passenger seat and reiterating his instructions, the wave of worry had grown into a full-on cascade of emotion.

Zhen ordered Bryce not to deviate from the highway. He was to drive all the way north. To the gate outside of a city. A city that Zhen promised had lights and running water. And other kids and teens his age.

Finally, their former captor said that to stop was to die. For if the engine were turned off, the battery wouldn't have enough of a charge to get it restarted.

"Do you understand?" asked Zhen, a certain menace to his tone. "This is your one and only chance to save yourself. You are very lucky the war ended when it did. You and the rest of your family were one day away from being transported to the fields. Instead of living out the rest of your lives as slaves in service to the Communist Party of China, I'm granting you freedom."

Bryce didn't know what to say. He was too busy worrying the twins were going to start bombarding him with questions he didn't have the answers to—chief among them: Where is Mom, Dad, and Uncle Jack?

Remaining tight-lipped, he nodded that he understood, climbed behind the wheel, and waited for the signal.

The signal came after the soldiers had removed the motorcycle and closed the van's rear doors. It was a single rap on the sheet metal that was still reverberating in his head as he let off the brake and steered for the nearby on-ramp.

Tears welled in his eyes when he thought of his parents and Jack being thrown around inside the tin can as it plummeted to earth. He hoped they had died on impact instead of having been burned alive as Yong had suggested. Bryce suspected the man was lying. Pushing his buttons. From the first day in captivity, the tall Asian had taken to tormenting Bryce and his siblings.

Though Bryce's eyes were clouded with tears when he looked at the passenger side mirror, he was certain he saw the bike, complete with rider and passenger, speeding off toward the golf course.

Chapter 39

Raven, Duncan, and Daymon were still hunkered down in the master bedroom when the dirt bike carrying the two soldiers ripped across the distant fairway.

As Duncan tracked the bike with the Steiners, he concluded that Scarface was in control. The taller soldier, bullpup slung across his back, looked goofy sitting ramrod straight and gripping the underside of the seat with both hands.

Sitting cross-legged by the window, silhouette broken up by the floor-to-ceiling drapes, Daymon was busy looking out over the backyard.

From the time the van had driven off, up until about a minute ago, Bernie had been stretching the tether to its limits and walking a continuous circle. Something out of sight had the Z all worked up.

Over the span of a minute or so, the reason for Bernie's increasing agitation had been showing up in twos and threes. Now, from the cement pad below Daymon's perch to the uneven strip of grass bordering the green, the backyard was overrun by Zs.

Clearly, it was the helicopter that was drawing them in from the street.

Daymon did a quick count of the bobbing heads down below. *Thirty.* It was a ballpark figure, and they were still coming.

Some of the first zombies to arrive had taken an interest in Duncan's pickup. They were crowding the driver's door, craning to see inside. Others, their attention drawn to the returning motorcycle, were making a beeline for the green.

Duncan watched the riders dismount the dirt bike and leave it propped up alongside the remaining shuttle van. The subordinate went to work ripping the rows of seats out of the van. When he was finished, the van was gutted, and the jumble of seats discarded on the tee box stood nearly head-high to him.

While the subordinate was busy with something inside the van, Scarface pulled out a satellite phone, tapped on its face, and pressed it to his ear.

Working autonomously, the crew chief had removed the camouflage netting, folded it into a square, and stowed it away in the Z-9's troop compartment.

As Scarface finished the call and dropped the phone into a cargo pocket, the helicopter's turbine fired and the rotors started to spin.

A handful of seconds after Scarface had ended his call, the crew chief was inside the helicopter with the cabin door closed.

With the Z-9's rotor blades picking up speed and beginning to merge into a single blurry disc, Duncan said, "Second helo inbound. Eleven o'clock. Low and slow."

Since the moment the van with the kids inside had sped off, Raven's attention had been pulled nonstop in three different directions. There were the dead showing up in the yard below, the activity in and around the helicopter on the practice green, and the Thuraya clutched in her left hand.

The phone to her was like Lord Sauron's Ring was to Gollum. Though she was aware of the idiom *A watched pot never boils*, and knew full well what it meant, she couldn't resist the urge to lift the phone to her face and see with her eyes what her ears could confirm. Though it had been ten minutes since she had sent the lengthy text to her father, the chime to alert her that it had been received still had not sounded.

Bracketed by Duncan and Daymon, the spotting scope peeking between the closed blinds, she pressed her eye to the rubber cup and began searching the sky for the new arrival. When she finally acquired the light gray helicopter, she said, "What kind is this one?"

Duncan tracked the inbound chopper using the Steiners. "Markings are similar to the other. It's definitely a PLA bird. But it's a different model. Trade me." He handed over the Steiners, crouched down behind the spotting scope, then spent a few seconds watching the helicopter orbit the clubhouse. As it slowed and began to descend toward the second practice green, he said, “It’s a Harbin Z-8. Multi-role platform made by Aerospatiale. Looks unarmed. Probably transporting troops.” He rattled off a few more specs then went quiet.

Raven had been composing another text to her father as Duncan was speaking. She left the text unsent and watched the helicopter settle on the green.

The helicopter was much bigger than the first. It, too, had tricycle landing gear and a single rotor overhead. Unlike the Z-9, the Z-8’s tail rotor was not housed inside a protective shroud. It was currently a horizontal black blur scything the air.

Even as the door opened and a pair of soldiers and three other men in civilian attire spilled out, the turbines maintained their high-pitched howl.

Duncan said, “They’re keeping her hot. Ready to launch at a moment’s notice. Better add that to the book you’re writing.”

“It’s a text,” Raven shot. “I don’t want to leave anything out. Quit breaking my …” She left the rest unsaid. Figured Duncan could use his imagination to fill it in.

Daymon was up and pacing a hole in the carpet. He said, “All that noise is just going to bring out more biters. Maybe we should be thinking about getting out of here.”

Duncan said, “And have the Z-9 put a heat seeker up my tailpipe? I’ll take my chances right here. Hell, if the biters break down the door, we can always retreat to the attic.”

Stopping in his tracks, Daymon said, “That’s what I’m afraid of.”

Raven said, “I’m with Duncan. Besides, I think they’re up to something big. I owe it to my dad to pass along as factual a SITREP as possible. If he doesn’t respond soon, I’ll run it up the chain.” She nodded at Daymon. “I have General Nash on speed dial. She’ll know what to make of all this. At the very least, she’ll send in the cavalry.”

Duncan was going to comment on Raven’s perfect use of military nomenclature but was sidetracked when he saw the Z-9’s crew chief run the ramp over to the Z-8. Then, with the help of a crew chief wearing a helmet and identical jumpsuit, they positioned the ramp in the open door. Together, the crew chiefs rolled two more dirt bikes from the helo, pushed them across the green, and left them at the shuttle van with the other two.

With the Z-9 spooling up off his left shoulder, Zhen snatched the ramp from the Z-8's open door and hustled it over to the van. After bringing the two recently arrived members of his Cobra Force up to speed, he instructed Staff Sergeant Xian Chun to take the wheel. Zhen then ordered Sergeant Wen Bao to help the crew chiefs load two of the dirt bikes into the van.

Everything was falling into place. The Z-8 launching behind him was ranging ahead to scout out a safe place for them to rendezvous once the second phase of Operation Blanket was commenced.

The American spawn were well on the way to their destination. He wasn't stupid, though. No way he was going to leave it all up to the teenager to unknowingly deliver the weapon. Already going light on her gear, the Z-9 was going to fly ahead and shadow the van to track its progress.

If anything should go awry—if Bryce's free will got the better of him and caused him to disobey orders, or the van suffered a mechanical breakdown, or a herd of jiangshi got in the way—it wouldn't be the end. In fact, this was only the beginning. There was still plenty of the new Whirlwind virus to go around. As Zhen mounted his bike and waited for Chun to get the van turned toward the clubhouse, his play on words brought a smile to his face.

The helicopters were thundering off to the west when the pair of riders gunned their bikes and rolled out ahead of the van.

Raven watched until the only thing moving outside the mansion was the parade of Zs streaming toward the clubhouse. After adding a few more lines to the SITREP, she read it one last time. Unable to think of anything else to add, she sent it on its way.

Duncan said, "Now we wait."

Standing at the window, palms pressed to the glass, Daymon looked to Duncan. "If we do end up in the attic, you better have enough rounds for that shotty of yours to open up a big ass hole in the roof. Because I'll be damned if I'm putting my back into it like I had to in Hanna. My spine hasn't been the same since."

"That's old age creepin' up on you," quipped Duncan. "Get used to it. Ain't nothing that can stop the march of time. Or keep the Reaper at bay when he comes a callin'."

Eighty-five miles southwest of New District, Jedi One was clipping along at a hundred and seventy knots. It wasn't her top speed, but Ari was pushing it pretty close. He was taking very seriously the return-to-base order.

Fifteen hundred feet below the black helicopter, Great Sand Dunes National Park and Preserve, a three-hundred-and-thirty-square-mile sand deposit, was a mosaic consisting of the tallest sand dunes in North America, grass-covered plains, marshy wetlands, conifer and aspen forests, and the occasional alpine lake.

The beautiful landscape did nothing to assuage the feeling of disappointment that had been nagging Cade since the hasty Albuquerque exfil. The culmination of the mission, spanning two states and hundreds of miles, rang eerily similar to the one at Fort Meade in Maryland.

Zhen and his Cobras had slipped the noose that day, too. The Pale Riders had missed the special forces team by a matter of minutes. President Clay diverting the Pale Riders to the Archives Building in Washington D.C. to retrieve the founding documents had just added insult to injury. It was a side trip Cade had not foreseen. Still, serving at the pleasure of the president, he had swallowed that bitter pill and executed the new orders to the letter, bringing the documents home for the people to see. To derive hope from. Hope that America would soon push the People's Liberation Army into the sea, defeat the zombie scourge roaming the nation, and then rise again from the ashes, stronger than ever.

An incoming text vibrated the Thuraya clutched in his hand. He'd been checking it every fifteen minutes or so since boarding Jedi One. He was about to do so for the fifth time when the tremor coursed his glove.

As he read the pair of long, detailed messages, he sensed all eyes on him. Finished, he looked around the cabin. Judging by the looks directed back at him from behind their D50 masks, to a man, his teammates' curiosity had been piqued.

Cade texted back: **Stay put! Sending help.** Hailing the op center at Peterson, he reread Raven's texts with both Nash and Smokey on the line. After the oration, he reminded them of the van full of kids that had been saved by the Stryker crew. Letting that sink in, he mentioned the PLA scouts Raven had caught on video shortly thereafter. He then posited his theory that the van full of kids witnessed leaving the golf course was the delivery system. They were infected, and the van was a modern-day Trojan Horse.

"Every one of them passed quarantine with flying colors," Nash said. "We're days out from that incident, and New District isn't in the grips of a new pandemic."

Cade said, "That was a dry run. What my daughter witnessed today is the real thing."

Nash said, "Agreed." There was a short pause, after which she added, "Smokey concurs. We'll bring POTUS up to speed."

Though neither of them had asked Cade for his input, he recommended an interdiction force of medical personnel and shooters be formed. Agreeing, Smokey indicated he would get the 160th SOAR assets lined up and two teams of shooters to the tarmac.

Nash promised, come hell or high water, the birds would be wheels up in ten. She also indicated that one of her satellites had been re-tasked and would soon be passing over Arizona and New Mexico.

While the satellite might be on station in time to help, Cade knew the ball was in his hands right now. Ending the call, he started crunching numbers. Concluding that the first van's thirty-minute head start should put it nearly equidistant to Pueblo and New District, there was no way his team was going to be involved in the interdiction. With that in mind, he decided it was on them to find and intercept the responsible parties. With two enemy helicopters already in the air, a van and two riders on the move, the search was going to be akin to searching for needles in an Everest-sized haystack.

Having been listening to the SITREP and follow-on conversation, Ari didn't need anyone to tell him what to do next.

Working the pedals, stick, and collective in unison, he got the bird tracking for Pueblo at top speed.

QSZ-92 pistol clutched in his left hand, Zhen steered the softly idling Yamaha with the other. As he closed the distance to the pack of dead, he threw the safety and thrust the pistol out over the handlebars.

The creatures were spread out across the entrance to I-25 southbound, leaving only a yard or so between the shoulder and right-side guardrail. Their appearance was a direct result of the earlier activity on the overpass. Zhen had spotted them wandering the streets a few blocks west of the highway and had expected them to follow the retreating van.

That they didn't was not a problem. Because if all went as planned, there would be thousands of jiangshi streaming north, their arrival at Colorado Springs timed to coincide perfectly with the start of the massive die-off wrought on the Americans by the aptly named Whirlwind virus.

Adjusting course to avoid a miasma of pulped flesh and splintered bone spread across the eastbound lane, Zhen pressed the trigger, sending the jiangshi nearest to him crashing to the road. Slow-rolling the bike forward, he shifted aim and sent a second monster to its final sleep. Expending the entire magazine, Zhen left a trail of jiangshi bodies in his wake and opened up a path wide enough for the van to safely pass.

With Yong on Zhen's six, and the van following close behind Yong, Zhen led the three-vehicle procession down the ramp and onto the highway.

Choosing a spot on the highway where it shot off laser-straight to the south for as far as he could see, Zhen pulled over and dismounted his bike. To his right, up a small embankment, was a used car lot. The vehicles were all blackened husks resting on tireless rims.

Adjacent to the northbound lanes, up a steeply angled hill and separated by chain-link fence, was the south end of Pueblo Mall. A large, boxy building housing something called Hobby Lobby was on the opposite side of the fence. Its glass facade was punched through with bullet holes. The windows at ground level were mostly broken out. Dozens of dead bodies, most mummified by the high desert sun, lay scattered about the sidewalk and parking lot. A full-sized import SUV was wedged in one of the store's two entrances. Already the sound of the van's engine was drawing the dead out of the other door.

While Zhen's team wired the van with explosives, he rode on ahead, beeping the bike's tinny-sounding horn as he stayed to the center of a car-sized gap cleared from the jammed-up traffic.

After riding south for a mile or so, his thumb never lifting off the horn button, Zhen stopped and turned the bike around.

He put the bike in neutral and released the clutch. Steadying the bike's vibrating mirror with one hand, he focused on the off-ramp reflected back at him. He'd only been waiting for a minute or two when the jiangshi began to appear. At first, they showed up in twos and threes, heads bobbing, eyes searching for the source of the noise. All of the first arrivals had been burned to one degree or another. After another minute or so, the jiangshi were cresting the top of the ramp in waves and pouring down the decline.

Seven minutes had slipped into the past before Zhen was satisfied with the number of jiangshi his horn had coaxed from the burned-out city.

The technique he was employing was akin to siphoning gas from a vehicle—something he was no stranger to. Get the gas flowing from the tank, then let gravity do the rest.

While Zhen had already started the flow from the city, the van bomb was designed to sustain it.

Then, when the lead element reached the van, Zhen and his Cobras would be the *gravity* that kept the burgeoning horde flowing northbound in the southbound lanes. At first sight of the fresh meat Zhen and his men represented, he was confident the jiangshi would lose any and all interest with the burning van and give chase.

Zhen looked at his watch. He'd been gone for ten minutes. Plenty of time for his expert demolition man, Chun, to finish his task.

With the stink of death coming off the approaching jiangshi causing his eyes to tear, Zhen engaged first gear and rode slowly north. For the first half of the ride back to the van, he stayed just out of reach of the bell cow, blipping the engine and honking the horn to further excite the African American jiangshi. Once Zhen had the van in sight, he kicked the bike into third gear and sprinted the rest of the way.

When Zhen reunited with his team, they were astride their bikes, engines running and helmet straps cinched tight.

"How many jiangshi?" asked Chun.

"One hundred, maybe two," answered Zhen. "There will be more." He stole a quick peek at the Hobby Lobby. Jiangshi now stood shoulder to shoulder and three deep at the fence. Their combined weight was bowing the fence outward. Judging by the sharp angle the fence posts had adopted, the entire run was close to failing.

Chun handed over the detonator. It was the size of a pack of cigarettes. A red plastic shroud covered the firing switch.

Zhen pocketed the device then tore off to the north. After traveling roughly five hundred meters, he slowed his bike in the shadow of an abandoned UPS box truck, looped around back of it, and dismounted. He left the bike running and stepped aside to make room for the other bikes.

While he waited for the others to take cover, he checked in with the pilot of the Z-9. Da Yin, an ultra-confident city-dweller whose parents had been hardwired into the CCP since the Tiananmen Square incident, had jumped ahead of the line and was fast-tracked through training. A green aviator when the virus escaped, Yin had quickly honed his skills ferrying party elites to the bunkers they all thought would be their salvation. They were mistaken. Some of them had brought Omega inside with them.

A big fan of American cinema, Yin had chosen his own call sign. A big no-no for an army aviator. Acceptable when your peers had been failing to return from missions in ever-increasing numbers.

"Ice Man, Zhen. How copy?"

Yin loved hearing his call sign come over the radio. Smile blooming beneath the helmet's deployed visor, he said, "Good copy, Zhen."

Zhen said, "Do you have eyes on the vehicle?"

"Affirmative," Yin replied. "But they've only covered fifteen kilometers."

Zhen had had a hunch, due to the teenager's tentative nature and lack of experience behind the wheel, that the going would be slow. But not glacially slow.

"Keep overwatch as long as possible. They *must* reach Colorado Springs."

After receiving a rather terse sounding "affirmative" from the self-proclaimed Ice Man, Zhen fished out the detonator and flipped up the shroud. Alerting his team, he started counting down from five. Arriving at *one*, he said, "Fire in the hole," and threw the rocker switch.

The command traveled via radio frequency from the detonator to the RF receiver attached to blasting caps embedded in each of the two one-and-one-quarter-pound bricks of C-4 plastic explosive. The RF receiver fired the blasting caps simultaneously.

The explosion was near instantaneous and rocked the UPS van front to back. Debris rained down on the highway, a twisted bumper falling dangerously close to Zhen and his team.

If Zhen had been watching, he would have seen the shockwave slap down the first thirty or so jiangshi. Though the lead element had closed to within a hundred meters of the van prior to detonation and had been peppered with glass and shrapnel, they were rising up from the debris-strewn blacktop before Zhen and his Cobras had rolled their bikes from cover.

Straddling his bike, Zhen looked south. The initial fireball had already subsided. The van was still fully engulfed. Burning plastic, vinyl, and rubber contributed to the thick, black smoke plume roiling skyward. Gray smoke from the melting tires poured from the wheel wheels.

Zhen sounded his horn, keeping the button depressed. The seconds ticked away as he waited for the dead to make their appearance.

Walking Stick Golf Course

Raven had been standing by the window overlooking the backyard, watching close to a hundred zombies cutting a path toward the distant clubhouse, when she heard a hollow boom. A beat later, as the windows vibrated in their frames, she looked to Duncan.

"What was that?"

"An explosion," Duncan replied.

Having been pacing the master bedroom since Raven's back and forth texts with her father, Daymon stopped long enough to peer out the window. Seeing the dead beginning to about-face, he spit a couple of choice epithets and then resumed pacing.

"No duh," said Raven. "What do you think it was, and how far away did it happen?"

"Sounded like some type of high explosives. I'd put it somewhere south by west of here. A mile, maybe two out."

Peering out the window, Raven said, "The biters are all heading back this way."

Daymon stopped again. "Of course they are. We're going to be trapped in here. I can never catch an effin break. I come all this way, I show you the honey hole, and then this happens. Ever heard of snatching victory out of the jaws of defeat?"

Raven shook her head.

"That's definitely not you, Daymon." Duncan chuckled at his funny. "You have idiom dyslexia."

Daymon shot Old Man the bird. "You knew where I was going. Pisses me off we'll be leaving all this stuff here."

Raven said, "You spoke too soon, Uncle Daymon. Looks like the biters are forgetting all about us. They're bypassing the yard and heading for the street."

"When they're all gone, I'm getting the hell out of here," Daymon declared.

"I have the keys," Duncan said. "And we have orders from on high. We're staying put until the cavalry arrives. And five gets you ten that Cade's idea of 'cavalry' is a Chinook or Black Hawk."

Incredulous, Daymon said, "You're just going to leave your truck here?"

"What's your buddy Eazy E say? Something along the lines of 'throw it in the gutter, go find another.'" Duncan winked at Raven. "That's what I'm going to do. Sage advice."

Raven said, "I can't leave. I promised my dad I would hang tight."

"Ditto," Duncan said. "Captain America always comes through in the end."

"Fine," Daymon said, his tone that of a petulant child. He plopped down on the bed. "Two against one. And the losing streak continues."

I-25 Pueblo, Colorado

Three minutes after detonating the bomb, with the van settling on bare rims and flame still licking the empty frames where window glass used to reside, the train of staggering jiangshi parted the ground-hugging smoke.

Zhen kept the horn blaring and led the team away, at slow speed, toward the nearby Cesar Chavez overpass.

Reaching the overpass, the team parked in its shadow, killed their engines, and dismounted.

Doing the math in his head, Zhen figured it would take the fastest jiangshi of the group close to ten minutes to trudge the half-mile to his position.

This was to be just one stop of many the Cobras would make over the course of the next dozen or so hours. The game of cat and mouse would go into the night and stretch to first light. By then, Zhen's job would be done. The horde would be fully formed, an unstoppable and insatiable mass of decaying flesh and bone within striking distance of America's largest stronghold.

Smiling at the thought of the walls coming down under the weight of so many undead Americans, Zhen retrieved a cereal bar from a pocket, peeled back the wrapper, and took a bite.

Before Zhen had swallowed that first bite, he felt a sensation deep in his chest that could mean only one thing: An American stealth helicopter was rapidly approaching.

Cursing himself for leaving the man portable missile in the helo, Zhen hunched down over the bars and searched the sky for the incoming threat.

Chapter 40

Viewed through the Ghost Hawk's fuselage window, South Pueblo looked like it had been hit by a low-yield nuclear bomb. The only thing left standing taller than the scorched trunks of what were likely the largest trees in the city prior to the inferno were the remnants of steel-framed and brick buildings. The intense heat had reduced the former to mounds of malformed girders that resembled the famed Hindenburg zeppelin's superstructure as it lay in ruins on the field at Naval Air Station Lakehurst in Manchester Township, New Jersey.

The latter resembled the smattering of structures left standing in London after the Nazi Luftwaffe unleashed their Blitzkrieg on the English capital.

As the corpse-choked Arkansas River came into view out Cade's window, Ari abruptly cut the helo's speed in half and nosed her into a steep dive.

Over the shared comms, he said, "We've got a smoke plume. Twelve o' clock. Four miles out. Dropping to one thousand AGL."

Breaking in, Haynes said, "Bringing optics up."

Griff scowled at Cade. "And here I thought I was going to get to take this damn mask off sometime in the not too distant future."

Cross said, "Enjoy your time in the wild while you can. When we get back to base, we're probably looking at an extended stay in quarantine."

"Damn surfer boy," Griff shot. "Always champing at the bit to burst my bubble."

Ari parked Jedi One over I-25. The stretch of highway was bordered on the west by razed business concerns and to the east by train tracks. Fountain Creek, reduced to a trickle due to the lack of rain, meandered south on a serpentine path parallel to the tracks.

Haynes said, "Migrating video to the cabin monitor."

All eyes in the cabin went to the monitor. The run of car-choked highway displayed on the screen was cut in half by a thin plume of black smoke, the source of which was a mystery due to the standoff distance.

Cade said, "Zoom in." No sooner had he requested it than the source of the smoke was growing exponentially larger on the monitor. When the camera ceased zooming in, and the image snapped into clear focus, there was no denying they were looking at the remnants of one of the shuttle vans described in the text. The clear proof was the driver's side door that had ended up fifty yards away. Emblazoned on it in red letters was the golf course's name and all of its contact information.

"That's one of the course shuttle vans," Cade acknowledged. "Lots of smoke. Hard to tell if there was anybody inside when it went up."

Nat said, "Looks like they hit an IED. I don't see a crater, though."

"Dead giveaway that it wasn't an IED," Axe noted, "is that the majority of the glass ended up on the ground *outside* of the minibus."

Ari said, "I can hover close to the wreckage. Rotor wash will scour the smoke and give you a better view of the van's interior."

Cade said, "Haynes, pull back and pan down. There in the foreground. Seems to be a lot of movement between the vehicles a quarter-mile south of the van."

Haynes said, "Roger that. Coming up."

Simultaneously the van grew smaller on the screen and, as Haynes manipulated the camera in the gimbal, the stretch of highway due south became the focus.

Commenting on the new image on the monitor, Cross said, "That's got the makings of a full-blown horde. A couple, maybe three hundred rotters is a solid nucleus."

Cade said, "Ari, can you bring us in closer using the smoke as concealment?"

"I can park us in the middle of it if you want," Ari offered.

"Just put it between us and that overpass."

Griff said, "PLA scouts?"

Cade nodded. "The van is the lure. They're the bait. They've got to be loitering somewhere close by. It's mid-eighties out there. If it was me drawing the Zs north, I'd do my loitering in the shade."

Ari said, "What's the call, boss?"

Cade said, "Go to thermal and check the underpass. If the enemy is still nearby, that's likely where we'll find them."

"Copy that," Ari replied. "Haynes, go to thermal. Skip, ready both guns."

As Jedi One went nose down and began to creep slowly forward, Skip powered open the right-side door and both of the weapon bay doors.

In rushed hot air thick with the combined stench of decaying flesh and kerosene-tinged jet exhaust.

Deploying the right-side Dillon, Skip looked to Cade. "Which one of your guys is going to man the left-side mini?"

Only obvious choice was Nat. While he was the biggest of the group and took up more than his share of cabin space, with his messed-up toes he would be a liability if he were to go boots on the ground with the team.

Making room for the big operator to slide by, Cade said, "You're up, Nat." Looking to Axe, he added, "You got overwatch. If we encounter riders, try to wing them."

Anticipating the call, the Brit had already begun assembling his custom Remington MSR sniper rifle.

"If we go boots on," Cade said, looking to Griff and Cross, "I'm point. Cross, you take rear guard."

Cross nodded and flashed Cade a thumbs-up.

Shaking his head, Griff said, "Always making good ol' Griff the meat in the sandwich."

Cade said nothing. He was staring intently at the monitor.

Ari pulled Jedi One out of the dive roughly two hundred feet above the long snarl of scorched cars on I-25. Applying pedal, the SOAR aviator side-slipped his bird through the smoke plume.

Though keeping the helo's right flank facing the underpass provided the enemy a huge target to shoot at, it allowed Ari a perfect view from the right seat, Skip a two-hundred-and-seventy-degree field of fire with the right-side minigun, and Axe—prone on the floor with his long gun trained downrange—as stable a platform to shoot from as humanly possible.

All business, Haynes said, "Enemy contact, eleven o'clock. Four bodies on motorcycles. Heat sigs indicate all four engines are hot."

Flicking his eyes to the threat warning screen, Ari noted the absence of radiation indicating the presence of an activated MANPAD.

What Haynes had described, Cade was seeing on the cabin monitor. "I concur," he responded at once. "Engage at will."

As Skip fired a short burst from the Dillon, Cade double-checked his safety harness. If they were going to take fire, the rounds would soon be incoming. No sooner had he thought it than he saw a star-shaped muzzle flash erupt in the shadow of the overpass.

Having withdrawn deep into the shadow of the overpass, Zhen had dragged binoculars from his pack and was busy scanning the southern sky. While he could still feel the disconcerting and barely perceptible resonance in his chest, he could now *hear* the faint thrum of something scything the air far away. If he didn't know any better, if he hadn't been in the presence of the evil black helicopter on more than one occasion, he would probably attribute the audible sound to a rising wind. Maybe explain away the sensation in his chest to a rapid change in barometric pressure. But he did know better. It was out there somewhere. And it was on the hunt.

With the dead marching steadily toward the only viable cover for blocks around, Zhen had a difficult decision to make.

He could recall the Z-8 from the loiter LZ and risk losing the remaining bioweapon stockpile. Another option would be to place a distress call to Yin and order an immediate exfil. The Z-9 was armed with missiles and might just level the playing field. Or the most logical of the three: Recall Yin, wait until he was seconds out, then split up the team and rabbit in multiple directions. This third scenario would, in theory, kill two birds with one stone. First, it would flush out the enemy, who would then find themselves so preoccupied with chasing the mice that the returning dog just might succeed in catching the cat unaware.

Zhen had just delivered the order to start option three into motion when, from out of the smoke plume, the black helicopter revealed itself. It was coming fast from the south and had just cleaved through the rising smoke plume.

Twisting the throttle to the stop, Zhen released the clutch and put his weight over the tank. As he wrenched the bars left, kicked out his left leg, and the rear tire grabbed the road, all hell broke loose around him.

First, the patch of asphalt he had just vacated seemed to erupt, and he was peppered with fragments sent airborne. They banged off the bike. A few jagged shards found flesh, burrowing deeply into his right upper thigh, forearm, and shoulder. At first blush, he categorized all three as superficial. Already his system was being flooded with pain-deadening endorphins.

Zhen's right-hand man, Chun, had been anticipating the attack. And though he was able to empty an entire magazine downrange, the distance was too great. He had just let go of the rifle and was transitioning his hands to the bike's handlebars when the enemy rounds found him.

In his headset, Zhen heard Chun grunt. That was it from the man. Judging by the condition of the torso careening through Zhen's right side vision, the man wasn't getting up. With just one leg and a bloody stump for an arm, he was seconds from bleeding out even if he had survived the volley.

Following Bao and Yong, already powering their bikes up the embankment, Zhen radioed the former, ordering him to slow down and allow him and Yong to overtake him.

As Bao let off the throttle, Yong shot past him on the right, already angling to make the sharp turn at the top of the ramp.

Engine nearly redlined, Zhen coaxed every ounce of horsepower out of the Yamaha's 450cc engine. He would need it when he crested the hill alongside Yong.

Prior to the helicopter's arrival, Zhen had split the team into pairs, each with its own protocol should they come under attack. He and Yong were the bait. They would sprint for the nearby business cluster, hopefully drawing the attacker's undivided attention.

Meanwhile, Chun and Bao were to lag behind. Once the enemy was on the hook, they were to go in the opposite direction, cross the overpass, and find somewhere to go to ground.

Zhen was angry at himself for letting his team get caught out in the open.

He wasn't surprised by Chun's death. The young man wasn't the first to die under his command, and he certainly wouldn't be the last.

No battle plan survives first contact with the enemy.

On his stomach, safety tether biting into his hip, Axe steadied his breathing and drew up a few pounds of trigger pull. The Leupold scope allowed him to see the entire stretch of road where the off-ramp fed Cesar Chavez. It was where he was anticipating the riders to reappear.

Through the scope, he had witnessed one rider's body come apart. As the shredded corpse and motorcycle went their separate ways, he asked himself what he would do next. The obvious came to him at once. His hunch was confirmed when two riders appeared, cresting the hill, their bikes leaned hard over to their right.

Skip had been on the same page. Great minds and all that. The MSR and Dillon spit lead at the same time.

Both attempts failed.

The short burst from the minigun carved a man-sized canyon into the pavement in front of the riders just as they were making their turn. If either was hit by lead or debris, it wasn't immediately evident.

Undeterred, Axe kept the scope trained on the overpass and swung the Remington's barrel a few degrees to the right.

When rider number three's head and upper body came into view, Axe exhaled slowly and pressed the trigger. Moving at close to thirty-three hundred feet per second, the .338 Lapua match-grade round hit the rider a full six inches lower than where it was supposed to. Instead of creating a fist-sized hole in the rider's face, it struck his neck, square on, severing the helmeted head from the torso.

Bike, rider, and head went in three different directions.

The headless corpse was thrown backward off the bike. It landed in a fetal ball, tumbled across the blacktop, then came to rest splayed out at the feet of a pair of zombies, who instantly dropped to their knees and dug claw-like fingers into bloody flesh.

Engine still delivering power to the rear wheel, the riderless bike continued on for a dozen feet before crashing to the road, where it spun around two full revolutions before going still.

Moving like a misshapen soccer ball struck by David Beckham, the rider's head skipped across the boulevard. After hitting a first turn square in the junk, the head came to rest at its feet, the road-rashed face staring skyward.

Immediately, Axe swung his barrel left. He caught sight of the retreating bikes at the same moment Skip ripped off another short burst with the Dillon.

As rounds from the mini chased the riders, more asphalt was churned up on Cesar Chavez, and sparks erupted from the rear of the trailing bike.

Cade had moved a seat over and was watching the action on the monitor. As soon as the second rider was relieved of his head, the helicopter began to spin on axis and grab altitude.

Addressing Skip, Cade said, "I think you hit the bike. Hopefully, it'll slow them down."

Skip was craning to reacquire a target. "Lost them in the trees, damn it. That miss is all on me. Didn't anticipate them laying their bikes down sideways and taking the turn like they did."

"Never seen a dirt bike ridden like that," Griff added. "A Suzuki Hayabusa, sure. But a Yamaha on knobby tires?" He shook his head. "Never seen anything like that on pavement."

Cross said, "Desperate times call for drastic measures."

The Ghost Hawk was picking up speed and leveling off, tracking west along Cesar Chavez. On the left side, everything was razed by fire. Only the signs remained. Jack in the Box, Dairy Queen, Pizza Hut, a coin-op laundry, a battery and light bulb store—they were all reduced to ash.

Off to the right of the Ghost Hawk, save for the zombies and trash in the streets and lack of working traffic signals, everything appeared normal. Down below, fronting the boulevard and sharing a vast parking lot, was a Lowe's home and garden store and a strip mall full of small businesses.

The darkened windows and signage made Cade think of *The Omega Man*—a Charlton Heston film he had watched with his father at the Avalon Theater in Portland.

Behind the blocks-long commerce district was a residential neighborhood. It was bordered to the east by a cluster of fast food joints in view of I-25.

Beyond the sprawling residential area were miles and miles of desert. The landscape was crossed by rural roads and dotted with scrub. Here and there, a home surrounded by brown grass and obligatory pickets of wind-breaking trees could be seen.

The riders had quickly cut another right and disappeared under cover of a blocks-long copse of trees bordering I-25. It was double canopy. The optics couldn't penetrate it.

Ari swung the helo back around, cutting a clockwise arc above the business district that left Nat looking out over the one- and two-story homes and Skip with a clear view of the trees the riders *should* be hiding in.

Cade said, "If Skip did ding the bike, they're probably doubling up on the other one as we speak. If it were me down there, I'd squirt into the business park to the west. Lots of cover. Easy to get lost in there."

Griff said, "They *could be* aiming a MANPAD at us as we speak."

"Negative," replied Skip. "I only spotted rifles and sidearms."

Over the shipwide comms, Ari said, "Still nothing showing on the sensors. If they had a man-portable that we didn't see, and they do paint us with it, they'll have to come out in the open to do so. The second they power it up and activate the seeker, we'll know all about it."

Cross said, "I didn't see NVGs on their helmets. What do you say we deploy ours and go in the woods and flush them out?"

Cade said, "Advantage noted." Addressing Ari, he went on, saying, "I need an orbit around the grove. Give us a better feel for the battlespace." On his mind was the Omega-tainted ammunition. He'd already lost one Pale Rider to the disgusting tactic. He wanted to expend all other avenues before rushing in.

Ari said, "Roger that," and started the helo tracking on a clockwise orbit that initially took them out over I-25.

Skip was alert, both gloved hands on the minigun grips.

Now sitting cross-legged in the open doorway, MSR tucked in tight to his shoulder, Axe was focusing his attention on the grove's many shadowy alcoves.

As they came around the grove's east side, Cade saw that the headless PLA soldier had drawn quite a crowd. The first zombies on scene were already on their knees, faces buried in the dead man's chest. Others had wormed their way in and were bent over and stripping flesh from the soldier's limp appendages.

A handful of Zs had pursued the riders and was just entering the grove from the south, at roughly the same spot Skip had last seen them.

More walking corpses were arriving steadily from the east and west.

Cesar Chavez was quickly becoming a dangerous place to be.

On a low ridge three-quarters of a mile northeast of Peterson Air Force Base, Xehua Peng was occupying the same patch of ground he'd been lying on when he witnessed the beginnings of a large-scale aerial operation.

Now, hours later, he had been in the sun so long that a thin sliver of skin on the back of his neck not covered by the ghillie suit was severely sunburned. Also, there was the ant problem: like miniature jiangshi, they had come at him from all sides, the sting of their tiny pincers adding to his overall discomfort.

With the sun finally behind the distant mountains, and a cooling breeze lifting up from the west, Peng was counting the seconds until full dark, when he would be able to move from the ridge and put some food in his belly.

He had his sights set on the laundromat. It would conceal the flame of his white gas stove as he boiled water to add to his instant noodles. If he had enough left over, he promised himself a half cup of freshly brewed tea.

Resisting the urge to crush an ant angling in for an attack, a flurry of motion at the distant air base drew Peng's attention.

Lifting the binoculars, he glassed the base. Already several helicopters had lifted off from the tarmac. They were actively patrolling the air space over the entire area. Fearing he would be spotted, he had remained motionless—until now.

Men in various stages of undress and carrying weapons were rushing toward a pair of Black Hawks. As the helicopters' rotor blades began to move, more people—men and women clad in hazardous material suits—arrived aboard a pair of golf carts. Carrying helmets and portable oxygen units, the new arrivals jumped from the carts and hustled for the helicopter.

A cold ball forming in his stomach, Peng lowered the binoculars and went to fish the Inmarsat from a pocket.

He was dragging the phone out when he heard the same tell-tale scuffing noise he'd been hearing intermittently all day long.

Ignoring the wandering jiangshi—the odds of them discovering him next to zero—he tapped in the unlock code. When the screen flared to life, two things happened back to back. As he felt the kiss of cool steel being pressed to the inflamed dermis at the base of his skull, in his side vision, he saw a gloved hand snatch his rifle from the ground.

With the destruction of the sat-phone taking precedence over all else, Peng smashed it repeatedly against the ground. Simultaneously, training kicking in, his free hand shot for the pistol in the holster on his thigh.

Having been advancing on his quarry for the better part of an hour, the ghillie-suited Marine scout sniper had crawled to within ten feet of the enemy spotter when the air base below erupted with the flurry of new activity.

Knowing the arriving personnel and helos going hot had everything to do with the ongoing operations near Pueblo, and that he couldn't let the spotter get the word out, the young sergeant rose up off the ground, suppressed Glock in hand, and rushed the prone form.

Now, literally having the upper hand on the enemy, the Marine growled, "Be still," and brought his knee down hard on hand going for the sidearm.

There was a snapping sound, and the jagged ends of Peng's ulna and radius lanced the skin of his inner forearm. This was followed by a vicious blow to the temple that knocked him unconscious and immediately stopped the destruction being wrought on the sat-phone.

The Marine flex-cuffed the enemy spotter and emptied the ammunition from the captured weapons. Stowing the damaged sat-phone in a pocket, he radioed the Black Hawk circling high overhead and requested an immediate exfil.

Chapter 41

According to Cade's Suunto, Jedi One had been orbiting the grove for nearly ten minutes. With each passing second, it was becoming evident the riders had gone to ground. It was almost a certainty that going boots on would be necessary to bring them out. Dead or alive, Cade really didn't care at this point.

Word had just come in over the net that the pair of helos scrambled from Peterson had just intercepted the shuttle van. It had been traveling northbound on I-25 and closing with Fountain when a sharpshooter in one of the Black Hawks stopped it with a single round to the engine block.

A team specializing in biological warfare agents was on station and locking down the site.

Another bit of news had come in shortly thereafter. Nash's people had been poring over brand new satellite imagery of the desert southwest of Pueblo and indicated that they may have found one of the Harbin helicopters. The Ospreys returning from the Arizona mission were closest to the remote location and just minutes from getting eyes on.

On the heels of the spate of good news, Jedi One was completing its seventh circuit of the grove and moving slowly above the straight stretch of I-25 when a whole lot of things happened all at once.

Cade heard a warning tone in his headset. Judging by the reaction of the men all around him, they too heard the piercing warble. It was followed by an artificial female voice warning of a missile launch.

As if Ari and Haynes were grafted neurally to the helo, they reacted to the threat instantaneously. While Ari was coaxing max power from the gas turbines and jinking the bird hard to the right, a maneuver meant to put the southern tip of the grove in the path of the inbound missile, Haynes was deploying flares and initiating electronic countermeasures.

Caught staring out his left-side window, Cade saw ground and sky seemingly trade places. As he was pressed hard to his seat by loading G forces, time seemed to slow to a crawl. To his fore, both hands gripping the minigun, eyes wide and mouth a silent O, Nat was saved from pitching over backwards by his safety tether.

While Axe's expression was stony, the second the helo had heeled over, the SAS shooter let go of his rifle and grabbed ahold of the door frame to his left.

Though Griff knew the Brit was tethered to the bird and was in no danger of being ejected, he took a handful of the man's fatigue blouse and held on tight.

Meanwhile, Cross was sitting tight, back to the bulkhead, arms crossed over his weapon, silently petitioning God to intervene and divert the missile.

Craning around, Haynes picked up the missile contrail. It was an expanding gray gash cutting the blue sky off his left shoulder. Releasing the air trapped in his lungs, he said, "Missile missed us. Be advised … we have an H-9 on our six."

"Not for long," replied Ari. The Ghost Hawk had turned the corner and was just leveling out over the business district. With the ship close to maximum speed, he added, "Hold on," and hauled back hard on the stick.

Cade was just getting his bearings when, once again, the ground and sky traded places. Only this time, it was happening on a different axis—fore and aft, versus side to side.

Unlike the first evasive maneuver, this one didn't quickly level off. It seemed to last forever, with everyone aboard going weightless at the apex, then being pressed back into their seats after the helo nosed over and rocketed groundward.

Cade's first time completing a full loop in any type of aircraft. Seeing as how it felt to him as if his stomach had remained at the apex, he hoped it would be the last.

As the craft rushed toward the ground, he saw that the hunter had become the hunted. The sleek Harbin was now in front of Jedi

One and trying desperately to turn the tables. It jinked left and right, eventually diving so close to the deck that the Lowe's sign atop the boxy building was in the way of Skip getting off a clean shot.

White as a sheet, legs and tethered rifle dangling out the right-side door, Axe rolled over onto his stomach. It took a combined effort by Griff and Cross to haul the Brit into the cabin.

To Cade's right, just as Axe was getting his butt into a seat, the minigun belched lead. The noise of the long burst filled the cabin as Skip walked the orange stream across the enemy helo's tail. Licks of flame were just erupting and the craft was yawing to the right as a follow-on flurry of tracers cut into it amidships.

Ice Man was still trying to process the maneuver he had just witnessed when the Z-9's cockpit was assailed by a number of tones alerting him of multiple system failures. He was angry the TY-90 air-to-air missile had lost its lock. Aside from the American Comanche attack helicopter and a French prototype whose name he couldn't recall, he had never seen performance on the scale the black helicopter had just displayed. He was on the cusp of warning the Cobra leader that he was about to make a hard landing when bullets pierced the cockpit glass to his right, killing him instantly.

The Harbin was on fire as it plunged the final hundred feet to the parking lot fronting a convenience store a block west of I-25. The subsequent fireball bloomed over the nearby strip mall.

As the Ghost Hawk finished the turn and overflew the crash site, its rotor wash split the rising smoke and sent it roiling away like a pair of breaking waves.

"Not survivable," Haynes intoned.

Ari said, "Good shooting, Skip. You've got another air-to-air kill decal to apply to your bird."

From the moment Zhen had entered the grove, he had been in constant radio contact with the Harbin pilot and waiting patiently for the missile attack. When he heard the *whoosh* of the missile launch and follow-on *pops* of the stealth helicopter deploying multiple flares, he instructed Yong to hold on. Wounded by a fragment of the bullet that had disabled his bike, Yong tightened his grip around his commander's midsection. Though Yong had recently been a passenger aboard this very motorcycle, this time, due to the tourniquet applied below his right knee, his leg from there on down had gone completely numb. Unable to feel the peg against his boot sole put him in danger of falling off.

When Zhen popped the Yamaha's clutch, a rooster tail erupted from the bike's rear tire. As the approaching jiangshi were pelted by dirt and gravel, Yong's feet came off the pegs.

Leaning forward to keep the front wheel on the ground, Zhen heard the missile detonate somewhere far off to the south. *Certainly a miss.*

The howl of turbines working hard overhead reached his ears through his helmet and headset. Hearing the ripping noise of the stealth helicopter's minigun, he tightened his grip on the bars and aimed for the fast approaching fissure of daylight.

The thunderclap-like boom of a nearby explosion reached Zhen's ears just as his bike shot from the grove. Swerving to avoid a head-on collision with a pair of wandering jiangshi, he caught a fleeting glimpse of the resulting fireball. A millisecond later, the shockwave hit him head-on, causing the bike to get a case of the death wobbles and Yong to nearly be thrown off the back.

Accompanying the report was the sensation in Zhen's chest that told him the source of the roiling fireball was *not* the stealth helicopter. This realization was followed closely by an overwhelming urge to chance a sprint across open ground, to the nearby cluster of businesses, where he and Yong would find better cover than the grove of trees. It was a hundred meters or so distant. Doable solo. A risky proposition with the added weight of the injured passenger.

The instant Zhen witnessed the slow-moving enemy helicopter blast through the rising column of thick black smoke, common sense won the mental tug-o-war occurring in his head. Again warning Yong to cling to him, Zhen cut a tight circle in the middle of the deserted street, planted a foot to keep the bike upright, then twisted the throttle wide open.

Engine sounding like a nest of pissed-off hornets, shocks sagging under the weight of two bodies, the Yamaha jumped the curb. It bounced and shimmied as it cut a path through waist-high grass. As Zhen angled the bike for the same shady alcove from where they had initially emerged, the ground all around him was tilled up by a short two-hundred-round burst fired from the Dillon.

"Damn it, Nat," Griff shot. "If you would have just led them a tad more, you would have spared us from the side trip into Sherwood Forest."

"Lock and load," Cade ordered. "Keep your masks on." Addressing Ari, he asked that his team be infilled at the grove's northern tip.

"Roger that," Ari responded. "Know that each of you will receive the soon-to-be-coveted *I survived the Pueblo barrel roll* patch. And you all get a brownie button for doing so without joining the puker club."

Ignoring the banter, Cade said, "Let's confuse them with a couple of false insertions."

"Bringing her around," Ari answered. He came in hot on the grove's east side and hovered for a two-count. Finished, he backtracked and performed the same maneuver near where they had last seen the bike.

As the helicopter was completing the clockwise orbit, the north tip of the grove dead ahead, Cade said, "In case they circled back, guns hot and eyes peeled."

Griff readied his MP7, then established eye contact with Nat. "If those bastards shoot out of there again, think Kubrick's *Full Metal Jacket*." He paused as he unbuckled his safety harness. "You got to *lead* them."

Dropping the three-man team off on the spit of brown grass due north of the grove and a stone's throw from the I-25 embankment, Jedi One backed away real slow, fifty feet off the deck, Skip covering the Pale Riders' approach with the right-side minigun. Once the team was in the shadow of the grove, Ari resumed the orbit, intent on performing a couple of more false insertions before assuming the agreed-upon overwatch position.

The more confusion they could sow for the enemy, the better.

Chapter 42

Cade entered the grove ahead of Griff. They were keeping good separation, so he was inside by himself for a couple of beats. Immediately, he noticed that the place hadn't seen a public works crew for quite a while. At least a year since the fall, and likely another year prior to that. With the wounds from the collapse of the housing bubble still fresh, and the money in state coffers all but dried up, it had been the same in Portland pre-Omega. Grass growing out of control on freeway exchanges. City parks sorely in need of upkeep. The homelessness was rampant, with tents popping up on sidewalks and vacant lots. Drug use was off the charts. Graffiti everywhere you looked.

It was very dark inside the grove. The temperature had dropped fifteen degrees.

Cade deployed his NVGs. Looking up, he learned that he was under very dense double canopy. Having served in Vietnam, Duncan would feel at home here. Swinging his gaze slowly left to right, he learned that he was not alone. A dozen yards to his right, likely drawn into the grove by all of the activity, was a lone female first turn. It was making a hell of a racket as it fought to wade through a thicket of low scrub.

Cade took a knee a few feet inside the grove. Making eye contact with Griff and Cross—both with NVGs deployed and MP7s at the ready—Cade tapped the IR strobe on the back of his helmet. Switching it on prompted Griff and Cross to activate theirs. Nodding to indicate that their beacons were activated and strobing, Cade motioned for Griff to range left, then directed Cross to go right.

Once Griff and Cross were in position, all Cade could see of them were the intermittent flashes of the IR strobes affixed to their helmets. While splitting the team up wasn't optimal, their advantage in numbers offered the best chance of catching the enemy in a crossfire.

Heel and toeing it along a game trail, head on a swivel, Cade was coming up empty. He couldn't see any signs of the bike having come through here. If a person on foot had used the path, they hadn't left a trace. No boot prints. No tire marks. No broken and bent branches. *Nothing.*

Cade was beginning to think the adversary had either slipped the noose or had found a real good hide—a hollow tree or natural depression—when opposing volleys of suppressed gunfire shattered the still.

Crows in a nearby tree took flight, cawing in displeasure at having been disturbed.

The entangled female Z became more animated, hissing and clawing the air to her fore.

The gunfire had come from Cade's left. The opposing volley was definitely from Griff's MP7.

"SITREP," Cade radioed.

Cross checked in at once.

Griff did not. Very troubling. The man lived to add his two cents to any conversation. If he had dinged his attacker, he would have quickly answered the SITREP request and claimed his scalp.

Compounding the uneasy feeling brought about by the radio silence, Cade had lost sight of Griff's IR strobe. Taking a knee, weapon aimed where he figured the exchange of gunfire had occurred, he said, "Cross. Do you have eyes on my strobe?"

"Affirmative," Cross radioed.

"Griff's?" Cade asked,

"Negative," Cross reported.

"Close on my position," Cade ordered.

As Cade waited for Cross to reach his position, the IR strobe informed him of the SEAL's progress. At first, the flashing orb was moving slowly, right to left, stopping every few feet. After covering a third of the distance, the strobe abruptly disappeared.

No doubt Cross had taken a knee, pausing to look and listen. Make sure he wasn't walking into an ambush. Or being stalked.

In most circumstances, the full-color four-tube NVGs offered a great advantage over the naked eye in dark and dim light environments. They worked best when employed inside a darkened building with all of its flat surfaces and sharp edges. However, when the surrounding foliage matched the camo pattern the enemy was wearing, if the enemy were savvy and remained still, he could be five feet away and go undetected. Cade had a bad feeling that was what had befallen Griff. And he was out there, either wounded or dead.

Slow is smooth. Smooth is fast. Something Griff liked to hammer home to anyone who would listen. Rushing to his aid wasn't an option.

Cross was on the move again. He was a dozen feet away when a burst of suppressed gunfire rang out. It had come from somewhere near Cade's eleven o'clock. He'd been looking away and couldn't lock down exactly where. He was still crouched down next to a mature tree, his attention divided between his immediate surroundings and watching the SEAL's approach, when a volley of incoming fire chewed up the tree trunk a foot in front of his face. He felt his left shoulder suddenly go numb, and he was pelted about the face and chest by splintered wood.

Cross's MP7 stuttered. A short volley quickly followed by a radioed warning for Cade: *One tango. He's between us. Moving in your direction.*

Jedi One was making a pass off of Cade's right shoulder. He couldn't see the helo. Still, its rotor wash rustled the leaves overhead, creating a racket as tremors coursed the branches and boughs of the upper canopy.

Taking advantage, Cade slipped from cover, moving laterally in a combat crouch, SBR shouldered, the suppressor parting the grabbing branches. He wanted to flank the tango. Catch him as he moved on the bullet-riddled tree.

Cade was ten steps from his last position, curling around clockwise, left to right, trying to get to where he thought the gunfire had originated, when he picked up a flash of movement in his side vision. It was off of his right shoulder. A dozen feet away. Definitely not Cross, who was clad in desert-tan camouflage fatigues.

Freezing in place, Cade watched a PLA soldier slipping wraithlike from tree to tree. Knowing that Cross had gone to ground and was somewhere out there, behind the enemy, which would put him in the line of fire, Cade went to ground. Carbine never leaving the unsuspecting soldier, he radioed Cross. "Eyes on one tango. He's still between us and on the move. Be advised, one tango is unaccounted for." He paused for a beat. Then, in a funereal voice, he added, "Griff is down."

"Copy that," Cross replied grimly. "I hear the creeper. He's real close. I *do not* have eyes on."

Jedi One had moved off to the south. Silence returned to the grove.

The soldier reappeared a dozen feet in front of Cade. He was searching the ground near where Cade had been.

I'm harder to kill than that was what Cade was thinking as he radioed Cross, warning him to keep his head down. Bracketing the soldier with the EOTech, he added, "Taking the shot," and pressed the trigger three times in rapid succession.

The soldier grunted and crashed to the ground, out of sight.

Cade radioed, "Tango down." Rising up, weapon trained on the last place he had seen the enemy, he crept forward.

Cade found the soldier prostrate on the ground a few feet from the chewed-up tree trunk. He was face up and tangled in some underbrush. It was Zhen. No doubt about it. The scarring on his face—the dead giveaway. He had taken a round in the right shoulder and, judging by the blood wetting his fatigues underneath his right arm, at least one to the torso.

Zhen was grunting in pain and struggling to bring the bullpup rifle to bear.

"Drop it," Cade bellowed.

Zhen didn't comply, so Cade shot him once in the left shoulder. Coincidentally, the recoil sent a fresh wave of pain radiating from Cade's own left shoulder. He was pretty sure he hadn't caught a bullet. Nevertheless, the possibility was real that a fragment may have found its way in along with all the wood splinters.

Announcing his presence, Cross materialized from a thicket off Cade's left shoulder. He went down on one knee, MP7 aimed at the woods behind Cade, where the sound of branches breaking was rising in volume. He said, "Someone's coming," and placed his finger on the trigger.

The "someone" was not concerned in the least with noise discipline.

"It's a Z," Cade warned, then quickly returned his attention to Zhen. A quick once-over told him the gunshot wounds to the shoulder weren't life-threatening. The one to the right was oozing blood. The bullet was still in there but hadn't hit anything major. The other was a through-and-through and had rendered the arm useless. It was exactly the outcome Cade was expecting when he had fired the shot.

Cade relieved Zhen of his sidearm and knife. Next, he stripped off the bloody chest rig and plate carrier. There was a gaping entry wound between ribs six and seven. It wasn't sucking air, so Cade dumped some QuikClot into the wound and slapped a makeshift bandage over it.

Three down, one to go.

The noise in the brush was growing louder, branches snapping a few feet in front of Cross. Without warning, he squeezed off two rounds. The shell casings were still arcing through the air when, like a felled tree, a face-shot first turn on a one-way trip to the ground parted the bushes. It landed with a hollow thud, the majority of its brains splashing Cross's boots.

Staring Zhen in the eyes, Cade said in Mandarin, "Where is the other soldier?"

Nothing.

"Suit yourself." Cade rolled Zhen over and flex-cuffed his wrists behind his back. Planting a knee on the prisoner's back, he then used another pair of cuffs to secure the man's legs at the ankles. Then, being far from gentle, he zip tied Zhen's ankles to his bound wrists.

The man looked like a trussed pig. Only thing missing was the apple. In its place, Cade stuffed a fist-sized wad of gauze bandages.

Whispering into Zhen's ear, Cade said, "Stay put. I'll be back." Twisting the proverbial dagger, he added, "Better pray the jiangshi don't stumble across you first."

When Cade and Cross left Zhen, the bound and gagged man was last seen eyeing the woods all around and struggling mightily against his restraints.

***

After a short search, they found Griff a dozen yards from the grove's eastern edge. He was facedown and motionless. Before Cade got within ten feet of the fallen Pale Rider, he spotted the deep furrow creasing the top of his teammate's ballistic helmet.

Not fifteen feet from Griff was the man who had gotten the draw on him. It was the unaccounted for PLA soldier. He was sitting with his back against a tree, arms at his side, eyes wide and glazed over. On his lap was a suppressed bullpup rifle.

A tourniquet had been applied just above the dead soldier's left knee. The pant's leg from there on down was wet with blood. But that wasn't the cause of death. The pair of dime-sized entry wounds just above the reach of the man's ballistic vest were the culprits. Cade had missed them initially. They were hard to see thanks to the downward tilt of the man's head.

A Yamaha dirt bike was on its side in the underbrush nearby. The exhaust pipe and swingarm on one side was a mess of twisted metal and coated with a dark red fluid.

Hustling to Griff's side, Cade dropped to his knees and rolled the man over onto his back. Immediately, he saw that not only had the man taken a round to the helmet, but he had also been hit twice in the chest. At least one round had either penetrated or had skipped past the outside edge of the ceramic chest plate. Griff's Crye Precision top was wet with a dark and sticky substance. It was also oozing from one of the holes punched through the chest rig.

Cade ripped off a glove. Pulling the armor away from Griff's chest, he slipped a hand into the narrow space and probed around with his fingers, searching for the entry wound.

Instead of finding a wound, Cade received one. Something sharp in there cut deeply into his pointer finger. *Bullet fragments?*

As he withdrew his hand, the scent of blackberries and alcohol reached his nose.

He loosened Griff's plate carrier and retrieved the item that had caused the cut. It was the half-pint flask bequeathed to him by Lopez. A gaping hole was punched in one side. There was still some liquid in the flask.

Cross said, "I can smell it from here. Gotta be blackberry brandy. Or sloe gin."

Cade pressed two fingers to Griff's neck, checking for a pulse. Feeling a flutter, he said, "You in there, Griff? Can you hear me?" He continued talking and rapped his knuckles on top of the man's ballistic helmet.

Cross said, "Drop and show me your best sugar cookie."

Griff's eyes snapped open. "Where am I? Coronado? Is Hell Week over?"

Cade said, "You're in Pueblo. Hold still." Careful to not disturb the mask's seal, he removed Griff's helmet. Though the man's red hair was matted and sweaty, there was no visible wound. "You took one to the helmet. Got your bell rung real good."

Inspecting the helmet, Cross said, "Lucky it wasn't a hand's width lower. Instead of a concussion, you'd have an extra eye."

Cade undid the Velcro on the other shoulder and peeled back Griff's plate carrier. Peering underneath the sweaty undershirt, he said, "Not a scratch. Just a thicket of chest hair."

Cross had picked up the flask. Shaking it, he said, "Hear that? Bullet's still in there."

Looking to Griff, Cade said, "Lopez saved your ass posthumously. That means you're going to have to pour out a little extra for him."

"When we get out of quarantine," Cross said.

Looking up at Cade, Griff said, "You going to join us at FU-BAR this time? Pour one out for Low Rider yourself?"

Without missing a beat, Cade said, "I'd be an asshole if I didn't. And there are plenty of other good men who have passed who deserve the same." He looked to Cross, a finger pressed to his headset, listening. A beat later, he cracked a rare smile. "More good news, gentlemen. Cat Scratch Two-One located the other Harbin. The scientists are detained, and their weapon stockpile is under lockdown."

After texting Raven the latest news, making sure she knew to stay put and that the Chinook was inbound and five minutes out, Cade stowed the Thuraya and helped Griff to stand. Since he was a bit wobbly on his feet, Cade and Cross each took an arm and walked with him as they retraced their steps.

Zhen was basically where they had left him. A worn path in the dirt suggested he had managed to wriggle worm-like a few feet forward. Cade would have given him an A for effort if this was a SERE course. But it wasn't. This waste of skin had the blood of hundreds on his hands, many of them friends and loved ones.

Cade rolled the special forces captain onto his back. Looking down on him, he said, "You're a hardy one. Multiple gunshot wounds and still you try to escape."

Despite the gauze in his mouth, Zhen tried to speak.

Unable to understand a word of it, nor tell if Zhen was speaking Mandarin or English, Cade removed the makeshift gag.

Drawing a deep breath, in flawless English, Zhen said, "You killed my entire team. You're an alpha. You and me … we're cut from the same cloth. We're warriors. The rest of them, they're all sheep. Breathing. Eating. Dying." He swallowed hard. "From one warrior to another … I ask that you grant me an honorable death. Let me die on the field of battle."

Cade had remained stoic as Zhen spoke. No facial expressions. Just a stony stare from behind the mask.

"You don't know honor. You and me are nothing alike. You're evil. You kill innocents. Kids and adults alike." Just getting started, Cade planted his hands on his hips. "Your people … Communist Party loyalists were here long before your comrades released the virus on us. Your college indoctrination centers infected our youth. Started them turning against the American way. Questioning our founding documents. Disrespecting the flag. At the same time, you were busy blackmailing our politicians on both sides of the aisle. If you couldn't get them with sex, money always worked." He shook his head. "I really want to kill you. Indirectly, you killed my wife and her family. You killed some good friends of mine. Multiple brothers in arms. Your country's negligence has altered my way of life more than I can put into words. Hell, your negligence set the world back centuries. Maybe even sent some societies back to the Stone Age. Every fiber in my body is screaming for me to put my dagger into your heart. Or, better yet, let you become infected, turn into a jiangshi, and then kill you. But that isn't going to happen. I made a promise to someone way above my pay grade. You're going into quarantine. So am I, probably. When I get out, I'm going to watch your trial. And after you're found guilty for crimes against humanity, I'll be there with my popcorn, waiting with bated breath to see your neck get stretched."

Looking to Cross, Griff said, "That's the longest oration I've ever heard come out of your mouth, Wyatt. Didn't know you had a Gettysburg Address in you."

With a certain tilt to his head, Cross said, "Color me amazed."

Cade said nothing. He was all out of words. Dragging the Gerber from its scabbard, he rolled Zhen onto his stomach. Part of him wanted to grab hold of the front of the man's helmet, draw his neck back close to the point of breaking, then saw his fucking head off. That would be selfish of him. The people of New District needed to see the enemy defeated. See them pay. Eventually, rest easy with the knowledge every single one of them had been killed or run out of the country.

Resisting the bloodlust rising within him, stuffing the fury back into the lockbox in his chest, Cade cut the tie securing Zhen's wrists to his ankles. Lifting the enemy soldier to his feet, he radioed Ari and requested an immediate exfil.

Epilogue

Two Weeks Later

Raven's grip on the wheel was white-knuckle tight as she steered the Cushman golf cart across uneven ground east of Schriever Air Force Base. Heat shimmer made the distant tent city seem to undulate as she drew nearer.

Already pushing ninety degrees at a quarter till nine in the morning, today was shaping up to be another scorcher in a long run of them.

Turning the Cushman onto a graded dirt parking lot, she saw that already several dozen people were assembled outside the twelve-foot-tall hurricane fence surrounding the large assemblage of dome-shaped yurts and Army-issue canvas tents.

Erected not so much to contain the inhabitants of the tent city as to serve as a visual reminder of the seriousness of the situation that necessitated it be built, the fence was plastered with pictures drawn by the children of New District. Notes of encouragement to the quarantined inside were taped to the fence here and there. The gate bristled with bouquets of plastic flowers, many of them already sun-faded. On the ground was a colorful mountain of plush stuffed animals.

The lone entry was manned by an MP sitting on a folding chair set up beneath a red nylon sunshade.

Fingers laced through the fence, men, women, and children were lined up beside the gate, waiting for friends and family to emerge.

Raven parked the cart well away from the bystanders. To keep from being enveloped by the drifting plume of dust that had seemingly followed her all the way here from the edge of the distant tarmac, she dismounted quickly, SBR in hand, and scooted off toward the fence.

Emerging from his yurt with only the clothes on his back and a copy of George R. Stewart's *Earth Abides* in hand, Cade immediately turned his attention to the nearby gate. Using the thick tome to blot the low-hanging sun, he caught sight of Raven. Though he had told himself he wasn't going to, as soon as he saw her clinging to the fence, he broke out in a full-on sprint.

Arriving at the fence chased by the rising cloud of dust kicked up by his Danners, Cade met Raven's gaze. "Good to see you, Bird."

She threaded her fingers through the fence. Interlaced them with his. "You too, Dad." She blinked away a stray tear. "I thought I had lost you like I lost Mom."

Cade hiked up his shirt sleeve. Displaying the constellation of pink scars on his deeply tanned bicep, he said, "Splintered wood did all this. Thank God no tainted lead found me. It's still a little sore. Hurts like hell when I do my push-ups."

Looking toward the gate, where the MP was working his keys in the lock, she said, "We need to get you home so you can shave and everything."

He looked a question at her.

"Big day today. The kids who died from the virus are being recognized. A statue in their honor, I think." A twinkle in her eye, she added, "General Jinlong, Captain Zhen, and a few others are set to hang at high noon. You and your team have been invited to sit in President Clay's box."

Craning to see the distant cluster of vehicles, he said, "Where are the others?"

"They're already staking out front row seats. Well, except for Peter. He's manning the register at Daymon's new store."

"Store?"

"Long story. I'll fill you in during the drive."

"I expected Duncan or Daymon to show. Lord knows I need to thank them for getting you back from Pueblo."

Smiling coyly, she said, "It was kind of the other way around."

Cade chuckled at that. "How are the Uncles D?" he asked.

"Glenda took Duncan back in. I asked if he wanted to come with. Said his knees are bugging him. He's getting a little long in the tooth. His words, not mine."

"Daymon?"

Raven made a face. "He's got some phobias and women issues. He'll be there, though."

Arching a brow, he said, "So who drove you?"

"I did."

"Black Beauty?"

She nodded. "Left her parked by our old quarters. Drove a golf cart here."

"Your feet reach the pedals now?"

"I'm as tall now as Mom was when …"

"About Mom," he said, looking off into the distance. "We *will* bring her home. One way or another, I am going to make it happen."

Changing the subject, she said, "I already got out your dress uniform. It's ironed and lint-free. All the medals and pins are squared away. The shoes will need a shine, though."

Thanking her, Cade said, "Does this store of Daymon's have all the same stuff Lola's does?"

"And then some."

"Good," Cade said, "because today's festivities wouldn't be complete without *popcorn*."

THE END

To be continued in a new *Surviving the Zombie Apocalypse* novel in early 2022.

Thanks for reading! Reviews help us indie scribblers. Please consider leaving yours at the place of purchase. Look for books in my bestselling series everywhere eBooks are sold. Please feel free to Friend Shawn Chesser on Facebook. To receive the latest information on upcoming releases, please join my no-spam mailing list at ShawnChesser.com.

Shawn's Facebook Author Page:
www.facebook.com/SurvivingTheZombieApocalypse/

Shawn on Twitter: http://twitter.com/@sdchess

ABOUT THE AUTHOR

Shawn Chesser, a practicing father, has been a zombie fanatic for decades. He likes his creatures shambling, trudging and moaning. As for fast, agile, screaming specimens ... not so much. He lives in Portland, Oregon, with his wife, two kids and three fish. This is his eighteenth novel.

www.ingramcontent.com/pod-product-compliance
Lightning Source LLC
LaVergne TN
LVHW020526100826
845148LV00010B/1350

* 9 7 8 1 7 3 7 1 1 0 6 2 0 *